UMBERTOUCHED

New York Times Bestselling Author
LIVIA BLACKBURNE

ISBN:978-1-940584-11-9

To Amitha, Rachal, Jen, Emily, Coral, and Peta. First readers, and dear friends.

ONE: DINEAS

You can tell plague guards by their fear. Some hold their sword hilts as if trying to crush them to dust. Others jump at the slightest brush of wind. Still others look fine from a distance, but up close, you see how wide their eyes are, how their gazes jump from bird to grass to stone.

You'd think that guarding a quarantine of civilians would be easier than fighting a battle. I mean, you're not staring down a line of archers or charging into a wall of spears. But somehow it's worse. Maybe it's because there's no fighting to heat up the blood, or because you can't kill a fever with a sword. Whatever the reason, every soldier guarding the walls of Taof is terrified, and the citizens pay the price. This morning, a woman strayed too close to the perimeter and ended up with seven arrows in her back.

Which is why I stay low as I creep forward in the knee-deep grass outside the city, cutting as narrow a path as I can through the sharp, scratchy blades. Taof sits at the edge of the northern grasslands, where the plains start giving way to hills and shrubs. A road of flattened weeds and wagon ruts runs past the city gates, though I don't walk on it—it's far too easy to be seen.

It's sundown, and the light is fading fast. My crow Slicewing circles around my head, ready to call a warning if anyone draws near. The other two crows are back in the hills with Zivah. Since the entire empire is looking for an umbertouched man traveling with a rosemarked woman, it's safer for me to scout alone.

It's been a month since Zivah and I barely escaped Sehmar City with our lives. A month since Commander Arxa unmasked me as a spy and Emperor Kiran started amassing an army to invade our homeland. We should have returned by now, but instead we've doubled back one league for every three we've traveled. We've gotten lost, run in circles, and huddled, starving, in caves as soldiers camped within steps of finding us. Finally, we managed to get as far north as Taof, only to run straight into a rose plague outbreak. Emperor Kiran's declared a quarantine, and the river crossing ahead of us swarms with plague guards.

If we don't find a way through soon, we'll have to double back and follow the river for days upstream or downstream. Even the thought of doing that is maddening. Every day we lose makes me wonder if this will be the one that lets the Amparan army overtake us, that leaves our kin in Monyar to fight without our help.

"Lies!"

The shout sends a jolt through my entire body. I freeze, then realize that the speaker is too far away to have anything to do with me. Peering over the grass, I see a crowd of people outside the wall dressed in travel leathers. They look familiar. A big, grizzled man seems to be speaking to an official on their behalf.

"Lies," the man says again. "We've been camped outside the city the whole time, and the horse market was across the river from the outbreak. None of us are a danger. If you put us within the quarantine, you might as well murder us all."

Horses. Now I see the herd of them a short distance away, and I realize why these people look familiar. There's no mistaking the elegant lines and long silky manes of Rovenni steeds. I had a run-in with this tribe back in Sehmar City. It wasn't exactly a friendly visit, but Neju knows I don't wish the plague on them.

I sneak closer.

"It's Emperor Kiran's decree," the minister says in an oily voice. "You must be kept in the city because of new plague laws."

"Lies. The emperor wants us all dead so he can take our stallions for his army."

I remember this man. His name is Nush, and he once accused me of being a horse thief.

"Think carefully before refusing a direct order from the emperor," says the minister.

It seems now that the soldiers guarding the gate all turn to watch.

Finally, Nush speaks again. "Keep us here if you must, but put us outside the walls. If you try to force us in, we'll fight, and we have nothing to lose." There's enough threat in his voice that any smart man would take heed.

I don't think the minister will bring in soldiers, but I can't afford to wait and see what happens. Grass bends and crunches under my feet as I hurry away, and soon the ground starts to slope downward. The river is a thousand paces wide, swollen from the spring rains, and the water splashes and froths as it rushes past. It's deep too, judging from the boats I saw earlier in the day. I don't know what I'm looking for. An abandoned boat? A secret log bridge? Stone jutting up from the river at convenient intervals? It really isn't the type of river to ford or swim, even for those as desperate as me and Zivah, and the only proper bridge is currently the centerpiece of the Taof quarantine.

Slicewing caws. I freeze. A lone soldier walks the grass toward me with wide, swaggering steps. He's not looking in my direction, though, and I duck down into the grass. With any luck, he'll walk right past. But since we've been short on luck lately, I wrap a hand around the hilt of my knife.

As he comes closer, I see he's a typical Amparan sentry in standard armor. Not as scared-looking as the others now that he's farther from the city, but I'm not impressed with the way he's keeping watch. He looks like he's daydreaming rather than scanning for fugitives. I notice he's rubbed mud on his skin to look like umbermarks. It's not the first time I've seen someone try to fool the plague that way. Zivah says it doesn't work.

The soldier swivels his face in my direction. His eyes widen.

Maybe not so much of a daydreamer after all. I tense my muscles to spring.

And then his face shifts. His skin darkens. His eyes grow more wide set, and his cheekbones more pronounced.

My knife falls from my hand. "Masista?"

The man's face shifts back to that of a stranger. Gods, what was that? I grab on to my confusion and use it to propel myself into the man. For a moment, we're a tangle of limbs—his neck is slick with sweat, and he smells like swamp mud—and then I catch his ankle with mine and throw him down. He hits the ground with a grunt as I sprint away.

"Halt!" he shouts.

What self-respecting fugitive has ever halted? I double my speed, plunging blindly through the grass. The soldier screams for reinforcements. I flinch as an arrow flies past my head, and I swerve toward the hills. Once I get there, I can disappear into the shrubs, but it's at least a quarter league away. Hooves thunder behind me now, sending vibrations through the ground, and I bite back a curse, reaching for any last bit of speed.

It's not enough. I skid to a stop as a soldier on horseback cuts me off, his warhorse kicking dirt into my face. Two other horsemen take their places behind me. That's the problem with Amparans. They never want to give you a fair fight.

"Halt," says the soldier in front of me, "or we'll grind you into the mud."

This time I halt.

I call myself all sorts of names as I put my hands up in the air. If the Amparans don't beat me senseless, I'm tempted to do it for them. What kind of good-for-nothing fighter mistakes an enemy for a friend and drops his knife? There are toddlers in my tribe who could have done better.

The soldier who'd threatened to trample me dismounts now and raises his sword. He's an ugly brute with a scar that makes his eyebrow look crooked.

"Who are you?" he asks. "What is your business out here?"

A sliver of an idea. Since I dropped my knife, that first soldier might not even know I'd drawn a weapon. "Sirs, there's been a misunderstanding. I was just out to gather wood for our cooking fire."

"You run pretty fast for someone with nothing to hide."

It's not hard to fake a nervous laugh. "I was afraid I'd be cut down on the spot."

"You might be cut down yet."

"I'm umbertouched, sir." I reach for my sleeve, and Crookbrow raises his sword. "I'm just rolling up my sleeve," I add. "I'll move slowly."

He doesn't relax, but he doesn't skewer me either.

"I have no reason to fear the plague," I say, pulling up the fabric to reveal my skin, "but my fellow Rovenni do. We must boil river water if we want any chance of surviving, and wood from the riverbank burns hotter than grass."

Crookbrow stares at my arm. In the moonlight, it's hard to see the dark splotches that mark me as someone who survived rose plague and emerged immune, but you can find them if you're looking. Crookbrow's gaze moves from my umbermarks to a scar on my wrist. "He bears a Rovenni brand," he tells the others.

5

If he were more observant, he would see that my brand is unevenly applied, the work of an amateur rather than a Rovenni elder. But I don't bring that to his attention.

"Please," I say. "I don't want any trouble. Perhaps this evidence will be more convincing." I detach a small bag from my belt and toss it at the soldier's feet. He picks it up, his eyebrows rising at the heft of its jingling contents. My fingers curl into claws. It's hard not to snatch the pouch right back out of his hand. That's the last of our money, the leftovers of a purse I lifted from a traveling priestess of Mendegi. Maybe this whole thing is the Goddess's wrath for stealing from her.

Crookbrow frowns as he weighs the bag in his hand. I wonder if he's going to take the money and kill me anyway, but then he slips the pouch beneath his cloak. "We'll escort you back to your kin, but if you leave again, we'll shoot you like any other plague fleer, umbermarks or no."

"Thank you, sir."

Truthfully, though, I don't know whether to be worried or relieved as the soldiers march me back toward the city. On the one hand, they didn't recognize me. Still, I'm now at the Rovenni's mercy. A word from them, and this entire charade will be over.

Outside the city gates, some haphazard wooden fences have been set up to form a corral. Several large square tents have been erected inside, and a handful of Rovenni mill beside them along with their horses. I see men and women, young traders and old. Amparan soldiers stand sentry outside the fence. As my guards bring me closer, the Rovenni gather around the gate, looking warily at my escorts and then at me.

The man Nush stands closest to the gate, legs planted wide as if he were still astride one of his steeds. I catch his eye. "I told you it was folly to send me out there, brother," I say loudly. "Brother" might be too much, but I don't exactly have time to send a subtle message. "Almost got me killed."

Nush's eyes are intent on my face, and his thick beard does nothing to hide his frown. I can tell he finds me familiar, though I'm not sure he can place me.

Crookbrow jerks me toward the gate by the sleeve of my tunic, rattling my bones. "You are all to remain inside this enclosure. Even the umbertouched."

Nush stares at me, and I stare right back. If only we could send thoughts through our eyes.

Finally, the Rovenni grunts. "Kill this one if you want," he says with a noncommittal shrug. "I won't shed a tear."

The soldier guffaws. "Your friend doesn't seem overly fond of you," he says. But he pushes me through the gate and returns to his horse, probably eager to go count his money. I stand next to the fence, painfully aware of all the traders' eyes on me.

Nush clamps a large hand on my shoulder and pulls me toward the center of the enclosure. "Good to see you safely back, *brother*." His arm is so heavy it's a wonder I don't sink into the ground. He steers me between tents until all Amparans are blocked from view, then whips me around to face him. "Who are you? I've seen you before." He furrows his eyebrows again, and a flicker of recognition flashes in his eyes. He grabs the lapel of my tunic and yanks me closer. "You're the umbertouched horse thief!"

I grab my tunic to keep the fabric from choking me. Do I look like a good target to push around? I used to cut a more intimidating presence. "I never stole any horses from you." I pick my words carefully. Even though I never stole their horses, I did steal something else. To be fair, I was in some pretty desperate circumstances at the time.

Nush's eyes flicker down to my wrist. "What is..." He grabs my arm and then runs his fingers over the brand. It tickles when he brushes the edge of the scar tissue. Comprehension dawns on the Rovenni's face. "Why, you scoundrel," he says. He holds my arm up for all around him to see. "This is the man who stole our branding iron," he says.

I grit my teeth as murmurs sound all around. Everyone stares at me, and not in a friendly way. I cringe to think how far Nush's voice might have traveled.

I step closer to him and lower my voice. "I can explain. And I can be useful to you. Just hear me out." I don't actually know how I'd help them, but I'll say anything at this point.

Nush's gaze doesn't soften. "Our brands are legacies from the founders of our tribe. Our men and women train for years in horsemanship to make themselves worthy of the mark. It's core to everything that makes us Rovenni, and you stole the iron as if it were no more than a horseshoe."

I have a feeling that more lies will get me killed. "You're right. I did steal your brand. I was a spy in Sehmar City and needed it to throw Arxa off the scent of who I really was."

There's a brief silence as Nush puts together my words. "You're the Shidadi spy the emperor has been trying to capture."

Disconcerting how quickly he figured that out.

"Where is the healer you travel with?" he asks.

"She's in a safer place than this," I say. "But there's no need for us to be enemies. I know you have no love for the empire. I can help you get out of the quarantine."

The Rovenni man snorts. "Help us? You're locked in here just like we are. You have no weapons and no horse."

"I can help in other ways. Not all weapons are made of wood and metal."

"You Shidadi might have a fearsome reputation, but you think too highly of your skill if you think one man can make a difference."

I wrack my brain. "My companion the healer has some...unconventional tools. She'll be able to help you." *Prove me right, Zivah.* "We also stole a Rovenni stallion from the palace stables. You can have him back."

Nush's fingers spasm around my wrist. "You have Natussa?"

"If that's the name of the roan stallion the emperor forced you to sell to the army, then yes."

A change comes over Nush at the mention of that horse. Now he looks at me as if I'm a bug to brush away, rather than a bug he wants to squish. "Say your friend can help us. That means we'll be raising arms against the empire's soldiers. We'd become fugitives."

"You can't avoid it," I say. "Kiran's already forced you to sell your breeding stock to the army, and you know he's trying to sicken your people. Unless you want to hand over your life's work and the legacy of your ancestors, you'll have to start fighting him soon, whether you want to or not."

Murmurs erupt around us again. I hadn't realized that the others had come closer.

"Help never comes free," says Nush. "What do you want from us in return?"

This I can answer. "Create enough of a distraction so Zivah and I can cross the river without being seen. Help us flee north to Monyar."

Nush glances around at the others. Perhaps what he sees is encouraging, because he looks back at me. "Tell us more about what your healer friend can do."

TWO: ZIVAH

I clench my fists, my eyes fixed on the torchlight dancing far below my hiding place. It's too dark and I'm too far above the plains to see the people involved, but it doesn't look good. Slowly, the flames travel in a ragged line toward the city. Will they kill Dineas, or will they take him prisoner?

Now the torches turn toward a corral outside the city—a Rovenni encampment, judging by the horses I saw when it was still light. My snake, Diadem, senses my alarm and hisses, tightening her grip around my arm. On my shoulder, Scrawny the crow flutters his wings, while his wingmate Preener caws curiously from a branch above. I run my fingers through Scrawny's feathers. "Why would they take Dineas to the Rovenni?"

Perhaps it hadn't been Dineas they'd captured after all. Perhaps he'd convinced them he was one of the horse traders. If he's safe, he'll find some way to send me a message. If he's not...

"We'll give him until morning." The crows show no sign of hearing me.

Scrawny resumes poking his beak through my hair. I hope it's for leaves and dust, rather than anything living. That thought makes me shudder, though, after weeks of travel, I wouldn't be surprised if he found something. I rub anxiously at the dirt on my arms. My bones are sharp beneath my skin, and my skin sports scratches and bruises on top of my rosemarks. I wish, not for the first time, that Dineas and I could fly across the continent like the crows. Perhaps then, we'd be back home by now, helping our people prepare against the upcoming invasion. It's been months since I've had any news of my family back home: Leora, now a married woman, Alia, with her constant chatter and impish smile, and my parents, who must be desperate to know how I am. I wonder if I'll see them again. I have to believe that I will.

On my arm, Diadem gradually relaxes, though her tail flicks when Scrawny's wing beats encroach into her space. She hadn't welcomed Scrawny's company at first, but after a few weeks, the crow's persistence had worn her down. Now the two of them coexist, if not in a completely friendly manner, then at least in a civil one. Perhaps they take their cues from their humans.

A soft flutter sounds above me, and my heart quickens as a third crow—Slicewing—touches down in front of me. Slicewing, who was with Dineas. There's a parchment tied to her leg.

Thank the Goddess.

Quickly, I untie the message. I'm barely able to make out Dineas's scrawl in the moonlight. We've written enough notes by now that I decode the cipher in my head.

Rovenni will help us cross river if we help them escape. Can you make potions?

I fold the note between my fingers, relief warring with incredulity in my chest. He's alive, and the empire doesn't know he's here. For that, I send up a quick prayer of thanks. But is he really depending on my potions to save us? We've been on the run for a month. I've nothing but the clothes on my back and the animals with me. And despite what Dineas might think, I cannot mix potions out of moonlight and dirt.

I rub the bridge of my nose, where a light but insistent headache lingers. "What do I do?"

Scrawny fluffs his feathers in what I imagine could be a bird shrug.

I look at the shrubs around me, scouring my memory for herbs I glimpsed on our journey here. In my pouch, I have sweetgrass for stomachaches and puzta flower for wounds—proper healer's tools from the plains, but nothing that will get someone past a guard. My three remaining blowgun darts are dipped in sleeping potion, but I'd need five different ingredients to make more, none of which are native to this area. There's nothing I can forage out here that can help me.

Dineas's note was short, but I can guess much of what he didn't say. He's out of immediate danger, but not for long. It's only a matter of time before someone recognizes him.

I look back out toward the city. If the quarantine is set up like most Amparan quarantines, they'll have cleared out one corner for the actively ill. There will be healers there, with stocks of useful herbs.

I turn to the birds. "Would you like to come on a mission?"

The climb down the hill is tricky in the dark. Bushes catch at my tunic, and small, spindly trees gouge yet more scratches across my hands and face. Diadem hisses once or twice when a wayward twig hits her, while the crows circle impatiently overhead. Our Rovenni stallion is tied near the bottom of the hill and huffs at my approach. I give him a quick pat and promise to return soon.

A year ago, I would have never thought myself capable of sneaking around in the dark, dodging Amparan soldiers in an unfamiliar land. The past months have changed everything, but still, my blood pounds in my veins as I leave the safety of the hills. Once in the open grassland, I set the crows to scouting. A chill wind stirs up strands of hair that have escaped my braid. The soldiers are concentrated toward the river, but these grasslands are still too exposed for comfort. I feel for the blowgun at my waist, reassuring myself that it's still there.

Taof is surrounded by a low earthen wall, barely higher than my head. It's easy enough to find the area they've set apart for the fevered. There's no hint of the shuffles, clinks, and murmurs you'd expect to hear over a city wall at this time of night. I'm alert for guards as I approach, but I don't see any outside the walls. They're probably all stationed inside to keep people from fleeing. No one in her right mind would try to enter the quarantine.

I stand on tiptoe to peek over the walls. The street on the other side is empty except for an umbertouched soldier patrolling its length. Farther down the road, several domed tents are set up. A few look like living quarters for healers, but there's a larger one that's likely for supplies. I whistle quietly for the crows and point over the wall to the tent.

"Fetch," I say. They take wing. I let out a long breath through my mouth.

A few moments later, Preener drops a beaded necklace in my hand.

"It's beautiful, Preener, but that's not really useful." He snatches it back and manages to toss it into the air so it drapes over his wings.

Slicewing comes back with bukar root, a fever reducer. Scrawny gifts me a grimy washcloth.

I hold up the bukar root. "Something more like this." - Slicewing plumps her feathers as Scrawny wilts.

After the crows take off again, I hear footsteps on the other side of the wall.

"I see they set up the big tent," says a young man. "Guess he's coming after all."

"You know he likes his comforts," says another.

The first one snorts. "Someday, when I'm a renowned rose

plague physician from the Imperial Academy, I'll have tapestries in my tent too."

My breath catches.

His companion snorts. "You'll be lucky to become the mayor's chamber pot inspector, the way you shirk your duties."

There's only one rose plague physician from the Imperial Academy....

The crows land in a flurry of wings. Slicewing brings the same root again. Preener brings dried vel flower, and Scrawny brings a fuzzy leaf. When I break the leaf in half, a milky liquid with a cloyingly sweet scent oozes out.

I rub the sticky sap between my fingers. This might do, aged in sunlight and snake venom, though my master, Kaylah, wouldn't like me using it this way. *The knowledge given to us by the Goddess is not to be abused. Your potions are to be used only to heal.* It's been six months since I left Monyar as an idealistic young healer, and two months since I ripped my healer's sash in shame for having broken too many vows to be worthy of it. I've broken more vows since then, though the guilt doesn't get any less.

"More of this," I say to the crows. "Bring me much more of this."

THREE: DINEAS

The next day, all three crows come into the Rovenni encampment with small packets on their legs. Slicewing bears a note as well.

Smoke is an emetic. Don't kill.

And then on the next line...

Baruva is here. We can't leave yet.

I read the last part several times before I can fully believe it. When Zivah and I were in Sehmar City, we learned that Emperor Kiran had intentionally infected his own troops with rose plague so he could cast the blame on our people. Baruva was the healer who'd helped him. We had to flee the city before we could find proof of their guilt, but if Baruva's here, it might give us a second shot.

Of course, that would mean giving up our chance to flee with the Rovenni.

I write a note back to Zivah. *Do you want to stay?*

Time goes slowly as I wait for a reply. And when it comes, the handwriting is shakier than usual. *We must.*

If we stay, who knows how many days we'd lose. From what we've heard, the Amparan army left Sehmar two weeks behind us. It marches more slowly than two fugitives on a stallion, but we've also had to double back. I try to guess how many days we have to spare, but there's just too many unknowns. I suspect Zivah's right about staying, though. If we can find evidence that Kiran raised his hand against the empire's own troops, it would discredit him completely. And discredited emperors have a hard time waging wars.

I write her back: *Meet me at the quarantine wall when the Rovenni run.* I hope I don't live to regret this.

Upon closer inspection, Zivah's sent us bundles of leaves with some kind of milky white paste on the inside. They smell like something that's been dead a week.

Nush coughs and makes a face when I show him. "What is that foul poison?"

"Something that should incapacitate the guards quickly and quietly. But you have to swear to keep them alive."

"Why?"

I shrug. "Healer's vows. I don't understand them either." The answer's enough to satisfy Nush, though my words set me to wondering how well I really know Zivah these days. Back in Sehmar City, the other version of me had been close with her. Would he have understood?

We make plans over the course of the day, taking care to keep every conversation short and out of sight of the Amparan guards. The Rovenni pick their best fighters. Then there's nothing to do until sundown.

I'm restless as the sun crawls across the sky. Nush and the others keep busy tending their horses and packing what belongings they can without raising suspicion. Meanwhile, I have nothing to do except torture myself over my capture last night. I still can't make sense of what happened down by the river, how that soldier's face shifted into that of my friend from the Amparan army. Right before we escaped Sehmar City, when Zivah restored my memory permanently,

16

she told me I'd taken the last of her potions and that I should be back to normal. If that's true, then what's wrong with me?

As night falls, everyone gathers around the campfire. An older rider with a dark, windblown face tells a story of how their ancestors tamed their first horses. A bowl of water is passed unobtrusively around, and everyone dips a cloth in. As the story winds down, I meet Nush's eyes, and we exchange a nod. The ten Amparan guards outside the enclosure aren't paying attention, but we'll have to act fast nonetheless. Nush points to each fighter and then to a guard. I'm to take care of a tall, right-handed swordsman near the enclosure gate.

Quietly, we tie our wet cloths to cover our noses and mouths. Then Nush takes out Zivah's packets, puts them into a copper bowl, and holds them to the fire, angling his body to hide them from view. As they start to smoke, he fishes them out with tongs and quickly drops each into its own wooden bowl. A putrid odor fills the air.

"Act quickly," he says.

We scatter. I grab my bowl and run for the fence, lobbing it toward the guard, who stares at the packet and starts coughing. The smoke is something fierce. Even with my mask, my eyes water.

I vault over the fence, fighting the urge to gag. My stomach wants to roll out my throat, but the Amparan soldier has the worst of it, doubled over with his hand over his mouth and nose. I rap him over the head with the butt of my knife. As he falls, his arm comes up, and a sharp pain slices across my bicep. Scars, that was careless of me.

A neigh rings through the night, and a Rovenni mare jumps the fence, her rider crouched expertly in her saddle. Other horses follow suit, some with riders and some without. Shouts sound from the city as the guards finally realize something's awry.

I need to get to Zivah. I turn toward the city, when a black stallion leaps the fence and cuts in front of my path.

Nush looks down from the saddle. "You're sure you don't want to leave with us?"

I shake my head. "I have duties here."

He gives a matter-of-fact nod. "When you leave Taof, take the eastern trails north to Monyar Strait," he says "The garrisons there are expert card players and not good at much else. You'll have the easiest time sneaking past them. May the gods watch over your journey."

And with that, he gallops away.

FOUR: ZIVAH

It's easy enough to tell when the Rovenni launch their escape attempt. The shouts of surprised guards carry clearly over the grass, and hoofbeats of fleeing horses shake the ground. As I wait in the shadow of Taof's walls, our own stallion tosses his mane.

"Wait," I say. "Dineas will take you to your herd."

But he takes a mighty leap toward the commotion, ripping his reins from my hand and disappearing into the night. And though we'd been planning to return him, panic stabs through my gut. If it's taken us so long to come this far, how much longer will it be now that we must travel by foot?

Dineas comes barreling out of the shadows and stumbles to a stop. I can't see his face, but I recognize his speed, the readiness of his crouch. He casts around, not seeing me. "Zivah?"

"Over here."

The crows fly celebratory circles around his head as he joins me. "Any trouble?" he asks.

"Not yet." I hand him his sword, bow, and his quiver, which he straps on. "Are you hurt?"

"Only a little." Which, coming out of Dineas's mouth, is not reassuring at all.

"Will the Rovenni make it away?"

"I hope so." He stares in the direction of the commotion and wipes the sweat from his brow before turning back to me. "This is the only diversion we'll get. You're sure you want to use it to get inside?"

I wish he wouldn't tempt me like this. Haven't I been away long enough? But finding Baruva's secrets would do far more to protect my family than anything I could accomplish in Monyar. "I'm sure if you are."

Dineas hesitates the briefest moment before giving me a confirmatory nod. He steps to the wall and boosts himself over the top.

"No guards," he says. They must have been called to contain the Rovenni. I climb after him and drop into the middle of an empty street. Not a single sound drifts out from the houses in front of us. Not a single window has light coming from its shutters.

Soft footsteps drift down a side street, and Dineas and I exchange an alarmed glance. He pushes on the door of the nearest house. Locked. The one I try swings open, and we rush inside. As Dineas closes the door, I peek out the window just in time to see a harried-looking healer shuffle by. The street falls silent again.

Dineas curses softly. "I'm dripping blood."

I resume breathing. "Of course you are. Come here." I make room for him by the window, where a beam of moonlight offers just the slightest illumination. "Where's the cut?"

He points to his upper arm.

"Take off your tunic."

There's a rustle of cloth as he pulls his shirt over his head. I reach for the dark shape of his arm and pull until he's positioned to make the most of the light. "Everything moves as normal?"

He responds by wiggling his fingers. "I'm fine."

"Your fingers aren't controlled by your biceps."

He sighs and extends his arm, raising an eyebrow at me as if to ask if I'm satisfied. The gash itself is four fingers long but relatively shallow and straight. I probably don't need to stitch it, which is good because I don't have a needle. As I look once more at the wound, my eye is drawn to the rest of him. Like me, he's lost weight since we fled Sehmar City. His limbs are wiry and lean, the muscles more clearly delineated. I adjust my grip so that only my fingertips are touching his bare skin, rough from our weeks of travel but still warm. The darkness makes it harder to bandage him up, but part of me is glad he can't see my eyes or my face.

I reach for my waterskin and splash a small amount of water on his arm, as much as we can spare. "You can't count on me to keep making weapons for you," I say. "I'm a healer, not an arsenal."

His forearm tenses under my grip. "I'll aim to be more considerate next time I'm trying not to die."

I sprinkle puzta petals over the cut. "I'll do what I need to keep us alive. I have so far, haven't I? It's just...vows to the - Goddess aren't meant to be taken lightly."

"If your Goddess wants you to keep your vows, maybe she can do a little more to help us out."

I've had the same thought myself, but I'm not in the mood to agree with him. I drop his arm and feel my way around the darkened room. There are some pallets on the floor with blankets on them. I cut a piece off the one that smells cleanest. "What happened out there? You've scouted places far more crowded than that riverbank without being caught."

He doesn't answer.

"Dineas?"

"I got careless."

I know him well enough to tell when he's being evasive. I also know it's a waste of breath trying to get him to say more. I layer some sweetgrass over the cut and bind it all with blanket strips. If I'm a little rougher than I need to be, he doesn't complain.

"Is it too bulky?" I ask. "Can you move?"

"Well enough."

Silently, we gather our things. Dineas opens the door a crack and peeks out. "Where to first?"

"Let's look around. See if we can find Baruva or his quarters."

It's still eerily quiet outside, the only sounds the occasional shout from the direction of the river. As we head down the street where the healer had gone, I wonder how large an area has been cordoned off for the sick, and how many have been struck thus far. Strewn outside the doors and windows of the houses we pass are hundreds of tiny handmade sculptures made of woven twigs and leaves. The Amparans call these sculptures "promises to Hefana," and they symbolize offerings the maker will sacrifice to the goddess of healing if she would keep his household safe. Passing from door to door, it's as if there's a miniature city at the foot of the real one. Tiny horses of braided grass stand with their forelegs propped on thresholds. Twig wagons wait below windows. There's even a wooden wine jug decorated with pressed flowers. They all lie abandoned now, and I wonder which of these prayers Hefana will answer. As if in response to my question, the wind shifts and smoke blows in our direction. It comes with the smell of burning flesh—a funeral pyre.

Finally, we reach a large building with light coming through the windows. I glimpse rosemarked patients through a crack in the shutters, but no healers. Like the hospital in Sehmar City, care of patients during the night is probably left to one or two assistants.

Dineas cocks his head at me, asking if I want to go in. It's a good question. Baruva's probably not there now, but we might find something useful. I push on the nearest door. It swings open, and the scene inside is familiar in the worst way. Fevered patients lie on pallets along the walls, the occasional delirious cry piercing the underlying layers of moans. As I walk through the room, their suffering seeps into me. One patient, a small boy, wails piteously as he tosses back and forth on the floor. I crouch next him and lay a hand on his forehead. His wails die down to a whimper.

It doesn't matter where I am, or which people are involved, the rhythm and language of illness stays the same. Though this group of patients isn't as badly struck as those in the other outbreaks I've seen. I remember, back in the Sehmar City rose-marked compound, the cries would be so loud that Jesmin and I often had to leave the room to converse.

I long to tell these people everything will be all right, but it would be a lie. The vast majority of people who contract rose plague die within days. Only one in ten beat it completely, becoming umbertouched like Dineas. And then there are those, like me, who survive the first bout of fever but don't expunge the disease from our bodies. Our rash stays red, and we live a few more years before the fever comes back to claim us. Those years must be spent in isolation, because our touch remains infectious.

The patients need care, but I dare not stay long. I catch Dineas's eye, and we go out to the corridor, then into the next room. This one too is filled with the plague-stricken. It amazes me how many there are. In the crowded Amparan cities, one infected person is enough to sicken dozens.

The unmistakable sound of a door opening and closing echoes down the corridor, and multiple footsteps come toward us. I stop in my tracks. Are the healers still here? I cast around. There's a small storeroom along the wall next to me, and I step inside. It's a musty space crammed with tables, chairs, and bolts of cloth. This place must have been a weaver's shop before it became a makeshift hospital. There's barely enough room in this closet for me to fit, and when I look for Dineas, he signals for me to close the door before ducking out into the corridor. A few patients watch our exchange, but without comprehension.

In the closet, I hold my breath, listening for any hint of what's happening outside. I can see a sliver of the room through a crack at the edge of the door, but nothing of the corridor or Dineas.

The footsteps come closer, and three people walk in. One is a tall, thin man with a narrow face, sharp eyes, and a flat, wedgelike nose. He wears a rich blue robe with a gold overcoat. The other two, a man and a woman, wear rough homespun tunics and carry themselves as if to take up less space. Slaves.

The rich man walks down the center of the room as the two slaves start to work, going from patient to patient, giving them water and wiping their brows. They're very skilled—not as adept as a full healer, but certainly as comfortable with the sick as a good apprentice. The patients seem genuinely calmer after their ministrations. My eyes linger on the slaves' plague gloves, and that's when I realize that neither they or the rich man have any marks of plague.

He gives the type of instructions a healer would. Extract of bukar root for one feverish patient. Valerian root for another who's so panicked from his hallucinations that he can't sleep.

He has many slaves to help him with the more dangerous aspects of his work.

Those words, spoken by a physician in Sehmar City about Baruva, run through my head. And I know that I've found the empire's leading scholar of rose plague. It's hard to contain the wave of disgust I feel at the sight of this healer who avoids danger, who wears fine robes instead of plague gloves and forces others to take the risk that should be his.

Baruva and his slaves remain in that room until my muscles ache from staying still. Finally, after close to an hour, Baruva speaks again. "We're done for today. The assistants should be able to care for the patients overnight."

Quickly, efficiently, the slaves pack up their supplies, empty the water basins out the window, and extinguish all but one lamp.

I wait until the footsteps fade before I step out. I'm standing in the middle of the room, trying to shed my lingering disgust for Baruva, when there's a shuffling at the doorway. I jump, only to sigh in relief at the sight of Dineas.

"That was him," I say. "Baruva."

Dineas wrinkles his nose. "Fancy fellow. He left in the direction of some tents. Do you think he lives there?"

"Probably. Let's search his quarters tomorrow."

In the closet where I'd hidden, we find some tunics that resemble the homespun worn by the slaves, then find a place to lie low for the rest of the night. Dineas pries open the shutters of a nearby house, and we settle down in a room with six pallets on the floor and a child's cloak hanging on the wall.

"I wonder if this family was in the hospital, or if they fled the quarantine," I say. *Or if they're already dead.* It feels wrong to be thinking this as I curl up on their floor.

"Better not to wonder," says Dineas.

He's probably right. There's a steady throbbing just behind my temples, and I squeeze my eyes shut.

"Are you all right?" he asks.

"Just tired."

He makes a skeptical noise in his throat and removes his weapons for sleep. His swords go on one side of him, and his bow and a small quiver on the other. He runs his thumb over the top curve of his bow. I've seen him do it before, and I lean surreptitiously closer for a look. A Shidadi letter is carved into it. The weapon itself is old, with chips and dents in the wood.

"That bow looks well loved," I say.

"It was my mother's," he says simply.

I'd never thought about what Dineas's mother and father might have been like. I'm curious, but he's already laid his head down and closed his eyes. A few moments later, his breathing becomes slow and even. The moonlight through the shutters bathes him in gray light. His brown hair curls lightly over his eyes, and he wraps his elbow around his head. I'm struck by how relaxed he looks in his sleep, how much more at peace. This was how he'd looked in Sehmar City, when he'd had no memory of his past. In the capital, I'd gotten a glimpse of the man he might have been, had he not suffered so much at the hands of the empire.

When I restored Dineas's memory for good, we'd both felt the loss of his other self. For him, it meant a return to facing his demons. As for me, I lost a friend. Or, if I'm honest, someone who might have been more. It's for the best—nothing good can come of a friendship with half a person, even if the half removed had endured more than his share of pain. Still, life as a rosemarked person is lonely, and for a brief while in Sehmar, it had been less so.

Dineas flinches and startles awake with a hoarse cry, casting around to get his bearings until he realizes where he is. His breaths rasp against the darkness.

"Are you all right?" I ask.

He pauses before answering. "A fly landed on me."

It wasn't a fly. It was the beginning of a nightmare, and perhaps in another time, he would have told me what ghosts had chased him out of sleep. I wonder how much longer we'll keep dancing around each other like this, pretending we don't know each other as well as we do. Pretending that we hadn't been in love.

Dineas groans and stretches before settling down again. "Why are you frowning?" he asks.

"Thinking about how best to search Baruva's quarters." The lie comes glibly, sliding out with the ease of practice.

He nods, turns over, and goes back to sleep.

I suppose I can't blame Dineas for lying if I also lack the courage to tell the truth.

MORNING BRINGS voices and footsteps from outside. When I peek through the shutters, I see the occasional healer, assistant, or slave walking the road. One of the slaves is rosemarked, and I wonder if he was assigned to quarantine work after he fell ill. Dineas and I share a quiet meal of dried fruit and put on the tunics I'd found at the hospital. Then he opens the shutters a crack and whistles for the crows. Scrawny lands on the windowsill first, only to be knocked off by Preener. Slicewing settles on the ground outside, too dignified to join in the fray.

Dineas clouts Preener across the wings, eliciting an indignant squawk. "No more horseplay. We've a mission to do."

We pick a moment when the street's empty to leave the house, then hurry along as quickly as we can. I'd thought the quarantine would be less disturbing during the day, but somehow it's worse. Bright sunlit streets should be crowded with merchants, wagons, and children, but everything is empty. A few times, we pass healers on our way, but they hardly notice us in our slave clothes. The crows trail us to the edge of the quarantine, where several tents had been set up. One is twice the size of the others. We crouch close and listen intently. No sounds coming from within. Rather than untie the entrance flap, Dineas pries up one of the tent stakes.

"Scout," he tells the crows. And then we duck inside.

The interior of the tent is as opulent as Baruva's clothes. A plush maroon rug covers the ground, and colorful tapestries hang on the tent walls. A sturdy bed and chest stand on one side of the tent, across from a desk of fine hardwood and a shelf stacked with scrolls.

"What are we looking for?" asks Dineas.

"Records, notes, anything that will tell us what he knew. What he did." I pull on a pair of gloves and start toward the shelves.

Dineas gives my gloves a funny look. "Even for him?"

"It would be against my vows," I say, somewhat defensively.

Dineas shrugs.

To be honest, I'm not even sure myself why I insist on putting on gloves. It's tempting, knowing what I do about Baruva, to touch his possessions with my bare skin and leave his fate to the gods. Besides, I've broken plenty of my healer's vows already, vows made to a Goddess who allowed me to fall ill the same month I dedicated my life to serving the sick. Sometimes I wonder if I keep the remaining ones out of habit rather than deep conviction.

I start at one end of the bookshelf, unrolling the scrolls one by one and shuffling through stacks of clay tablets, cringing at the occasional clink. One set of tablets turns out to be letters to his brother in the capital. Another long scroll looks like a daily journal. I put that aside, as well as a scroll of medical notes.

"Nothing much on this side," says Dineas. "Just treatises from the imperial library."

A crow caws, and I freeze. Footsteps sound in the distance, as does Baruva's voice. "I don't like her poking around in our work. She's not a physician. Rosemarked or not, she has no business here."

I snatch the two scrolls I'd set aside and we move toward the back of the tent, away from Baruva's voice. I put my ear between two of the tapestries. Muffled voices come through that side as well. We can't slip away unnoticed.

Baruva's voice comes closer. "You'll likely travel the same

path as her caravan. Stop and talk to them if you can. See if we can catch them in a violation—incorrect travel papers from Sehmar, forbidden foods in their wagon. Her father's stature can't protect her from everything, especially with his recent disgrace." The door flap shakes as someone pulls out the ties that hold it closed. Dineas sets his jaw and moves to the far side of the flap as I duck behind one of the tapestries. Then the door opens, revealing Baruva and another healer, though Baruva's the only one who comes in.

Dineas elbows Baruva in the ribs before the tent flap has fully dropped. He doubles over, and then Dineas is behind him with a hand over his mouth and a knife to his throat.

"No noises," he says to Baruva. And then to me, "Rope."

Rope? Sometimes Dineas forgets he's not on a mission with his fellow equipped-to-the-teeth soldiers. But I rummage through the chest at the foot of Baruva's bed and strip the sashes from two of Baruva's silk robes. Dineas gags him with one and uses the other to tie him to a chair. Baruva looks from Dineas to me, and recognition dawns on his face. I suppose there aren't many travelers who fit our descriptions.

Dineas moves closer, brandishing the knife. "You'll be quiet, won't you?" Baruva nods, eyes rolling in panic, and Dineas eases his gag.

"My bodyguards will come looking for me," he says.

"You don't have bodyguards," I say.

The healer's mouth presses tightly together. I have to give him credit, as he's already suppressed most of the panic I saw just a moment ago.

Dineas turns to me. "Is there anything you want to ask him?"

I look at Baruva. "We know you poisoned the Monyar battalion under Kiran's orders."

If he shows any surprise at my words, it passes quickly. "I have no idea what you're talking about."

Dineas takes a menacing step toward him, and Baruva

sneers. "You want to beat the answer out of me? Try to do that quietly in this tent."

"I don't have to hit you to do you harm," says Dineas. "Zivah simply has to take off her gloves."

I glance at Dineas's face. He certainly looks like he believes I'd carry out that threat.

Baruva dismisses the threat with a sideways glance at me. "She wouldn't break her vows. And if not for her vows, then to save her own skin. I'm the last chance she has at life."

Last chance at life? Dineas looks at me for an explanation, but I just shake my head.

A crow caws again, and we hear more footsteps. A calculating look crosses Baruva's face.

"Dineas—" I say.

Dineas lunges for the healer, but it's too late. Baruva draws a quick breath and shouts, "Help me! Intruders!"

FIVE: DINEAS

S cars, I'm a fool. I raise my arm to clout Baruva over the head. He flinches, but I let my hand drop. The damage is done.

"To the back!" I hiss. I slash a gouge in the wall. Zivah slips through first, and I squeeze out after her. Then we're sprinting away.

A gruff voice shouts behind us, "There they are!"

I risk a look back, thinking maybe it's just a few healers, but no such luck. Looks like the quarantine guards have returned from chasing the Rovenni.

A parade of miniature stick animals watches us flee. The sandy dirt-packed road is slippery under our feet as we race down a narrow side street. We near the next main road, but shouts sound from the other direction, and we skid to a stop. As the footsteps behind us get louder as well, my eyes fall on a supply wagon by the side of the road, its open back covered by an oilcloth. Most of it's tied down, but I flip up the end. Zivah climbs in, and I dive after her, hitting the bottom of the wagon with a hollow thud and yanking the oilcloth back over.

Yellow light filters through the cloth into the wagon. It's

mostly empty, though burlap sacks and a handful of dried beans scattered across the bottom give a clue as to what it was used for. We crawl up against the far end of the wagon bed and curl up as small as possible. I stuff the burlap sacks between our feet and the opening we came through. It's not good cover at all. Anyone could brush aside those sacks in a few heartbeats.

Zivah lies completely still next to me, her eyes fixed on the cloth above us. I can feel the heat from her body and sense her trying to quiet her breathing. As footsteps come closer, I reach for my dagger and hold it between us. Zivah's eyes flicker to my knife, and a hint of a smile pulls at her lips. I wonder if she's thinking of our first meeting, when I threatened her with a knife and she turned the tables on me with that wretched snake of hers.

When I first met Zivah, I'd thought her rosemarks disfiguring. Slowly, though, as my other self had fallen in love with her in Sehmar, she'd become beautiful. Now that my memory's been restored, I keep expecting my old impression of her to return. But I still catch my gaze lingering on her profile, the curve of her lips.

The footsteps pass without slowing. We stay there, stock-still, as others run by. Gradually, the sounds become more distant. Zivah looks at me, her features aglow in the strange light. I'm about to breathe easier when a movement catches the corner of my eye. I bite back a curse when the movement resolves into a hairy palm-sized spider lowering itself from the oilcloth above.

Sweat breaks out on my skin. Scars, I hate these things. It's all I can do not to move as the spider dangles less than a hand's width away from my face. *Crawl back up. Crawl back up.* Give me a dozen soldiers any day. I glance at Zivah. The hint of a smile I'd seen earlier is more than a hint now. She reaches her hand up, slowly, until it's right below the spider. The disgusting creature sets one spindly leg onto Zivah's palm, and then another, until Zivah closes her hand around it. Slowly, she withdraws her hand and rests it back by her legs.

I give her a sheepish grin, and her eyes crinkle. Funny that the first time we share a joke after Sehmar would be under circumstances like this. She got along far better with the other version of me—I suppose he was easier to get along with. It's a strange feeling, to be measured against yourself and found wanting.

A door closes. More footsteps. My stomach plummets as I hear the click of horse hooves. The wagon creaks and shifts as someone gets in the front.

Well, this wasn't part of the plan, but it might not be a bad thing if the wagon leaves the quarantine. After some more creaking and shifting, the wagon starts rolling. I strain my ears for clues about where we are.

"Halt right there," says a voice. The wagon trundles to a stop. "Just need to take a look."

I grip my knife. Footsteps approach the back of our wagon. We really should have come in feetfirst.

Zivah catches my eye. "Wait," she mouths. She shifts her weight.

Light streams through the sacks at our feet as someone throws open the oilcloth. "Food rations?" the guard asks.

There's a muffled reply from the wagon driver.

More light comes through as sacks are brushed away. I coil my legs for a kick.

"Agh!" yells the guard. And then we hear laughter as someone scrambles away from the wagon. "Cursed spider ran right across my hand. Big one."

I suppose spiders aren't so bad after all. The guard lets out a string of curses, and there are more replies from the wagon driver.

"Damned quarantine has everything acting unusual," says the guard, and we hear him come closer again.

Zivah's mouth tightens. I suppose it was too much to hope that the guard would be put off by a spider.

There's more talking, and a shadow blocks the light streaming in. I plan my next few steps. Kick his hands against the wagon hard enough to make his eyes water and get him to step back. Push off the board at my head toward the opening at my feet, then sit up, twist, and come out with my dagger.

"What in the—" Again, the guard dissolves into curses, and again he steps away. More laughter now, and are those crows I hear in the background?

"Blackbird's graced you with a crown!" comes another voice.

"Better plant some seeds while the manure's fresh!"

Could it be...Did one of the crows relieve itself on the guard's head?

More raucous laughter. Then someone yanks the oilcloth shut, and the wagon trundles away. Zivah stares at me, her mouth agape. I can hardly believe it either. The crow who did this is going to get double rations for a month—if I can figure out which one it was.

The roads are rough, and the bouncing feels like it's going to leave bruises, but the important thing is that we don't stop. It's hard to judge the angle of the sun through the oilcloth, but I think we're heading north. Once in a while, I hear other horses and wagons, but it's mostly quiet around us. That, combined with the bone-rattling bumps and divots we roll over, makes me think we're taking back roads.

My limbs stiffen as we trundle along. Zivah fidgets ever so slightly, straining and curling her fingers in an obvious effort not to move more than she has to. I think on our next step, whether it's better to wait for a stop or jump out while the wagon is going. Either way, we'll likely be seen.

Finally, the driver says something, and the wagon rolls to a stop. There's muffled voices in the distance, and I hear our driver walk off. I look at Zivah, who shrugs. Carefully, I cut a slit in the oilcloth and look through.

It looks like we've stopped at a creek. There are several wagons nearby, and a group of people at the river already watering their horses. An umbertouched man in healer's robes, probably the driver of our wagon, walks toward the river to join them. I recognize him as the man Baruva was talking to before he entered his tent.

I duck back down. "If anyone's paying attention," I whisper to Zivah, "they'll see us getting out, but I don't think we'll find a better chance."

She gives a quick nod. I hand her my dagger, and she cuts a wide slit in the oilcloth behind her, on the side of the wagon facing away from the river. I say a quick prayer to Neju as she clambers out, then follow her. I drop next to her behind the wagon, and we run, keeping low, toward a cluster of bushes by the riverbank. Almost there.

Zivah reaches cover first and turns to check on me. I dive into the shrubs a moment later and wave her forward. We're still too exposed for comfort.

She doesn't move. I gesture at her again, but she simply stares past me at the caravaners, her eyes wide with shock.

"Zivah!" I hiss. And then I finally follow her gaze.

SIX: ZIVAH

I blink several times, trying to clear my vision, trying to clear my mind. The healer whom we'd seen with Baruva stands near the river, but it's the woman he's talking to that has me mistrusting my eyes. She shouldn't be here, but there's no mistaking the dark blond hair and wispy aristocratic frame of Commander Arxa's daughter, the rosemarks on her cream-colored skin. Next to her is a plague veil that she's cast off to drink from the river.

I turn to Dineas. "Is that Mehtap?"

Dineas nods, looking as perplexed as I feel.

We're weeks away from Sehmar. The rosemarked need special permission even to leave our compounds, yet there she is. But she's different. The girl I'd befriended in Sehmar City had been isolated, lonely, and desperate. This woman, though, stands straight and speaks to Baruva's healer with a clear, steady voice. After they're finished talking, she climbs back up the riverbank toward a caravan of three wagons, frowning at the oilcloth covering of one and readjusting it. Mehtap talks with each of the wagons' drivers as well—all of them are umbertouched. I get the sense that she's issuing commands. In all the time I've known her, I've never seen her so resemble her father.

You'll likely travel the same path as her caravan. Stop and talk to them if you can. See if we can catch them in a violation—incorrect travel papers from Sehmar, forbidden foods in their wagon—her father's stature can't protect her from everything, especially with his recent disgrace.

I turn to Dineas. "Baruva's trying to sabotage her."

"Sabotage what?"

I don't know. One of Mehtap's drivers, a tall, umbertouched young man, approaches her with a ledger. They stand close, foreheads bent together as they look it over. What could she be doing? What is she delivering? I don't know if Mehtap and I had parted as friends or enemies, but I don't like the idea of Baruva scheming against her. She's still worth a hundred of that loathsome physician.

I edge toward the open. "I need to warn her about Baruva."

Dineas grabs my shoulder. "Are you out of your mind? That's Arxa's daughter!"

Yes, it would be folly to reveal ourselves to the daughter of the man who's hunting us across the empire. But Mehtap helped Dineas and me escape Sehmar City. She likely saved both our lives. I can't leave her without a warning.

A shadow passes over my head. The crows! I signal Scrawny down and rummage through my pack for a scrap of parchment. *Baruva is trying to discredit you. Be careful not to be caught violating the quarantine rules.*

Scrawny drops the note into the seat of her wagon. We don't stay to see if she finds it.

"You might as well have handed that letter straight to Arxa," says Dineas. The glare he shoots at me is milder now that we're safely away, but still, he's not pleased.

I know he's right. After all that work to throw Ampara off our path, a note like that, if Mehtap recognizes my handwriting, could ruin everything.

"She did save our lives," I say stubbornly. "You'd still be in the dungeons if not for her."

"She saved our lives as one last favor, because you didn't tell her father that she killed the emperor to make him a general. You'd be naive to think there's more to it."

Actually, there *is* more to it. Mehtap had asked a favor in exchange for her help. She made me swear that Dineas and I wouldn't harm her father. Dineas does not yet know about the promise.

"Do you think she's all right?" I ask.

"I guarantee you she's faring better than we," says Dineas.

We walk in silence for a while, heading east as Nush had advised. The terrain is hillier now and scattered with white boulders. Occasionally a groundhog jumps out of a hole and races away from us.

"I wish we'd gotten more from Baruva," I say after a while.

Dineas gives me a curious look. "What did Baruva mean, saying he was your last hope?"

That question has been haunting me as well. "Perhaps he wanted me to think he had a cure, but I've heard of no such thing."

"Could he know something you don't?'

"If he had a cure to the rose plague, he wouldn't be able to keep it secret. Someone would find out." At least, I think they would. I can't afford the distraction of hoping for more. "There might be more to know in his scrolls. I'll start working through them."

We travel as fast as we can. It seems Nush was right about the garrisons in the northeast—if there indeed is a search for us, it is a half-hearted one. As we go farther north, the plants progress from grass to bushes, and finally to small trees, and the air becomes heavy with moisture and salt.

A week later, we stand on a ridge overlooking the black and choppy waters of the Monyar Strait. Foreboding gray clouds loom above. As I stand there, buffeted by winds that threaten to knock me over, I think it's the most beautiful sight I've seen in a long time.

Dineas steals a boat from a fisherman's shed, and we drag it to an isolated beach. He holds the boat steady in the water and gives me a crooked smile. "Ready?"

It's one of his more charming moments, waiting there with that rakish grin. I think of our journey out here, getting on a boat to leave Monyar, barely able to stand each other. I don't think I ever truly expected to return.

The boat rocks on the waves as we start rowing, and the occasional spray comes over the side. The sheer black cliffs on the Monyar side grow steadily taller until we can see the rocky beaches below them and the bamboo forests beyond. As Dineas pulls the boat onto shore, I rake my fingers through the sand and squeeze a grainy handful between my fingers. I'm home, yet I can't shake the feeling that we're bringing back disaster with us. When I glance at Dineas, I see the same mix of emotions cross his face.

"It seems like so long ago, doesn't it?" I ask.

He scans the edges of the beach. "The cliffs make the beach easier to defend," he says. "As long as we hold those, we'll have at least some advantage."

What little joy I felt shrivels at his words. "That's it, then, isn't it? Our home is now nothing more than terrain on a battle map."

He looks at me, and his mouth twists. "I've never lived in a home."

I think about the forest around my village, the long days I used to spend wandering the hills gathering herbs with my mother. "What's the point of fighting if there's no place to return to afterward? Herbs won't grow in a trampled field."

"They say there are some plants that thrive on blood."

His cynicism scares me. "I refuse to give up before we even start." I strike off ahead of him toward the forest.

"Zivah!"

I turn, another retort on my tongue, but Dineas is looking past me toward the bamboo. He signals for my silence with a quick lift of his hands. Casually, he picks up his sword from the ground, shaking it loose from its oilcloth wrapping. I reach for my blowgun.

"I know you're here," Dineas calls. "Show yourself!"

For a long moment, we stand there, muscles taut, scanning the edge of the forest. Finally a voice calls out, "Dineas and Zivah, is that you?"

Two young Shidadi men step out from the forest. Dineas lets out a relieved breath and jogs past me toward them. "It's all right," he says over his shoulder. "Frada and Gaumit are from my tribe."

Frada is a heavyset warrior about Dineas's age with pock-marks and a star-shaped scar below his eye. The second Shidadi is slightly younger, skinnier, and hunches when he walks. To my surprise, I see that he's umbertouched. Other than Dineas, he's the first umbertouched Shidadi I've seen.

Frada clasps Dineas's arms in greeting. "We've been looking for you for weeks."

"We made some detours, but they may pay off," Dineas says.

"Detours? Or did you get lost again? You're not great at finding your way around."

There's a stiffness to Dineas's smile. "If I remember right, it was you who got lost overnight on the eastern coast."

Frada guffaws, radiating confident nonchalance. "That wasn't getting lost. Just some exploring that took longer than usual."

A muscle twitches in Dineas's cheek. "How are things here?"

"Quiet so far. Kiran hasn't sent any troops since he's announced his plans to attack," says Frada. "He knows we wouldn't let them in. Shall we send word to Gatha that you're back?"

"No," says Dineas quickly. "We're going straight to the village and can send word from there."

Frada shrugs. "Suit yourself."

We enter the shade of the bamboo. At first, the wind whips the leaves around us, making it sound as if the waves have followed us onto land. But as we go deeper in, it quiets. Dineas doesn't speak.

"I can't tell if you and Frada like or dislike each other," I say.

Dineas gives a wry smile. "I find him arrogant and obnoxious," he says. "But I can't dislike him too much."

"Why?"

"He..." Dineas furrows his brow. "Frada carries my hair and blood."

"What?"

"If someone saves your life, you give them a lock of your hair sprinkled with your blood. It's an acknowledgment of blood debt that you'll repay one day. Frada took an arrow for me some years back."

"And you find him obnoxious even though he saved your life?"

The corner of his mouth raises slightly. "I find him *more* obnoxious since he saved my life."

Slowly, the paths become more familiar. I recognize the field where I used to gather my cloudweed, and a small pond where we swam in the summers before I became rosemarked. The landscape is beautiful, and far too delicate.

"We're nearing the village," I say. "I can't go much closer." I try to keep my voice neutral, but Dineas's gaze softens.

"I'll let people know we've arrived. Will you be all right staying here?"

"Yes, of course."

But my heart is pounding and my head feels light. It's not that I want to run away. I'm desperate to see my family, but I'm also terrified of what I will find. Will they look the same? Have they changed? Will they find me different? Beyond that, has anything I've done in the past months made any difference? I've traveled so far and made so many mistakes. Have I really done anything to protect them, or have I made things worse?

After Dineas disappears down the trail, I pace back and forth. I strip the leaves from a stalk of bamboo and shred them into pieces. Footsteps approach, and my stomach does a somersault. I toss the leaves to the side, straining to identify who it is. If it's not my family, I'll have to get out of their way. But I see with a jolt that it's my younger sister, Alia, charging down the path, followed by my mother and father.

"Zivah!" shouts Alia, and my heart swells. She skids to stop in front of me so abruptly that I jump back in case she's forgotten to keep her distance.

My mother puts her hands to her mouth to stifle a sob. "Thank the Goddess."

She's older, and the bones of her face are more prominent. She raises her arms as if to embrace me but settles for hugging Alia's shoulders instead. Father beams at me, his eyes moist. He too looks thinner.

"Where's Leora?" I ask. Then I see my older sister coming around the bend. She walks slowly, rocking from side to side with each step, and I notice the roundness of her belly. Her eyes light up when she sees me.

Something overwhelms me—joy, hope, or grief, I can't tell. "Leora, you didn't tell me!"

She lays a protective hand over her belly. "News travels slowly across continents."

"You must stay away from me," I say. "For the little one's sake."

"I do not wish to," she says. But she doesn't come any closer, and I feel the distance in the innermost part of my chest.

It's a relief when Alia claps her hands. "Come. We will go to your cottage and clean it up."

"I should probably see Tal," I say. Our village leader was the one who sent me on this mission, and he'll likely be awaiting news.

"He's sending word to Gatha and the other Shidadi leaders," says my father. "He'd like you and Dineas to meet with them later today."

"So you have nothing to do now. Come on!" Alia says, and runs back the way she came. I'm about to follow when I see Dineas standing off to the side. There's a strange expression on his face.

I meet his eyes. "Will you go find your people?"

He nods. "I'll see you when the council meets." He doesn't look nearly as eager to find the Shidadi as I'd expect.

I take a step toward him. "Is everything all right?"

"Everything's fine," he snaps.

I stop, thrown back by his tone. He walks away before I can say any more.

I stare after him, aware of my family's eyes on me and wanting to throttle him. But Alia calls for me to hurry, and I resolve not to let Dineas's moods vex me. I keep expecting him to be someone else, when that person is long gone.

Alia keeps up a constant stream of talk as we head to my cottage. She tells us of her escaping goat, and of how the river flooded and three carts got stuck in the mud on the same day. Perhaps I imagine it, but her chatter doesn't have the same old shine of enthusiasm. She's more careful, her laugh just a little slower to come. When she runs ahead, I address my parents.

"How are things in the village? How does everyone respond to the news of war?"

"Most are scared," says Father. "The Shidadi have started teaching our young men and women to fight. It is good of them, and we're fortunate to have their help. But it's not what any of us wanted for our people."

I try to imagine Leora or Alia fighting, and the pictures just won't form. But then, had I ever imagined that I would break someone out of an imperial dungeon?

I hold my breath as we come into the clearing where I used to live. Part of me is surprised to find my cottage still standing, though it's been less than a year. It's certainly in need of repair. A corner of the roof collapsed in the rain, and the neighboring portions show signs of decay. The door to the shed has come off its hinges and is nowhere to be seen.

My mother walks ahead and stops to pick something off the ground. She frowns at it and then tucks it into her apron.

"What is it?" I ask.

She waves her hand. "Nothing important. Why don't you see how your cottage looks on the inside?"

I push open the door to my cottage, steeling myself for the worst, but it's not as bad as I'd feared. Cobwebs decorate the corners, and everything is covered in a thick layer of dust. A small animal has chewed through one of the legs of my cot, leaving some droppings on the floor next to it. I find my broom still in its old place. As I sweep the floor, Alia, my mother, and my father gather leaves to weave new thatching for my roof.

Leora comes to my door to keep me company as I sweep. She's careful not to lean against the frame. "Tal told us about the truth of your mission. It was very brave of you."

It's a relief to no longer lie to them, though I'm ashamed that they know I did. "I certainly didn't feel brave when I was doing it."

She smiles as she rubs her belly. "I suspect most heroines of history don't."

"I didn't want to keep it from you, but it was safer that way."

"I understand why you did it. We all do." She hesitates just a moment. "What you wrote to me about Dineas. That was true, wasn't it? At least the part about his memory loss in the capital, and what it was like to relate to him."

I slow in my sweeping. "Yes," I say carefully. Somehow, it was easier to speak with Leora about Dineas when I was an empire away. "It was a strange experience for both of us."

Leora moves out of the way as I sweep the dust out the door. "Would you say you know him well now? The real him?"

"He's harder to get to know. More guarded."

"And more human, I suspect," says Leora. "Are you still friends?"

"Allies for certain. Friends? Perhaps, though we don't always see eye to eye."

Leora tilts her head. "You've changed," says Leora. "You act more sure of yourself now."

I pause for a moment and consider her words. How indeed have I changed? I arrived in Sehmar City a healer, and I left a spy. What would Leora think if she knew that I've thrown scorpions into the face of a prison guard, or threatened a soldier with my blood? In the past year, I've helped people, and I've killed people. I've saved lives, and I've narrowly escaped death. But I am still rosemarked. I will still die. That has not changed.

SEVEN: DINEAS

I shouldn't have left Zivah so abruptly, but it was too hard to stay. Even now, there's a pit in my chest. It's strange to see her go back to her family. Of course I've always known our mission would end and we would head our separate ways, should we survive. It just takes some getting used to, after watching each other's back for so long.

Seeing Zivah with her family reminds me that I have none of my own to return to. My father's been gone for years, and my mother died in battle the first time I was imprisoned by the Amparans. I'm far from the only orphan in the tribe, and for the most part, we act as family for each other. But still, there's something about having your own mother and father, to be one of three siblings instead of a hundred.

Slicewing comes soaring down, chattering happily.

"Did you find the others?" I ask.

She hops onto a nearby stalk of bamboo and caws at me. Our tribe cycles through several campsites nearby, and she's likely found one of them to be inhabited.

"Give me a moment," I say, striking off in a random direction and ignoring Slicewing's caws. Preener and Scrawny fly in circles, clearly confused about what I'm doing.

I need more time before facing my people. Facing the knowledge that I'd killed my own kin in battle, thinking they were my enemies. And facing the memory of my Shidadi warlord Gatha stabbing my Amparan comrade Naudar. I'd hated her at that moment, wanted nothing more than to put a sword through her throat. Hate like this doesn't disappear when you get your memory back. It's an ember underneath my rib cage, and I fear that it will burn everything down.

But what did I really expect? That I'd live and fight alongside the Amparans, then come back and continue on as before? Truth is, before I left Monyar I hadn't thought much about what would happen after I came back. Perhaps I didn't really think I would.

Slicewing's chatter gets more and more insistent, and I give in. "Fine, lead me."

The bird flies off with an air of relief, stopping every so often to make sure I'm following. Preener makes a game of landing in the exact same place Slicewing does. At first he touches down before Slicewing leaves each perch, but after a few squabbles, he settles for diving in right after. I haven't gone far when a familiar voice calls out to me.

"Dineas." Gatha steps out of the foliage, looking much as she had before. Strong, and sturdy, the force of her personality showing through her stance.

"Gatha." This is the warlord I've followed from birth. A brave and fair leader, and a Shidadi warrior of the truest kind. I should be happy to see her.

Gatha looks me over with pride and squeezes my shoulder. "I was starting to worry you were waylaid."

It's a relief, at least, that I don't flinch at her touch.

"You did well," she says. "Very well."

"Feels like I just brought the Amparan army here earlier." I'm embarrassed as soon as the words leave my mouth. This is something only a green soldier in need of assurance would say.

"It was not an easy mission you had," says Gatha. "But now we have warning of the invasion, and we have your insider's knowledge of their tactics."

Gatha's praise had always been enough to make me stand straighter. For the most part, it still does.

She gestures behind her. "Your fellow fighters are eager to greet you."

Other Shidadi emerge from the forest, calling my name, slapping me on the back. "Dineas!" "You made it!" "Quite the mission, was it?"

Hands guide me to a small fire circle, where one of the older fighters hands me a rack of goat that sets my mouth watering. "Sit! Eat!"

My stomach reminds me that I haven't had a hot meal since we left Sehmar City. The bone is hot enough to burn my fingers. The meat is unseasoned but juicy, with an aftertaste of smoke.

Gaumit sits down on a log across from me. He and Frada must have just returned from their scouting rounds at the beach. "Tell me about Sehmar."

He doesn't make any effort to hide his envy as I tell him of the giant city, the marketplaces with all kinds of foods, and the palace with its carved facades and beautiful gardens. From Gatha's letters, I know that Gaumit fell ill with the rose plague shortly after I arrived in Sehmar City. It was a freak case of illness. No one else in our tribe caught it, and Gaumit still doesn't know where he picked it up. I wonder if he wishes he'd gotten his umbermarks earlier, so he could have been sent instead.

At least Gaumit will talk to me. More than one person quietly leaves the campfire as I speak. Then Mansha, a woman from our tribe, comes to sit down. At the sight of her, an image flashes through my mind.

I'm fighting next to my Amparan comrade Walgash. Mansha charges at me. I block her blow and slice my sword across the side of her face. She clutches at her bloody ear.

Mansha's long hair is tied in a loose ponytail that obscures her ear. I'm sure, though, that it's at least half gone. I look Mansha in the eye. "I'm sorry."

She raises a hand halfway to her head before dropping it. "You were doing your duty," she says. But she doesn't look me in the eye.

Frada steps between us at that moment, cutting across the campfire to sit a few paces from me. He eyes me with the same air of obnoxious challenge that he'd sported at the beach. "I'm intrigued by what this healer did to your memory," he says. "Did you really remember nothing of what you were?"

I tear off a bite of meat and chew it well. "Nothing. It was uncanny."

"Must have been hard to be among the Amparans and not want to kill every last one of them."

"It wasn't," I say steadily. "I couldn't remember anything."

He flicks a piece of gristle back into the fire. "Any news of Tus?"

The circle goes silent. I chew deliberately, aware of all the eyes on me waiting for an answer. The meat takes a few swallows to get down my throat. "Tus is dead."

I could say more—that the Amparans had tortured him beyond saving, that I'd given him my dagger so he could end his own life. That I'd been the one to capture him in the first place, convinced he was the enemy because I didn't remember who I was....Only later did I realize Tus had held back in that fight, and for that he'd paid.

Of course, everyone here knows I'd captured Tus. Half of them had been there when it happened.

"Dineas!" All eyes go to Gatha as she approaches the campfire. "Are you eating your fill?"

"Getting there," I say.

She's holding a knife in her hand. Her hair is tied in a stub of a ponytail, and she pulls at it now and cuts a lock loose. The crowd goes silent as she draws the knife across her palm and sprinkles the blood on the strands before twisting them into a quick braid.

"On behalf of the tribe," she says, presenting the lock to me.

I stare at her. Blood and hair from a warlord is given only for the highest examples of bravery and sacrifice. I haven't yet saved any Shidadi lives, have I? If anything, I've taken more lives than I've saved. If Gatha is trying to send a message, I'm not sure how it's being taken. Looking around, I see some nods of approval while others stare at me with open hostility.

Then it happens. Gatha's face shifts and lengthens. The jawbone becomes more pronounced. Stubble appears, and I'm looking at Arxa.

Arxa is dressed for training like the rest of us, in a short tunic and light leather armor that goes to his knees. "Don't be afraid to fight your best," he says to me. "Sometimes the new recruits think I want them to throw the fight."

"Not many men can claim the privilege of sparring with you, sir. I won't squander the opportunity."

"Take your stance, then."

I feel a thrill down my spine as I raise my sword.

Arxa is not nearly as aggressive a fencer as I expected. He's conservative, blocking and parrying rather than coming on strong. He's calm, though, and quick enough to block everything I throw at him. The few times I try to feint or surprise him, he doesn't fall for it.

We continue back and forth for a while, with no clear advantage on each side. What's frustrating is that thus far, he's just responding, and I can't get a good sense for his style. Little by little, I scale up my attack. My arms burn, and we both breathe heavily. The sun is still high, and I'm absolutely drenched with sweat, so much so that I worry about my grip on my swords.

Finally, I catch signs of him tiring. His sword is just a little slower to meet mine each time, and gives just a little more. I press him, knowing that I have to beat him before I tire as well. He takes a step back under my attack, and then another.

My foot catches on uneven ground. As I stumble, Arxa swings at my head, and my desperate attempt to block makes me lose what balance remains. The ground comes up, and Arxa's sword grazes my throat.

"You're younger," says Arxa. "You're faster and stronger than a man my age. Because of that, you rely too much on your skill and your strength. That will only get you so far in war. There's a reason I chose to spar with you when I knew the ground would be trampled from riding exercises."

He helps me to my feet. "In battle, you must use all the advantages at your disposal. Don't ever face your enemy on equal footing if you can help it. Pick terrain that favors you. Do you have greater numbers than your enemy? Use them. Do they lack cavalry? Deploy yours wisely. Our army's might does not simply lie in the skill of its soldiers. Do not discount our engineers, our supply trains, and our tent makers.

"Know your enemy. Know how much he's willing to sacrifice. Know yourself. Know when you're beaten, when you need to take risks, and when to be safe. Learn these lessons well, and you'll easily become one of Ampara's best."

The memory fades away. Sweat erupts all over my skin, and a fist squeezes my lungs. But when I look back at Arxa, he's no longer there. It's Gatha again, still holding out the lock of hair.

"Thank you, Warlord." I manage to loop it to my belt without dropping it.

Gatha studies my face, and I wonder how long that vision had lasted. "Come, it's time for us to go to the village."

I don't look anyone in the eye as I leave.

Gatha doesn't say anything else until the others have

dropped out of earshot. When she draws breath to speak, I steel myself.

"Some trouble from the others is unavoidable after a mission like yours," she says. "But it'll only come from a few. In time, most of your brothers and sisters will understand what you did."

If they do, then they will know me better than I know myself.

Dara looks about the same as it did before I left on my mission. It's a sprawling, messy network of trails and bamboo cottages that stretches down the length of the valley, interspersed with terraced fields. We pass the occasional villager on the narrow grassy trails, and others gathered around wells and clearings. We also run across Shidadi, but they're always hurrying through, and they're never talking to the Dara. As Gatha and I pass one well, a Dara man glares at us with unmistakable venom.

"Are we not welcome here?" I ask Gatha after we've passed him.

"Some of them blame us for bringing the war to them," says Gatha. "It's not all of them, or even most of them."

"Seems unwise of them to make enemies of us at this point," I say.

"There are all types of people in a tribe or a village," says Gatha. "You soon learn which opinions matter and which don't."

Gatha leads me to an open field away from the houses. Not a usual meeting place, I gather, but Zivah's not allowed in the village proper. There are four people waiting for us, and Zivah's seated on a mat set off from the other three. A plague veil lies folded next to her, along with a hat. Of the others, I recognize the Dara leader, Tal, but the remaining two are unknown to me.

"Dineas," Gatha says. "Let me introduce you to Vidarna and Karu." She gestures toward a tall, muscular Shidadi slightly older than herself. "Vidarna is the warlord of the tribe in the northern wetlands."

The man looks familiar.

"You may have met Vidarna when you were a child," says Gatha. "Our tribes used to cross paths in Southern Ampara. Vidarna and I fought side by side more than once in our youth."

Vidarna extends a hand. "From all accounts, I hear you do our bloodline proud."

A caw sounds, and Preener dives out of the sky right at Vidarna.

"Preener!"

A black-and-white pigeon launches itself off Vidarna's shoulder and flies into the trees. Preener follows, still chattering loudly.

I'm going to roast that crow for dinner. "I'm so sorry."

Vidarna looks like he's trying not to smile. "I'm sure White-claw can fend for herself."

Gatha raises her eyebrows at me, then indicates the woman next to Vidarna. She's very young for a warlord, about thirty years old, handsome, with long dark hair tied back. One of her eyes is covered by a patch, and she's umbertouched. "Karu is warlord of a tribe on Iyal Island," says Gatha.

Karu nods a greeting. There's something about the way she looks me over that gives me the acute sense she's looking for faults. She doesn't speak.

Two tribes came to our aid, then. Gatha had contacted four. "Any word from other tribes?" I ask.

"Our messenger wasn't able to find our tribe in the Eastern Provinces." That was bad news. I've never met anyone from the group that fled east fifteen years ago, but they'd numbered almost seven hundred.

"And our kin in Mishikan?"

Gatha presses her lips together and shakes her head. They'd

said no, then. I want to blame them but can't muster up the energy. Maybe they have their own troubles.

Tal looks at all assembled. "Emperor Kiran is sending armies our way. He accuses us of infecting a battalion of Amparan soldiers with rose plague, but we know that it was he who actually ordered the troops infected."

"It's a foolhardy move that could spread panic through his troops," says Gatha. "Does he command the respect of his soldiers? Will they follow him into battle against an enemy who supposedly wields the plague?"

"I think they will," I say. "The troops respect Kiran because he trains with them. They call him the warrior prince. We see him on the training fields, and he can hold his own. Also doesn't hurt that he's generous to the army out of his coffers."

Karu leans forward. "You say Kiran deliberately sickened the troops. Do you know how he did it?"

"I have some ideas," says Zivah. The council turns toward her. "He wrote that mixing the blood of the sick with weak vinegar strengthens the disease essence, perhaps enough so that it could be added to a battalion's food stores and not dissipate. We took possession of some of Baruva's notes and journals on our journey back, and I will do my best to find more clues."

"Do you know enough to sicken the troops yourself?" asks Karu.

Zivah freezes. "That would be an inappropriate use of healing knowledge."

"Do not be alarmed by my question," says Karu. "It's simply wise in these times to know all our options."

Gatha clears her throat. "What do you know of the army headed our way?"

"My best guess is that the army started marching two weeks after we left," I say. "They could get here within days. Ten thousand troops at least, maybe more."

A long silence follows my words.

"We have three thousand fighters at most," says Karu. "And that's counting the Dara villagers, who will be of questionable usefulness."

Tal's jaw tightens.

"It's not simply numbers that determine the outcome of a war," says Vidarna. "Our warriors are braver and more skilled."

"We're outnumbered, that's true," says Gatha. "But the peninsula gives us several advantages. The Amparans have to cross the strait to get to us, and the cliffs limit the places where they can make landfall. Our beaches are too rocky for their warships, so they'll have to come in by rowboat, which limits both their mobility and their supply train. If we choose to hold them off at the beach, we can deploy archers and rock flingers on the cliffs, and soldiers on the beaches to meet them. Or we can melt into the forests. Either way, we meet the Amparans on our terms, not theirs."

"What of their leadership?" asks Tal. "Is General Arxa still in charge of this campaign?"

"All we have to go by are rumors," I say, "but it seems Arxa was censured once Zivah and I were found out. He is no longer in charge of this entire campaign, but he is still commanding a contingent."

"That's all he faced?" asks Vidarna. "Wasn't he the one who brought you and Zivah into the capital in the first place?"

"Yes, but Arxa knows Monyar better than anyone else. They can't afford to remove him if they want to attack us. I'm guessing his friendship with Kiran protected him as well." Truth is, my first reaction when I heard of Arxa's fate was one of relief. I'd thought him a good and fair commander when I served under him, and somehow I can't shake the feeling that I'd betrayed him. On the other hand, he had me beaten bloody once he found out who I was and would have tortured me further if he'd had the chance.

Vidarna's gaze sinks into me. "And you, Dineas. You fought

alongside the Amparans and trained under their general. Can we trust you still to be loyal to our side? Will you be able to raise a sword against your old commander?"

For a moment, I wonder if Vidarna can read my mind. Then Gatha cuts in. "Dineas is one of my best. He would never—"

I stop her. "No, it's a fair question. I did fight alongside the Amparans, but my heart is Shidadi."

Vidarna nods, seemingly satisfied. If only I were as easily convinced as he.

EIGHT: ZIVAH

Returning to my people means becoming an outcast anew. Once again, I live alone in a cottage set apart from the rest of the village. Once again, all who come to see me must stay five paces away. It seems there are only two choices available to me: live shoulder to shoulder with strangers who share my fate, or exist at arm's length from those I love.

All around me, people prepare for the invasion. The Shidadi patrol the shores, watching for signs of the coming army. The Dara work day and night to stockpile food, blankets, and clothing. After months in a place where I had a role to play, I feel restless and useless. For the first time, I come to truly understand what life might have been like for Mehtap in the rose-marked compound.

One morning, I'm awakened by a thud against the wall of my cottage. It's a rock with an unsigned note tied around it.

May the Goddess judge you for bringing the Amparans upon us.

The words are large and stark, scrawled with such force that they leave indentations in the parchment. A chill spreads through me. I remember my mother picking something off the ground when I first returned to my house, and how she'd so quickly hidden it away.

Who sent this? I run through my recollection of fellow villagers, seeing their faces in my mind and sifting through everything they've said, before realizing the pointlessness of the endeavor. It could be anyone. One person may have written that note, but I'd be naive to think that only one person felt this way.

When I tell Tal about it, he doesn't seem surprised. "I'm sorry, Zivah. I'm to blame for this. I broke precedent by allying us with the Shidadi and sending you in secret. We're a people of harmony and compromise. We'd always made decisions by consensus until recently."

"Why did you do it?" I ask. Tal's led us for at least fifteen years. I've never known him to dictate anything before.

"We were slowly being bled to death by the empire, even before your mission," he says. "I had to take action before we became too weak to fight at all. The others would not have seen this."

I wonder at the conviction in his voice, and I wonder if it's warranted. "Do the people still follow you?"

"For now."

It's a disconcerting answer.

As battle preparations continue without me, I turn my attention to Baruva's notes, poring over them word by word. It feels distasteful to go through a man's private thoughts like this, but there's too much at stake. Baruva is a meticulous note taker. Every day has an entry, and his script is clean and even. Upon looking more deeply, I see a shrewd, manipulative man. He has notes on his fellow physicians—weaknesses, strengths, mistakes, details about their private lives. It's the type of knowledge that could be used to befriend and influence, or to threaten and blackmail.

As for Kiran, Baruva mentions meeting with him but never talks about what they discussed. There's far less about Kiran than there is about any of Baruva's colleagues. It appears that the healer is not a fool. He'll write down nothing to implicate himself.

Two days after I come home, my old master, Kaylah, appears at the top of the path to my cottage. There might be more gray in her long dark hair, but otherwise she is the same. Round face, wide, patient mouth that relaxes into a smile when she sees me.

"Goddess be praised for bringing you back."

Kaylah's always had an aura of peace about her. I've seen her touch soothe many a fevered patient, and even the healthy grow calm in her presence. My heart warms at the sight of her, yet I find myself fidgety as I lead her under the awning where I entertain visitors, with the four chairs that I never touch.

"You return from seeing the world," she says. "Tell me. What was it like in the capital?"

I sit back, unsure where even to begin. I think of the vast expanses of desert, the dilapidated rosemarked compound, the hospital filled with ailing. "It was good to be healing again, but it was hard to live in the compound. The conditions there are more desperate than I could have imagined." There was so much more—the months of deception, the desperate escape, the double life as healer and spy. But how do I speak of those things to Kaylah?

She lays a stack of clay tablets on the ground in front of her. "I've been reading through the notes you wrote for me."

"I'm glad they arrived safely." In Sehmar City, I'd recorded what medical knowledge I learned in the capital and sent them up north to Monyar. Scrolls would have been better, but tablets can be passed through the fire to dispel any lingering rose plague essence.

"What you wrote about Amparan surgeries was fascinating, especially the amputation you watched Jesmin perform. There must have been so much blood loss. How do the patients not bleed out?"

"Jesmin sutured each vessel independently as he worked. He says apprentice surgeons must practice on a hundred pigs before working on their first human patient."

Kaylah's hand goes to her mouth. "It must be horrific without anything for the pain."

"It was." I shudder now, remembering the man's screams. "The most they give for the pain is strong wine, and patients have to be held down. That's why Jesmin was so excited to learn about our potions."

"It's a pity we don't have the same surgical training in Dara. It would be quite useful in the coming months."

A pall falls over our conversation. I'm reminded that even those of us sworn not to kill will be affected by the war. It will no longer be illness, childbirth, and accidents that we tend, but sword wounds and arrow piercings.

"Will we have enough healers?" I ask.

"We've been training helpers in the binding of simple wounds. Beyond that, we'll just have to trust in the Goddess."

Kaylah has always had such faith in the importance of the work we do and the sacred nature of our vows. When I first spoke to her about going on my mission to Sehmar, she'd expressed grave doubts over the possibility that I would be pressured to break my vows as healer. I thought that her warnings wouldn't haunt me once I left Monyar, but even now, after I've returned, they tug at me.

I finally say it. "You still think I shouldn't have gone to Sehmar."

Kaylah takes a moment before replying. "You are a full healer now. I am no longer your master. You made a difficult decision. And we will have many more difficult decisions to come."

I know Kaylah. She won't accuse me or call me a liar. If I tell her that her worries were unfounded, that I went to Sehmar City and came back with my conscience clear, she won't challenge me.

But I would see the truth in her eyes.

I look away. "There's one thing that worries me. Now that we know Kiran infected his own troops, I fear the Shidadi will want me to use the rose plague against our enemies."

"And will you agree?"

The fact that Kaylah would even ask that question is more damning than any accusations she might have made.

"No. Of course not. That is a step too far."

"Then stand strong and have faith in the Goddess."

Kaylah's composure feels stifling. "To do what? To protect me from rose plague? To deliver us from the Amparans?" Kaylah blinks at my raised voice, but I can't stop. "What has she done to help us? I can't be like you, Kaylah. I can't simply trust in the Goddess to take care of us."

"And your own efforts to save us. How have they come out?"

"Better than—" I fall silent, because I still have no answer to that question. I killed men in the capital. Some fell to the snake I raise for venom, and others came to harm after I put them to sleep. I used my disease as a weapon to threaten others, and there were times when I was tempted to go beyond a simple threat. Yet after all this, I am still rosemarked. After all this, Ampara comes ever closer to destroying us.

I CATCH a chill the day after Kaylah's visit, and I'm confined to bed for a day with headache and nausea. When the fog finally lifts, I decide that I've had enough of staying in one place. I don my plague veil, put Diadem on my arm, and set out into the forest with my blowgun.

I had to give up treating patients when I became rose-marked, though I still helped harvest venoms for cures. These cures will be in great demand over the months ahead, and my collection of venomous creatures has long scattered. It's time I rebuild it.

The best way to go hunting depends on the type of creature. Spiders, scorpions, and frogs are best found by looking in nooks and crannies with a basket at the ready. Snakes, depending on their size, temperament, and habits, are best caught with snares or a blowgun. The same with star voles, the only mammals we keep, whose immunity to snakebites makes their blood useful for cures.

I set up a few traps in the hills near my cottage and catch a red-ringed spider off its web. Though I look over each bamboo plant with care, I don't see any snakes. It's a nice warm morning, though. The air smells green and fresh, and birds trade songs above my head.

There's a clearing not far from the village that I used to visit with my sisters. Blue coneflowers bloom there at this time of year, and I make my way toward it. As I get closer, I hear raucous laughter and what sounds like sticks banging against each other. If there are people at the meadow, I should turn around. But curiosity gets the better of me and I creep closer.

Dineas stands at the far side of the meadow holding a segment of bamboo as if it were a sword. He's fencing with someone whose back is turned toward me—a girl, from the sound of her laughter and the length of her hair. That shouldn't surprise me. I've always known the Shidadi have both male and female fighters. They trade blows back and forth, Dineas shouting tips over the clash of bamboo. Occasionally, the student stumbles or gets her sword in an awkward position, and that's when the giggling happens.

I edge closer for a better view, ignoring the twinge of...something...that grips me with each new peal of laughter. It strikes me how Shidadi Dineas looks. Now that we're no longer on the run, he's returned to carrying his weapons in the open. He has his swords on his back and several long knives at his belt. Beyond the weapons, though, there's something wilder about him. The fierce independence I remember from our first meeting shines through unrestrained.

Dineas and his pupil circle the edge of the meadow, maneuvering in and out of reach of each other's swords. Then they turn so that I see the girl's face, and I almost drop my blowgun.

It's Alia. She's quick on her feet—quicker than I would have expected—and she engages Dineas with surprising intensity. I step in for a closer look, and the movement catches her eye. She pauses, yelping when Dineas raps her on the wrist, and squints in my direction.

"Zivah?" she asks.

I take off my plague veil and hat, feeling like a child caught playing in the goat pen.

"Zivah!" Alia runs toward me. "Did you see? Dineas says I'm a quick learner!"

"She is," says Dineas, coming up behind her. He wears an easy smile, and a sheen of sweat covers his brow. His tunic is damp and clings to his broad chest and shoulders. I haven't seen much of him since our return, and I find myself searching for clues as to how he is. He's shaved off the unkempt beard he sported on the road, and he's trimmed his hair. The circles under his eyes remain. He's studying me as well, eyes flickering from my face to my clothes to the insect cage at my belt. I'm suddenly self-conscious about the wrinkles in my dress and the hair that has come out of my braid, even though I was often in worse shape during our travels.

"I didn't know Dineas was helping you," I say to Alia. She looks so pleased with herself that I do my best to match her mood, though the image of her fencing plays and replays itself in my mind's eye. My sister, wielding a sword. My sister, going into battle against Amparan soldiers.

"Just this morning," she says. "We ran into each other at the village. It's generous of him to take some time." Generous indeed. Thankfully Alia's chatter saves me from speaking.

"Leora wants to know when she can come visit you. She says you haven't responded to her message."

Leora has indeed asked to come see me, and I've put off replying, worried that I would endanger her baby.

"Tell Leora I'm sorry. I've been busy." Alia's eyes don't leave my face. I wish she would look away. "Do you still help at the fields in the afternoon?"

Alia glances up at the sun and grimaces. "Yes, I should be going."

Dineas gives her a cheerful punch on the shoulder. "Well done today."

"Send my love to Mother and Father," I tell her as she rushes off. And then it's just Dineas and me.

Without the immediate threat of Amparan soldiers at our heels, it's no longer obvious what there is to say. The image of Dineas punching Alia on the shoulder flashes across my mind. It was a brotherly gesture, but still a bitter reminder that he can touch Alia when I can't, that once again I'm alone.

In Sehmar City, Mehtap had been generous with her embraces. Dineas as his other self had been affectionate as well. Even before we thought ourselves in love, there had been playful nudges and pats on the shoulder. And in Jesmin's hospital, I'd been a bestower of touch, laying my hand on my patients' foreheads when they needed comfort, taking their hand when they were in pain. Now, back in Monyar, there are no more patients. My sisters are forced to keep their distance, and Dineas...things are different with him as well.

"You're settled now, back with your people?" I say.

"For the most part." He doesn't sound very convinced of it. "And you?"

I indicate the caged spider at my belt. "I'm rebuilding my collection."

Silence. I wonder where the crows are. "I thought the

Shidadi leaders promised that Dara youth were not to join in the fighting," I blurt out.

"They won't be forced to, but those who are willing and able will be welcomed."

"And Alia. You'll welcome her into your ranks?"

"She's a quick learner."

"She's fifteen years old."

"That's how old I was when I joined Gatha's elite fighters."

"And you would wish that on someone else?"

The hazel in his eyes seems to disappear, leaving them darker. "I didn't *wish* anything on anyone. Alia asked for help with her swordplay. I would think you'd want her to be as prepared as possible."

I try to choose my words wisely. "I do want her to be prepared, but she's young. She's impressionable and eager for excitement. It's a game to her. By the time she learns that it's not, it may be too late."

"You can't hide her away, Zivah."

"You would rather I put her in the front lines? Just because your people rush to destruction, does that mean we must as well?"

I regret my words as soon as they come out of my mouth, but I can't unsay them.

Dineas stares at me—incredulous, furious.

I take a step back. "Dineas." I stumble over my words. "I'm sorry. I—"

His expression doesn't change. This wasn't how I'd planned for the conversation to go.

I draw breath to speak again, but my eye is drawn to a movement in the forest. Alia reappears at the edge of the meadow.

"I'm glad you're still here," she says, running toward us. "There's a man in the village looking for the two of you. He says his name is Nush."

NINE: DINEAS

Alia slows as she nears, her gaze going uncertainly between me and Zivah. I school my features and see Zivah doing the same. Apparently we agree about keeping our fights private.

"You're certain this man's name was Nush?" I ask Alia.

"Yes. He told the scouts that you were a guest of his near Sehmar City, and that you two met again in Taof."

I suppress a snort at that. If that's hospitality, then I'd rather be an outcast. But I'm intrigued. This is far to travel, even for a Rovenni trader. "Take us to him."

Alia leads the way back to the village. I glance at Zivah as we walk, and a fresh wave of frustration comes over me. I'd forgotten how naive she could be. If she thinks she can protect her sister by keeping her ignorant of swordplay...

Though I have no reason to doubt Alia, I'm still surprised to see the big Rovenni man waiting for us. He seems unintimidated by the two scouts from Karu's tribe escorting him, though he looks inexplicably smaller without his horses.

"Nush." I extend a hand in greeting. "How did you get here?"

Nush looks me over as his Shidadi guards and Alia leave,

taking special interest in my weapons on display. "We sell some of our horses to sea traders. There are a few that owe me favors, and I've been curious to see Monyar." He shifts his gaze to Zivah, who has come to a stop several paces back. "And you are the healer whom the emperor seeks," he says. "I must say, I'm impressed the two of you made it back."

"We owe it to your advice on which roads to follow," says Zivah. "Have your people encountered any trouble since you left Taof?"

"We know the continent better than the emperor himself. There are places we can go to avoid trouble. With the war coming, he does not concern himself with chasing us." He looks at me. "We hear that the emperor is dispatching a fleet of warships and his most talented engineers to Monyar. You'd do well to watch the shore diligently. The empire's engineers have won many a war for Ampara."

Indeed, I've heard the histories—generals who redirected rivers to starve out a town, troops who constructed walls or drained swamps overnight.

"Thank you, we'll be on our guard."

The Rovenni nods. "I didn't come just to deliver a warning. We owe you our lives after Taof. Our elders have sent me to offer you what aid we can. We won't raise arms against Ampara, but we travel far, and we can be your eyes and ears on the continent."

Zivah and I exchange a glance. Winds are indeed changing if the previously neutral Rovenni are taking active steps of rebellion. "Eyes and ears we can certainly use," says Zivah. "Would you be willing to be our mouth as well?"

"How so?" asks the Rovenni.

"We learned things about the emperor while we were in the capital. First and foremost, we learned that Kiran ordered Baruva to poison a battalion of Amparan troops."

I'm surprised to hear Zivah bring this up, but I suppose there's no reason to keep it secret.

Nush scratches his beard. "Why would he hurt his own army?"

"Think about it," I say. "Kiran wants to expand the empire, but he needs to rally his people behind the cause in order to justify the expense and lives lost. If a battalion falls mysteriously ill in one of the outer territories, where it's already known that there are unsubdued rebels, who would you suspect? Who would you blame?"

"These are serious accusations. Do you have any proof?"

"I trust the man who told me," says Zivah, "but I can't prove it to you. We had to flee the capital before we could find any evidence."

He squints in the direction of the strait. "Gods know the empire has done worse than that to her subjects. I take it you want me to spread word of Kiran's misdeeds? Most won't believe it."

"But some will," says Zivah.

Nush frowns. In the past, I would have thought him displeased, but now I realize he's simply thinking. "Very well. We'll see what comes of it."

"Thank you." I look around for my crows and catch a flash of wing in a nearby stand of bamboo. When I whistle, Scrawny and Slicewing land on my shoulders while Preener comes to perch on my head.

"Take Preener with you," I tell Nush. "He can carry messages from the continent, though if you want a reply, you'll have to stay in the same place and wait until he returns." Preener gives me a perplexed look, and I pat his head. "Go with Nush. He'll show you some interesting places."

Nush extends a skeptical hand to the bird, who steps gingerly onto his finger. The crow looks at him, and at me, and then starts picking through his wing feathers. The Rovenni man turns to me. "I will do my best to be of help," he says. "Be careful. The road you go down, there's no turning back."

TEN: ZIVAH

K aylah continues to visit me, though we don't speak of Sehmar City or sacred vows after that first day. She brings the tablets I'd sent her on Amparan medicine and studies them while I read through Baruva's journal. Occasionally she asks questions about what I'd written, and I answer to the best of my ability.

Though I've turned up no evidence against Baruva or Kiran, his notes still contain valuable medical knowledge. He has a theory of rose plague as a disease that starts in the blood and settles in the skin, and he's written many lengths of parchment dedicated to the search for new ways to fight the illness. There are no cures here, but plenty of methods to ease a patient's suffering. There are potions for treating the plague's initial symptoms: managing the high fever and improving clarity of mind in the throes of the illness. A second section is dedicated to alleviating the headaches, tremors, low-grade fever, and blurring of vision that signal the fever's return in the rosemarked.

I have to admit the man's genius. He's thorough, observant, and insightful, and I can't help but wonder if this is why the plague patients at Taof had seemed better off than the ones I'd previously treated.

I'm reading through lists of esoteric treatments when something catches my eye: *The suona flower grows only in the mountains of the Mishikan Empire, above the snow line. Its pollen, red with a hint of yellow and iridescent in the sunlight, is rumored to extend the life of the rosemarked.*

I have to read the line over several times to make sure I'm reading it correctly. A treatment for extending the life of the rosemarked is far different from the palliatives he'd written about up to now. Was this what Baruva meant when he said he was my last chance at life? I glance up at Kaylah, fighting the absurd feeling that I'm looking at something I shouldn't. She's engrossed in her own studies.

The most credible report comes from the story of Nia, brother of the previous king of Mishikan, who became rosemarked in his thirtieth year. To save his brother, the king instituted a modified tribute system. People living in the mountain regions were required to submit a basketful of suona flowers as part of their yearly tithe. Nia took a pinch of pollen in his tea every morning and lived rosemarked for fifteen years before finally succumbing to the fever.

The rarity of these flowers may render interest in this herb to be purely theoretical, as only someone with a monarch's resources could gather the amount of pollen needed to keep even one person alive. Attempts to grow the flower in other climates and soils have failed, though it's rumored that Mishikan royalty have started storing suona pollen in case another member of the royal house falls ill.

A bitter taste forms in my mouth. So that was why I hadn't heard of it. Because it's a plant found outside of the empire, rare enough to be used only for kings. There's a note in the margin of the scroll. It's Baruva's handwriting but written very small.

Slow dysentery, plague incubation length.

Does he mean that the suona pollen would slow dysentery? But dysentery is not a common symptom of rose plague. And what does that have to do with plague incubation length? I wonder if this was simply an unrelated note, a scrawled thought to be remembered later. But Baruva has always been so meticulous.

"Did you find anything interesting?" asks Kaylah.

I glance up with a start. "Nothing important," I say, and I move on to the next section of notes.

ELEVEN: DINEAS

Naudar is impeccably dressed, as always. His belt buckle shines like a mirror, there's no trace of stubble on his chin, and his tunic is as wrinkle-free as a statue's. He's also surprisingly cheerful, considering that he's dead and wandering the camp of the people who killed him.

He steps carefully over sleeping bodies, looking curiously at the faces of my kinsmen. They don't stir, which I suppose makes sense. Though when I follow in Naudar's footsteps, my progress isn't nearly as smooth, as I trip over blankets and kick dirt into snoring faces. More than once, someone stirs and panic grips my chest, but no one wakes.

"I'm disappointed in you, Dineas. You should at least press your tunics," Naudar calls over his shoulder. "Especially with all these maidens fighting alongside you." He pauses. "Isn't that distracting?"

"It only seems like it'd be distracting because you're not used to it. I mean, there's less facial hair and sweat, I suppose. And you have to look around before undressing or taking a piss. Otherwise, it's about the same."

"People shouldn't be answering nature's call in the open anyways.

It reflects badly on the empire. Where is your warlord, by the way? I didn't get a good look at her in the battle."

There are all kinds of reasons why I shouldn't lead him there, but this is a dream, and ghosts do what they will. We cross the camp, stepping over body after body.

"We had some good times in Neju's Guard, didn't we?" he calls over his shoulder. "Remember that time they tied us naked to the rooftop?"

"I wouldn't really call that a good time."

"Let's just say you gain some perspective when you die."

He comes to a stop by Gatha's bedroll. My warlord is sound asleep, even though she usually wakes up at the slightest sound.

Naudar furrows his brow. "She's a decent commander. I'll allow that. And I can't fault her fighting skill. But why follow her when you can fight under Arxa?" He gestures toward the hills around me. "Why this, when you can serve the glory of Ampara?"

I shift uncomfortably. "I'm Shidadi. I always have been."

Naudar's eyes narrow. "Really? Because you didn't seem very Shidadi in Sehmar City."

"That was different. I lost my memory—"

He cuts me off. "You know what really makes me angry? It's that I expected so much better from you. You seem like such a soldier's soldier. Live by the sword, die by the sword, and all that. Sure, the emperor has assassins and spies, and all those slippery types, but I wouldn't have expected that of you."

"I—"

"No excuses, Dineas. You took that potion. No one forced it down your throat. Walgash, Masista, and I, we took you in, showed you Sehmar City and made sure you were successful in the army. And then you come around and stab us all in the back."

Suddenly he's holding a knife.

"Naudar, what are you—"

He looks straight at me. "Kind of like this."

And then he plunges the knife into Gatha's chest.

My scream wakes me up. I'm on my feet, reaching for my

knives, before my eyes have completely opened. My breathing is ragged and coarse as my bedroll falls away and the predawn breeze brushes my skin. I look around, trying to see if I've awakened anyone, but it seems I haven't. I've been sleeping away from the others, because this is not my first nightmare.

There's something about waking up in a Shidadi camp after dreaming of your Amparan comrades that makes the morning feel extra cold. I have an urge to find Gatha and make sure she's alive. It's a foolish thought, I know, and I wouldn't be able to find her anyways. She sleeps in a different part of the camp every night, makes sure she spends time with everyone in the tribe. Plus, she's up before dawn, tending to the day's business.

Why her when you can serve under Arxa?

Arxa was good to his men. He had a keen eye for skill and pushed us to be the best of our ability. But when Neju's Guard traveled, Arxa slept in a tent in the middle of the camp, surrounded by the men but separate from them. That distance was part of his power. He had a mantle of authority, of someone who knew more and climbed to greater heights.

With Gatha, there's no distance. She's in the mud with us, living and fighting day to day. Arxa might give educated speeches, but I've seen Gatha lay a hand on a boy's shoulder, say two words, and make him burst into tears. They're often painful, uncontrollable tears, but he'll sleep better that night and hold his head higher the next day.

I wonder, if I told this to Naudar, whether he would understand why I'm loyal to Gatha. I wonder if he would forgive me.

I make my way toward a small campfire where Frada and Gaumit sit warming their hands. Next to them, a young woman from Karu's tribe plucks a tune on an Iyal finger harp, so quietly I can hardly hear it over the fire's crackling. Rounding out the circle are two fighters I don't recognize, playing some game involving hand gestures and a lot of grimacing. Our campfires tend to segregate by age rather than tribe, a habit from the old days when we still traveled the central continent. Whenever tribes crossed paths, we'd camp together for a while. There'd be tournaments, songs, and performances around the campfire. Couples would meet, flirt, and fall in love, though I was never old enough to join in any of the festivities. By the time I came of age, we'd already fled into Monyar.

"Morning," Gaumit says. His umbermarks dance in the flickering firelight. "Water?" He passes me a hot mug. It burns my tongue, but the warmth is worth it.

"Any plans this morning?" I ask.

Frada shrugs. "This and that." I don't care enough to coax more out of him. I catch a glimpse of the lock of my hair that he wears on his belt. Why is it always the jackasses that save your life?

Gatha's voice drifts over from the edge of the camp. "She should take more care where she steps. Something was bound to happen." She and Vidarna walk into view, and her eyes land on the campfire. I double-check for a knife wound on her chest.

"Do I see idle swords?" she says to us. "Mansha sprained her ankle crossing a creek. I need a replacement for her scouting round."

"I'll do it," Frada says too quickly.

"Go now, then. Her watch starts in a quarter hour." She turns and yells at a cluster of children throwing knives at a tree. "Stop cheating, Riyo. I saw you step over that line."

As they walk off, I hear her consulting with Vidarna on the best combat formations to use on the Monyar mountainside. The two are always discussing strategy, both with each other and with the rest of the fighters. Karu rarely joins in. She talks a lot with those of her own tribe, but I hardly ever see her with the other two leaders.

After Frada leaves, Gaumit hunches over, seemingly preoccupied with the fire.

"Didn't know Frada was so fond of scout duty," I say. *Almost as if he didn't trust me to do it.*

"He's probably restless, needs to walk it off," Gaumit says. Though he still doesn't look at me.

I've had enough. "Thanks for the water." I stand to hand the cup back to him, but it slips out of my hand. I lunge, barely catching it before it hits the dirt. Gaumit throws his arm over his head.

"Sorry, Gaumit." I straighten myself and hand him the cup. Only then do I realize that he's reached reflexively for his knife.

He drops his hand. "Good catch."

I'm careful not to make any more sudden movements as I step away.

I take a trail into the forest, walking quickly as if faster steps would trample my frustration. Frada doesn't trust me to scout. Gaumit doesn't trust me to sit next to him without killing him. My own kinsmen see me as an enemy.

Every so often, a rustling in the leaves alerts me to some creature scared away by my approach. The early morning breeze filters right through my tunic, but I don't feel it. The mission's over. I'm back with my people. Why am I still haunted by ghosts?

When I step on the trail leading to Zivah's cottage, I stop pretending that I hadn't been headed this way all along. Zivah's up already and seated outside her front door. I'm not surprised to see her up early, since this is her favorite time of day. She likes to watch the sunrise and reflect on the day to come. The other me had learned this in Sehmar City.

Zivah's incredibly still as she studies a scroll in front of her. Occasionally, she wrinkles her brow or brushes a strand of hair from her eyes, but otherwise, she might as well be a statue. She cuts a regal profile in the morning light. It's such a peaceful scene that I wonder if I should turn back.

But then she looks up. "Dineas. You're out early."

"Are you busy?" I ask, like the lumbering ox I am.

"No. Just looking at Baruva's notes again." She motions me toward a chair.

I sit, but the chair is far too restrictive and I stand again. "Find anything?"

"No."

If it had been the other me dropping by, there wouldn't be any of these stunted exchanges. She would have brightened to see me and found some way to slip away from her hospital duties. We would have gone for a walk, talked of everything and anything, and the time would have gone by too quickly. The other Dineas wouldn't have stood here wondering how much to say, how much to reveal before she fears me like all the others, before she realizes, truly realizes, that I am nothing like that bright-eyed soldier in Sehmar City.

"I dreamed about Ampara last night," I say.

"Who did you dream about?" Not *what* did you dream about, but who. That one word gives me the courage to continue.

"Naudar." Poor, dead Naudar. His loss feels fresh again after that dream. "I can't come back from there."

Her eyes soften. "I'm sorry."

Once the words come out, it's hard to stop. "Maybe it would have been different if I'd been a normal spy, if I'd known I was lying from the beginning. But I can't simply cast off a whole other life that I lived." I stop. "And it's not just me. I can see it in their eyes too."

"Who?"

"The others of my tribe. They remember how I spilled Shidadi blood. They say they forgive me, but they don't." I wave my hand disgustedly. "They don't trust me, and who's to say they're wrong? When I go into battle, I might see Arxa again. I might see Walgash or Masista. Can I kill them when the time comes?"

"Do you want to kill them?" she asks.

"Does it matter?"

I spoke more loudly than I meant to. The birds around us go quiet, and my face goes hot.

But Zivah seems unperturbed. She looks down at her hands. "I dream about Mehtap and Jesmin, sometimes even Arxa. And I try to tell them I'm sorry."

"What do they say?"

She frowns, as if surprised I'd ask this question. "Sometimes they forgive me. Most times they don't. Sometimes I think, 'Why should I be sorry? I'm the one who's sick because of the empire's abuse. I'm the one whose homeland has been invaded.'"

"Were Mehtap and Jesmin friends to you?" I ask, strangely curious. "True friends?"

"At the time, yes," she says with a sad smile. "Who knows what they think of me now. Mehtap—" She stops abruptly.

"What?"

She shakes her head. "Nothing, I just miss her."

I'm tempted to let the conversation end here, keep her from knowing the extent of my madness. But it's not a secret I can bear by myself any longer. "It's not just dreams for me."

She looks up. "What do you mean?"

"That night on the riverbank near Taof. You ask me how it was that they captured me. It's because I saw a soldier's face turn into Masista's. It was only for a moment, but it was enough."

Her brows furrow.

I keep talking before I lose my nerve. "It still happens. Gatha turned into Arxa the day we came back."

She blinks. "And this happens without warning?"

"Yes."

Zivah frowns. "It must be the residue of the memory potion. Your mind is used to living that other life. It intrudes now."

"So I'm still two people." I'm still split into pieces. "Will it stop?"

She shakes her head, and I see deep, helpless grief in her eyes. "I don't know," she says softly. "The potions were never meant to be used for these purposes."

She'd warned me of this when she first treated me, that there were things we didn't know. If something went wrong, I could lose myself. She looks at me now as if expecting me to hate her. And I suppose I should, but I can't muster it up. We've been wandering in the dark this entire mission, taking steps as best we could and hoping not to trip and fall. I could yell at Zivah, tell her she should have done her part better. I could point at the shattered parts of myself and tell her that it's her doing. But then I would still be stumbling in the darkness, only this time, I'd be alone.

I don't know why it took me so long to admit it to myself, but I miss her. "Remember those walks we used to take in the rosemarked compound?"

It takes a moment for her to understand me. "In Sehmar?" I wish she wouldn't look so surprised that I'd bring them up.

"When we'd circle the compound, or go sit inside Mehtap's villa."

A faint smile comes across her face, and it warms my chest. "I suppose we made the best of that place, even though it wasn't exactly the emperor's garden."

"Well, there *was* the courtyard of Mehtap's villa. The shady spot underneath the cedar."

"And the pool of polished stones," she says. "I loved those colors."

"I used to snack on your herb garden," I say. "I'd pick the leaves off the plants and chew them while I waited for you to come out."

Zivah laughs. "So it was you who did that? My poor seedlings kept wilting. I spent so long trying to find the culprit."

I throw up my hands. "It couldn't have been *just* me. I only took a little from each plant. I swear I know better than to massacre innocent herbs like that."

She crosses her arms over her chest and tries to pull off a frown. "It was always about your stomach, wasn't it?" There's a sparkle in her eye, but somehow it makes me uneasy. "I still remember the candied rose petals you brought me when you first joined the army. Those early weeks, I was so worried about you being found out, and instead there you were, eating your way through the marketplace."

I realize what it is that bothers me, and with it comes a lance of bitterness. "I should go."

She blinks. "So soon?"

"I have scouting rounds." A lie. I wonder if she can tell.

She touches me lightly on the arm. "Will you be all right?"

"I will." I try not to pull away, but a flicker of hurt still crosses her face.

"If there's anything I can do to help..." she says, uncertain now.

"Thank you," I say. "I may come back later if Gatha doesn't need me." But I know I won't. Because just now, I've realized two things. One, that I'm still in love with her. And two, that she's still in love with the Dineas from Sehmar City. The version of me that never existed.

TWELVE: DINEAS

A scout comes sprinting into camp two days later, shouting loud enough to wake the emperor of Mishikan: The Amparans have arrived on the opposite coast. Before that scout catches his breath, dozens have already taken off running toward the ocean. Several hours later, a crowd of us gathers, breathless, atop the cliffs to watch the soldiers pouring onto the opposite shore. So many of them, so few of us. It's just a matter of time before they attempt a crossing.

We move our own camps close to the shore, within marching distance of the three beaches they're most likely to attempt. As the native warlord, Gatha has high command of our fighters. She divides all the Shidadi into scouting groups of three. I'm put in command of two warriors. Hashama is a fighter under Vidarna who's the same age as me. He's tall, broad shouldered, and I've never seen him crack a smile. He has a strange habit of gazing over people's heads when he's walking or talking, and seems like the type of person who would have been bullied mercilessly as a boy, except that he's one of the fastest runners I've ever seen and a solid fighter all around.

Sarsine, from Karu's tribe, is fifteen years old, as tall as

Gatha but half as wide, with a hooked nose and stubborn chin. If humans grew like trees and she keeps adding rings, she might look like Gatha in thirty years. Over the past weeks, I've gotten the sense that Karu's tribe had a hard time surviving on Iyal Island, which is saying a lot considering the rest of us weren't exactly living in luxury. Almost every Karu fighter I've met has been skinny and scarred. Most of them act pretty beaten down. Sarsine is skinny and has her share of scars, but she also has quick, intelligent eyes and a constant energy that gives the impression she might run off in three different directions. She also reminds me of myself. For one thing, she's a devil with dual swords. She's also umbertouched.

I can't help but notice that Gatha has put me with soldiers from Karu's and Vidarna's tribes, instead of my own. Part of me wonders if this should bother me more, but it's a relief to have some respite from the suspicious glances and veiled comments coming from those who should be my family.

We're assigned to scouting rounds every two days, walking along cliffs where we can get a good view of the Amparan shore. As we scout this morning, Sarsine holds forth on the implications of rose plague for fighters. "It's like a different sort of battle, isn't it?" she says. "You against the gods. There's no way to train against it, really."

"Does Karu let you talk this much on a mission?" I ask.

"No. But it's not as if the Amparans will hear us from the opposite shore." Without missing a beat, she draws a bow and shoots something in the underbrush. Hashama frowns as Sarsine wades out of the forest with a skewered quail. "See? I'm paying attention."

I turn my head to hide a smile. I shouldn't encourage this kind of insubordination, but I can't bring myself to discipline her. My friend Walgash in the Amparan army was much like her, sounding off on all sorts of topics at length. The habit was annoying at times and strangely comforting at others. I'm not the only one who lingered close to Walgash's campfire on long missions to be entertained by his chatter. After Naudar died, Walgash spent an entire evening recounting stories about him, from pranks to battles to everything else in between. That, more than the memorial service weeks later at the capital, had been what really laid Naudar to rest for me. Of course, the last time I saw Walgash, he'd found me out for a traitor. And the last image I have of him is the anguish in his face as Arxa ordered him to beat me into submission.

We stop to look out across the strait again. What used to be beach is now covered with soldiers, flags, and tents.

"What's that?" asks Sarsine. I look where she's pointing to see two giant warships skirting the Amparan shore toward the enemy camp.

"I thought warships were useless on our shores," says Hashama.

"They are. We have too many rocks for them to maneuver around." At least I thought so. I whistle for Slicewing and scribble a quick note to Gatha. We keep watching.

The ships get closer and closer to the Amparan camp, though they make no move to cross the strait. One stops parallel to the shore, and the other one pulls up next to it on the Monyar side. In the distance, two more warships make their way closer.

"They're boarding," says Hashama.

Indeed, a handful of soldiers are boarding the ship that dropped anchor closer to the beach. My pulse starts to race. Is this it?

"Give me the horn," I say.

Hashama hands me a ram's horn, and I blow an alarm call to the troops below. From my vantage point, I see our people spring into action. Those on the beach run to their stations as others march in from the forest.

But something's off. There's only one ship being boarded,

and now a third ship comes and takes position on the Monyar side of the other two ships, parallel to the shore but nowhere near it. Then the crews start taking down the sails. Half an hour passes, and then an hour. Men scurry around the decks, but the ships don't move. If anything, it looks like there's construction going on, pieces of wood getting moved about and hammered into place.

Our army's might does not simply lie in the skill of its soldiers. Do not discount our engineers, our supply trains, and our tent makers.

A fourth ship pulls into place. And the realization dawns on me with disbelief and dread.

"I know what they're doing," I say. "We need to talk to Gatha."

The hammers of the empire ring in my ears as we hurry down the cliff.

"They're building a bridge across the strait."

I'm back at the clearing where Zivah and I first met with the leaders. She sits next to me, watching me with a puzzled expression. Vidarna and Karu stare at me as if I've lost my mind. Even Gatha and Tal look doubtful.

I continue. "They're lashing warships together to form a bridge, and then they'll bring their entire force on us at once."

"You're talking about hundreds of ships," says Gatha. "Lashed together, against the waves and the wind?"

"A bridge will make much better use of their numbers," I say. "They can send their cavalry across even as they deploy boats on the side. Our fighters aren't trained to stand down a cavalry charge in battle. They'd roll right over us."

"They wouldn't employ a cavalry in the mountains," says Karu.

"But they could send it in simply to overrun the beach if they need to," I say. "Ampara has resources."

"If that's true, it would be a waste of lives for us even to try and hold the beach," says Vidarna. "We need to move to the second part of the plan. Disappear into the forests. Leave nothing behind that they can use. Burn the houses and the fields. Fill in the wells."

Zivah blanches at the suggestion.

"Out of the question," says Tal. "I can't ask our people to abandon a lifetime of work."

"Either we destroy the village, or they do," says Karu. "If you cling to your houses, you'll lose your lives."

Gatha frowns. "He may be right, Tal. Staying here would just be inviting a slaughter."

"But to abandon our village without even trying to defend it?" says Zivah.

"I owe my people better than that," says Tal. "What if you attack the bridge preemptively? Keep it from being completed?"

"Send our warriors out in rowboats against warships?" says Karu. "They'll pick us out of the water like so many fish."

Our home is nothing more than a piece of terrain. The words ring in my mind with the force of Zivah's anger. I can see why the Shidadi leaders don't want to defend the beach, but if Dara had been our ancestral village, I don't think we'd be so quick to abandon it.

I clear my throat. "If a full attack is too dangerous, maybe we could try a smaller sabotage mission. Go at night for cover. Bring pitch and fire arrows to burn what we can."

Zivah looks at me in surprise.

Gatha makes a doubtful sound in her throat. "You'll be dashed against the rocks without light to see by."

"Some of us know this beach well enough to navigate blind," I say. "I can lead it."

"Sending a small group of volunteers may not be entirely foolhardy," says Gatha. "We wouldn't risk greater casualties that way."

Karu narrows her eyes at me. "You would lead such a dangerous mission? Your kinsmen don't even trust you to live among them."

I stare at Karu in disbelief. Am I so hated by my tribe that even the other leaders would speak openly about it?

"Karu," Gatha warns.

Vidarna lets out a resigned sigh. "Karu may have been out of line in saying it," he says, "but she does raise a good point. Dineas may not be able to lead an effective attack if those under him don't trust him."

"If no one volunteers, then we won't go," I say. "Don't gnash your teeth on my behalf. Just tell me if you'll let me try."

"You have no objections from me," says Gatha.

"If your warlord approves," says Vidarna, "then it's not my place to stop you."

All eyes turn to Karu.

"If it's only volunteers," she says, "I have no objection."

THIRTEEN: ZIVAH

I catch Dineas by the shoulder before he has a chance to leave the field. "Thank you."

He meets my eye just briefly. "Don't get your hopes up," he says. "Those army engineers know their trade. That bridge will be hard to damage."

"But you're willing to try. That means a lot to me."

He tilts his head at me.

"To all of us," I add.

He shifts his shoulders as if I'd laid a too-warm cloak on his back. There are hollows in his cheeks. I wonder when was the last time he'd slept, and I feel the heavy truth that the ghosts keeping him awake are of my making. I was never foolish enough to think our troubles would disappear at Monyar's shores, but somehow I thought our burdens would at least lighten.

"Have you been sleeping?" I ask.

His mouth quirks. "Have you?"

Again, our eyes meet. I look away. "When will the mission go out?"

"Tomorrow night, perhaps. The sooner the better."

If he's going out to face the Amparans, I have to tell him about the promise I made to Mehtap on his behalf. I don't know why I've put it off so long, when I'm not even sure it would upset him. But even now, it's hard to get out.

"What is it?" Dineas asks.

I suppose I'm not as good at hiding things from him as I thought. "There's something I haven't told you about Mehtap."

He waits.

"Back at the capital, when Arxa had you imprisoned, she was the one who helped me sneak into the palace to break you out."

"I know."

"She also asked me to swear that neither you nor I would harm her father."

He frowns, not quite comprehending. "You made a promise for me?"

"I was trying to get us out of Sehmar City."

He still looks as if he's trying to unravel my words. "You promised Mehtap I wouldn't harm Arxa?"

"She wouldn't help me otherwise."

Disbelief begins to color his voice. "So you felt it proper to make a binding oath on my behalf?"

"It wasn't a binding oath. The gods wouldn't hold you to it."

He rubs his temple. "But you let her believe you could convince me to go along. You shouldn't have done it."

"If you'll remember, I didn't have many other options."

Dineas shakes his head. He speaks deliberately, as if trying not to lose patience with a child. "You have no idea what a vow like that could do in battle. A moment's hesitation on my part when I'm surrounded by enemies—that's all someone needs to slip past my guard and kill me, or, worse, kill one of my kinsmen. And I assure you, Arxa won't have the same hesitations about me."

His self-righteous indignation tries my patience. "You're right. I don't know what it's like on the battlefield," I say. "But I know what it's like to be tossed into an Amparan prison. I know what it's like to fight my way out with a handful of scorpions and drops of my own blood. And I know what it's like to break into a dungeon full of Amparan soldiers to rescue someone from its depth. Would you rather I had abandoned you there?"

"Do you know what Arxa did to me?" I flinch at the same time he realizes how loud he is, and he lowers his voice, stepping closer and continuing in a hiss. "What he did to the other Shidadi he captured? He would have tortured you too if we hadn't escaped."

We're so close we're breathing the same air, but I refuse to back down. "Don't act as if the man's your sworn enemy. You've said yourself that you might not be able to kill Arxa. He was good to you once, and he was good to me. Mehtap saved both our lives, and her father is all she has."

He makes a disgusted snort. "You speak of Mehtap as if she's an innocent child. She's an assassin with a child's face, and she's lived an easier life than most."

"You owe her your life, Dineas. Doesn't blood debt mean something to your people?"

He blanches, and his face twists with loathing. "You really know nothing about us, do you? Blood debt doesn't mean 'something' to us. It means everything. That is why it 'upsets' me so much. My fellow Shidadi already don't trust me. If word gets around that I owe my life to an agreement with Arxa's daughter, that I've been sworn not to raise my hand against an Amparan commander...You should have left me in that prison. At least then, I'd still be able to hold my head high."

As he storms away into the forest, I wonder if he may be right that I don't know anything about his people, or him, at all.

FOURTEEN: DINEAS

My fight with Zivah haunts me as I make preparations to scout the bridge. It's an arrow lodged in my ribs, working its way in even as I try to ignore it. Every time I let myself think we understand each other, something like this happens to make me realize how little she actually knows.

A nagging voice comes to me. *Is the promise really what's bothering you? Or is it that when you heard the promise she made, part of you grasped at it? You've long doubted whether you'd be able to fight your Amparan comrades. This oath would make that decision for you, at least for Arxa.*

That thought, I bury deep underneath the rest.

Thirty of us responded to Gatha's call for volunteers—ten boats of three people apiece. As night falls, we gather on the beach to ready the attack. The water around the beach is rocky, and in this darkness, we won't see the rocks until it's too late. We'll be relying on our memory and our instincts to keep from being dashed on them. I'll be surprised if all ten of the boats make it to the bridge. Seven would be a good number. If the winds work against us, the number could be as low as five. As I consider the risks, I realize how foolish I was for not going to see Zivah again before the mission. If something were to happen to me tonight, I don't want that fight to be our last conversation.

The waves beat a steady rhythm on the sand as I strap my swords to my waist, and my quiver and bow to my back. Our shields go on the bottom of the boat, along with jars of pitch. All around me, I hear muffled thuds, the swish of clothes, and the clink of metal as the fighters make their own preparations. When I'm done, I peer out onto the ocean. Somewhere in all that darkness, there are the darker shadows of ships, but I can't see them.

A hot wind blows across my face. It's high noon. Sweat drips down my forehead as I stand in formation with Neju's Guard. Arxa's voice echoes over the field.

"Look around you. These are your brothers-in-arms. You are one creature. If one dies, all die with him."

A surge of pride fills me at his words.

Not the best flashback to have when I'm about to launch an attack against the empire's ships. I turn the memory around in my head, try to make Arxa's words about the crew on the beach. Try to pretend that the pride that surged up within me was for being Shidadi.

Sarsine nudges Hashama. "Don't look so glum. We haven't even left yet."

Hashama raises his eyebrow. "Glum?"

She throws up her hands. "What was I thinking? You always look this way."

I turn my head to hide a smile. I'm glad Gatha's assigned them to my boat.

It's time to go. I whistle into the darkness—the signal to leave—then bend down and take a hold of the boat. Sarsine and Hashama do the same behind me, and we push out into the water. My veins start to thrum with the familiar anticipation of battle. The vessel rocks on the waves as I hoist myself in and get my bearings. The sliver of a moon does give us some light. I can see a few boat lengths in front of me, and I make the most of my vantage point, whispering directions to the others.

"Big rocks off starboard. Be careful."

Far behind me, I hear a scrape and a muffled curse—one of the boats has hit a rock. I don't look back. They're close enough to shore that they can make it back if they've capsized. Still, it's early to be losing a boat.

I stop talking as we row farther out. Soon, we're floating in what looks like an endless expanse of water, and then the outline of the first warship materializes. The bridge has lengthened quite a bit in the past days. It now reaches almost halfway across the strait.

I put up a hand, and we stop rowing, letting the current carry us the rest of the way. And now I finally look over my shoulder to see who made it. Four boats trail a short distance behind us. As we drift closer, Sarsine sticks her oar behind us like a rudder and adjusts the angle. Each bob of the waves carries us closer to the bridge. I reach out to touch the damp hull of the warship.

Something hums through the air above my head, setting every nerve in my body to buzzing. I dive to the bottom of the boat and raise my shield over me as an arrow thuds into the side of our boat. Behind me Hashama yells and clutches his arm.

Shouts sound, both from our own boats and from the bridge. On the deck of the warship above us, torches flare to life, illuminating rows of archers lining the edge. How are there so many of them?

I call over my shoulder. "Hashama, are you hurt?"

"Grazed my arm," he says through gritted teeth. "Could be worse."

Zenagua, goddess of death, take them. They knew we were coming. If we stay here, they really will pick us out of the water like fish.

I give three high-pitched whistles in a row—the signal for retreat. It hurts to give it. We were so close.

"Row back to shore!" I call over my shoulder.

"We won't get another chance!" yells Sarsine from the back.

"She's right." Hashama forces the words out like a growl.

I have to admit, I'm thinking the same thing. It kills me to get so close to the bridge and not even get a chance at it, but I can't risk the lives of those under me. "Hashama needs a healer."

"I'm fine," he shouts.

An arrow pings off my shield.

"Sarsine, is he lying?"

A short pause, then she calls. "He's telling the truth."

Well, in that case, let's at least give the Amparans a proper greeting. "We stay. But only I go on the ship, and you two cover me from the boat."

I pass my shield back to Hashama, and he holds it over our heads as I row furiously away from the archers. Water splashes into the boat, both from my oars and from the arrows coming down around us. The onslaught lightens somewhat as we reach the relative cover below the prow. Sarsine picks up her bow and starts directing shots at the archers nearest us. Other Shidadi boats must have had the same thought as us, because arrows are now arcing onto the deck of the warship, some with flaming tips.

Well, it won't get any easier. "I'm going!" I shout.

I throw my grappling hook over the side of the ship and tug to make sure it's caught. Then I sling two jars of pitch over my shoulder and climb. The rope swings back and forth with the waves, and my feet slide on the slippery hull. I flinch as an arrow grazes my arm but keep going. An arrow whistles past my head from Sarsine's direction, and an archer falls over the side of the ship.

When I pull myself over the railing, the deck of the boat is in chaos. A handful of archers stand at the edge of the boat, shooting arrows over the side. They're more concerned with whatever's down there than with me, but that could change at any time. I smash one jar of pitch against the ground, then pick up a flaming arrow smoldering next to me and set the pitch alight.

A thud shakes the deck behind me, and I turn, drawing my blade. It's Sarsine.

"Get back to our boat!" I yell.

"Go!" she shouts at me, and removes her bow from her shoulder. I'm not going to waste time arguing with her. Two soldiers run to meet me as I sprint toward the next boat, only to be felled by Sarsine's arrows. Behind me, the fire I'd started crackles and grows.

Wooden planks span the space between this ship and the next—the skeleton of what will become the bridge. Breathing a quick prayer, I hop onto one plank and teeter across, then mash another jar of pitch on the deck and jump down after it. I look for fire to set it alight, but there's nothing nearby.

An arrow strikes the ground by my feet, sending a vibration up my legs. I dive to the side and scan the deck for the archer. At the other end of the boat is a huge and very familiar shape —Walgash.

My old friend doesn't nock another arrow. For a moment, we simply stare at each other.

Metal flashes in the corner of my eye. I throw myself to the ground just in time to keep my head on my shoulders. The swordsman behind me raises his blade for another strike, and I roll away from him.

Then his mouth opens. Blood seeps through the front of his tunic, and he falls to the ground. Sarsine stands behind him.

"Be glad I'm disobedient," she says.

Another group of swordsmen charges toward us.

"Over the side!" I shout.

She sheathes her sword and runs for the railing. I look again for Walgash. He's still watching.

I sprint for the side of the ship and throw myself over.

FREEZING water rushes through the gaps in my armor, soaking through my clothes and forcing the breath from my lungs. For a moment, I'm paralyzed as the weight of my gear drags me down. Then I regain my senses. I yank my daggers out of my belt and let them fall. My quiver goes as well, but I keep my swords and bow. I pull madly at the water, propelling myself away from the ship until my lungs are about to burst, and then with one last surge of strength break through the surface.

Choppy waters toss me about, splashing into my nose and mouth when I try to breathe. Flames sprout from the closest warships as yells and screams carry across the water. Liquid seeps into my boots, freezing my ankles and pulling me down again. I search desperately for the beacon fire that was supposed to be lit from shore after the attack began. It's hopelessly far, scarcely the size of a candle flame. I'll freeze to death before I'm even halfway there.

Oars splash behind me. Someone grabs me by the collar. Hashama's only using one arm, but it's enough to let me hook my elbow over the side of the boat. I nearly capsize us climbing in.

"Sarsine?" I gasp, looking around.

"Right here," she says behind me.

I toss my weapons to the floor of the boat, peel off my waterlogged equipment, and grab the oars. I'm shivering so hard it shakes the boat, but I don't feel cold at all. I throw my back into the rowing, and the arrows don't follow us.

Shidadi meet us at the shore, pulling us onto the sand. Someone throws a blanket over my shoulders and pushes me toward a bonfire. I stagger to it, holding my hands up to the blessed heat.

I look back out at the flames flickering across the water. It's hard to see, but I'd guess that six of the ships are burning. Significant damage, but they'll make up for it in just a few days. That's the problem when fighting against Ampara. There are always more ships. There are always more soldiers.

As warmth slowly radiates through to my bones, pins and needles attack my limbs. I scan the faces around me, trying to figure out who made it back. There's Sarsine and Hashama, and I count fourteen total who'd been on the boats. At least eight are nursing injuries. Gatha will do a full head count in an hour, and we'll know what the real toll was.

I stand next to Walgash in the practice field. A short distance away, Naudar and Masista load sacks of sand onto a small catapult and launch them one by one into the air. Walgash draws his bow and shoots each of them. Every single arrow hits right through the center.

"You need to spend more time at the campfires, Dineas," he says between arrows.

"Why?"

"Because you're new. The men don't know you, and they won't trust you until they see more of you around."

"Do I need them to trust me?"

He looks at me like I'm the world's greatest simpleton. "When we go to battle, who will be keeping you alive?"

"Fair point."

Masista launches five targets in succession, and Walgash handles them with ease. The last target must have been worn thin, because the bag explodes in a rain of sand, prompting curses from Masista.

"Did you buy the armory steward a skin of Desoraf wine?" Walgash asks me.

"Last week."

He looks at me expectantly. "And?"

"He looked at my armor and told me the leather was dry. Then he found me a newer set."

Walgash's grin is as smug as a crow who'd stolen a meat pie. "See?

Uncle Walgash will take care of you, if you care to listen."

The fire crackles, and I snap back into the present. Walgash's arrows never miss their target. Not by accident, at least. Why didn't he kill me? I wonder what I would have done in his place. I wonder if he would do the same, should we meet again.

Footsteps crunch in the sand behind me.

"Report, Dineas." I jump at Gatha's voice.

"They knew we were coming," I say.

Gatha's face turns stern. "You're sure of this?"

"They were waiting for us with torches and arrows. Either their scouts can see like owls, or someone warned them."

She turns her head to see if anyone heard me. Accusations of treason are not something to be made lightly. "Is there anyone you suspect?"

I shake my head. "None more than any other." I notice now that several Shidadi are sneaking glances at me. I wonder how many people are having a similar conversation right now, and how many of them think I'm the traitor. I wonder if Gatha is one of them.

"What did you see on the warship?" asks Gatha.

"Nothing of use. What little I saw of the bridge looked sturdy."

"And the soldiers. Anyone you recognized?"

A twig cracks in the fire, sending sparks into the darkness. I step back to avoid them.

"No one I knew well."

A movement on the other side of the campfire catches my eye. Sarsine's looking at us. I wonder how much she can over-hear from where she stands.

Gatha glances at Sarsine and then at the others around the beach. "I feel for you younger fighters," she says. "You've known nothing but war."

It's a strange time for Gatha to start feeling maternal.

"When I was a girl in Central Ampara," she continues, "a

Shidadi child growing up could have many Amparan playmates. My favorite was a boy from a small village that we passed by several times a year. He was skinny as a snake, born with a shriveled left hand, but tough enough to run and tumble with the Shidadi children. I always looked forward to visiting his village."

The story makes me uneasy. I look for an excuse to leave, but everyone else has drawn away from us.

"When we grew older, his family fortunes changed, and he left to join the army. I didn't give much thought to him, because Emperor Kurosh was ordering more attacks against us by then. Over the next years, the Amparan army drove us north. Our warlord died, and I was chosen to succeed him."

I know where she's going now.

"One winter, our scouts reported an army supply train moving north. We were desperately in need, since we hadn't built up enough stores. I led a band to raid that caravan. As we were coming up, I saw him guarding the wagon. It had been ten years at least. He was a grown man now, broad of shoulder and square of jaw, but I noticed the way he propped up his shield with his arm. I saw his hand then, and I looked more carefully at his face. I could have killed him—should have—but I ordered our band back. Said something about how the guards had seen me."

She shakes her head, her eyes dark with grief. "We lost twenty to sickness and starvation that winter. I think about those dead every time it gets cold. I never saw my friend again."

"Why are you telling me this?" Gatha doesn't trust me either. Somehow, I feel betrayed to know this, even though I'm the one who just lied to her.

Gatha sighs. "You are not the only one who has had to face friends across the battlefield," she says. "You're not as alone as you think."

And then she leaves me there.

FIFTEEN: ZIVAH

I feel especially useless today.

It's morning. The village must have news of the bridge attack by now, but there's no way for me to hear it. If I were a true healer, I'd be on the beach or waiting at the village for the fighters to come in.

I tell myself it should have gone fine. If we were able to return to Monyar from Sehmar City, then Dineas should be able to make it to the bridge and back alive.

As I pace the ground in front of my cottage, a shadow flits across the sky. Scrawny? Dineas sends the crow once a day to check for messages. The crow who lands, though, is not Scrawny. It's a very dusty Preener.

He may not be Dineas, but I'm still glad to see the bird back here safe. "How are the Rovenni treating you?"

Preener caws crankily and extends his claw. There's a note rolled on it.

We've been spreading news about Kiran. Rumors unearth other rumors. There's long been talk about Khaygal outpost. Slaves warn each other not to eat food from there, and the name Kione keeps coming up. She was a former slave at the outpost and fell ill with rose plague around the same time as Arxa's battalion. Regrettably, we cannot talk to her because she resides in the Khaygal rosemarked compound.

Preener looks at me expectantly, and I throw him a large piece of taro bread. After all that time looking for evidence in Baruva's notes, I've come close to admitting failure, but now I wonder if perhaps there is more out there to be known. Hope, though, comes tempered with reality. Kione is in a rosemarked compound in Central Ampara. That's far away in the best of times, and now with Amparans at our doorstep...

A ball of black feathers dives at Preener, stirring up a cloud of dust. Scrawny flaps and chatters, dancing circles around Preener as the latter shakes dust from his feathers and caws his indignation.

"With a welcome like this," I tell Scrawny, "Preener might not come back again."

Scrawny continues his dance, and I notice a note tied to his leg.

"Come here, Scrawny." He ignores my first two whistles but reluctantly flits over after the third.

This note is much shorter.

Request your presence at meeting with leaders in clearing.

My stomach drops when I see it's not Dineas's handwriting. It doesn't necessarily mean that something has happened to him, since Gatha sometimes borrows his crows. Still, I'm quick to throw on my plague veil and race down the trail.

I strain to identify the voices in the clearing before I arrive. When I break through the foliage, I glance quickly from face to face—Tal's stern dark eyes, Gatha's stubborn chin, Vidarna's regal profile, Karu's sneer...and then I see Dineas and relief floods through me. He slumps where he sits, as if straightening up is too much of an effort right now, though other than a bruised jaw he has no immediately visible injuries. He catches my eye and his face brightens. There's no hint of anger from him, and I realize that I don't feel any toward him either.

I take my spot at the opposite pole of the circle, a safe distance from the others. The tension is palpable. Everybody's looking at each other, yet nobody speaks. And for once, it's painfully clear what this gathering of people really is: strangers forced together by fate.

Gatha clears her throat. "Zivah, the others know about the outcome of the bridge mission already. The Amparans discovered us very early on. Our fighters caused some damage to the bridge, but not nearly enough, and now we must be realistic about what choices lie before us." She turns to Tal. "I know your people are attached to their homes, but there's no way we can defend a village like Dara against an army of that size. Dara has no walls, no fortifications. Your houses are too spread out. If we face the Amparans in fair battle, we will lose."

My heart sinks at Gatha's words.

"Do what you must," says Tal. "But do what you can to ensure we have a home to return to."

"It's in all our best interest to keep the lands habitable," says Gatha. "And we will keep looking for ways to shorten this fight." She looks at me. "Zivah, you've been looking for more evidence against Baruva and Kiran. Have you found anything?"

"Baruva's too careful to put anything incriminating in his notes," I say. "But we heard today from a Rovenni messenger about rumors in the rosemarked colonies. There's a former slave at Khaygal outpost who may be able to tell us more about how Arxa's battalion was infected."

"It's not clear to me," says Karu, "how a slave a continent away could be of any use to us."

"I could go find her. I've made the trip before."

"You made the trip with Dineas," says Gatha. "And we can't spare him now, not with the Amparans so close."

Dineas frowns at that, though I'm not sure what exactly upsets him.

"Send someone else with me, then," I say. "I can't row across the strait, but I know the continent."

"You've risked your life once already," says Karu. "It'd be folly to send you out again. We know the positions of the main force at our shores but can't account for other forces that may be moving into the region."

Karu had never struck me as someone particularly concerned about my well-being. "Everyone else is doing their part," I say. "I must as well."

"You're not useful to us if you die thousands of leagues away in pursuit of an imaginary woman," she says. "There's one way you can be most useful to us, and it's time we stop avoiding the obvious."

"Speak plainly, Karu," says Gatha.

"You know what I'm saying." Karu's voice is sharp, pointed. "We cannot continue to survive if we cling to our notions of honorable battle."

It takes me a moment to understand what she means. "I won't infect the troops. It's not just a matter of blindly following my vows. Sickening that many people who live in such close quarters, there would be no way to contain the disease. The plague could spread back through the supply trains to the rest of Ampara."

"Karu." Gatha's voice holds a growl of warning. "Your words are not worthy of a Shidadi."

"In a generation, there will be no Shidadi," Karu snaps. "If we must make some changes to survive, so be it." She looks to Vidarna and Tal. "And you two agree with me. Don't hide it."

Gatha looks at Vidarna, who looks away. "I don't completely agree with Karu," he says, "but in times such as these, we would be foolish to dismiss any tactic out of hand. Kiran gazes on Monyar from his warship, and we're nothing but fleas to him."

Gatha turns incredulously to Tal, who stays silent a long time, staring at the ground. Finally he raises his head and looks at me. "Is it worth it, Zivah? Is it worth losing our home and our lives?"

The chills that had been spreading along my skin turn to ice. If even Tal has abandoned me...

"Taking this path is too high a price," says Dineas. "If we infect the Amparans, we would no longer be Shidadi, and no longer worth saving."

His vehemence surprises me. I look at him, grateful for support, but he's glaring at Karu.

"Strange words from one who is hardly Shidadi himself these days," says Karu. "How did the Amparans find out so quickly about the attack, Dineas?"

Dineas jumps to his feet.

"Enough!" says Gatha, her voice a thunderclap over the field. "Everything that can be said has been said, and no good will come of staying here further. We adjourn now and go our separate ways for the night. We'll reconvene tomorrow, when heads are cooler."

I'M in a daze as the leaders disperse. My heart races as if I'd been in a battle, and I suppose I have. Perhaps I might have expected Karu or Vidarna to pressure me into breaking my vows, but to have Tal turn against me as well...

Dineas storms out without a second glance at any of us. Gatha gazes after him, then sighs. "This is war, Zivah," she says. "It's a messy affair."

Tal simply shakes his head. "Goddess help us." He doesn't look at me either.

I'm restless after I return to my cottage. Words from the meeting echo in my mind. Am I a fool to hold my ground? I don't know why Dineas left so quickly, or what he's thinking right now, but I need to talk to him.

My best chance of finding Dineas is through Scrawny, who seems to be around more than strictly necessary these days—I think he's taking a liking to me. To summon him, I fasten a blue cloth to my roof and wait. Sure enough, a flurry of black feathers appears on my windowsill a half hour later.

"Good to see you, friend." I give him a few crumbs of bread.

He snaps them up almost before I've dropped them all, then gives me a baleful glance.

"Was that not enough?" I spread out a few more, and this time he settles down.

I write a short note and tie it to Scrawny's leg. "Find Dineas."

Scrawny takes off in the direction of the mountains. I can tell by his confidence that he knows where to find him.

The afternoon goes slowly by. At first I try to read Baruva's scrolls, but they just taunt me about the decision I must make. Am I wrong to say no? Am I turning my back on my family, on my people? I think of Leora and her unborn child, and I wonder if I'm bringing about their doom.

Finally I hear footsteps on the trail to my house. I rush outside, but it's not Dineas at the top of the trail. It's Karu.

I stop in my tracks. Compared to the likes of Gatha, Karu looks slight and rather young, but her expression is chiseled in stone.

"Warlord," I say.

"No need to pretend to be glad to see me," she says, walking right past me. "We face hardships enough without creating new tasks for ourselves." She stops at the chairs in front of my cottage. "May I sit?"

It takes me a moment to respond. "Of course."

I sit in my usual chair. Since she's given me permission to avoid any pretense, I refrain from making conversation. We look at each other without speaking, and then after a moment Karu nods as if satisfied.

"You're idealistic, as are my people," she says. "It's admirable, to be devoted to such noble concepts as honor and fair play."

"I appreciate your words," I say. "But I imagine you will now tell me why we can no longer be so devoted."

Karu gazes at the forest. "My tribe used to number a thousand," she says. "More than that before I was born. We lived in Central Ampara like Gatha's tribe. Emperor Kurosh was brutal toward the Shidadi in the early years of his reign. He sent wave after wave of soldiers at us. Sometimes we held them off, other times we retreated. But then a rose plague outbreak took our best fighters. The Amparans came upon us in force as soon as we recovered, and this time we could not match them."

Her eyes bore into me. "Have you seen rivers of blood? Gullies that run red with the life of your kin? Your soldiers murdered, their weapons piled up for the Amparans to divide among themselves? Have you seen entire families wiped out, infants dashed against rocks, old men beheaded? Save your honor for those who have honor themselves. Keep your piety for those who don't spit on the gods. When you see your kin falling to Amparan swords, your people enslaved and sold across the empire, we'll see what you think of your vows."

I curl my hands over the side of my chair. The images Karu's words evoke in my mind are all too vivid.

Karu stands. "I've said my piece. I trust you will make the right choice."

She leaves me then without waiting for a reply, and I don't know how long I sit there, staring after her. Nothing Karu said was unexpected. In fact, it felt all too familiar, perhaps because I'd already imagined those things myself.

Wings beat above me, and Scrawny lands on my shoulder. The note on his foot has been removed, but there's no reply. Sharp disappointment lances through me.

"Did you find him?" I ask.

The bird squawks, which could either be a yes or a no.

As hours pass with no sign of Dineas, my disappointment turns into anger. Where is he? Why would he leave me to this? After the meeting today I thought we'd put our arguments behind us. Perhaps I'd been wrong.

Night comes without any news. When I finally sleep, I dream that I'm looking down on the Monyar Strait from above. One side is lush and green with bamboo. On the other side, the Amparan army gathers before swarming across the strait into Monyar. Then blood oozes out of the earth, filling up the valleys until it overflows back into the ocean.

SIXTEEN: DINEAS

I tear through the forest, knocking plants out of my path and sending rodents and birds scattering. When was it that my people became strangers to me? At what point did they change into something I was ashamed to be a part of? I was raised to believe that war was a test of strength, skill, and bravery. Spycraft was barely tolerated—assassinations, a method of the cowardly. But now Karu and Vidarna are talking about using rose plague against the entire Amparan army. Have things changed so much? Or was I just too blind to see how things really were?

In my mind's eye, I see Zivah facing down our leaders. I see the cynicism in Karu's eyes and the desperation in Tal's. Zivah will only be able to hold out for so long. Sooner or later, they'll wear her down.

I try taking my frustration out on the bamboo around me, and quickly lose that fight. Cradling my bruised hand, I slink back into camp. My legs ache from the long night and hike back up the mountains. At this time of day, it doesn't look much like a camp at all—no fires, no bedrolls, just a handful of Shidadi milling about, resting, eating, and talking. The few people who look in my direction take one glance at my face and go back to what they were doing.

I settle down at the base of a fat stalk of bamboo, away from the others. Carefully, I remove my weapons and lay them out before me. There's a dry patch on one side of my bow, so I work a chunk of lard and beeswax into the wood. The mindless, repetitive task helps for my frustration—somewhat.

A shadow falls across me, and I look up to see Frada's characteristic smirk. He'd been one of those who chose to attack the bridge despite my signal to retreat. It might have been out of loyalty, though given that Frada doesn't even trust me to scout around our camp, I wonder if he stayed to keep an eye on me. Whatever the reason, he sports a bandage across his brow for his efforts. I know I owe him for lending me his sword, but I'm in no mood to chat. I return pointedly to my work.

"Feeling put together again?" he asks.

So he's not going to take the hint. "I didn't have anything that needed treating. Just a few bruises."

"Huh." There are layers of accusation behind that word.

"You would have done well to follow my signal to retreat," I say. "That face of yours doesn't need any more decoration."

"My sword was getting thirsty."

"You know, an Amparan soldier would get in a lot of trouble for staying when the leader calls a retreat."

"We all know you're an expert on Amparan customs."

My wax block slips, sending my knuckle burning across the wood.

"Did you enjoy paying respects to your friend on the bridge?" Frada asks.

A slow prickle of ice spreads up my arm and down my spine. "What did you say?"

"The Amparan archer. The one who didn't shoot you."

I stop working the wax. "You're mistaken."

"I have eyes," says Frada. "And I'm not a fool." He crouches down to look me in the eye. "You know what else I saw? What you did to Tus on that mountainside before you hauled him off to the imperial dungeons."

My heartbeat drums in my head. I grip my bow until my knuckles turn white.

Frada leans closer. "Tell us what happened to him in the capital, Dineas. How did he die? Peacefully? In his sleep? Or did he rot to death while you were busy playing emperor's favorite soldier?"

An animal sound escapes my throat as I launch myself at him, one hand going to his neck as the other pulls back for a punch. He must have been expecting me to attack, but he still falls back at the sheer fury of my onslaught. We roll on the ground, ramming each other into stalks of bamboo and struggling for an advantage. I'm vaguely aware of shouts, which I ignore until someone drags me up by the tunic. Pain explodes on the side of my face, and I land stupidly on my backside.

Gatha stands between the two of us. "Fools! Maybe the two of you should take up hammers and help the Amparans build their bridge, since you're so intent on doing their work for them."

Frada tries to come at me again, but two Shidadi grab him under the arms. "If you had any honor, you would have saved Tus!" he shouts at me.

Gatha moves so that she's squarely in front of Frada. "I gave the order to leave Tus in the Amparan dungeons. If you have a problem with how Tus died, you take it up with me." She looks at the men holding him. "Remove him to the other side of camp." As they drag him away, she casts her eyes at the gathering crowd. "Back to your business."

I stand in a haze as the crowd disperses. After a while, I'm vaguely aware that I'm alone with Gatha, but I can't look her in the eye. *If you had any honor, you would have saved Tus.* Sometimes truth comes from the mouths of people you trust and respect. Sometimes, it comes from arrogant bastards who know nothing but are right about you nonetheless.

"Look at me, Dineas." The way Gatha says it, it's not a request.

I look up at her. She's fierce, protective, and completely wrong about me.

"It was my order to leave Tus there. Do you hear me?" she says.

"Yes, Warlord." It was her order, but it was my dagger that killed him.

"Do you hear me, Dineas?"

"Yes." I sound dead. I feel dead.

She shakes her head in frustration, but she waves me away. I pick up my weapons and charge up the mountainside. When the path splits, I take the one headed more steeply up. I repeat that several times until the trail ends at a ridge overlooking the ocean. I'm on one of the highest cliffs in the area. The waves frothing below look like mere ripples, and the warships like child's toys.

I'm surprised to find a pyramid of stones here—a monument made by a Shidadi priest to Yaras, god of the sky. The Amparans worship the gods in temples, but our ways are to honor them in the temples of their own making. The priest who built this altar must be from one of the other tribes, because ours was killed several years ago. I wonder how long it will be before all of our priests are gone. We fight so hard to keep our identity as Shidadi, but it seems we're losing ourselves nonetheless.

I take a seat at the edge of the cliff and dangle my legs above the dizzying drop. In the distance, the boat bridge stretches back to the Amparan shore. Their army camps at the other end —massive, powerful, unstoppable. Are we really doomed if Zivah doesn't infect them with the plague?

There's a crunch of dirt behind me, and I grab my knife. Sarsine stands a few paces away, hands held up.

"Careful there, sir. Our numbers are small enough as it is."

That they are. "You followed me up here?"

She shrugs. "I wanted to go somewhere quiet. I figured after that fight at camp, you'd be looking for somewhere quiet too, and since you know this place better than me..."

"How much of the fight did you see?"

"Pretty much all of it. I'm a decent eavesdropper, even when people *aren't* shouting at the top of their lungs."

A decent eavesdropper. I remember her on the beach last night, listening as I told Gatha that I hadn't seen anyone I knew on the warships.

"You were right behind me when we attacked that bridge," I say.

She nods sagely, and I know she saw what happened between me and Walgash.

"Why didn't you back Frada up?"

Sarsine shrugs. "It was obvious you knew that archer, but it's not as if you gave him all our secrets. I think you're loyal to our people. No reason to complicate things."

"You think I'm loyal even though I lied to Gatha?"

"I think you have to bend some rules to be truly loyal. Our warlords are only human after all." She taps her fingers on her leg. "Maybe I'm wrong. Maybe you'll murder me one day and use my corpse for animal feed."

I look at her carefully. "Do you really believe that?"

"That you'd use me for animal feed?"

"That sometimes you have to bend some rules to be truly loyal."

She returns my scrutiny. "I love my people. I love my tribe. But I make my own decisions. Why do you ask?"

SEVENTEEN: ZIVAH

"*Z*ivah, wake up!"

Dineas's voice is an unlikely counterpart to the nightmarish images haunting my sleep. I bat the voice away, annoyed that I'd be so needy as to imagine him when he doesn't show up in person. But he keeps calling, and finally a gentle nudge on my shoulder rocks me awake.

I open my eyes and spring away from the touch. Fear crawls up my spine. It's the middle of the night.

"Zivah, it's me," whispers Dineas.

It *is* him. I can make out his shadow crouched next to my cot. Even in the darkness, I sense how tense he is, coiled as if ready to leap into battle. Heat emanates from his skin, and I half expect him to glow like a dying ember. The faintest trace of his breath tickles my cheek. "What are you doing?"

"You need to leave."

"What?"

"Leave the camp tonight. I'll help you."

What is he talking about? As I shake off my sleep, all the anger and hurt from yesterday comes rushing back. I prop myself up on my elbow. "Are you mad? Where were you yesterday? Why didn't you acknowledge my note? And now you just break in here in the middle of the night and order me to leave?"

I'm sitting now with my blanket clutched around me, staring him down in the darkness. There's a long silence.

"I'm sorry," he says. "I should have come. I was foolishly wrapped up in my own troubles. But I'm here now, if you'll hear me out."

I offer no words of conciliation, but I wait for him to continue.

Dineas lets out a breath. "You need to leave before we meet with the warlords again. They'll just keep at you to poison the Amparans, and soon you won't be able to refuse."

Have you seen rivers of blood? Gullies that run red with the life of your kin?

"Maybe they're right to urge me," I say.

"Maybe they are. Maybe they're not. But it should be your choice."

It dawns on me that he's serious. He really wants me to leave Dara, right now. "But that's impossible."

"Why? I'll help you get past the scouts."

"I can't just run away. I won't leave my family to fend for themselves."

"Don't run away," he says. "Go find this Kione. Find out what she knows."

"How would I cross the strait?"

"One of my fighters will go with you."

He's thought this through. And I do want to find Kione. But how can I just pack up and go? "And you?"

"I have to stay. They need me to help plan the defense." He stops abruptly. Is that regret in his voice? "You can go to Khaygal, or cross the strait and come back after thinking things through, but if you stay, you won't leave Monyar until we defeat the Amparans. Or until they kill us all."

I think of the vast army gathered on the beach, of the bridge that comes closer day by day. Dineas is right. It will only get harder to leave Dara once the fighting starts. If the warlords don't let me go to Khaygal now, they never will. And if I'm stuck here, that leaves me only one way to help with the war.

I kick my feet off the bed. "Do I have time to pack?"

"Some," he says, and he sounds relieved.

"Turn around so I can get dressed."

He pivots to face the door. I wait a moment to make sure he doesn't turn again, and then spring into action. Now that I've made the decision, I feel surprisingly at peace. I open the window shutters to let in more moonlight and shed my night-gown for more functional tunic and trousers. It doesn't take long to put together what belongings I need. My blowgun already lies next to a bag packed with darts, an assortment of dried herbs, a bracelet of snake fangs, and a few bandages. I store the bulk of my healing supplies on my shelves, but I've had this bag ready for weeks. I suppose part of me must have known I might have to leave on short notice. I throw some leftover taro root and bread into the bag. For other food, I'll have to forage along the way.

There's one more thing to do. I go to my shed where I keep my venomous creatures and open all the cages. My blackarmor scorpion clicks out of its cage the moment I open it, as does a brownhead serpent who flows down the shelves and out the door. Setting these creatures free is easy until I get to Diadem. The snake's pale green scales shimmer gray in the darkness, and she lifts her head when I approach.

"It was good to know you, friend. But I can't let you risk your life again for my sake. Not when I know this time how dangerous it will be."

Diadem flicks her tongue and stays in the cage. I leave the door open for her, fighting the lump in my throat.

"I'm ready," I say to Dineas.

Outside, the moonlight gives the forest a ghostly sheen. Insect calls ring over the muffled sound of our footsteps. Dineas leads the way, forgoing the trails and leading us directly through the bamboo. We hike up the side of the valley and make a large circle, giving the other houses a wide berth. Soon my clothes are damp with dew.

As we travel, I can't help but wonder about Dineas. He creeps through the forest with the stealth and agility of a warrior. Yet when he looks back, there's a fierce protectiveness in his gaze. Finally, as the sky turns gray, he slows and looks around, his entire body alert to the sounds of the forest. An umbertouched Shidadi girl steps out of the shadows, and Dineas beckons her over.

"We should be past most of the scouts," Dineas says, his voice unusually solemn. "Sarsine will help you get to Khaygal. She's the best kind of warrior. I'd trust her with my life. I trust her with yours."

Sarsine beams. "Karu will be furious with me," she says, though she doesn't seem to mind.

Dineas whistles, and Scrawny lands on his shoulder. The crow doesn't complain as Dineas carefully transfers him to my hand.

"Scrawny likes you more than he likes me these days," Dineas says with a wry smile. "It would break his heart to be left here."

Perhaps it's the arrival of daylight, but suddenly the magnitude of what I'm about to embark on hits me, as does the gravity of what Dineas has done. I have a hundred questions to ask him, and I wish we had more time. I wonder what price he will pay for this.

Dineas opens his mouth to speak, and I hardly dare to breathe. But instead, he looks away.

Sarsine clears her throat. "I'll wait for you beyond that hill."

We both watch her disappear. Cicada calls fall like a curtain around us.

I struggle for words. "You betray your people to help me. Why?"

Dineas casts his eyes downward. "I thought you a coward before," he says, his voice soft with shame. "I know better now. I know your vows to the Goddess, and what they mean to you. If you do as the council asks, it will shatter your soul. There are some things you can't recover from."

He speaks with the conviction of one who's had his soul shattered. I think of his anguish over his double life, and once again, I'm deeply aware of my part in his suffering.

I search his eyes. "Do we part as friends?"

Something flickers across his face at the word "friends," but it disappears just as quickly. "Of course."

"Will you look after my family? Keep Alia out of the fighting if you can. I—I'm sorry I faulted you for helping her with her swordplay. She'll be safer with what you taught her."

"I'll look out for them," Dineas says firmly. And then he furrows his brow. "I don't know how the battle will play out here. When you come back, stay at the beach you leave from. I'll send Slicewing once a day to look for you."

I nod. So many logistics to arrange, yet I can't shake the feeling that there are more important things to say. I see the same frustration mirrored in his expression.

"Zivah…" He swallows. "I said some things when we argued about Arxa…I'm sorry."

The regret in his eyes surprises me. "We've both said foolish things. There's nothing to be sorry about."

"There's plenty to be sorry for. There's plenty to regret." His voice dies down to a whisper. "I know I'm not him."

He said it so softly I'm not sure I heard him right. "What do you mean?"

"I'm not the man you knew in Sehmar City. But..." He stops and shakes his head with a sad smile. "I really made a mess of things, didn't I?"

"Dineas, I don't understand..."

My words grow weak as he steps closer, then die away completely as Dineas takes my hand. I shiver, transfixed by the depth of yearning in his gaze, and find myself paralyzed as he leans forward and brushes his lips against mine, so lightly that I'm not even sure we actually touch. My heart stutters, and I draw a sharp breath. In a fraction of a heartbeat, he's stepped away. The cold wind brushes my fingers where he'd held them.

Dineas stares at me, eyes wide. "Forgive me," he says. "I—"

"There's nothing to forgive." My mind can't make sense of it, but my mouth tingles where our lips came close. The scent of his skin lingers, the warmth of his breath.

Hope comes into his eyes, but it's a resigned hope. "Be safe. Come back."

I'm struck by the urgency in his words, the fear of someone who had already lost too much. And too late, I realize how strong my fear of losing him has become as well.

"I will."

His gaze drifts over my face, committing me to memory before turning away. And then, all too soon, he's gone.

THERE's a spark in Sarsine's eye when I come over the hill. "Come," she says. "We want to move fast."

Making conversation is beyond me right now, but thankfully she doesn't seem to expect a reply. Sarsine's confident for someone so young, moving quickly and deliberately through the tangles of foliage. She swivels her head from side to side as we walk, pausing every so often at any suspicious sound. I follow as best as I can, feeling slow and clumsy in her wake. I wouldn't be able to match her in the best of circumstances, much less as I am now, with my mind a whirlwind of thoughts and my heart yearning toward the forests behind me.

I know I'm not him.

True, Dineas is no longer the man I loved in Sehmar City. I'd thought anything between us beyond friendship had disappeared when I restored his memory. But if that's true, then what was that look in his eyes? Why this tug at my chest? I wonder now if I've made a grave mistake in leaving.

By afternoon, we reach a small beach I'd never seen before. The ground is covered almost entirely with rocks bigger than my fist. Tidewater fills in some of the larger gaps, and the entire beach smells of seaweed and barnacles.

"Have you kept watch before?" Sarsine asks.

"Dineas and I alternated watches when we traveled together."

She purses her lips, then seems to accept Dineas's judgment of my vigilance. We find a sheltered spot near the edge of the tree line. I take first watch, then Sarsine takes over while I sleep. When she wakes me, the sun is low over the horizon.

"Come." Sarsine leads me to a boat buried underneath the rocks. "Between the land breeze and the boulders, the Amparans stay away at night."

She starts heaving rocks out of the boat, and I follow suit. The stones are cold, heavy, and caked with slippery sand, but with the two of us working, we soon have them all tossed to the side. Sarsine makes a slow circle around the boat, checking for damage. Then we lug it to the water, taking care not to twist our ankles on the uneven ground.

Sarsine hands me a set of oars. "We'll both need to row. Don't want to be dashed on the boulders."

"Is it that dangerous?" The boat wobbles under me as I climb in. Scrawny perches on the side and flaps his wings for balance.

"There's a reason the Amparans avoid this beach." She pushes off before I have a chance to reply.

This beach would be beautiful if it weren't so deadly. Giant boulders jut out of the sea to the height of several men, their brown surfaces glistening red in the fading sunlight. There's no chance to admire them, though, because waves meet us immediately. Our boat tilts, and we drift toward one particularly menacing rock. I start rowing.

"Good, good," says Sarsine. She steers us to the left. "Keep going."

We drift past the first rock, and then the real current hits. The boat pitches back and forth, turning my stomach, and Scrawny takes off with a squawk as frigid water splashes over the sides. Though I'm rowing as hard as I can, the water carries us straight toward a jagged outcropping. I wonder if I'd be able to swim back to shore should we capsize.

"Harder!" Sarsine yells.

Any Amparans around would surely hear us, but they were wise enough to stay away. I throw my back into each stroke. My muscles scream. Behind me, Sarsine grunts with exertion. We narrowly pass the outcropping, then skim another sharp boulder.

"Almost there!" Sarsine cries.

Salt water splashes into my face. I spit and cough. My eyes burn.

"Just past that next one."

That next one comes toward us at a frightening speed. A horrible grating sound rattles the boat. We lurch, and I almost drop my oar.

"Row harder!" Sarsine shouts again. It's a wonder we're still upright.

And then we shoot past the last rock into the open ocean. Sarsine lets out a hoarse sigh. The rhythm of her paddling slows, and I take that as a cue that I can slow as well. My heart gallops in my chest, my arms burn, and it hurts to breathe. The Amparan shore, a thin line in the distance, taunts our efforts.

I hear a strange cackling. At first I think it's some kind of seabird, but I then I realize it's Sarsine laughing maniacally behind me. When I turn around, she grins.

"See, that wasn't so bad, was it?"

EIGHTEEN: DINEAS

"Where is Zivah?" Gatha's face mirrors her frustration. It took the leaders a day to notice Zivah had left. Enough, hopefully, for her and Sarsine to be well on their way. And now, I stand facing my warlord in the clearing outside Zivah's cottage, steeling myself to face the consequences.

I set my chin. "She's gone."

"Gone where?"

"I would never lie to you, Warlord, but I will say no more."

"Is Sarsine with her?"

I don't answer.

Gatha sighs. "It's not like you to act alone like this."

"I acted alone," I say. "But I acted on Shidadi values. We're stooping to tactics that we would have condemned in the past. Zivah's taken vows to her Goddess. She shouldn't have to destroy herself to win our war."

"It's her war too. It's her people."

"Maybe, but it should be her choice. If she stayed, you would have made the choice for her."

"So instead, you and she have forced all our hands. We'll have to clear everyone out of Dara, set up camps deep in the forests." Gatha rubs the bridge of her nose. She looks as though she'd just fought a week-long battle. "I don't know what to do with you, Dineas. Karu is pushing me to exile you back to Ampara. Vidarna doesn't go so far, but he harbors his own suspicions after that failed bridge raid. You've always been one of my most loyal fighters, but there have been questions asked about you since you returned. I don't want to doubt you."

I don't want to doubt you. That's not the same thing as saying she trusts me, and it hurts. With my parents dead, Gatha is the closest thing to a mother I have. "I'll take whatever punishment you give me."

Disappointment settles over her countenance at my answer. "You're not to leave camp from here on out without my permission. No more wandering the mountainside, and definitely no scouting of the Amparans, unless you have an escort. Don't test these boundaries, Dineas. I can make them tighter."

She leaves without looking at me.

Zivah's cottage stands still and silent in front of me, taunting me with its emptiness. I have an urge to hit something, kick the walls of the cottage and yell. But what good would it do? Zivah would still be gone. My people would still think me a traitor. If Zivah restored my memories in Sehmar City, why do I know less and less about where I belong?

There's a rustling in the bamboo, and I reach for my sword. A pregnant Dara woman steps out into the clearing. My heart sinks when I recognize Zivah's sister Leora. I can see Zivah in her face. They have the same eyes, and the edges of their mouths turn up in the same way.

"They say you helped Zivah leave," Leora says.

Why does word travel the fastest when you least want it to?

Leora comes closer, stepping awkwardly under the weight of her swollen belly. "Will you tell me where she is? At least tell me whether she is safe. Will you keep news of her from her own family? We love her, and we worry for her."

She looks so vulnerable, so utterly defenseless against anything that might come. I think of the promise I made Zivah to protect her. How foolish I was to think I could keep that promise.

Leora takes a step closer. "You love her too," she says.

What does it mean to say I love Zivah? In Sehmar, I thought myself in love with her. I bought her gifts from the market, talked with her about anything and everything, lay awake at night thinking about what it would be like to kiss her. Now I try to talk to her and the words tangle in my mouth. I lie awake wondering if she's alive. And yet, there's still the memory of a kiss.

In Sehmar City, I'd implored Zivah to take a chance on love. *Nothing's promised us by the gods. Isn't that all the more reason to love while we can?* Those were the words of someone who hadn't lived through the horrors of war. Who hadn't watched his friends and family die, one by one, until he didn't think his soul could fragment into any more pieces.

"Don't give up on each other," Leora says.

She's still watching me intently, brow furrowed as if I were a note whose ink had been smudged, and suddenly I'm exhausted. Every single one of my battle injuries throbs in unison.

"I'm sorry," I say. And I find there's nothing more I can add. So I simply turn around and leave.

NINETEEN: ZIVAH

It's light when I wake. My bedroll lies between several craggy bushes with waxy gray leaves. Scrawny is poking his beak into a hole in the dirt, and Sarsine's nowhere in sight. Groaning, I stand and dust myself off. We're on a hill overlooking the strait. Occasionally, I smell salt water on the breeze. I've just folded up my bedroll and settled down to chew on some dry bread when Sarsine comes over the hill.

"Pretty impressive sunrises around here. Almost purple at first, and then the gold reflects off the dew," she says by way of greeting. "I've scouted the area and there aren't many people around. Traveling this stretch shouldn't be hard."

We head south at a brisk but much more relaxed pace than yesterday. I soon find that Sarsine's considerably chattier on this continent.

"Healer turned spy, huh?" Sarsine asks at one point. "Did you get bored or something?" She catches a glimpse of my stunned expression. "Oh, you like being a healer? Might be interesting in its own way." Though it sounds as if she doesn't think it very possible.

"I enjoyed my work as a healer," I say. "But I couldn't do much once I became rosemarked, and we needed a way to get Dineas into the capital."

"Ah, rose plague." Sarsine reaches up with an umbermarked hand to brush the hair away from her eye. "I'd much rather face an army than rose plague."

It's strangely refreshing that she doesn't shrink away from the subject. "But you've faced the disease and won. How did you fall ill?"

She shrugs. "I snuck off to a harbor town because I was bored, and struck up a conversation with a merchant who manifested rosemarks the next day. She died. I didn't. Coincidence or arm of the gods, who knows?"

I can't help but compare this journey to my first trip to Ampara. Dineas and I hardly spoke to each other as we made our way south, we'd despised each other so much. It's hard to fathom that less than a year later, I'd travel the same path and wish he were here with me.

Other than a few days when I'm feeling unwell, Sarsine and I make good time. Both of us are eager to complete our quest and get back to Monyar. Though we're careful to avoid notice—staying off the roads and keeping my skin covered—Sarsine seems to genuinely enjoy the journey. She discusses the sunrise with me every morning and stops often to watch an unfamiliar bird fly by. When we pass by one village, she runs out to "scout" and returns with a bag full of breads and cakes—half of which have bites taken out of them.

"I had to know which ones were worth taking," she says with a shrug.

I'm relieved when the village disappears behind us and there's no sign of an angry baker in pursuit.

It takes us a week to reach the grasslands. Once there, we steer clear of Khaygal outpost to avoid the troops marching by on the way to Monyar. Instead, we head east. A league from the outpost, crumbling mud-straw walls come into view. The brick work is uneven, and what buildings I can see on the other side have moldy roofs. There's no mistaking a rosemarked compound. The area enclosed by these walls is much smaller than Sehmar's compound—I'm guessing it holds perhaps three hundred people—but it has the same dilapidated conditions, the same sense of a place that's abandoned.

Of the four umbertouched guards watching the gate, two of them appear to be leaning against the wall. "Not going to be much of a challenge to sneak in, is it?" asks Sarsine.

I survey the scene, trying to figure out how we'll find this mysterious Kione. Three hundred people is too large a colony to simply walk in and hope we run into her. At the same time, the colony is small enough that I'd be recognized for an outsider if I go in and start asking questions.

"You'll have challenge enough," I say. "You have to walk in the front gate and convince the guards to tell you where Kione is."

"Shouldn't you go in? You're the one with rosemarks."

"I can't pose as a new resident without an escort of priest-esses. But umbertouched people are allowed into these compounds as private messengers. Only the rich can afford them, but we'll have to hope the guards don't think that hard about it. Can you do it?"

She sticks her tongue into her cheek. "More interesting than climbing that wall, at least."

I look her over for anything distinctly Shidadi. "Your swords have to go if you're to look the part," I say.

Sarsine makes a face as she reluctantly hands them to me.

"You carry two swords like Dineas," I say. "Is that how you like to fight?"

"I can best almost anyone on dual swords. People have

trouble with them because they think of their arms as two separate limbs. You really have to think of them as two ends of one long arm."

I confiscate Sarsine's bow too, though I let her keep her knives. After we're done, she looks like nothing more than an umbertouched girl turning her marks into extra income.

"Do I look the part now?" she asks.

"Close enough. I'll climb the wall on the easternmost end of the compound and meet you inside."

She tones down her usual saunter as she approaches the gate. The guards leaning against the wall don't even bother to straighten. I can't hear what she says to them, but they wave her through—they've always cared more about keeping people in than out. I wait a little longer to make sure there's no trouble, and then whistle for Scrawny to follow me to the eastern end.

Once we're at the right place, Scrawny takes off, circles, and then lands back on my shoulder. All clear. I jump and catch the top of the wall—it's gotten easier with practice these past months—and drop down on the other side. Sarsine's already waiting for me with a self-satisfied smirk. "She lives in the northwest corner."

This rosemarked compound is not as crowded as the one near Sehmar City. The houses there had been pushed up against each other, with makeshift dwellings erected in every conceivable space. Here, light actually falls between adjacent rooftops. All around us, people go about their day—sweeping doorsteps, running errands, relaxing in the shade. We get a few curious looks, but nobody stops us.

Eventually we come to a long rectangular building with a thatched roof. Sarsine looks to me for permission, and then raps sharply on the door. An elderly woman answers.

"I'm here carrying a message for Kione," says Sarsine. "I'm a private messenger from Sehmar City."

The woman squints at her, then looks at me. "Kione!"

A middle-aged Mishikan woman comes to the door. Her long black hair is tied into a bun, and she wears the same type of rough homespun tunic I'd seen on Baruva's slaves.

"Are you Kione?" asks Sarsine.

The woman gives us a curious look. "I am called Kione, yes." She speaks slowly, though I get the impression that it's a sign of thoughtfulness.

"I'm a private messenger—" says Sarsine, but I stop her with a hand on her shoulder. We need to be honest with Kione, if I want her to be honest with us.

"My name is Zivah. I'm looking for information about a man named Baruva."

Kione looks at me sharply. "Not really messengers, are you? How did you hear about me?"

"From the Rovenni."

Her eyes are shrewd. "Dara, rosemarked, and asking questions. You're the healer from the capital. The one stirring up trouble in the north."

I wonder, if she decides to call guards on us, how soon they would appear. "How do you know of me?"

Kione gives an amused smile. "Slaves are loyal friends, you'll find. I have friends with more freedom than I who bring me news from time to time. When you've suffered together as much as we have, you don't let something like the rose plague separate you." Without warning, she takes my hand and rubs at my rosemarks. "Verina, is she a real healer?"

The woman who'd answered the door sizes me up. "What are the three major organ systems?" she asks.

"I'm a Dara healer," I say. "We don't follow Ampara principles. But I believe them to be gut, blood, and sense."

"How would you treat a milk infection?"

"I'd engulf the breast in a steam bath infused with nadat root, and give vel tea to drink."

Verina looks at Kione and nods, then walks away.

Kione's posture softens the slightest bit, but not by much. "Why do you want to know about Baruva?" she asks.

"I suspect that he's wronged a great many people. I want to bring about justice."

"There is no justice in this world," she says calmly, "but I will tell you what I know." She motions us in. It's dim inside, and dust floats in the shafts of light coming through the small windows. Six beds line the interior walls. Besides the woman who answered the door and Kione, there are three other women of various ages.

"Zivah wants to talk to us," Kione says.

Us? I open my mouth to correct her, but Kione interrupts. "All of us were at Khaygal. All of us worked with Baruva. That's what you want to know about, isn't it?"

She's not really asking, so I simply follow. All the beds in the house leave little room for much else. Kione leads us to the far wall, where bags of dry goods are stacked. She sits on one and bids us sit as well. The bag feels like it's filled with beans. A seal on the cloth catches my eye.

"This is General Arxa's family seal, isn't it?" I ask.

"I don't know his seal, but these beans were brought here by his daughter," says Kione.

"Lady Mehtap?"

"That's the one. She's been traveling from compound to compound, delivering supplies. She passed through a fortnight ago on her way to the northern coast."

That must have been what she was doing at Taof when we hid in her wagon. "But how is she allowed to travel?"

Kione shrugs. "Permission from her father, special favors, who knows? Food is food."

"Are these paid for by Arxa's family?"

"Certainly not by the emperor."

I suppose what Kione says is possible. Mehtap had already

been interested in the governing of Sehmar City's rosemarked colony before I left. Perhaps this was the next logical step.

The other women gather around, taking seats on the sacks and the floor around us. They seem to defer to Kione, which surprises me because she's not the oldest.

Kione indicates three of the women. "Verina, Ali, and Ilia were hands for Baruva."

"Hands?"

"Assistants," says Verina. "He didn't like to touch the sick himself. I worked three years for him before I fell ill five years ago. Ilia came in last year, and Ali moved in half a year later."

I look to the last woman, who's tall and young, with strong shoulders. "And you?"

"Baruva didn't find me good enough to be his hands. I wasn't careful enough with the patients, so after a while I was put to work clearing out bodies."

The image of slaves wheeling bodies out of an outbreak makes me ill. It makes no sense to me how a man who cares so little for his slaves would be so concerned for his patients. "I'm sorry."

"We're the lucky ones." Verina's voice has a bitter edge to it. "Most of the others died."

"It's the greatness of the empire," says Kione. "Its vast reserves of knowledge. All of Ampara's glory is built on the backs of those like us."

I tally up the women so far. Three had been hands. One did menial labor. That left Kione.

"I worked in the kitchens," Kione says when I meet her eye. "We cooked mostly for the guards and for soldiers who passed through. Emperor Kiran, who was Prince Kiran back then, visited the outpost quite often. Baruva did as well. That's why Baruva had dedicated slaves here, so he wouldn't have to bring his hands from the capital.

"In the last few years of my service, Baruva and Kiran started showing interest in the kitchens. They came through and asked us questions. Kiran himself inspected our stores and supplies.

"One day we received a command to prepare supplies for a battalion. Fat cakes, dry bread, standard rations. But they gave us special flour to use. Said they were for the emperor's favored troops." She pauses and looks me in the eye. "Five of us in the kitchen fell ill with the rose plague a fortnight later."

A shiver dances across my skin. "Do you think it was the flour?"

Kione digs her palms into her makeshift chair. "That's what we thought, but what did it matter what we thought?" She pauses. "There was one more thing that was strange. The supplies were meant for a battalion headed to the northern swamplands. But Neju's Guard passed through the next day and the steward gave them the special rations, thinking that they were most favored by the emperor. I remember Baruva coming through the day after. Never had I seen a man so furious as Baruva when he learned of the mistake, furious and terrified. We all expected to be punished, but he did nothing. Later, I found out that the battalion headed to the swamplands had a commander who was very critical of Kiran. Said he involved himself too much in the army."

"Are you certain it was Baruva and Kiran working together? It wasn't just Baruva alone?"

"I see no other reason why Kiran would have been in the kitchen."

Sarsine and I exchange a look. "Do you know if there is any evidence we can find against him? Did Kiran give Baruva any written orders? Did either keep records of their meetings?" The word of a slave would carry precious little weight in Ampara.

Verina speaks up. "If Baruva keeps anything, it would be in his home."

"In Sehmar City?" My heart sinks at the thought of that long journey.

"No, Sehmar has too many prying eyes. Baruva has a summer home an hour northwest of Khaygal where he relaxes and entertains official guests. If he has any secrets, they would be there."

TWENTY: DINEAS

E very day brings the Amparan bridge closer to our shores. Crows and messenger pigeons crisscross the sky with news from our scouts.

Three more ships added to the bridge.

One more battalion spotted on the far shore.

The damage we did in the last raid disappears within days. It's clear to everyone now that another attack would simply be a waste of lives. So we wait, and we watch. And we prepare.

The order is given to empty the village. The paths fill with men, women, and children, bearing their most treasured belongings on their backs. It doesn't all go smoothly. Possessions go missing; squabbles break out over supplies. A Dara youth picks a fight with one of Vidarna's fighters over some insult I don't even understand, holding his own remarkably well before people finally pull them apart.

Still, the migration proceeds. I make sure Zivah's family gets out safely. In the mountains, we prepare hiding places and stockpile goods.

Every time a crow flies over my head, I think it's Scrawny with news of Zivah, but I know I'm being foolish. Zivah and

Sarsine will be traveling as fast as possible. They wouldn't waste time waiting for Scrawny to fly to me and then return to them. There's nothing I can do but push thoughts of them to the back of my mind. The worry is still there, though, lodged like a stone in my gut.

Gatha, true to her word, has removed me from scouting duties and assigned me to digging ditches around the village instead. It could be worse. Ditches, at least, don't try to shoot you full of arrows. But I don't exactly get a warm welcome from my fellow workers. The Shidadi from Karu's tribe don't even look at me, which makes me wonder how much has gotten out about what happened. To my surprise, it's the Dara who are more welcoming. After one long morning of labor, a tall man named Nuri hands me a waterskin.

"You're the first person who's looked at me straight on all day," I say, accepting a drink.

Nuri takes a swig himself. "I grew up with Zivah. We played together as children. I appreciate what you did for her."

"I wonder if you'll still think that once Ampara overruns your village."

He purses his lips as if I've made an excellent point. "Me too," he says, and finishes the rest of the water.

By now, we've dug pits and traps all around the village. We've excavated ditches with carved spikes underneath, and others with sharp rocks. Beyond those, there are also fire ditches to be filled with kindling. Dried bamboo explodes if set aflame with the compartments intact, which makes it bad for firewood but good for our purposes. The fire ditches were an idea of the Dara, actually, who've proven surprisingly good at adapting their knowledge to war. Their builders have several techniques that have proved useful—better ways to lash together bamboo spikes, closer weaves for mats to camouflage our ditches, ways to fill in wells so they aren't easily excavated again.

Today, we dig a ditch to be filled with rocks. "You know," says Nuri, looking down at his shovel, "brownhead serpents like to burrow in holes with plenty of dried leaves. They're very poisonous."

I raise my eyebrows. "They don't give you Dara enough credit. You have quite the devious mind." As we throw handfuls of leaves into the pit, I wonder if Zivah ever had a brownhead in her menagerie.

Soon, the village is emptied of most people, leaving only a few to set the trap. Some of this rear guard are Dara, but most are Shidadi veterans, milling around in houses not our own. The reports continue to come.

The final ships are lashed into place.

The bridge is complete.

A group of us watch from atop a cliff as the army starts to march. They lead with their infantry, pouring onto the bridge like black ink. The first segments of the bridge bob in the water, sending waves radiating out on either side, but the bridge holds.

We don't wait to see any more. Back in the village, the first wells are filled in.

With the passing hours come more reports.

They've arrived on Monyar.

Slowly moving north, widening the paths as they go.

They are close.

Two days after the Amparans cross the strait, the signal is given. Everyone rushes into position.

"Shoot well," Nuri tells me as I pick up my bow and head south.

"Neju give you strength," I say. "You know what to do?"

"Destroy everything, isn't that it?" His light tone doesn't quite mask the bitterness behind his words.

"Make them pay," I say. And then there's no more time to talk.

I take my place near the main trail leading into the village, swinging my bow over my shoulder as I climb one of the bigger stalks of bamboo. I settle at the spot where it forks; then I nock an arrow and wait. There were some Shidadi who wanted me to sit out the fighting, but Gatha argued that we needed all the fighters we can get. The compromise was to place me far from the center of action, but still close to enough fighters to keep an eye on me.

A flock of birds takes wing in the distance. Bamboo shifts underneath them. Rustles and cracks echo through the air.

Foot soldiers come into view, more than a hundred of them. They take positions alongside the paths and hack at the bamboo with axes. I take aim at the closest one and shoot. He drops. Though I can't see my fellow archers, I see their arrows strike and hear the screams of those they hit. The remaining Amparan soldiers drop their tools and flee. I shoot a few more in the back, and then I retreat to the village.

Gatha, Vidarna, and a handful of other fighters await us at the southernmost cottage.

"Rest while you can," Gatha says as another crew goes out. The plan is to give the Amparans no rest. Don't let them widen the paths without a fight. Make them decide to attack the village on suboptimal terrain.

As we wait, I gulp from my waterskin and swallow mouthfuls of dried fruit. An hour passes, and then another. Someone offers me a piece of deer jerky, which I chew into paste. Nearby, a cluster of Vidarna's fighters suck on swamp berries as they wait. They claim it quickens their reflexes for battle, but it also tints their mouths a disturbing shade of bluish purple.

Vidarna keeps his messenger pigeons flying back and forth between us and our scouts, commanding by waving different strips of colored cloth. Most warlords delegate communications to others, but Vidarna keeps a careful eye on what's coming in and out.

A crow caws. *Soldiers on their way.* We scatter. Once again, I climb a stalk of bamboo.

This time, the soldiers are expecting us. They stream down the trails as the surrounding forests sway with the movements of their comrades. I fire at the first man that comes into range and keep firing, focusing my shots to my left, forcing the soldiers toward traps that we've set. One Amparan falls, and then another. There's a crash, then yells sound in the distance, and I know the traps have been sprung. But the Amparans keep coming.

A Shidadi horn blasts. *Retreat.* Light blazes in the corner of my vision as a Shidadi sets fire to the first line of cottages. Pops sound as the bamboo starts exploding. I shoot four more arrows, then slide down. A soldier rushes me as soon as my boots hit the ground, swinging his sword at my head. I dive out of the way as his blade catches on a stalk of bamboo behind me, then knee him in the stomach and run.

The battle continues. Hide, shoot, burn, retreat. Hide, shoot, burn, retreat. Make them think the village is fuller than it is. Make them pay dearly for every bit of land they gain. Dara is a long string of houses down the length of the valley, and we work our way back little by little. I stay in the forest, just outside Dara's network of trails, taking down soldiers who push their way through the plants and leaving it to other fighters to fire the cottages as we go. The Amparan line falls ragged, but so does ours. Fewer arrows fly from our ranks with each successive fall back. My arms ache from shooting. My eyes water from the smoke.

The horn sounds again, this time a long, drawn-out blast. *Fall back to final position.*

I run into the village, breaking through into a clearing of several cottages. There are scattered clusters of fighting—the only Amparans out here are ones who'd been lured away from their units. Hashama fends off three attackers by a well, swinging the curved sword of his tribe like Neju himself. That man might not have a sense of humor, but his swordsmanship warms my heart.

An Amparan charges me as I approach. As our swords clash, his face flickers and turns into Naudar's.

No. It's not Naudar. Naudar's dead.

I grit my teeth and drive my attack, moving him back one step, then another until my sword slips through his guard and he falls to the ground. When I look at his face this time, he's once again a nameless soldier.

"Dineas," Hashama shouts. He's dispatched the other two.

"Go!" I yell, and we redouble our speed. Ahead of us stretches a trench packed with kindling. Gatha's on the other side, flanked by archers who fire past our heads. The ditch looms in front of us now, as wide as a man is tall. In one last burst of speed, I leap and land hard on the other side.

Gatha steadies my shoulders and pulls me away from the ditch. "Light the fire," she says.

The Dara man Nuri thrusts a torch into the kindling. The pitch catches fire immediately, and a wave of heat hits my face. Archers fire through the flames until the fire grows high enough we can't see past it. And then we run. The sound of the Amparan army grows distant behind us.

We retreat up the mountain until we reach a ridge over-looking the village. There, I finally look back. The valley, Zivah's home, is alight with flames. Somewhere down there, the Amparans are trying to regroup. Next to me, Nuri surveys the flames and unabashedly wipes a tear from his eye.

"This is it, isn't it?" he says. "We're at war."

I look at the smoke curling into the air, and the full weight of Nuri's words hits me. "This is it," I say, and something that's either dread or hope uncurls within me. "This is the last war we'll ever fight."

TWENTY-ONE: ZIVAH

S arsine doesn't say anything until we're well away from the rosemarked compound. When she does, her voice shakes with quiet fury. "What kind of man would do this? What kind of empire would allow this?" She's not really asking for an answer.

Verina's directions are easy enough to follow. There's a dirt wagon trail that leads northwest through the grassland. Though I take care to hide my rosemarks, we don't see a single other person on the road, which makes the manor all the more striking when we come upon it. It's an enormous compound enclosing an area the size of the emperor's gardens. The perimeter is marked by a brick wall, and on the other side I can a see the manor building's upper floor. The building itself only takes up a small portion of the compound. The rest, judging from the trees and hedges peeking over the top, is well-culti- vated foliage.

I stay a safe distance away while Sarsine does a preliminary scouting round. She comes back with her cheeks flushed from running. "Baruva's here," she says.

"You saw him?"

"From a distance. At least, I think it was him. Pompous-looking fellow, dressed in overly nice clothes?"

"That sounds right."

Sarsine gives an unladylike snort. "It's a big house. Twenty rooms, I'd say. We might be able to search some of them at night, but not his personal quarters."

"That's where he'd most likely hide anything important."

She nods in silent agreement.

That means we'll have to search his quarters during the day, then, and that didn't work out so well at Taof. "We can watch the gates for a day or two," I say. "Perhaps he'll leave the manor for a few hours."

With that settled, there's nothing to do but wait. Night is falling, and we set out our bedrolls in the grass a good distance from the road. We don't dare make a fire, but the night is warm, and the stars shine down brightly. Though it's my watch, Sarsine doesn't go straight to sleep. Instead, she picks a fistful of grass and holds it to her nose.

"It smells different down here, doesn't it?" she says. "Iyal Island smelled like mud. Monyar smells green. Here, it smells sweet. Sweet and dusty."

A gust of wind blows, sending ripples through the grass.

"We used to be nomads, you know," says Sarsine. There's a note of longing in her voice.

I turn to look at her. "What?"

"The Shidadi. My tribe. We used to be nomads in my father and mother's time, before the Amparans drove us into a corner. We prided ourselves on being tied to no land, strong enough to handle any terrain. 'Shidadi' means 'freedom' in our language, did you know that? Sometimes we lent our swords to others, or sometimes we simply fought to defend ourselves. But we were free."

She sighs. "Now we're cooped in. Iyal Island is small enough to circle in a day. We survive for months on swamp root. And the mosquitoes..."

She trails off, but I sense she's not finished.

"The elders always told stories of the main continent. Deserts that stretched for leagues, grassland like this, markets with fried sweet buns and music. I always wanted to see them for myself."

"Is that why you came here with me?"

She gives me a crooked grin. "Well, I mean, there's the part about loyalty and fighting for my people and doing what's right, but yes."

There's a beat of feathers over my head. Scrawny comes swooping down and settles at the foot of my empty bedroll. He tucks his chin, fluffs his feathers, and watches us.

Sarsine flicks a blade of grass toward the bird. "I mean, I'm not stupid. I've seen how long my kinsmen live. If I'm going to die soon, I want to see more of the world before that happens."

"You might not die, Sarsine."

"Well, I certainly don't plan to make it easy for them to kill me." She reaches out and gives the sword next to her a pat. "And Karu would be very put out if she lost another fighter."

This is the first time Sarsine's mentioned Karu on our trip. I think of my parting conversation with the warlord, as well as what Dineas told me about the traitor in the Shidadi camp. "Is Karu a good leader?"

"She's held us together," says Sarsine. "That's not easy to do. I mean, she's not the most pleasant to be around sometimes, but I wouldn't be either if I had her responsibilities."

"I see." I want to ask more—how far Karu would go to stay alive, whether her willingness to bend rules applies just to the enemy, or if she'd betray her own people as well. But I don't know how loyal Sarsine is to her warlord. "Do you find her...trustworthy?"

Sarsine looks at me. "Karu is Shidadi to the core," she says flatly. "I trust her with my life."

Of course, Sarsine wasn't there when Karu tried to convince me to infect the Amparan troops. But I sense it's not the time to push this further.

Sarsine lies back and folds her hands over her stomach. "So, is Dineas a good kisser?"

Apparently it's possible to choke even when your mouth is empty.

Sarsine gives me an impish grin. "I mean, that's what you were doing when I gave you time to say your good-byes, wasn't it? If not, then both of you are idiots."

I'm thankful we don't have a fire, because my cheeks are burning. "It's complicated, between us."

"Oh, I know. I heard about your mission. Almost too strange to believe, some of it. It still doesn't change the way he looks at you."

I think of our parting moment in the Monyar forest, the way he drank me in with his eyes, as if he could somehow keep us from parting by force of will alone. "We've been through a lot together. But I've also hurt him."

"Why do you say that?"

"I..." I've carried my guilt alone for so long now that it's hard to put it into words. "They must have told you that I gave Dineas potions to change his memory. Problem was, our potions had never been used that way before. It seemed a risk worth taking at the time, but he's suffered consequences I didn't foresee." I think about how the memory of his Amparan comrades haunt him still, and I remember his anguish as he confided in me. "He may suffer these consequences for the rest of his life. I'm a healer, yet I've caused him irreparable harm."

Sarsine weaves her fingers together and drums them on her stomach. "He's scarred, that's for sure," she says. "But we all are to some degree. And I have a feeling you've done more good for him than you realize."

"What do you mean?"

She shrugs. "Love is hard to come by. Even when it comes painfully, it's rare enough to hold on to."

"Perhaps you're right." I stare at the night sky, sending up one more prayer for his safety. I wonder if the Goddess protects those who are not her own, or if I should be praying to Neju instead.

"So you did kiss him," says Sarsine.

I throw a clump of dirt at her, which she deflects with a giggle before rolling over and pulling her cloak tighter around herself. A few moments later, I hear faint smooching sounds drift over from her direction.

"Go to sleep."

"You're no fun at all." But I can hear the grin in her voice. A few moments later, she's asleep.

WE HAVE a stroke of luck the next day when Baruva rides out in the morning with two servants. They carry baskets but no luggage, which means they'll likely be gone a few hours.

As we make our way closer to Baruva's home, I can't help but admire its beauty. It's constructed with bricks of alternating earthen red and deep purple. Though the building itself is square and solid, the arched windows of the second floor give it a refined air. We approach the outer wall from the side, out of view of the two gate guards in front. Sarsine scales it first. Then I slip on gloves and follow her into a courtyard paved with the same red and purple bricks. The ground-floor windows are open to let the breeze in, and we scramble through.

Inside, it's dark, cool, and colorful. This place would be a peaceful retreat under different circumstances. We come into a sitting room piled with red and gold cushions. There are no servants in sight, though I do hear footsteps echoing down a mosaic-lined corridor. Sarsine looks around, and then points down another corridor. We race along, passing several more sitting rooms, a dining room, and giant windows overlooking a garden before we stop at the foot of a fan-shaped staircase.

"Upstairs?" Sarsine mouths.

I nod. That's where Baruva's quarters will most likely be.

The landing at the top of the stairs goes in two directions. Sarsine frowns at the thick rug covering the floor, then points right. I realize she's looking at the pattern of wear on the rug. Sarsine leads the way, her eyes fixed on the carpeting. At one point, she stops, pushes me into an empty bedroom, and manages to close the door behind us without making a sound. She puts a finger to her lips, and sure enough, footsteps pass by soon after. We wait for them to fade, then continue on our way.

Finally, Sarsine stops at a door and tries the knob. It's locked, and she smiles in satisfaction. "No reason to lock a door if there's nothing to keep hidden."

I glance around nervously as she pulls out a set of lock picks. They scrape disturbingly loudly against the lock, but soon the door swings open. The suite inside is opulent and neat, with a bedroom to the left and a study to the right.

"I'll stand watch," Sarsine whispers, and I get to work.

I decide to start with Baruva's bedroom. His chest yields nothing out of the ordinary, and there's nothing between the tapestry and the walls. I check the lining of his clothes, as well as the edges of his pillow and linens. I even knock on the board at the head of his bed, but it yields nothing but a solid thunk. The bed itself sits on four feet carved in the shape of lions, and I check those as well. All solid.

Sarsine sticks her head in. "Find anything?"

I shake my head. I must have been here an hour now with no success. "I'll try his study."

Baruva's desk is piled high with medical texts, but there's

nothing here out of the ordinary, nor is there anything behind the scrolls on his shelves. I get on my hands and knees and knock on the floorboards one by one. When Sarsine comes to check on me, I just shake my head again. Could Verina have been mistaken? Or am I just looking in the wrong place?

"I think we need to leave," says Sarsine. "I don't want to push our luck."

As much as I want to stay, I know she's right. I look out the window, trying to judge how far the sun has moved since we came in. The manor building itself sits atop a hill, and the view of the gardens below is quite striking. There's at least one pond, an orchard, and an herb garden with plants in neat rows. From here, I can identify some of the plants.

"Can we leave through the garden?" I ask.

"It would mean more chances to get caught," says Sarsine. "Why?"

"A hunch."

Someone else might have asked for more of an explanation, but Sarsine simply nods. We duck down a side stairway and into a pathway lined with cypress trees. The lane passes a pond covered with fragrant lilies, and then a small court of yellow and blue wildflowers. After that comes the herb garden I saw from the window. I count twenty rows, each planted with different herbs—bukar plants, whose roots are good for fever; spineleaf bushes, whose sap soothes all kinds of ailments; karada shrubs, whose stems are boiled for dysentery.

Slow dysentery, plague incubation period. Those were certainly strange notes on the side of Baruva's journal.

I count the number of bushes in the lane. Thirty. The garden here is well maintained, but not as immaculately so as the rest of the compound. Perhaps this patch is tended only by Baruva and a few trusted servants. Perhaps this would be a good place to hide something important.

Sarsine has gone several steps ahead. "Zivah?"

"Wait," I say, and step into the garden. The plague incubation period is ten days. I count ten bushes. The ground at the base of the tenth bush looks the same as the rest of it.

I whistle for Scrawny. "Scout," I say, and start digging as soon as he takes wing. The dirt is moist but firm, and doesn't part easily under my fingers.

"What are you doing?" Sarsine hisses.

"Watch for anyone coming."

She looks around uneasily but doesn't say anything else. The smell of earth fills my nostrils. My fingers grow raw from digging, and I look around for a better tool.

"Here!" Sarsine tosses me a flat rock. I nod my thanks and keep digging.

Am I just imagining things? Those words could have countless meanings. But still...

I'm elbow deep now. Worms burrow frantically away as I uncover them, occasionally squiriming over my fingers.

"Zivah," says Sarsine. "We shouldn't stay long."

There's nothing here. My stomach sinks as I survey the growing mess around me. There's no way I can fill this hole well enough to blend in.

My little finger hits something hard and smooth—too smooth to be a rock. More digging, more clearing away of dirt. My fingers close around a wide-mouth jar, small enough to fit in my hand and sealed with wax against the moisture. Jars like this can preserve documents for years. My heart pounds as I jiggle it loose from its place. I glance at Sarsine, who's still looking up and down the path, and then I carefully break the seal. A sharp, astringent smell assails my nose.

There aren't any documents inside. Instead, it's filled to the brim with a red-orange powder. When I hold it to the light, I see the powder's pearly finish.

Red with a hint of yellow, iridescent in the sunlight.

I slam the plug back onto the jar, scarcely daring to breathe.

How had Baruva gotten a jar of suona pollen? Using slaves to protect himself was apparently not enough of a safeguard for him. Is this what Baruva meant when he said he was my last hope? I try to remember what his notes had said about the pollen. Prince Nia of Mishikan had taken a pinch of pollen in his tea every morning. At that rate, there's enough pollen here to last several years.

Scrawny caws.

My hands are sweating now, and I get the absurd notion that the jar will dissolve between my fingers. I could take this treasure and flee. We could be hours, even days away before he realizes it's gone.

I swallow a lump in my throat. Why does he live in luxury, when I am sick? Why do Kione and the other slaves die a slow death while he grows in prestige and reputation?

Someone grabs me by the shoulder. I swallow a scream.

"Zivah, didn't you hear me?" Sarsine hisses. "Someone's coming!"

She kicks the mound of dirt I'd piled back toward the hole. About half of it lands in, and she lets out a string of curses, grabs my sleeve, and hauls me deeper into the garden.

"You there, stop!" shouts a man behind us.

I turn and lock eyes with a guard near the path. We keep running.

A path leads off the garden at the other end. Sarsine and I race down its length and then cut through the flower garden. There's a wall of hedges past the flowers. Sarsine points to a gap near the bottom, scarcely large enough for a cat to fit through.

"We'll fit!" she says, and gives me a shove. Dirt rubs onto my sleeves and tunic and branches snag at my hair as I scramble through. Cobwebs brush at my face. I hope to the Goddess I don't get stuck in here forever, and then I burst out into yet another garden.

Shrubs carved in the shape of different animals surround a

central mosaic of red and black flagstones. Behind us, I hear the guards closing in. The jar of suona pollen is heavy in my hand, far too precious to lose if we're caught. As Sarsine fights her way through the hedge, I crouch beside the nearest shrub—one shaped like a trumpeting elephant. The base is a tangle of branches and leaves, and I thrust the jar of suona pollen as far in as I can, ignoring the sharp twigs scraping my skin.

"What are you doing?" Sarsine asks.

"Never mind," I say, brushing cobwebs off my arm. "Go."

We race past a small fountain with statues of the seven gods, and past an altar to Hefana. We're just a few sections away from the wall now. Just a little bit farther.

One more turn, and a wall appears in front of us.

And so do five guards.

TWENTY-TWO: ZIVAH

F ive guards stand between us and the wall. Another three close in from behind. Sarsine reaches for her sword, and I for my blowgun.

"Touch your weapons and we'll sever your hands from your arms," says a guard.

Sarsine's eyes flash as she looks from soldier to soldier. For a moment, I fear she may fight. But then she raises her hands in surrender, and I follow suit.

A familiar voice speaks behind us. "What is this?" Baruva strides into our midst accompanied by another man in official-looking robes. Baruva gets a better look at me, and his face reddens with fury. "Zivah."

"The fugitive healer?" says the official next to him incredulously. "The emperor will be eager to have them."

A spasm of irritation crosses Baruva's face. "Yes, we'll send word. Take them to the outside holding room."

Sarsine and I look at each other helplessly as the soldiers tie our hands and march us to a small building with barred cells. How could I have been so careless? An umbertouched soldier searches us. Sarsine scowls as they take her swords and daggers, while I fight the urge to hang on to my blowgun.

"Nothing else?" Baruva asks the soldier. "Are you sure? They stole some items from my tent last time."

Why don't you come pat me down yourself? I think.

The soldier shakes his head.

Baruva looks at me with a distaste usually reserved for leeches and flies. "It's a pity. By all reports, you are a brilliant physician, though admittedly backward in some ways. I suppose talent doesn't always come hand in hand with sense."

"If sense means letting slaves face the dangers of disease for me, then I am proud to be backward."

His smile is condescending. "My cures and treatments have helped thousands of patients. No one else can do what I do. Would you rather I contracted the disease two decades ago and let the world stumble on with the same treatments we've used for centuries? Should I have been like you? Promising, dedicated, and dead before twenty?"

His words empty my lungs better than any blow his guards could have thrown. Baruva gives me one last knowing smirk before turning to his companion. "Come. We've more pleasant things to attend to."

As the guards file out, a heavy silence falls in our cell.

"Don't listen to him," says Sarsine. "You are a hundred times the healer he will ever be."

Am I? His words echo in my head, sharp and painful in their truth. *Promising, dedicated, and dead before twenty.*

I slump against the wall. "I'm sorry. I should have run when you warned me."

"No use looking back in war," Sarsine says firmly. "Now we look forward. How do we get out of here?"

I do my best to take on her resolve. She's right. We've come too far to die out here, leagues away from anyone we know. The one window is too small to fit through. The door, as well, is shut tight. Sarsine starts prying pebbles from the earthen floor. "You can do a lot of damage with these. Do you think they will take us back to Sehmar City?"

"Perhaps," I say.

The room darkens. A crow-shaped shadow appears in the patch of sunlight on the floor.

"Scrawny!"

The bird puffs his wings as I run to the window. "Scrawny, can you bring us something? A weapon perhaps?"

He tilts his head.

"A weapon, Scrawny. You must know what a weapon is. A knife maybe."

He caws and flies off. A half hour later, he returns with a stick the length of my hand.

"No, not that." I send him off again.

Evening falls soon after. We have a pitcher of water but no food. Sarsine and I huddle together for warmth as the sun sets. Her breathing quickly grows even. It takes me longer, but eventually I drift into a fitful sleep.

THE DOOR to our prison slams open. Baruva stands framed in the doorway, his face illuminated in stark angles by the light of his oil lamp. He comes straight up to the bars and almost grabs them before remembering himself. "Where is it?" he hisses.

"Where is what?"

Next to me, Sarsine leaps to her feet.

"You know what," he says.

"I think you're mistaken," I say.

"You think you're safe because of your rosemarks?" he says. "I have an umbertouched interrogator I trust in the capital. And in the meantime, your friend poses no danger to the untouched."

Sarsine lifts her chin. "Just try and make me talk, old man."

Baruva gives her a dangerous smile. "Be cocksure while you can. We've broken the spirit of many a Shidadi at Khaygal. Eventually they scream and beg just like all the others." He turns for the door. "I'll return tomorrow, and you'll do yourselves a favor by confessing without trouble."

Baruva leaves, and we're plunged into darkness. I can hear Sarsine's shaky breathing next to me. "Do you still have what you took from him?"

"No," I say after a pause.

"Don't tell me what you did with it," she says firmly. "Don't even tell me what it is. Then I won't be able to give them anything."

"Sarsine, if it comes down to you being tortured, I'll give Baruva what he wants."

She looks at me as if I'm the world's greatest simpleton. "This is the only thing you hold over Baruva right now. If you tell him, there's no reason for him to keep either of us alive. Does he seem like the type of man who will keep his word?"

As horrifying as her words are, they seem all too plausible.

After a while, Sarsine speaks again. "Khaygal was where Dineas was imprisoned, wasn't it?"

"Yes."

"I see." She says no more.

Wind whistles outside our window. As the silence stretches, I think about the way Baruva stormed in. This is the first time I've seen him alone, without umbertouched soldiers or slaves to do his work for him. Why is that? Even this late at night, he should have the authority to command someone to follow him.

"He may be bluffing," I say abruptly.

"What do you mean?"

"I think he wants to keep the su—the thing that I stole from him a secret. If he tortures us, he won't be able to."

"I hope you're right."

Despite Baruva's threats, Sarsine falls asleep quickly. I

wonder if it's something the Shidadi learn early on, to sleep in the face of danger. As I lie listening to her breathing, I remember the haunted look in Dineas's eyes whenever he relives his time in the Amparan prison, and I resolve to do everything in my power to protect Sarsine.

I don't know when I fall asleep, but when I open my eyes, it's morning. An umbertouched soldier comes in and places two bowls of gruel on the ground for us. A short while later, Scrawny comes back with a shard of pottery, which we break into two sharp halves. The thought crosses my mind that if we can't get out, at least we could send him back to tell Dineas what became of us. But I push that thought away, because it's too early to think about giving up.

Sarsine spends the morning trying to pick the cell lock with the handle of her spoon. I walk around the edge of the room, looking at the points where the wall meets the floor, and for any small cracks.

"What are you looking for?" asks Sarsine.

"Scorpions. It's how I escaped prison last time."

Sarsine raises her eyebrows. "Can you get them to sting for you?"

"No, but they're useful as distractions."

She laughs. "I'll say." She stretches and takes a step toward the window, only to fall face-first onto the floor.

"Sarsine!"

She shakes herself and pushes onto her knees. "Must have tripped," she says.

There's something strange about her eyes. I drop to my knees and tilt her head to the light. Her pupils are dilated, and her inner lids are pale, almost white. Her breath comes slow and uneven. "Sarsine, how do you feel?"

She blinks, struggling to focus her eyes. "I..."

I catch her as she slumps, fighting back panic as I lower her to the floor. Her skin is cold and clammy. What is this? Disease?

Poison? I crawl across the room and pick up our empty bowls. Was it the gruel? Or the water? The water had tasted fine. The gruel...Now that I think of it, it did have a distinct aftertaste.

Sarsine rubs her forehead and wriggles on the ground. "I don't know what's wrong with me," she slurs.

I rush to her side. "Lie down and rest. See if it passes."

It doesn't. If anything, Sarsine grows more disoriented. Sweat beads on her skin, and her breathing grows more erratic.

Footsteps sound outside. I place a protective hand on Sarsine's shoulder as Baruva opens the door. He gives a satisfied smirk when he sees Sarsine, though his brow furrows slightly when he sees me. In a flash of recognition, I realize that the bowls of gruel were served to us together, in two identical vessels on the same tray. The water too was given in one pitcher. There was no way Baruva could have chosen which one of us to poison. He must have poisoned both, which means I'm supposed to be sick too. I let myself slump against the wall and unfocus my eyes. It's not hard to feign illness. After the past day's ordeal, there's a constant ache in the back of my head, and I feel hot and uncomfortable. Baruva takes a second look at me and relaxes.

"You see," says Baruva. "I have means of applying pressure, even in the absence of interrogators. This is a slow-acting poison. It starts with disorientation. In an hour or two, the pain should set in around your liver as the poison slowly eats it away. It's excruciating, from what I hear, and only grows worse over a course of days. Tell me what I want to know. If you tell me early enough, I'll give you the cure. If you tell me too late, I'll grant you a quick death."

"What did you give us?" I ask.

"I'm sure you would love to know," he says. And then he leaves.

TWENTY-THREE: ZIVAH

I rush to our bowls as soon as Baruva leaves, running my fingers along the bottoms and sniffing at what little gruel was left behind. They have a faint acrid odor I don't recognize. But I'm not sick.

"Zivah," says Sarsine. "What did he do to us?"

I lay the bowls back down and wipe my finger on the tray. "I don't know."

It wouldn't be the first poison I'm immune to. Dara healers are charged with harvesting venoms for cures. As part of our training, we inject ourselves with increasing amounts of venom to protect against accidents. I've survived bites from creatures that would fell men twice my size. Of course, none of this helps Sarsine.

She groans and presses her hands to her abdomen. "I think the pain is starting to settle in."

I run to her side again, wracking my brain. Is it a plant? A spider venom? There's a red-skinned frog in Monyar that causes similar symptoms, but I know of no poison that acts this slowly. Even if I were sure of the poison, I'd have no herbs with which to treat her.

Sarsine curls into a ball, whimpering. I bite my lip, willing my panic not to show. I need to stay calm for Sarsine. Getting her worked up may speed the poison's spread.

Could I treat her without knowing what the poison is? The Goddess tells us blood confers both strength and weakness. Sometimes with poisons, we'll strain out the blood of a star vole, which is immune to most snakes, and use it to treat the snakebitten.

Sarsine moans again, and I put my doubts aside. There's no time to dither. Either I'm wrong, or I'm right. I empty our water cup from breakfast and place it under my arm. The guards took my herbs before locking me up, but they didn't take my bracelet of snake fangs. I untie the cord and detach two of them. My hands shake as I dig the first into a vein in my arm. Blood flows out in a thin stream. I let it flow until the cup is half-full, and then press the bottom of my tunic against the cut until the bleeding stops.

"How do you feel?" I ask Sarsine.

"Like there's a knife between my ribs."

That kind of pain isn't a good sign.

"Hold still," I tell Sarsine. I pierce her arm with one of the fangs and leave it there. I can tell Sarsine's trying not to move, but she writhes despite her best efforts. By now, the blood I let into the cup is starting to clot into its elements, the red solids at the bottom, and the clear serum up top. "Red for vigor," I recite under my breath. "Clear for essence." I dip the other fang into the serum and feed a drop onto the fang in Sarsine's arm. The liquid drips into the wound, both along the outside of the tooth and through the hollow middle.

We keep at this for hours—Sarsine squirming on the ground and me feeding the drops one at a time into her vein. It's precise, exhausting work, and my arm shakes from fatigue. Though the residual venom on the snake fang helps against clotting, I still have to jiggle the fang regularly to keep things moving.

As night falls, I hear footsteps outside the door. As the latch turns, I hurriedly push the cup against the wall and slump against it. Baruva comes in, and I twist my face as if in pain. It's not a hard act to do.

"Have you thought about what I've said?" he asks.

"Zenagua take you." Sarsine's curse ends with a whimper.

The healer smirks. "The pain only gets worse. You have half a day before you're beyond saving."

The moment he leaves, we get back to work. Sarsine and I continue the treatment into the night. Eventually, she falls asleep, though I don't know if it's because the pain has decreased, or simply due to exhaustion. I too collapse soon after.

I WAKE to the sound of multiple voices outside our door.

"I would like to keep them longer," says Baruva. "They can be questioned just as effectively here. It may be dangerous to transport them, since they seem to have fallen ill."

"Emperor Kiran would like them in Sehmar City." I don't recognize that man's voice, but he speaks as to allow no argument.

Sarsine stirs and looks at me, bleary eyed. Her face is no longer strained with pain.

The door opens, and an umbertouched man in imperial purple walks in, followed by two umbertouched soldiers and a very displeased Baruva. The healer's eyes pass briefly over us, and then he stares. We look far too healthy.

The man points at me. "This one is the healer?"

Baruva nods, still looking from me to Sarsine and back. I allow myself a small amount of satisfaction at his obvious confusion, but it's tempered by the imperial soldiers about to take us away. There's something familiar about that man in purple, though. I wonder if I've seen him before in Sehmar City.

"And the other?" asks the man.

"Shidadi, but we know little else."

The man nods. "Get them ready to go."

The soldiers tie our hands behind our backs and march us outside, where we're herded into a closed cart. I'm heartened to see Sarsine walk out on her own strength. The wagon is a box on wheels with a door in the back—almost like a carriage without the fine trappings. I sit down on a bench lining the wall, and Sarsine crumples onto the one across from me.

"How do you feel?" I ask.

Her eyes go unfocused as she takes inventory of her body. "It still hurts," she says, "but not nearly as bad."

"That's better than I'd hoped." Now we just have to pray that it was good enough for a full recovery.

It's stuffy inside the wagon. A little light comes through cracks in the wood, but not much air, and the cart jostles every time we hit a bump. I strain at my ropes, but they're too tight to slip off. I start sawing them against the edge of my wooden bench. Sarsine does the same, but then she stops and peers out through one of the cracks.

"We're not going toward Sehmar," she says. "We're going north."

Something gives in my bindings. Quickly, I pull the ropes from my wrists. "I'm free."

Sarsine turns her back to me, and I dig my nails into the knots binding her wrists, working them loose.

The cart slows to a halt. We freeze.

Sarsine frantically casts off her ropes as footsteps approach our wagon. She pulls out a fistful of pebbles from underneath her tunic and presses them into my hands. "Go for the eyes," she hisses. She picks up the rope that had bound her and stretches it between her hands, a ready garrote. We creep—Sarsine still a little unsteady—toward the door and take our positions on either side. I shift my weight to leap at the person beyond.

The door opens. And I stop.

A lone woman stands outside. Her face and clothes are obscured by a cylindrical plague veil. Only her hands show from underneath, and there's something about them. They're mottled into the familiar rosemark pattern, but more than that, I've seen them before—serving tea, plucking a harp, clutching a bowl of incense.

The woman lifts her hands to her veil and parts it to reveal Mehtap's face.

All I can do is stare.

Next to me, Sarsine, her makeshift garrote still in her hand, looks warily between Mehtap and me, waiting for my cue.

Mehtap takes in my expression. "An imperial messenger with a secret, urgent message from Baruva to Kiran switched horses at a nearby outpost. It wasn't hard to guess what it was about, and not much harder to fake a return messenger." She indicates a short distance behind her, where the man in imperial purple stands grooming a horse. "Sisson used to be one of Kiran's guards at court, and he's very good at imitating the peacocks that spend their days there." Now I know why he looked familiar. I saw him speaking with Mehtap the last time we saw her caravan.

"You rescued us?" I still can't wrap my mind around it.

A flash of irritation crosses her face. "I've no great love for Baruva. The sycophant has stood in the way of all my recent efforts. It's time something doesn't go his way." She pauses. "It was you who wrote that note, wasn't it? The one warning me about him."

So she did find the note. "I overheard him talking about you at Taof."

"You should have been clear out of the empire by then," she says. "You promised you'd leave right away."

"It proved to be harder than anticipated."

She lets out a small huff and steps back from the wagon. "Don't you want to come out?"

The situation feels more and more bizarre as Sarsine and I climb out. We're still in the grasslands, and our cart is circled with the rest of Mehtap's wagons. There's a fire pit in the middle, and a basket of travel bread on the ground. The crew of her caravan walks between the wagons, busy with their tasks.

"Sit, eat," Mehtap says. She still has the same childlike face, and her rosemarks are as prominent as ever. But the differences I noticed near Taof are even more pronounced now. For one thing, she wears a torn brown travel tunic instead of the embroidered gowns she wore at home. Beyond that, though, she has an air of command that once again brings her father to mind. She's a far cry from the tormented soul I left in Sehmar City.

My stomach growls, and I decide that Mehtap has easier ways of killing us than giving us bad food. The bread is quite good—softer than most travel breads, with a nutty taste.

"Delicious, isn't it?" says Mehtap. "Remember Estir from Sehmar's compound? There's a woman in her group who makes this. It's called Zenagua's scales—the currants are good deeds and the raisins are bad. The baker decides the proportions."

This batch is markedly heavier in raisins.

"Your weapons are in the back of the first wagon," Mehtap says. "You shouldn't stay long. Take what food you need to keep you alive on your journey."

Sarsine needs no further encouragement and rushes to the first wagon, reminding me of Dineas the way she's so eager to get to her weapons.

I linger. "I heard you were traveling between colonies bringing them food and supplies."

Mehtap shrugs. "After everything happened in Sehmar, I didn't know what to do. I could lie down in my villa and wait to die, or I could continue the work we started. To atone for—" She looks at Sarsine and stops. "But I received news of the outbreak at Taof and that they were low on supplies. The emperor doesn't do anything—we know that. My father had to ask a few favors, but I was granted permission to travel if we stayed to the side roads and my crew handled everything outside the compounds. I want to be useful, Zivah. I want to make a difference. That hasn't changed."

Her answer shames me. I don't know why I keep underestimating her. "Thank you. You likely saved our lives."

She gives a bitter laugh. "You know what's maddening? I couldn't even hate you. You'd betrayed me in every way. Made my father look like a fool, took our kindness and threw it in our faces. I started running this caravan to escape everything, to forget all that's happened. But then, I wouldn't even have thought of doing this if it hadn't been for you. If you hadn't shown me that I could do more than just be locked up in my rosemarked villa with my servants. So should I be grateful to you? When you've done so much to hurt us?"

"I'm sorry." I wonder if those words hold any meaning at all anymore.

"If you're truly sorry, you'll tell me what you're doing back in Ampara. Am I handing an advantage over to my father's enemies by letting you go?"

I hesitate just a brief moment. Mehtap may not believe me, but I have to try. "Your father's enemies are not who you think they are."

Her expression flattens.

I continue. "Remember Utana, the minister of health? He made a confession to me before he died. He'd learned that Kiran and Baruva worked together to infect your father's troops with rose plague."

Mehtap furrows her brow. "Kiran and Baruva? Plotting against my father's troops?"

I nod.

"No. I don't believe it. Baruva is a craven puppet, but he wouldn't go that far. And Kiran is devoted to my father. He wouldn't harm his troops."

"Kiran didn't mean to. The food was meant for another battalion, but there was a mistake."

I think I see a flicker of doubt spread across her face. "You learned all this from Utana? Why didn't you have him tell my father?"

"He died before I could find out more, and there were pieces I had to fill in. A woman named Kione at the Khaygal rose-marked compound told me the rest. That's why I came back to Ampara. To find her."

Mehtap mouths Kione's name. "I don't understand. If this is true, why would Utana tell you, and not me?"

The answer is hard to say. I hesitate, considering different words, but there's no way to make it sound less damning. "I'd given Utana some herbs for pain. They...make some people more forthright than they usually are."

Mehtap rears back. "You have herbs that make people tell you their secrets? Who else have you given them to?" She pauses, aghast. "Have you given them to me?"

I throw out my hands, beseeching. "It was an accident. An unintended effect of the herbs. Mehtap, I would never—"

"Spy on my people? Learn our secrets? Lie to me and my father?"

I let my hands fall.

She turns her head, scrutinizing the horizon. "I think you should leave now."

"Mehtap—"

"These grasslands are too open. I can't risk being seen with you."

"At least—"

"I'm having headaches now, you know?" Mehtap says quietly. "My vision blurs sometimes at the edges."

My words die on my lips. "I'm sorry."

She gives a brave shrug. "It's not as if we didn't know it would happen." She gives a caustic laugh. "You know the real reason I rescued you? I wanted to see you one last time. I knew we were on different sides, but I kept on thinking about the good times we had. Dressing up for the festival, putting plans together for Utana...I wanted to say good-bye." She laughs, if something that wistful could be called a laugh. "Silly, isn't it? Silly and stupid."

Her despondence is like a brand on my skin. "Mehtap...You may not believe me, but I didn't want things to end this way."

Mehtap's eyes turn sad. "We all wish life could be different." She waves me away. "Go. Perhaps I will see you again in the afterlife. Maybe then we can rail together at the gods."

TWENTY-FOUR: DINEAS

The Amparan advance slows after they take the village, but it doesn't stop. Every day, they clear away more of the forest, and troops fill in the space that's left. They bring in foot soldiers, tents, supply trains.

As for us, we split our forces. The Dara fighters who'd stayed behind now join their people in the mountain camps, from where they'll keep us supplied with food and medicine. The Shidadi stay south. We do what we can, picking off Amparan scouts, harrying the troops that clear the forest. But there are just too many of them. Our fighters retreat farther and farther north.

Once a day, I send Slicewing to the beach where I expect Zivah and Sarsine to return. Every day, my heart sinks to see the crow flying back high and straight, not low and in bits and spurts like she would if she were leading someone. One day, she comes back agitated, chattering nonstop and ruffling her feathers.

"What is it?" Could something have happened? The next day, the same thing happens, and the day after that, Slicewing refuses to go at all. Something's wrong, and the crow's not talking. I need to see that beach for myself, but Gatha's confined me to the camp. Looks like I'm going to have to incur more of Gatha's wrath.

I start looking for chances to leave. I know that Gaumit's assigned to morning scouting rounds these days, and also that he dawdles near the scenic portions of his loop and sometimes leaves it altogether. He's never been good at staying where he's supposed to be. That's probably how he got the rose plague when everybody else in the tribe avoided it.

It doesn't take much effort to get past him. A well-timed walk and some help from Slicewing, and soon I'm safely out of the camp.

I travel south as quickly and quietly as I can. Once or twice, Slicewing calls out a warning, and I don't bother to check whether the soldiers are Shidadi or Amparan before ducking for cover. I get no trouble on the way down, but the back of my neck tingles as I near the beach. The sounds of the forest have shifted—not in a way I can put into words, but something's changed. Soon, I arrive at a narrow trail that leads down the cliff toward the water. I've just stepped onto it when Slicewing calls, and I dive into the trees.

An umbertouched Amparan soldier comes off the trail. His eyes skip lightly over the forest—I can tell he's the kind of scout who won't see anything at all before it's on top of him. I let the leaves close around me, and he walks past, but Slicewing calls again before I can come out. Another guard goes by, and then another.

This is strange. Could it be a passing battalion? I give up on the trail and pick my way through the underbrush to the cliff edge, peering over the side only to scramble back, biting down a curse. The beach below is swarming with soldiers. Why would they set up an outpost here? It's far too small and rocky to do any good, but I sure didn't imagine those troops. If Zivah and Sarsine come back now, it'll be straight into an ambush.

Or worse, what if they've already come back?

My skin crawls at the thought. Gingerly, I creep to the edge for another look. The outpost is split between the rocky beach and the cliff overlooking it. It's not a large camp—maybe a hundred soldiers. Sentries patrol the cliff up top. On the beach down below there's a bonfire with off-duty soldiers crowded around. If I listen carefully, I can hear their voices drifting up to where I am. There are at least five catapults on the beach, which seems silly since we have no cities with walls to knock down. A few rowboats lie on the rocks—none like the one Zivah and Sarsine would have left Monyar in, but then, the two of them might have taken a different boat back. A big tent is set up at the top of the cliff. Could it hold prisoners? In a fit of pessimism, I scan the beach for graves or funeral pyres.

I stay hidden in the foliage, watching the sentries pass one by one. They come in a regular pattern—one every quarter hour or so. After I figure that out, I sneak across the line toward the giant tent at the top. A peek inside reveals only a few musty cloaks and tiny bags of flour. Doesn't seem like the most well-provisioned of larders.

The only way down to the beach is by that single trail down the side of the cliff. There's no plant cover on the trail at all, and in a camp of a hundred soldiers, stealing an Amparan cloak wouldn't be enough to blend in. Is it worth the risk to go down there? I don't see any places where they could be keeping prisoners, but it kills me to leave without knowing for sure whether Zivah and Sarsine have been here.

Another sentry approaches, one who prickles my sense for danger with the way he scans the forest. He's a big man. There aren't many soldiers that size. I make a mental note of escape paths through the brush, just to be safe. And then the sentry comes closer, and I freeze.

It's Walgash.

I stare at his face, waiting to see if it shifts into something else, but it doesn't change. He has his bow slung over his shoulder and his sword at his hip, and I can see a slight frown on his face as he looks around. Walgash has sharper eyes than any of us, and I know better than to underestimate him.

Gatha would have my head, but I can't walk away. Why did he spare me in that battle on the bridge? I can't simply pretend that it didn't happen, or that the past year didn't happen.

Well, no one's ever accused me of exceptionally good judgment. Who knows, maybe he has news of Zivah.

I start to trail him, doing my best not to crunch the dirt underneath my feet. Slicewing trails behind me, flitting from branch to branch. Finally, I duck behind a thick stand of bamboo. I take my bow off my shoulder, careful not to brush any plants, and nock an arrow before calling out.

"Walgash."

He whips his sword out of its scabbard and scans the forest. "Who's there?"

"A friend. For today at least."

"Dineas?" There's disbelief and a bit of anger in his voice. He takes a careful step in my direction, and I loose an arrow toward the ground in front of him.

"Don't come any closer."

"Who's with you?" He holds his sword high, clearly expecting an ambush.

"It's just me. I come as a friend."

Walgash snorts. "Just like you came to the capital as a friend?"

"I mean you no harm, Walgash. I swear it on my sword. That's a sacred vow to our people."

He spits on the ground. "I'm not well versed in the vows of northern barbarians."

I nock another arrow. "Why didn't you shoot me on that bridge?"

"Because once in a while I'm a sentimental idiot."

"I'm glad you were sentimental this time."

He sweeps his head from side to side, scanning the trees. "Don't read too much into it. I serve my people, just as you do yours, and someday we'll kill each other like good soldiers."

We've both lived war long enough to know the truth of his words. "Maybe, but today I'm just looking for Zivah."

He stops short, and I can tell my question has caught him off guard. "Your fellow spy?"

"Have you seen her?"

"Should I have? And why should I tell you if I did?"

"She's not a soldier. I just want to know if she's safe."

"For someone who's not a soldier, she sure did a lot of damage." His gaze starts to narrow in on where I am. "And why would you think she's been here? Did she leave the island? For some 'not soldierly' purposes?"

I should know better than to underestimate him.

"She's saved countless Amparan lives," I say. "She may even have saved yours when Neju's Guard fell ill in Monyar." I pause. "Have you ever wondered if you're serving the wrong lord, Walgash? Have you heard the rumors about Kiran? How he was the one who poisoned Neju's Guard? They're true."

Walgash whips the bow off his shoulder and aims an arrow right to my hiding place. "You really are a shameless liar, aren't you?"

I step to my right. His aim follows me, even though I thought I'd made no sound. I'm beginning to see downsides to my brilliant plan. "Think about it, Walgash. You know Kiran's always wanted to expand the empire. He just needed an excuse."

"Get out of here," Walgash growls. "Or I won't miss this time."

He's serious. I didn't live this long without learning to tell when someone's ready to kill me. "You may not believe me, but I took no joy in deceiving you and the others. Knowing that I betrayed you haunts me still."

I can't read Walgash's expression, but his voice softens a bit. "I'll tell you what I know of Zivah."

"What?" I brace myself for the worst.

Walgash looses his arrow. I throw myself onto the ground, my own shot going wide as Walgash's arrow flies through the air where my head had just been. As I pick myself up, coughing, he rams into me and we go flying. There's a burst of pain in my shoulder as I collide with a stalk of bamboo, and then I hit the ground with an impact that knocks the breath out of my lungs.

Walgash positions his bulk squarely on top of me. "Why don't you apologize to my face, you coward!"

I'm too busy trying to keep him from pummeling my face into mush. Shouts sound in the surrounding forest, and I hear people crashing through the brush. I'm still pinned to the ground. Walgash is *heavy*.

A black blur flies overhead, and Slicewing yanks at Walgash's hair. As Walgash grabs at his head, I grit my teeth and surge up with all my strength, throwing my fist into his chin. He falls sideways with a grunt.

I scramble to my feet and run as fast as I can.

TWENTY-FIVE: ZIVAH

Our journey north goes quickly, thanks in part to provisions from Mehtap. It takes us a week to get to the strait, and once there, Sarsine proves every bit as skilled a boat thief as Dineas. We set out for Monyar in the late afternoon, timing it so that the light will be fading just as we reach land. We've had no news at all from our people, and I'm both eager and scared to learn what has happened since we left. Does the village still stand? Has Alia stayed out of the fighting? Is Dineas still alive?

As we draw close to the Monyar shore, something doesn't feel right. I squint through the darkness. There's a boat on the water off the beach—smaller than a warship but bigger than a rowboat, with an enclosed cabin on the deck.

"Do you recognize that ship?"

Sarsine shakes her head. "It's not a Shidadi ship."

And it looks like no Dara vessel I've ever seen.

"Are those campfires on the beach?" asks Sarsine, her voice sharp.

She's right. Two or three campfires wink on the sand. I don't know why I didn't see them before.

Sarsine scans cliffs on either side of the shore. "It's the right place..." she says uncertainly.

But now, as we row closer, we can see soldiers on the rocks —far too many, and moving far too rigidly, to be Shidadi.

Sarsine lets out a string of curses. "Row! We're turning around."

We paddle frantically, drenching ourselves with our frenzied efforts. Sluggishly, the nose of our boat turns and we pull painfully slowly back out to sea. When the Amparan soldiers once again become specks on the sand, we start to row parallel to the shore from a distance. The light is fading, though, and it's getting hard to see. Despite our recent exertion, I start to shiver.

"There!" says Sarsine. She points to a small stretch of empty beach. Both of us are shaky from cold as we bring the boat in and hide it among the rocks. Every time a seagull screeches, I jump. Every time the wind blows over the sand, I think it's an Amparan soldier.

Finally, the boat is hidden. Sarsine finds a sea cave that opens just above the high tide line, and we rush inside to flee the wind.

"We were so sure the Amparans wouldn't go there," Sarsine mutters. She sits on a rock shelf above the mouth of the cave, frowning at the waves below.

I think of that beach covered with soldiers. What does it mean for the war if the Amparans have come this far? What does this mean for the village? "We can't wait at that beach for Slicewing to find us," I say. "It's too dangerous."

"Maybe we can go directly to Dara," Sarsine says uncertainly. "Maybe the village still stands."

She doesn't really believe it, though, and neither do I. Scrawny's huddled in the corner of the cave, smoothing out his wet feathers, and I call him over. "Find Dineas," I tell him.

He's grumpy, but takes off after a few indignant caws. I feel some cautious hope as he flies confidently eastward, but no sooner has he disappeared than I realize he's simply going to the old camps. There's no telling if Dineas will actually be there. Sure enough, an hour later he returns with nothing tied to his leg, cawing sheepishly.

"Nothing?" I ask Scrawny. "What about Tal or Gatha? Can you find them?"

Scrawny jumps around apologetically, but doesn't leave.

"The village is empty isn't it?" says Sarsine quietly. "Otherwise he would go."

She's right. I struggle to contain my own dashed hopes. "If our people have abandoned Dara already," I ask Sarsine, "how hard will it be to find them?"

Sarsine prods her cheek with her tongue. "Depends on where they flee. These are big mountains and it's easy to stay hidden in the bamboo. If our fighters are moving around, it could take weeks for us to find them, even with Scrawny lending us his eyes. And that's assuming we don't have Amparans in our way."

Weeks to reunite with our people? Weeks of wandering enemy territory on our own? "Do you think they might have left any hint of their whereabouts at the village?"

From the way Sarsine grasps at my words, I can see she's just as frightened as I. "Maybe.... It might be worth the risk."

We sleep fitfully that night in the damp cave, haunted by the sound of waves crashing and by our own fears, and we're up early the next morning. Scrawny scouts for us on the trail. His shadow falls over us as he circles over our heads. I find it reassuring, though it also reminds me of Dineas. I wonder if he's still alive, and whether he tried to find us at that beach. I tell myself that if we were able to avoid the Amparans there, then Dineas would have been able to as well. I have to believe that he's still safe.

As we near the village, we start seeing signs of Ampara. Trails have been widened, and the ground is torn up. Both of us fall quiet, our ears sharp for Scrawny's warning call. Soon we start seeing rust-colored streaks on the bamboo. Sweat breaks out over my skin.

"Should we keep going?" asks Sarsine.

I'm not sure how to answer. I feel as if we've stepped into a land inhabited by ghosts. If I don't go any farther, I can still pretend that it's not my home. But I can't walk away. Not until I know just how bad it is.

"Scrawny hasn't called," I say. "Perhaps we can go a little farther."

Soon, the rust-colored streaks are joined by char marks. Sarsine points to something dark beyond the trees, and my stomach sinks at the sight of a burned cottage. Only the blackened frame is standing. The thatching's completely gone, and large chunks of wall have collapsed. What furniture was inside has fallen apart.

Whose house had it been? I try to remember, but I can't. The place looks too different, and I've lived outside Dara too long. Down the path, I can see other houses similarly burned. There's a ragged ditch in the ground, as if a giant had gouged it out with his fingers. I go toward it, only to back away at the smell of decaying flesh.

Have you seen rivers of blood? Gullies that run red with the life of your kin? Your soldiers murdered, their weapons piled up for the Amparans to divide among themselves. Have you seen entire families wiped out, infants dashed against rocks, old men beheaded?

Is this what happened here? Is this what became of my mother and father, of Leora and Alia? No. The leaders said they were going to move all the villagers into the mountains. They must have fled. Nevertheless, I hold my breath and force myself to the edge of the ditch. I'm relieved to see that the bodies wear Amparan armor, and then I'm ashamed of that relief.

"We should go," says Sarsine. She's fidgety, shifting her

weight and sweeping her gaze back and forth. I've never seen her this scared before. "There are bound to be troops nearby."

But there's one more thing I need to see.

"This way," I say, and hurry down the path before Sarsine can react. Up a hill here, then around a smaller trail. By the time my family's cottage comes into view, I've steeled myself for the sight of charred bamboo and ashes. Still I stumble when I see it, and have to stop and will strength back into my legs so I can approach the burned frame. It's empty inside, like all the others. No bodies—Dara, Shidadi, or Amparan. I reach out to touch the frame, but pull back just in time. If I don't touch the house with my bare skin, then there's still hope that someone can return and live here one day.

"We won't find anything here," I say to Sarsine. "Let's go."

She nods, relieved.

We hike quickly, trying to put as much distance between us and the village as possible. The ground slopes up as we leave the valley, and finally we stop to refill our waterskins at a spring on the hillside. The magnitude of the search looms ahead of us.

"You know your people," I say to her. "Where do you think we should go?"

"We might as well start on this side—go up into the mountains. I'll look for signs and tracks. See if we can get some more hints." She musters up a grin. "It takes a Shidadi to find—"

Sarsine stops then and raises her hand. A twig cracks in the distance. Amparan commands drift toward us.

"Run!" hisses Sarsine. We scramble away from the voices. The commands behind us turn into shouts, and an arrow whistles by our heads. Sarsine yanks me behind a cluster of bamboo, I fall into the thin stalks, my stomach dropping as they bend under my weight. Behind us, an archer and four swordsmen splash across the spring.

Sarsine scowls. "If only I had a bow."

I pull out my blowgun and fit a dart. My first shot hits the archer as he plucks an arrow from his quiver. My next shot misses. And then the other four are upon us.

Sarsine draws her sword and steps out to meet them. Three men surround her as the last one rushes at me. I step out from under his blade, blocking with my blowgun as Dineas had once taught me. The man's gaze rests on my skin, and a flicker of fear crosses his eyes. I spit in his face. As he scrambles back, horrified, his foot catches on a rock and he collapses. While he lies, stunned, I draw a knife from my belt and open a vein in his leg. It's easy, horrifyingly so. The man screams. From the way his wound bleeds, I know he won't survive.

I keep a tight grip on my knife and look around, bracing myself for the next attack, but the forest is eerily silent. My stomach flips as I realize I'm the only one standing. I look from body to body, counting the Amparan soldiers. One, two, three, four...

And then my heart stutters and stops, because lying in the center, lifeless, is Sarsine.

TWENTY-SIX: DINEAS

My bow is gone. My mother's bow, the only possession of hers that I have left, is gone. Walgash must have knocked it out of my hands, and I failed to pick it up. Of all the idiot things I could have done...

I lean over my knees, fighting to catch my breath and cursing myself for my carelessness. For a moment, I'm tempted to return for it. I could sneak back to where we fought Walgash. Maybe it's still there.

But the more I think about it, the more I know the folly of that plan. Only someone who wishes to enter Zenagua's kingdom would go back to an enemy camp for a bow, even one with my mother's initials carved into the wood. I have to leave it.

Gods, it hurts, though.

So this is what I have to show for disobeying Gatha. No bow, and no Zivah. And now I return to my people like a wayward pigeon and hope Gatha didn't notice that I was gone.

I slam my fist into my thigh, hardly noticing the pain.

I'll tell you what I know of Zivah, Walgash had said, right before he launched an arrow at me.

Was it any more than a bluff? Did he actually know something? My gut tells me no. I don't think Zivah's actually been to their camp. Or perhaps that's just something I need to believe.

The journey back is excruciating, as if a piece of sinew from my heart were attached to that beach and more of it tears off the farther away I go. I find it easier to run. The harder I push myself, the less energy I have to think.

As I get closer to the Shidadi camp, I start thinking about how to sneak back without being seen. Slicewing won't be able to help me, since Shidadi scouts listen for crow warning calls. I might as well have her announce my presence. My only hope is if the scout on duty right now isn't very alert. Gradually, I slow, scanning the foliage around me, crouching to stay out of view. When the wind picks up, every movement in the leaves looks like a Shidadi. I take one silent step, then another.

The leaves part, and Gatha and Karu step into view.

My lungs empty and I admit defeat.

Karu gives me a look of unbridled disgust out of her good eye. "Your fighter fails us again, Gatha. How long will you let this continue?"

Perhaps the worst thing is that Gatha doesn't look surprised. She doesn't look angry either, just resigned. "Where have you been?" she asks.

I look her in the eye. "Scouting the shore."

"What were you scouting for?" asks Karu.

Why is Karu here anyway? It's bad enough to be caught in disgrace, but if I'm to be disciplined, I want it to be by my own warlord and not some woman who's forgotten what it means to be Shidadi. I address my answer to Gatha. "I was looking for Zivah."

"You know where she is, then," says Gatha.

"Only where she was expected to return. There was a beach where I was supposed to meet her, but the Amparans have built an outpost there."

"Did you engage the Amparans?" asks Gatha.

I hesitate.

"Dineas." Gatha's a head shorter than me, but somehow still gives the impression that she's in the higher position.

"I engaged one soldier," I say. "Neither of us were seriously injured."

Karu turns to Gatha. "Will you make more excuses for him? You must do something."

Gatha simply looks at me, her shoulders heavy. I don't know how much longer her patience will last. Truth is, I don't know how much more patience I deserve. I steel myself for what she's about to say.

And then an arrow embeds itself in Gatha's ribs.

TWENTY-SEVEN: ZIVAH

Sarsine's dead.

I want to deny it, but her gaze is vacant, her body lifeless. My healer's instincts don't let me lie to myself.

Lying there, she looks so young. Without her weapons skill or her constant chatter to distract me, I remember that she's only fifteen years old.

Scrawny lands between the two of us and eyes Sarsine. Then he hops over beside me, subdued.

"She's gone, Scrawny."

A lump catches in my throat, but I swallow my tears before they come. There's no time to mourn, and no time to bury her. I cross her arms over her chest, murmuring a prayer to the Goddess, then add an awkward appeal to Zenagua, the Shidadi goddess of death. I take her daggers but leave her swords with her. I wouldn't know how to use them, and they belong rightly with her.

As I'm about to leave her, something about the fallen Amparan soldiers catches my eye. I'm not sure what it is at first. They look like any other soldiers, except...

I spent a lot of time in Sehmar City with Dineas. I remember the armor and equipment he was issued as a normal recruit, and then as a member of the elite battalion Neju's Guard. The armor and equipment worn by these soldiers are of a far better quality than anything Dineas had ever been given. Their cloaks are finely woven wool. Their armor is tough and supple. I see beaded inlays on the pommel of one man's sword.

Everything in me screams at me to run, but instead I edge closer to the fallen soldiers. One looks older than the others. Would he be in command? A small bag hangs from his belt. Inside is a ring with a purple stone. It's carved with a seal depicting a tree with the sun and the moon as fruit. With the ring is a piece of parchment.

Zivah: Black hair and eyes. Female. Fair skin. Slight build. Rose-marked. Eighteen years old.

Sarsine: Shidadi. Umbertouched. Brown hair and eyes. Short, stocky build. Younger.

Dara Village.

I start to shake as I read the note again. And then I'm running as fast as I can, up the mountainside and away from the village. I run until my lungs burn and I start tripping over my feet, until I finally collapse at the bottom of a cliff face. Scrawny lands in front of me and scolds me for my panicked exit.

I take out the ring and parchment and look at them again. These weren't simply soldiers that we were unlucky enough to run into. These men were waiting for us at Dara. They were sent to kill us. But who are they? Baruva's men?

"Scrawny, scout," I say. The crow chatters with nerves but obediently takes wing. After he's flown several circles without calling out a warning, my fear subsides a little.

I don't know where to go. Without Sarsine, I'm at a loss as to how to find our people, but I can't stay here. As it grows dark, I take shelter underneath a grove of bamboo. Night finds me shivering in my blankets. I imagine sounds of fighting in the distance, and morbid thoughts crowd my mind. What if everyone from Dara is already dead, and I'm the only one left? Sleep is impossible. The mountains to either side of me loom larger than ever. I think about wandering the forests alone for weeks or months, hiding from Amparan soldiers while trying to find some clue of where our people have gone.

Unless...what if Dineas is still sending Slicewing to the beach where we were supposed to meet him? Just because it was occupied by Amparans doesn't mean a crow might not fly overhead. I've no desire to march back into a camp full of Amparan soldiers. On the other hand, I might not need to go all the way there in order to see Slicewing and call her down.

Scrawny gives confused chirps the next morning when I start walking back the direction we'd come. I set him to scouting again. This time I have my blowgun at the ready, and I move as quietly as I can. After a while, I start to smell the ocean, and several times I run and hide as Scrawny calls a warning. When the trails start to look better traveled, I decide I've gone as far as I dare. I find a secluded spot off the trail, obscured by brush but with a decent view of the sky.

"Look for Slicewing," I tell Scrawny. He tilts his head at the strange request and flies toward the ocean. Meanwhile, I huddle in my hiding spot, ears attuned for any sound out of the ordinary.

A crash sounds above me. I gasp, barely holding in a scream, before realizing that it's just Scrawny. He's laboring mightily to carry something—it looks like a piece of wood tied to a string. The crow drops it at my feet, and I pick it up. It's the tip of a wooden longbow that looks as if it's been snapped off. The bowstring is still attached. I rub the wood between my fingers. Why would Scrawny bring me—

My hands pass over a symbol carved in the wood. A Shidadi letter I've seen before...

Dineas laying the bow reverently by his pillow as he lies down to sleep. Dineas running his fingers over the carved letter at the top.

"Dineas's bow," I whisper.

Scrawny perks up at Dineas's name.

"Where did you find this?"

Scrawny cocks his head.

I hold the bow fragment in front of him. "Where did you find this?" I say again, and my voice shakes.

The crow ruffles his feathers at my tone, but he seems to understand, flying a short distance and looking back for me to follow. I check for soldiers and then scramble after him. Little by little, spurt by spurt, we make our way toward the beach. Every step I take is painfully loud in my ears, every snapped branch a thunderclap. Finally, I see the trail leading down the cliff. Scrawny flies ahead and waits for me.

I shake my head. It's far too dangerous.

He caws and then launches himself into the air as two Amparan soldiers come up the trail. I stay huddled behind a boulder until they're gone. This trail is far too exposed, but perhaps I can find some vantage point to see what Scrawny wants to show me. I crawl through the underbrush until I finally break through to the cliff edge. From here, I have a clear view of the beach below, as well as the trail leading down to it. Scrawny lands on my shoulder and scares me half to death.

"No, Scrawny. Keep going."

He lifts up, flies a few circles, and then glides down onto the beach without me. He's careful to avoid the soldiers training in formation near the water, and he gives the campfires farther back a wide berth. Instead, he flies toward the edge of the beach and lands on a small pile. I have to squint in order to see swords, armor, and other weapons stacked up.

See your soldiers murdered, their weapons piled up for the Amparans to divide among themselves. Karu's words echo in my head.

No.

Maybe it was stolen. Maybe it fell off when he was scouting. But once again I see the look in his eyes as he runs his thumb over the bow, and I know that nothing short of death would part him from it.

I blink hard.

The sound of tearing cloth. A searing pain across my right arm. And then an arrow embeds itself in the ground in front of me. I clutch my arm and whirl around. An Amparan soldier stands ten paces behind me with an arrow trained at my heart.

I swallow. This was not the way I wanted to be reunited with Dineas.

The soldier frowns at the sight of my rosemarks and my clearly Dara features. I notice that he's umbertouched as well. "Who are you?" he asks.

"Mercy, please," I say. "I'm not a soldier." Warm blood trickles through my fingers.

He glances down at the blowgun at my waist. "Drop the weapon," he says.

I don't move.

"Drop the weapon," he shouts.

A blur cuts through the air, and Scrawny darts away with the arrow that had been at that soldier's bow. As he yells after the bird, I grab my blowgun and shoot him in the neck. And then, once again, I run.

Shouts sound behind me, but I don't look to check the pursuit. I simply flee up the mountainside as Scrawny flies overhead, thanking the Goddess that my wounded arm still works. An arrow whistles past my ear. As I duck and push myself to run faster, Scrawny turns and dives behind me. A man screams in pain.

And then there's a bloodcurdling shriek. A crow's shriek.

I turn to see an Amparan soldier clutching his eye. At his feet is a bundle of feathers and it's not moving. My heart jumps into my throat. I fumble for another dart and shoot the soldier in the arm. As the man's eyes roll back into his head, I run and scoop Scrawny off the ground. His eyes are open, and he twitches in my hand. I flee again, weaving between plants and scrambling one-handed up rock piles. My feet roll dangerously on the uneven ground, but I keep going. I have to get myself away. I have to get us both away.

I run until I lose feeling in my feet and legs, until my throat is a solid mass of pain. Finally I realize that there are no more sounds behind me. And even if there were, I don't know if I'd have anything left. I stop and hunch over my knees, taking in giant gulps of air, cradling Scrawny in my hands. First Sarsine, and now Dineas. *Please, not Scrawny too.*

As if in reply, the crow opens and closes his beak. His eyes focus on me. I want to cry with relief, but then I notice he's holding his wing at an odd angle.

I stare at it, feeling useless. I'm a healer for people, not animals. How in the world do I set a bird's wing?

"Would you take to a splint, Scrawny?" Somehow I don't think so.

I look at his wings again. Even if you can't splint a wounded bird, you can still immobilize the injury. Moving extra carefully, I fold Scrawny's wing close to his body. When he doesn't complain, I use a scarf to wrap it to his torso. That's as good of a treatment as I can make.

"How does that feel, you foolish bird?" I ask.

He gives a faint caw and what I hope is the crow version of a brave smile. I need a way to carry him. After some thought, I remove my cloak and tie it from shoulder to hip to form a sling. Scrawny doesn't object when I tuck him in.

Dineas's bow.

My hands go frantically to my purse and the pockets of my tunic. Nothing. I must have dropped it in the chase. Yet another loss to follow the others, but I swallow the lump in my throat. I need to be strong for Scrawny.

As I start walking again, my temples begin to throb. I hadn't noticed it in the excitement, but now the headache becomes more insistent.

"We need to find someplace to rest," I tell Scrawny. "We'll wait for you to heal up, and then we'll find the others. All right?" I'm not sure if I'm comforting him or myself.

Scrawny closes his eyes and opens them again.

I'm about to tease him for being taciturn, when pain shoots suddenly through my head, so strong that it leaves me gasping for breath. Along with the pain comes a fog at the edges of my vision. I fall onto the ground and curl into a ball, remembering at the last moment not to crush the crow tied to my body.

Scrawny gives a confused chirp, but I'm in no condition to respond. All I can do is squeeze my eyes shut until my breathing slows and the pain fades away. As the mountainside around me comes back into focus, so does the realization I've been denying for weeks now, the true meaning of the nagging headaches, the strange feeling of always being too warm, the tremors that overtook me in Baruva's prison cell.

My rose plague fever has returned. Sarsine is dead, and Dineas likely gone as well. Soon, I will join them.

TWENTY-EIGHT: DINEAS

G atha stumbles back, clutching at her chest. I catch her under the arms as she falls, stumbling under her weight. Where had that arrow come from?

Karu draws her sword. "Ambush!" she yells.

"Move, Dineas," Gatha snaps through clenched teeth. "Get your guard up."

I help her to the ground and draw my sword.

The forest comes alive. Amparan soldiers stream out from the bamboo. Karu and I move to flank Gatha on either side, and then the first soldiers are upon us. An Amparan sword comes down on mine with a jarring clang. Behind me, Gatha struggles to get to her feet but falls again, cursing. She grabs a horn at her belt, puts it to her mouth, and blows a short blast, only to clutch her ribs in pain. But she takes another breath, and the second peal nearly shatters my eardrums.

An Amparan slashes at me and then sidesteps to get at Gatha. I move with him, blocking his way, and he suddenly collapses. I look down to see Gatha on one knee, her sword through the Amparan's gut.

A distant cry splits the air. "To Gatha!"

"To Gatha!" a crowd of voices answers, closer now.
Arrows fill the air. Our arrows.

WE MAKE A RAGGED, pathetic procession through the forest. Some of us are lucky enough to walk. Others limp along, leaning on the shoulders of their comrades. Still others have to be carried. We sustained heavy injuries during this fight, but we can't afford to rest. We need to get out of here and erase traces of our passing before more soldiers find us.

There's an air of suspicion as we walk. After we defeated the Amparans, one of Vidarna's men found a Shidadi scout's body hidden a short distance away. That's how the Amparans had been able to get to us without warning. We'd been lucky that it had been a small group of soldiers—we counted fifteen bodies. If the Amparans had brought the full might of their army against us, or even a tenth of it, we wouldn't have stood a chance.

Which leads us to the question of why they'd sent such a small group. The fact that the first arrow hit Gatha was a disconcerting clue. Large armies are too obvious. We would have seen them coming, even if they'd managed to kill our scout. A smaller group to assassinate a leader, though—that might slip through our defenses. But small, targeted raids like this can only happen with information. Someone had told them where our camp was and where Gatha was likely to be.

Gatha raises a hand. "Quarter-hour rest," she says. Her chest is bandaged now, and she'd waved off any offer for help getting around. Our healer says her ribs had stopped the arrow from going far in. Still she's lost some blood. Her face is lined with pain, and far too pale.

At Gatha's command, people drop to the ground. There's hardly any talking as fighters quietly adjust bandages and gulp down water. Quite a few simply lean back and close their eyes.

A man from Karu's tribe doles out packets of healing herbs prepared by the Dara. I hear him tell someone that we're down to his last few.

I sit alone, apart from the others. Even from this distance, the weight of the suspicion on me is heavy, and a knot of worry grows in my gut. Since my return, I've been disobedient and a bad soldier—that I'll admit to. But now, after the attack, I realize I might be blamed for much more. As I try to ignore stares and dirty looks, I see Vidarna and Karu crossing over to talk to Gatha. My warlord doesn't look particularly happy to see them. They talk quietly. Actually, it's mostly Vidarna and Karu talking. Gatha just nods heavily.

Finally, Vidarna comes to me. "Gatha wants to speak with you."

I was expecting this, though that doesn't make me dread it any less. *I'm not a traitor, Gatha. Not in the way they're saying.*

Gatha leans against a stalk of bamboo. She looks exhausted, as if her very spirit had been torn from her body and weighed down. Part of it is because of the wound, but I've seen her bear worse injuries before and not look so utterly defeated.

"Did you know anything about this attack, Dineas?" she says. "About who killed the scout?"

"I had nothing to do with this attack, Gatha." My words come out fast, rushed. I wonder if there's anything I can say that doesn't make me sound like a liar.

Gatha's expression doesn't change. "Are there any witnesses who can vouch for where you were these past days?"

"I was alone, at the beach as I told you."

"A beach with an Amparan outpost," says Karu. I shoot her a glare of pure fury.

Gatha frowns. "I've tried to stand by you, Dineas. I've known you all your life, and you've served me well. But that trust can only go so far. I need some solid evidence in your defense. Some witness who can corroborate your story."

I wrack my mind, trying to think of something, anything. "Gatha, any traitor in the camp would know to make it look so I'm the guilty one." I wish I didn't sound quite so desperate, but I'm starting to panic. "If I really was the traitor, would I be so stupid as to time the attack so close to when I was gone?" I point at Karu. "She was also there before the attack happened. Why don't you suspect her? We already know she has no honor."

Dead silence. One of Karu's soldiers hisses. Karu herself simply sneers.

When Gatha speaks again, there's a grief in her voice that I'd never heard before. "I wanted to believe better of you, Dineas. I really did."

Her words eviscerate me.

"Warlord, please." My voice shakes. Every bit of me is aware of how pathetic I sound, but as the reality of what's about to come sinks in, all my dignity leaves me. "Please, Gatha. Give me a chance to prove myself trustworthy. I've disobeyed your orders many times, I admit, but I would never knowingly lead our people to harm."

"We have no solid proof against you," says Gatha.

I want to grasp at the hope her words offer, but there's a heaviness in her voice that's horrible to hear....

"That's why I'm letting you leave alive and unharmed," she says. "You're banished from the camp, Dineas. You have an hour to leave. If you return, you will be received as an enemy of the tribe."

TWENTY-NINE: ZIVAH

The night that follows is even colder than the last. I dream about Dineas. He's buried under a pile of armor and weapons and asks me why I've abandoned him.

I lie on the ground after I wake, feeling his absence like a tear through my insides. Part of me refuses to believe he's dead. He's careful, he's skilled, and we'd made it out of so many hopeless situations before. Perhaps there's an explanation. Perhaps.

It's hard to remember, right now, why I'd tried so hard to keep my distance when he wanted more than just friendship. If it was to avoid pain for myself, then I've failed. If it was to protect him...did I even succeed in that?

I stare up at the leaves, wishing I could stay here forever, lie here and let the world do what it will. But then, next to me, Scrawny flaps his good wing. He looks at me, his dark crow eyes subdued. It's because of me that he was hurt. He can't fly right now, and he can't forage for food on his own. If I give up, both of us will pay the price.

So I get up. Scrawny ruffles his feathers as I settle him into his sling, and he gives a satisfied click of his beak. Then I start to walk.

I run across a creek and give the wound on my arm a good washing. Thankfully, the cut is shallow and has scabbed over cleanly. My headache, as well, seems to have dissipated. After I refill my waterskin, I follow the creek, thinking that perhaps our people would settle near water. After a while, I start to worry about enemy soldiers, so I move farther away from the creek bank, still following its path but staying in the cover of the plants. Around midmorning, a sight stops me short.

The first body lies at the base of a small shrub. The rest are scattered a short distance beyond. Five bodies total—four Amparan and one Shidadi, so recently dead that their muscles have not yet stiffened. I stumble back at the sight, grabbing for my blowgun and looking wildly about for soldiers. There's a rustling behind me, and I whirl around. It's a pack mule, tied to a stalk of bamboo. Hand to my chest, I stare at the animal, willing my pulse to slow.

Then I hear the moan. It's low-pitched and weak, so soft that I might have missed it if I'd been walking closer to the river. My heartbeat quickens again. I grip my blowgun tightly—more as a club than something to shoot with—and make my way carefully toward the sound.

I find him collapsed on the ground twenty steps past the dead soldiers—a dark-skinned soldier barely old enough to grow a beard. There's a deep gash in his side, and his glassy eyes look up at me without recognition. He wears the Amparan livery that I've feared my entire life. He's far gone. Even if his wounds were bandaged now, he's more likely to die than recover.

It's a strange experience to look at someone who needs healing and decide to keep walking, but that is what I must do. I wonder, as I look down at him, whether he was one of the troops that burned my village. Has he killed anyone I know? He looks into my eyes. There's a flicker. He struggles to move his lips.

"Water," he whispers. His raw suffering lashes at my conscience.

You've made vows before your Goddess.

Why would I cure this man, when he would simply go right back to killing my people? The Goddess asks too much. I turn and walk away.

"Water," comes the plea again, even more desperate than before, though I hadn't known it was possible. And I know I'll continue to hear that plea, even if I keep walking and never stop.

I go back to him.

He has a waterskin hanging from his belt. It's half-full, and I pour a tiny stream into the space between his slack lips. He sips. Chokes. Licks his lips.

There's the problem of my rosemarks. It's dangerous enough for him if I touched him while he's fully healthy. But he has open wounds, and if our blood should mingle...

But then, if I don't touch him, he'll certainly die. If I try, he may still have a chance.

I rummage through my bags for gloves. He groans weakly as I pour water over his cut, then utters a sharp cry when I pull away the clothing stuck to the wound. There's some vel flower left in my bag, which I sprinkle onto the gash.

What am I doing?

I cut a strip off his cloak and clean it as best I can before binding it around him. As I work, his eyes gradually drift closed. I would think him dead if not for the tiniest movement of his chest.

I leave him alone for the rest of the day. What he needs most is to rest undisturbed as his body knits itself together. The next morning, his color is better, and the bleeding has slowed considerably on his wounds. Late that afternoon, I deem him well enough to be moved to a small cave in the cliffs nearby. I'm not sure how I'll move him until I remember the abandoned mule, whose suspicion of me lightens considerably after I feed him some stale travel bread. Bamboo, cloth, and rope from the mule's pack serves to make a rough sled, and I wrap the soldier in a cloak before dragging him on.

We make our way painfully slowly, threading our way through wider spaces and stopping every few steps to clear out a path, or when I need to rest. At least I have the mule to lean on as we hike. Finally, I settle the soldier safely in the cave and rest an hour before heading back out to hide our tracks. It's impossible to erase all signs of our passing, so I settle for dragging the sled along many paths to camouflage the real one.

In the shelter of the cave, the soldier recovers much more peacefully. Soon, he's opening his eyes for brief periods of time. Once, when a gust of wind blows across the cave mouth, he startles awake. I lay a gloved hand on his forehead.

"Be at peace," I say. "The gods watch over you."

Though I wonder, if the Goddess really is looking in on the two of us in this little cave, what she is thinking.

THIRTY: DINEAS

They give me half a day to get out of scouting range. Half a day to separate myself from my flesh and blood and never return. Part of me wants to beg them to give me another chance, but I scrape together some dignity and stay silent.

Gatha's generous with provisions—more generous than people want her to be, considering the glares I get from around the camp. As she hands me what looks like a few weeks' worth of dried meat and bread, I check her eyes for any wavering, any sign of changing her mind, but her gaze is steady and grim.

I can't hate her. She gave me plenty of chances to regain her trust.

As I stuff my extra tunic into my bag, Hashama comes to speak to me.

"I don't believe you to be a traitor." He's solemn as always, but this time it seems appropriate.

I clasp his hand. "I'm honored to have had you and Sarsine under my command." Beyond that, there's not much to say.

Hashama doesn't see me out of the camp, nor does anyone else. I walk alone past the stares of my kinsmen. Out of the corner of my eye, I see people stop what they're doing to watch me, but I keep my gaze straight forward. At least I have Slicewing. The loyal crow flies circles over my head, diving down occasionally to peck for worms before taking flight again. The camp grows quiet behind me, so quiet that it's hard to tell how far I've walked. But I don't look back.

Already the forest around me feels darker, more dangerous. Somehow, in the span of months I've gone from being a man of two peoples to a man with none. Any Amparans I run into will kill me on sight, and I don't know what the Shidadi would do. Though I don't see or hear anything unusual, there's a prickling at the back of my neck, as if threats I can't detect linger just out of reach.

After several hours of walking, my stomach starts to growl, so I sit and break out a portion of my food. That's when it hits me. For the first time in my life, I have no orders to follow, no one to fight for. No direction on where to go. It's this thought that finally sets my mind spinning and makes my skin break out in sweat. I might as well be one of Slicewing's lost feathers, floating from tree to tree until it falls apart.

Calm down, Dineas. If you can face dozens of Amparan swords, you can handle making your own way.

But can I? The forest, which was already feeling dark and dangerous, now feels impossibly large. I almost wish for enemy soldiers to walk out of the bamboo so I can fight them. But that's ridiculous, isn't it? Yet my heartbeat won't slow. Something constricts in my chest, and the world starts to tilt.

Claws dig into my shoulder. Slicewing peers around and eyes me with worry. I'm not alone, not completely.

I reach over and scratch her neck. "Thank you."

I'm too restless to stop for long. Soon I'm walking again, with Slicewing flitting along behind me. I try once more to get my bearings. If Zivah and Sarsine are still alive, I want to find them. But how? I don't even know if they made it back to

Monyar. Do I go back to Central Ampara and try to retrace their steps? Where do I even start?

Slicewing gives a warning call. Something swishes through the trees. Pain explodes in my calf, and I pitch forward.

I'm running out of a Central Amparan outpost with soldiers hot on my heels. A bowstring twangs, and an arrow embeds in my calf. I tumble head over heels, struggling to break my fall. I won't let them catch me. Won't let them torture me.

No, that's just a memory. That's not real.

But another bow twangs, and I roll to keep from getting skewered again.

These arrows are real. And it's only a matter of time before one of them kills me.

Slicewing folds her wings and dives out of the air. The forest shakes where she hits it, and someone yells. She's distracting the archer, but not for long. I grit my teeth and climb to my feet. My calf is bleeding, but there's no arrow embedded in it, and it holds my weight.

Roaring at the top of my lungs, I charge toward the place I heard the yell, crashing through leaves and pushing branches out of my way. An Amparan scout claws at his face as Slicewing dives and swoops. He lets out a surprised grunt as I tackle him, and we tumble to the ground. In the tangle of limbs, I reach for the knife in my boot and bury it in his neck. Hot blood flows over my hands. He shudders.

I'm wrestling with Tus on top of a mountain. He pins me to the ground and raises a knife, hilt first. I brace myself.

The Amparan's dead now, but there might be more. I throw the body off me and stagger to my feet. As the archer's body thuds to the ground, his face shifts, and suddenly it's Zivah lying there. Zivah, on the ground, bleeding out. I let out a ragged cry.

Slicewing flutters to the ground in front of me, staring at me.

"You're real, right?" I whisper to Slicewing, lurching toward her. The crow hops away with an alarmed caw and then flies to perch on a stalk of bamboo. The bamboo flickers as if underwater, and faces appear in its green bark. Walgash, Masista, Naudar, their faces one on top of each other.

"Traitor," says Masista. "You're a disgrace."

I scream.

THIRTY-ONE: ZIVAH

Over the next days, the Amparan soldier continues to improve. I'm certain now that he'll live, though that brings other worries. How certain am I that I have not infected him? I've been careful not to touch him with my bare skin, even while transporting him to the cave. But what if I slipped up, or my gloves became infected?

As he gets stronger, I leave food and water laced with restorative herbs next to him, and I hide at the edge of the cave to watch him wake. He sits up, puts his hand to his temple, and looks down at the roast fish and bamboo segments filled with water. Then he puts a hand to the ground and laboriously pushes himself up. He falls forward onto his knees, and I have to suppress my urge to rush in and help him. Does he still have an injury that I missed?

But then he clasps his hands together. His lips move silently.

He's praying.

I tell myself that his prayers have nothing to do with me, but I can't shake my unease.

The soldier eats and he sleeps, gaining strength. When he doesn't fall ill after five days, I start to feel more optimistic. As weakened as he was, the plague essence would have overcome him sooner than the usual ten days. He continues to pray upon waking each time—not the perfunctory prayer of those absorbed in their lives, but the earnest, grasping prayer of one who has seen the gods. It's with great relief several days later that I watch him get up and walk south back toward the Amparan camps.

The respite I gain from his leaving only lasts a half day. That afternoon, I find an Amparan archer with a deep gash in his arm, as well as a broken wrist and leg. This time, I don't hesitate before bandaging his cuts and setting his bones. As I gather scrap bamboo to build him a fire, I find another foot soldier with a bad head wound. Despite my best efforts to stanch his bleeding, he dies an hour later, moaning in pain as I hold his hand.

The archer fares much better. I give him sleeping potion for the first day, and when he awakes, he's alert and doesn't appear to have much pain. I watch from a distance as he hobbles around and fashions himself a crutch. It's a far walk down to the Amparan camps, but he might make it if he's determined. Or he might run into his comrades along the way.

I act before I have much chance to think, stepping out into his path. "You must stay," I say.

He stops. Looks at me in shock. Takes in the sight of my rosemarks and stumbles back.

"I treated your wounds and set your bones," I say. "I took care not to touch you, but you must stay until I'm sure it is safe for you to rejoin your comrades."

He reaches for his sword before realizing he doesn't have one. "Stay away from me," he says. He walks a wide circle around me, eyeing me as if I were a coiled snake. I tamp down on my growing anger, but I don't move to block him. The soldier passes me and gives me one last suspicious look before hobbling away.

I reach for my blowgun and shoot him in the nape of his neck.

It takes me a half hour with the mule's help to drag him back to the cave. Once there, I watch him sleep, sending more than one complaint to the Goddess as I do. Is it worth it, to spend my strength on someone like this? And what will happen once he returns to his countrymen, now that he's seen me? Even if he doesn't recognize me for who I am, someone else might guess.

A noise outside the cave catches my attention. I'm not even sure what exactly I heard, but the hairs on the back of my neck stand on end and I instinctively know I must be silent. The sound of footsteps drifts in from outside, along with the occasional clink of metal.

I hold my breath, thankful that my patient is unconscious, and trying to remember how well hidden my cave is from outside.

A voice drifts in, speaking Amparan. "...somewhere around here...says he walked two days south from where he woke up..."

A thrill of fear shoots down my spine. I cast my eyes around the cave. The comatose archer lies sprawled out against the back wall. Scrawny lies a short distance away, asleep in a nest of leaves. On the opposite side of him, my blowgun leans against the wall. Carefully, I crawl toward it.

"...says a goddess saved him...it can only be the healer..."

I grab the blowgun and fit a dart, then crawl on one hand to the cave mouth. The opening itself is as high as my knee. There's some grass in front to conceal it, but not nearly as much as I'd like. I chance a look out and see two men walking a stone's throw away. They're wearing unmarked armor, like the men who killed Sarsine, and they're umbertouched. Are they the only two, or are there others?

"I think she'll be farther north," says one. "She'll be eager to join the others."

"But it's hard to travel with all the fighting," says his comrade.

They've stopped now, and the first one examines the ground in front of him. Did I leave a footprint? He's so close. I lower myself onto my stomach and prop myself onto my elbows. I take aim.

"Something was dragged here," says the soldier.

My stomach knots.

His comrade walks up for a closer look and then turns his face toward the cave opening. He squints.

I shoot.

As he crumples, the first soldier jumps to his feet, scanning the rock face around my cave.

Don't panic. Don't fumble. Reach for another dart.

My dart catches the second soldier in the hand. He slaps at it, as if swatting a mosquito. And then he too collapses.

THIRTY-TWO: DINEAS

G uilt.
    Waves of it. Guilt that gouges a hole in my core. I curl in on myself, claw at my arms, my neck, my face, anything to make it go away.

The dead parade in front of me. Naudar, Tus, the myriad Shidadi I killed when I fought in Neju's Guard. In my visions, I cut down my kinsmen over and over. They die, and when I'm finished screaming, they die again.

"Forgive me!" When did it get so dark? Cicada calls assault my ears, and the night is bitterly cold. Once more I curl into a ball.

There's fire all around me. The air smells of lamp oil, and heat sears my skin. Smoke overwhelms my lungs. I cough uncontrollably.

Walgash draws his sword. "You're not leaving here alive."

I don't want to fight him, but I must.

I'm thirsty. Grievously thirsty. I grope for my waterskin and lift it to my lips. A trickle of water comes out, but no more.

I'm in the dungeon. Chains chafe my wrists. My back is sticky with blood, but I would take ten more whippings if I could just have a sip of water. Footsteps sound outside, and fear flares in my chest. Not again. I can't take any more. Please, just let me die.

I'm by the river. It's light again. How did I get here? In front of me, water swirls cold and fresh. I submerge my mouth, drink, and never stop.

The interrogator grabs my head and forces me underwater. I sputter and choke, thrash and cough. I'm drowning.

A dusting of black feathers against my face. A click of beaks. Slicewing peers into my eyes. Behind him is...Preener? Didn't I send him away?

"Help me," I whisper.

Slicewing sticks her beak into my hair. I run my fingers over her feathers, and they tickle my palms. The two crows chatter to each other. I cling to their voices. This is real. They are real.

Preener hops to my side and nestles into my chest.

"Preener, you vain bird. What are you doing here?"

The darkness creeps up on me again, crowding the edges of my vision. But this time I don't dream.

THIRTY-THREE: ZIVAH

What have I done? I crawl out the cave opening, shaking like a spooked mouse as I scan the forest for more soldiers. Both of the men I'd shot lie motionless in the grass. I dash to the first one and lift him by the armpits. He's not a small man, and he drags like a sack of flour as I strain to pull him toward the cave. By the time I wrestle the second man inside, I'm exhausted and covered in sweat.

Panting, I look at the three comatose soldiers laid out inside my cave. I can't stay here. That much is clear. But what do I do with my prisoners? The archer has seen me and talked to me, and this time when he wakes, he'll be angry. And then there are these soldiers with unmarked livery, the ones sent to kill me....

I have a few hours before the potion wears off, so I gather my courage and venture out again. I feel hopelessly vulnerable without Scrawny scouting for me, but there's nothing to be done except to keep my loaded blowgun at the ready.

The forest is loud with chirps of crickets and cicadas. The first thing I do is find a forked stick and trim it to my liking. Then I start my hunt, looking for the darker corners of the forest, the piles of leaves in the shade. Hours pass. I grow thirsty because I left my waterskin at the cave. But then I spot the tell-tale black and yellow stripes of the soulstealer snake. Carefully now. These snakes are notoriously easy to scare. I take one step closer, and then another. The snake lifts its head as I bring my stick toward it, tasting the air.

Now.

I thrust my stick into the ground so that the forks land on either side of the base of its head. The snake writhes and hisses as I pick it up, though it relaxes just slightly to my low-toned whistles. He goes headfirst into an improvised sack, and I waste no time in returning.

Back at the cave, my prisoners sleep quietly where I left them. As they dream, I milk the soulstealer with a piece of leather stretched over a segment of bamboo. Then I mix one drop of venom with liberal amounts of ziko and nadat, enough so the venom will only erase memories from the past few days. I dip a snake fang into the mixture and scratch each man's skin.

The venom should keep them asleep two days. When they wake, they'll be ravenously thirsty from the venom, so I place canisters of water laced with the strongest sleeping potion I have. I hope this buys me five days at the least, hopefully more.

Scrawny gives me a reproachful look as I go to check on him. Either he didn't like being left here with the soldiers, or he knows more about my healer's vows than he's let on.

"Time for a new home," I tell him as I tie him into his sling.

I walk well into the night before I stop to rest. When I do sleep, I dream of Kaylah visiting me in the cave I just left. She comes in and looks at the soldiers, the soulstealer venom, and the tainted water. She puts her hand on their foreheads, listens to their confused mumblings, and wipes down their faces.

I beg Kaylah for news of my family. Is Leora's child still healthy? Was my father able to make the long walk to the Dara camp? Is Dineas alive? Please tell me he's alive.

I ask her what I should do with these soldiers. When that doesn't work, I yell at her to simply talk, to say anything. I don't want to die alone out here. Please don't let me.

But she stays silent.

THIRTY-FOUR: DINEAS

I have no idea how much time has passed. It might have been an afternoon. It might have been weeks. All I know is that it's still summer and I haven't starved to death. My bag of food is almost empty, and I can see my ribs clearly under my skin. I also have a strong memory of painful thirst, though now my waterskin is full again.

The hallucinations and dreams space themselves further and further apart, and in their place comes bone-heavy, incapacitating exhaustion. I sleep long hours beneath a granite overhang too low to sit up under. I'm caked in layers of mud, and dried scabs cover my arms and legs. Everything hurts. My bones creak, and my head feels like it's being crushed repeatedly with a hammer. When I'm not sleeping, I have enough of my wits about me to eat a few mouthfuls of food, maybe stumble over to the river that I somehow found in my madness. Then I return to my hiding place and fall into dreamless sleep. At least now, when I wake up, I can remember falling asleep in the first place.

Eventually, I stay awake long enough to wonder what's happened to me. Have I truly gone mad? My episodes had never been as bad as this. Was it the fight in the forest that triggered it? Or being kicked out of my tribe? My mind seems to be piecing itself together once more, but I wonder how long it will last.

And then there's the issue of the crows. There *are* two of them.

"What are you doing here?" I ask Preener as he struts a circle around me, fluffing his plumage. He's looking obnoxious and self-absorbed as ever, but I still remember the comforting brush of his feathers on my chest, and I know I owe him.

There's a note tied to his leg. As I reach for it, I get a senseless jolt of panic. This will be the first I've heard from another human in who knows how long. What if the words send me spiraling into confusion again? Or worse, what if the note blows away before I can read it?

Gingerly, I hold Preener's foot still with one hand while I untie and unravel the note. It's short.

We've learned that Emperor Kiran secretly set sail months ago on his private ship toward Monyar. I believe he wanted to take closer control over the attack.—Nush

Kiran's here? That information might prove useful, or at least it would be useful if it actually gets to my kinsmen. But it was sent to me, and I'm alone in the heart of the mountains with no way to pass this on to my people. Do I even want to? It's too much to think about now. I memorize the note and scrape off the top layer. Since I have no ink, I carve a "thank you" into the parchment and rub black dirt into the furrows.

"Thank you, Preener," I say to the crow.

I feel a bittersweet pang as the bird flies off toward Central Ampara. Then my stomach growls. It feels empty in a way I'm not used to, and that's saying a lot. I need to find more food before I grow too weak to fend for myself. Slowly, painfully, I gather my things. I still have all my weapons and my cloak, which is a miracle in and of itself. If the gods grant me several more, I just might survive this.

Slicewing flies circles over my head as I pick my way through the bamboo. I find a few tender shoots and chew on them as I go. Not the most filling, but better than nothing. I'm swallowing a particularly bland mouthful when Slicewing gives another warning call.

I freeze. The crow circles back and lands on my shoulder. Not for the first time, I wish she could tell me what she saw. Based on the direction she'd called from, I'd guess that she's seen Amparan soldiers. She looks pretty calm, so it's probably not a large group. Still, I don't have anyone to patch me up if I get wounded. Better to retreat to safety. On the other hand, they might have some supplies I could steal.

My stomach voices its opinion in a very loud way.

I move in the direction Slicewing came from. It's a relief, at least, that I can still move somewhat quietly without falling on my face. I've gone fifty paces when I hear voices up ahead. Amparan colors flash between the leaves.

Four soldiers are setting up camp for the night, laying out bedrolls and taking food out of their bags. They each carry a hefty pack, but they're keeping them close. I circle around to get a better look.

"Strange story." The words float over from the camp. "Do you think the forests are haunted?"

Haunted? That's usually a sign of Shidadi scouts. I creep closer and listen.

"Arshama from the second battalion wandered into camp some days ago," says a soldier.

"Arshama's alive?" asks another. "I thought the fleas got him in that ambush."

Fleas indeed. The Amparans call us that because we turn up everywhere. But fleas bite. They should know that firsthand by now.

"We all thought so," says the first. "But he came stumbling into camp, talking and breathing. Says he woke up in the forest and his wounds were bandaged. He also says he remembers a woman tending his wounds. Claims it was the goddess Hefana herself."

The other man snorts. "I think Arshama's wounds got the better of his brain."

"But it's strange, isn't it? None of our healers are out there, and the Shidadi wouldn't do us any favors. Who could it have been? If the gods really are looking out for us, then I'll say an extra prayer or two."

A tingle goes up my spine. In my mind's eye, I see a woman weaving through the trees, bending over the wounded and dressing their injuries with skilled, gloved hands.

THIRTY-FIVE: ZIVAH

I travel another two days, putting as much distance as I can between myself and my comatose attackers. Finally, I find another cave. This one is the size of my cottage, and the entrance is a crevice sheltered by an outjutting in the rock. There are vines growing above the crevice, and I pull some down to disguise the opening. Then I place the soulstealer snake among the vines.

I am far from alone in this part of the mountain. Injured and dead soldiers are a common sight when I forage for food. I bind what wounds I can and take the worst cases back to my cave. Though it's dangerous, the presence of so much fighting also gives me hope. It means the Shidadi are close. If I can find a way to make myself known to them, they can lead me to their camp. A few times, I hear the clash of swords, but the battle is over by the time I arrive. The Shidadi have fled, and the Amparans are bandaging their wounded. It's only by the grace of the Goddess that they don't see me.

The work of tending to patients takes its toll. My headaches, which used to come every few days, now come daily and linger for hours. During those times, I hole up in the cave and close my eyes. It's impossible now to see these headaches as anything but my rose plague returning.

As the disease slowly takes ahold of my body, I get the old urge to fight it, to try once again to find a cure. I'm harvesting syeb flower one morning, when a familiar scent wafts through the air. It's sharp, the kind of smell that goes straight to the top of your nose. At first, I don't know why this is important, only that some instinct urges me to pay attention. Finally I realize where I've encountered that scent before—Baruva's suona pollen. I bring the white petals to my nose. It has a faint floral smell, but that's all. Then on a hunch I pluck the yellow stem from the middle of the flower and crush it between my fingers. The scent comes out, sharp as that jar in Baruva's garden, and sets my mind racing. Scents are signposts from the Goddess about an herb's function. Could syeb flower also counter the rose plague essence? I pluck all the flowers I can find.

As I get sicker, Scrawny gets better. After a couple weeks, his wing looks sturdy enough that I leave it unwrapped. He still prefers to travel in his sling, but when we're back at the cave, I take him out and he attempts small flutters around. I pray that I've set his wing correctly.

There's no shortage of wounded. One day I find an older Amparan soldier with an infected leg. Red streaks radiate from a wound in his upper thigh, and it gives off a putrid smell. I wash the cut with hot water and treat it with infusions of nadat root, but his chances of survival are slim.

Once, as I'm replacing the leaves I use as bandages, the man groggily opens his eyes and looks at me. "They said Hefana was wandering the battlefields. I didn't believe them."

More and more of the soldiers have been mistaking me for one of their goddesses, and I've not become any more accustomed to it. "I'm not Hefana," I tell him. "I don't even have the power to heal myself."

His eyes latch onto me as he takes in my words. "I suppose I don't know why a goddess would wear such wrinkled clothes."

A smile pulls at my lips. "Your mind is sharp, at least." Truth is, sometimes I do feel like a god, or at least, a mortal playing with the gods' powers. Every day, I decide whether to treat someone or to let him die, to let him return to his comrades or to hold him in quarantine. It's not a responsibility any mortal should have.

"Perhaps you are not Hefana," says the soldier. "Or perhaps you are lying. Either way, I thank the gods for you."

That evening, I hear more fighting very close by. I creep closer to find a lone Shidadi woman facing off against an Amparan scout. Her right arm hangs limply at her side, and she's fencing with her left hand as the scout drives her backward. I fit a dart to my blowgun, but I must make some noise, because the Shidadi's eyes flicker toward me. In that moment, the Amparan's sword flashes in a circular arc, and the Shidadi's sword flies out of her hand. She jumps back to dodge a killing blow. I shoot my dart, but it glances off the Amparan's padded vest. It's enough to make him look my way, though, and in that moment, the Shidadi directs a kick at his stomach. As he doubles over, a knife flashes in her hand, and then he falls lifeless to the ground.

The Shidadi staggers and almost trips over her fallen opponent before reaching out to a bamboo stalk for balance. She lifts her head and blinks at me, confused. "Who are—" She takes a tenuous step toward me and collapses.

I rush to her side. Up close, I see her injuries are more serious than I thought. In addition to her broken arm, there's a gash on her head and a cut on her chest. I work quickly, washing her wounds with an infusion of spineleaf sap and binding them as best I can. Briefly, I consider dragging her closer to the soldier I'm already tending, but it seems that putting the two together would just invite trouble. I shelter her instead under an overhang of a nearby rock.

The next day is spent running back and forth between the two. Both of my patients are delirious from their injuries, and both cry out during their more active moments. I can't help but notice how pain sounds the same no matter whom it's coming from. The Shidadi's rants in her native tongue bring back raw memories of Dineas and Sarsine. Perhaps, though I could not save my friends, I can save her.

Late in the afternoon, the Shidadi opens her eyes and looks around. "Where am I?"

"On the battlefield," I say.

"I almost died."

"Yes."

She seems to have trouble focusing her eyes. "Who are you?"

"A friend."

She makes as if to get up, but I stop her. "You need more rest." I offer her a cup of sleeping potion, and she drinks in long, thirsty gulps. "Can you find your way back to the others?" I ask.

"I think so," she says. "If they haven't moved."

"Do you know Dineas from Gatha's tribe?"

She groans. Her eyes roll with the effort of keeping them open.

"Dineas. Is he alive?"

Her eyelids sag closed. She doesn't respond to anything else I say.

THE SHIDADI WOMAN grows better by the day. Part of me is eager for her to recover so I can follow her home. I thirst for news of my family, and I want to know what happened to Dineas, even if the truth may bring me grief.

As the woman begins to have more moments of clarity, though, I start to have doubts. How will the Dara and Shidadi receive me, after I've run away like this? How would I explain my long absence? What if someone's seen me treating Amparan soldiers? And there remains the biggest question: What will they ask me to do once I'm back? Can I say no to them if I no longer have Dineas to support my side? That last question is bitter to contemplate. Dineas and I disagreed on so many things, for so much of the time we spent together. And now that we finally understand each other, it's too late.

The Amparan with the infected leg improves as well. Against all odds, the red streaks subside and his wound closes up. He progresses quickly, which is good because he'll need to fend for himself when I leave with my Shidadi patient.

He's remarkably good-natured for a man in his state. Several times, he murmurs a thank-you when I change his bandages. Once, after I rouse him to drink, he stays awake.

"What is your name, Not-Goddess?" he asks.

I've grown accustomed to working alone, and his voice, gravelly from disuse, startles me. "It's better if you do not know."

"I suppose Not-Goddess will have to do, then. What are your plans for me?"

"You should gain strength steadily from here on out. I've been careful to keep from touching you directly, but you will still need to wait some days to be sure you do not have rose plague. And then you will be free to leave."

After that archer's response to my mention of rose plague, I'm worried how this man will react. But he simply purses his lips. "And I shall tell my comrades that I was tended by a rose-marked woman without a name?"

"I would prefer if you don't tell them anything at all."

He gives a wan smile, though there's the hint of a brighter smile behind it. "A mystery. I love mysteries."

This soldier spends more time awake than my other patients. Perhaps it's his constitution, or perhaps it's because I

give him less sleeping potion than the others after that conversation. I've no doubt things would be different if we met out on
the mountainside, but in the world of my cave, he is good
company.

Meanwhile, the Shidadi's wounds knit together. When she
gains the ability to sit up, I leave food and water next to her and
let her care for herself. Every day, I check on her, expecting to
reveal myself to her now that she's coherent. But every day, I
decide to wait.

It's hard to guess a patient's recovery time accurately, but
both the Amparan and the Shidadi progress at a predictable
pace. I estimate that the Shidadi and I will leave a few days
before the Amparan fully recovers. It should be no trouble,
though, because he's already strong and able to feed himself.

"I may have to leave you alone for the last part of your
recovery," I tell him.

"Returning to the land of the gods?"

I roll my eyes. "You can stay in the cave as long as you
need to, and there are enough provisions here to keep you
well fed."

"Or returning to a suitor perhaps. Do you have a young man
who awaits you?"

The pang that shoots through me at those words is harder to
brush off. "No. No young man."

"I've offended you," he says.

"You haven't."

He reaches up to scratch his brow. "I would like to know
your name at least," he says. "Shall we trade, my name for
yours?"

"A name by itself means very little. Just call me—" I stop,
because something on his skin catches my eye.

Faint red markings.

A pit opens in my stomach. It can't be.

I comb through every moment of the past days, trying to

remember what I'd done. I'd been so careful not to touch him. Where had I slipped up?

By now, he's seen my expression. He looks at his hand, and his eyes cloud over. "Oh," he says.

Why this one? Why him of all people?

"Call me Zenagua." The name of the goddess of death scalds my tongue. "I have failed you."

THIRTY-SIX: DINEAS

*Z*ivah's alive. She's alive, and she's in these mountains. I bet my sword on it.

The news fills me with hope. These mountains are vast, but I can find her. It'll just take some time. That is, assuming neither of us manage to get ourselves killed.

Though, why is she treating Amparan soldiers in the forest? Is she lost? Is she injured? And what of Sarsine?

Stewing on these questions would be enough to drive me back into madness. I'll find her first, then worry about the rest. Based on what the Amparans said, she must be south of me. If she's treating people's wounds, she must be near water, and she may have looked for a cave to sleep in. It's not much to go on, but it's enough for a basic plan. I'll work my way south, looking near rivers and caves.

It's funny how having a goal can make the day go by so much easier. I'm still tired, half-starved, and confused, alone in a forest full of enemy soldiers, but now it feels as if I'm on another mission. The terrain is steep, and there are plenty of Amparans to avoid. I get spotted once by a sharp-eyed scout, and I dive into a clump of underbrush to escape his comrades.

As they run past, one man's profile blurs into Sarsine's. My heart jumps at the sight, but I'm getting better at knowing what's real and what is not.

Early one morning Slicewing gives another warning call, but it's the higher-pitched chirp reserved for friends. I stop in my tracks. Shidadi.

Do I hide from them like the Amparans? Do I spit in their direction? I don't think they'll ever fully understand what they've done to me by cutting me off. Still, I can't bring myself to walk away.

"Lead me to them," I tell Slicewing.

She flits ahead, silently hopping from stalk to stalk. I follow her until a crow—not Slicewing—gives the friend call in the distance, and I know I've been spotted. Someone in a brown tunic comes toward me. I make sure my weapons are in reach.

Frada takes an abrupt step back when he sees me. I can almost imagine his hair standing on end like a cat's, but he recovers admirably. "Dineas," he says. He's carefully neutral in the way he says it, though I can see him sizing me up. I meet his gaze, daring him to say something about the state of my clothes and the scabs on my arms. He's no longer wearing my hair and blood on his belt.

"I don't mean to surprise you," I say.

"You didn't."

"Fair enough."

Slicewing and the other crow start chasing each other through the leaves.

"Is Gatha recovering?" I ask.

"Admirably." Though I get the impression that he would say the same even if Gatha were dead. "She's sent us on some extended scouting rounds."

There's no reason for him to tell me about the scouting rounds. No reason he'd *want* to tell me, which means he's lying.

"Neju guide your eyes," I say.

He nods curtly. "I appreciate it."

It'd be a bad idea to follow him. It would just make things worse. My kinsmen might not trust me enough right now to tell me their plans, but neither will they attack me. If I'm caught spying on them, though, that would change.

I fall behind him just before he disappears from view. His crow doesn't make a sound—must think I've joined the group. Twenty fighters wait for Frada a short distance away—ten from our tribe, plus an older woman from Vidarna's camp, a seventeen-year-old girl under Karu who moves like a cat, and eight more that I don't recognize. Then the woman from Vidarna's camp—Taja, I think is her name—gives a command and they start walking.

If this is a scouting party, then my sword's an embroidery needle. There are too many of them, and everyone's too heavily armed. They'll be attacking someone before the day is out.

After a while, Taja signals for everyone to stop and sends the Karu girl ahead. I follow in her wake. She's good—almost catches onto me several times as she goes up over a hill and across a small creek. Finally, she climbs a stalk of bamboo. I watch carefully as she draws her bow, lets loose one arrow, then slides down and runs back the way we came.

Once she's gone, I sneak forward and climb the same stalk. A short distance away, an Amparan soldier lies dead with an arrow through his throat. She'd killed a lookout but hadn't bothered to hide his body, which means the rest of the attack is coming soon.

From my vantage point, I can see the rest of the Amparan camp. Three soldiers huddle on the forest floor. No, not just any soldiers. I recognize them from Neju's Guard. The men aren't stupid enough to light campfires, though they sit in a circle as if they had one. Their bedrolls are laid out next to them. I count six bedrolls, so at least three of the party are not here. One must be the scout that the Karu girl just killed. The others...

The bamboo rustles on the far side of the men, and General Arxa steps into view. Though he's haunted my dreams since I left, the sight of him in the flesh is a fist around my lungs.

I'm running across the training field. It's high noon. Sweat runs down my back. I'm wearing full armor, and I stumble under the weight of a bag filled with rocks.

"Go. You're stronger than you think!" shouts Arxa.

My throat feels like it's been pierced through, and spots dance before my eyes. I stumble, yet I don't fall. The edge of the field is just a little farther.

"Go!"

I reach for one last burst of strength and surge forward. Cheers erupt from fellow soldiers as I step over the finish marker. They clap me on the back, but I stumble past them and vomit onto the ground.

Arxa comes to stand next to me. "Remember this moment. You are capable of more than you think."

My heart swells with pride.

The memory drifts away, and deep shame wells up in its place. I can't even be trusted to hate our enemies. No wonder Gatha kicked me out of the camp.

What do I do now? Despite what Frada thinks, I'm still Shidadi. I'd never warn Arxa about a coming raid. But can I be trusted to fight against him? Even if I could, Frada and the others would never let me join the fight.

Bamboo sways behind me in the distance. Frada's group is advancing. I slide down and crouch behind a boulder as they run past. The Shidadi fan out, the soft pad of their footsteps barely audible under the swish of the wind. Now that I'm on the ground, I can't see the Amparans anymore, and soon the Shidadi too disappear from view.

Shouts upon shouts tell me when the fighting begins. I wait for the clash of swords to reach a steady volume, then rush in closer. The cloying smell of blood and sweat drifts over me as the melee comes into view. Shidadi outnumber Amparans three to one—Arxa must have really wanted to evade detection to risk traveling with such a small group. A member of Vidarna's tribe lies dead already, as does an Amparan I don't recognize. A second Amparan struggles against two fighters.

But there's no question where the center of the fighting is. Arxa stands back to back with one of his soldiers, fending off a throng of Shidadi. As my people close in, I get a flash of another battle in the mountains where I'd fought alongside him the same way. Now Frada attacks Arxa from the front, and Taja cuts down the soldier behind the general, leaving Arxa's back exposed. I grit my teeth, waiting for the final blow to fall, but then Arxa slams his foot into Frada's chest, sending him stumbling back. Before anyone can react, Arxa lowers his shoulder and charges through the circle, sending two Shidadi flying and almost certainly picking up some deep cuts in the process. Frada regains his balance and moves to block him, but Arxa takes full advantage of his momentum and forces Frada back with a furious attack. I reach for my sword. Frada may not be my favorite person, but he did save my life. As I crash out through the bamboo, Frada snaps his head toward me. His eyes widen.

Arxa runs him through.

I bite back a scream. The general's disappeared into the bamboo before Frada's body hits the ground. The Shidadi give chase, and I follow.

Arxa flees through the forest with four Shidadi in pursuit. Four Shidadi, that is, and me, though I don't think any of them even know I'm here. Arxa may not be as quick a sprinter as a younger man, but he's good with terrain. Nothing slows him down, and he picks paths that make it hard to follow him. We're all running at speeds that would break an ankle with a misstep. No time to think, just react. Still the Shidadi have lived and fought on this mountain for years now. It's only a matter of time before they catch up to him.

Only a matter of time, unless...

Arxa's words come back to me. Know when you're beaten. Know how much the enemy is willing to sacrifice. Know when you need to take risks.

He's running straight toward a Dara tributary, a fast-rushing stream at the bottom of a steep ravine. He must know about it, since they came from that direction.

I turn away from the chase.

Arxa's fleeing certain death, and a cliff jump might be the only way to throw off his pursuers. I don't know how far his pursuers are willing to go, but I do know that the ravine flattens out downstream, and that it's much easier to get to the water from there. That's where I go now. Once again I barrel through the woods, sending rocks scattering, and bruising my elbows on plants in my way.

Soon, I hear rushing water ahead of me. As the ground softens and gets slippery under my feet, I break through the plant cover onto the riverbank. Mud sucks at my boots, and a slick rock almost sends me flying. More carefully now, I wade out toward the center of the water and stop there, looking at the cliffs upstream. And I wait.

I'll have to kill him. That much is clear. I've already failed Gatha and Frada. I can't hesitate anymore.

Time passes. My face and arms get wet with spray. My ankles grow so numb that I no longer feel the curious fishes nibbling on them. Maybe I'm wrong after all.

Then I see him, a dark form plummeting off a cliff. I don't see the splash he makes, and I have no way of knowing if he was dashed to death on the rocks. Even if he survived, he might climb out before he reaches me, but I'm counting on the fall to be enough of a shock to render him useless awhile.

Eventually what looks like a bundle of cloth appears upstream, tossed by the current. Arxa bobs lifelessly at first, and I think my job might be done for me. But then there's a hint of movement. One arm comes out of the water and plunges back down. Another arm comes out, and then he's actively trying to swim out of the current—not very successfully at first, but his movements get stronger. He'll make it out of the water, though not before he reaches me.

As Arxa floats past, I run down the riverbank after him, trying my best to stay out of his line of sight. Finally, he collides with the shore. He lays crumpled for several heartbeats, and then drags himself onto the riverbank. He stays on his hands and knees, dripping wet and coughing up mouthfuls of water. I dash toward him, drawing my sword. I won't have the element of surprise for long.

I'm still ten paces away, when Arxa staggers to his feet and points his weapon at me. "Dineas. Traitor. I taught you too well, didn't I?"

Impressive how he still sounds like he's in control, even after crawling half-drowned out of a river. Part of me still feels like I should salute him. "You can't win this fight after that fall, - Commander," I say. "Drop your weapon, and my warlord may yet spare you."

His mouth presses in a grim line. "If you've paid any attention at all, then you know I won't."

Water splashes my eyes, and I flinch. As I realize I'd let him maneuver me to face the river's spray, Arxa charges me. I bring my sword up in a desperate block. *You're an idiot, Dineas.*

Then we're fencing, trading jabs and parries, moving up and down the slick riverbank. It could almost be a training drill back in Sehmar City, except our swords are deadly sharp.

"Still not paying attention," Arxa shouts over the water's rumble. "Still relying too much on your own skill."

It's disconcerting, getting advice from the man you're trying to kill.

You've said yourself that you might have trouble killing Arxa. He was good to you once, and he was good to me.

I'm a split second late to block Arxa's blow. It's only with a dive to the side that I don't end up decapitated.

There's no one in the world who thinks Arxa's an easy foe. That's because everyone who's underestimated him is already dead. Though I'm stronger and faster, he sees every mistake I make and exploits it. What gives me hope, though, is how tired he is. I just need to keep pressing him, and sooner or later he'll make a mistake too. As he starts to breathe more heavily, I press him back toward the river. Twice he tries to rally, but I stand my ground. Then he slips on a rock and stumbles.

That's my opening. I knock his blade out of the way and direct a thrust toward his chest. The sword slides in smoothly between his ribs. Shockingly smoothly, and slides out just as easily.

And then Arxa falls at my feet just like any other man.

THIRTY-SEVEN: ZIVAH

The Amparan soldier's rose plague drives me into a frenzy. If I tried hard to save this man before, now I work ten times harder. Any potion that might help, I brew for him. Any food that would give him strength, I find and prepare. I stay up with him at night, tending the fire and giving him water. To strengthen his humors, I trap a bird and feed him the liver mixed with congealed blood. I'd had such success with patients until now that I'd gotten careless. I realize this now, and I'm determined this man not pay the price. My headache becomes a constant throbbing at the back of my brain.

As the Amparan fights the fever, my Shidadi patient continues to improve. Scrawny comes with me to check on her, flying short hops from branch to branch as I walk. Every time we see the Shidadi, she's stronger. In a matter of days, she will be gone. I know I must make myself known to her, but if I do, what would become of the Amparan? If I leave with her, he'll surely perish. If I ask her to wait, then I'll be exposed for a traitor. One morning, I see her hobbling around her shelter, and I know that she'll be gone in two days, perhaps even one. Still, I make no move to approach. As I walk away back toward my cave, I feel a stirring of doubt that dissipates as quickly as it came. I don't return to check on her again.

Meanwhile the rose plague tightens its hold on the Amparan. He drifts in and out of delirium, and it seems that no remedy grants him clarity or peaceful rest. In desperation, I take out the syeb flowers I'd gathered and spread them before me. The thought of using an unknown cure on a patient is abhorrent to me, but I don't see what else to do. I think through what I know of the rose plague. If I follow Baruva's theory that it starts in the blood and settles in the skin, then a poultice might be the best. I mix five pinches of pollen together with ground nadat root to draw out the plague essence. The soldier doesn't even stir as I smear the concoction over his skin. I continue to give him vel flower tea for fever and keep him warm throughout the night.

The next morning, I heat a pot of water over the fire to start washing the poultice off. As I wipe the man's arm, he stirs and opens his eyes. They're remarkably clear.

"It smells horrible," he says.

Hope flares in my chest. "Yes, it does."

He falls back into the fever after that, but the exchange gives me a renewed determination. I clean him off, give him half a day of rest, then make another batch of poultice with my remaining syeb flowers. He wakes again when I apply it to his chest.

"What do you think the afterlife is like?" he asks.

"Don't think about the afterlife just yet."

He makes a weak gesture toward me. "But you must have thought about it."

"I suppose I have," I say. "But never for very long. It seems too much like giving up. You shouldn't give up."

"I spoke with a priestess of Zenagua once." I'm not sure he even heard what I just said. "She told me that Zenagua's realm is beyond wondrous. There are fields ripe with fruit, rivers that shine like jewels. Zenagua herself resides in a city of liquid silver."

The Amparans have a much more specific view of the afterlife than we do. The priestesses of the Dara Goddess tell us of peace after we die. Peace and rest, though they say little beyond that.

"Wait a little longer before you eat that fruit," I tell him.

"I'll do my best," he says.

That night, his fever spikes. Sweat pours from his forehead, and he's trapped in a world I cannot see. I can only watch as he talks to ghosts and hallucinations. A few hours earlier, he'd looked as if he might throw off his fever, and now he's as bad a rose plague case as I've ever seen. I do what I can, giving him more vel tea, wiping his brow.

Later that night, his eyes snap open. "Should I fear death?"

"No, of course not," I tell him.

His eyes unfocus. "No, I don't think I should. It's simply another journey. Another step. I see that now."

"Don't take that step. Not yet."

But he's asleep again.

I, on the other hand, don't sleep at all. I'm barely aware of the passage of time, just that my eyes grow dry and my limbs grow heavy. My vision clouds over, and my own skin burns like his. Still, I stay with him. After his restlessness this evening, he sinks into a deep slumber. I can only tell he's alive by the slight movement of his chest.

As the morning light starts filtering in, he coughs. I run to his side and take his hand.

"My name is Miza," he says.

"I am Zivah," I whisper.

An hour later, he is dead.

. . .

SOMEHOW, I manage to bury Miza. Somehow, I manage to drag his body outside, dig a grave, and lay him to rest with a prayer that is half blessing and all rage. After that, I stumble back to my cave. It's dark and smoky inside from the fire. The air stinks of poultice and sweat. I lie down and close my eyes. A steady drumbeat pounds at my head.

It gets lighter outside, and then dark again. In a distant corner of my mind, I feel hunger and thirst. The air grows cold and I start to shiver, but I stay still. Why move? Why fight?

Outside, metal clashes against metal. Soldiers yell war cries and rocks fall. I stare at the ceiling of my cave and watch the play of dust in the sunlight.

The noises fade. Night falls. The air grows cold.

A moan of pain drifts through the cave opening.

I shut my eyes and will the world to go silent.

Another moan.

I'm done. I'm finished. Just let me be.

A voice calls in the darkness. "Gods, have mercy." He cuts off with a sob.

I clench my fists, grit my teeth. A vision appears before me. A woman with eyes like granite and skin the color of new bamboo stands by a veil that hangs from empty air. She pulls it aside with slender fingers, revealing a darkness that shifts and roils like the Monyar strait. But she doesn't beckon me in. She simply holds it open and looks at me, asking what I will do.

So I open my eyes. I get a drink of water and take a bite of dried taro. Then I sling my bag of herbs over my shoulder and step out into the night.

THIRTY-EIGHT: DINEAS

It's surreal, the sight of Arxa lying on the ground before me, his hand pressed uselessly against his bleeding wound. Anger smolders in his eyes, but it's helpless anger. He knows he's lost. I raise my sword for a killing blow. Finally I can avenge what he's done to my people. Finally I can repay what he did to me.

But I can't do it. My arms won't move. Is it my memories of him? Or Zivah's voice whispering "blood debt" in my head?

Next thing I know I've ripped off my cloak and I'm tearing it into strips. Arxa looks on with bemusement as I wrap the makeshift bandages around his chest. The cloth soaks through with blood at an alarming rate, and the general's eyelids slowly drift closed.

I may be too late. Or maybe Neju knew my weakness and he's helping me finish the job.

Slow, deliberate footsteps sound behind me. The slink of a sword being drawn. Slowly, I turn around.

Walgash stands five paces away, a vengeful giant with his sword raised to kill. "You'll die for this."

There had been six bedrolls in the Amparan camp, and five Amparan soldiers in the battle. Now I've found the sixth.

I resist the urge to go for my sword. I'd never get it out in time. "He's alive," I say.

"I should have killed you when I had the chance," he says.

"Arxa is alive, Walgash," I say again. "I didn't kill him, but he needs help."

My words finally seem to sink in. Walgash steps cautiously around me to get a better view of Arxa.

I hastily raise my hands as his eyes narrow dangerously. "Think, Walgash. You can attack me if you want. You might kill me. I might kill you. Either way, you'd be wasting precious time while your commander bleeds to death. I bandaged his wounds, but he needs a real healer."

"Then he might as well be dead," says Walgash. "He won't make it back to camp like this."

He's probably right. Arxa is very close to gone. But a wild idea comes to me. "You don't need to bring him back to camp."

"What do you mean?"

Dear gods, let this be true. "Zivah can help him."

"She's here?"

"You must have heard of the woman roaming the hills, healing the sick. That must be Zivah."

Suspicion clouds his gaze. "You don't know?"

"I know Zivah, and this is just like her. I can find her." It occurs to me that I'm being less than convincing. "Look, you have nothing to lose. Do you want to take a chance to save him or not?"

Walgash glares at me with a mixture of fury and distrust. I'm tense, ready to duck out of the way if he attacks, but he doesn't move. Finally, he lowers his sword. "Neju help you if you're lying."

Neju help me indeed. How am I going to find her? Search all the caves around here? Arxa would die before we're even halfway through. Send Slicewing to look for her? She's probably hidden beneath the foliage. Wander around aimlessly? Honestly, it doesn't seem a worse plan than the others.

Walgash is still watching me, getting more suspicious by the moment. "I'll find her," I say again, though now I'm trying to think of ways to buy time. Maybe Slicewing could create a distraction. She and Preener had this routine that they used in order to steal from market vendors. Preener would fall to the ground, pretending to have a hurt wing and soaking up the crowd's attention while Slicewing stole her choice of treats. I get a bizarre vision of the crow falling dramatically in front of Walgash while I slip away.

No, that wouldn't work. But the crows stick in my mind. Zivah might be hard to spot, but Scrawny, if he's still alive, spends his days circling the sky, especially if Zivah's asked him to scout.

I whistle for Slicewing, who takes one look at Walgash and hops out of his reach. "Find Scrawny," I tell her. Slicewing cocks her head. She's not used to being asked to find another crow. I repeat the command, and finally she takes off.

"Scrawny's with Zivah," I tell Walgash. "Once Slicewing finds him, he'll be able to lead us to her."

"How long?" he says.

"An hour at most," I say glibly.

And then it's just the two of us. I keep my hands casually by my sides, never far from my swords. Walgash puts his back to a cluster of bamboo and watches me like a burly, murderous eagle. Arxa lies between us. If not for the motion of his chest, I'd think the general was dead.

"We'll need a stretcher," I say. Mostly, I just needed to say something to break the tension. I eye a stalk of bamboo that's the right width for a frame and wonder how hard it would be to chop it down. Walgash growls a warning, and I realize I'd reached absentmindedly for my sword. "Easy," I say. "I'm just looking for materials."

Walgash jerks his head toward some debris on the ground. "There's some dead ones we can use."

Fair enough. Chopping down that stalk of bamboo would have killed my sword anyway. Walgash rummages through the dead stalks and carries them over. Then he stands back and watches grumpily while I lash them together with what's left of my cloak.

The silence gets to me. "How does Kosru fare?"

Walgash looks up from tying his cloak to the bamboo frame. "Kosru?"

"The silent giant you're fond of. Your better half. Remember him?"

"He's on another mission." Walgash doesn't offer any more details.

"And Masista?"

"He took an arrow to the ribs. The general sent him back to the central continent to recover."

"I'm glad he's alive."

"How do I know you didn't shoot that arrow?"

I take the corner of the stretcher and jiggle it, testing the knots. "I'm a soldier, Walgash. You can't blame me for fighting."

Walgash takes two large steps toward me. I go for my sword, but he reaches for the stretcher and snatches it out of my hands. "You think I blame you for fighting? No. If you were a mercenary, I'd respect that. You'd have no loyalties, but you'd wear that plainly. But what you are is a liar."

He spits out the words with rage, and I feel my own anger bubbling up to meet it. "Damn you, Walgash. I'm done hearing this. That mission took everything from me. Those potions split my soul in two. And then I did such a good job of blending in, I was such a good *liar*, that my own people turned me out because they feared I'd become an Amparan spy." I stand up to my full height. Still unimpressive next to Walgash, but I don't care. "Yes, I'm a traitor many times over. Yes, I've spit in Neju's face with the way I've broken the bond of soldiers, but I've paid the price. And I'll tell you something more. Had you been in my place, had you watched your people get slaughtered by Ampara, had you spent months deep in the emperor's dungeons begging the gods to let you die, you would have done the same thing."

Walgash's nostrils flare, and his face turns red. I take a step back, wondering if he's finally going to attack.

Then it happens again. Walgash's face blurs, and in its place is Tus.

My heart freezes in place. Tus, the Shidadi I captured and took back to Ampara. The one who died painfully to protect my cover. A choking sound escapes my throat.

"What in Neju's name are you playing at?" says Tus. But it's Walgash's voice at least, and I grasp at it, telling myself that what I see is not real. I squeeze my eyes shut and grit my teeth. By the time I open them, it's Walgash who stares at me. There's a flash of uncertainty in his eyes, and I can't tell if he's about to move toward me or away.

The knot loosens in my throat, and I cough out the rest. "You have no idea the price I've paid." My knees go soft, and I crumple.

Walgash is still watching me. He says nothing.

"Think what you want," I say. "I'm done."

A shadow crosses my vision. At first I think it's another hallucination, but then Slicewing soars to a landing in front of me, followed by—my heart leaps—Scrawny.

"You found him!"

Slicewing fluffs her feathers as if to say I should never have doubted her. Walgash steps back and watches the crow. I still can't tell what he's thinking.

"Scrawny," I say, trying to keep a rein on my hope. Is Zivah alive? Have we found her? "Take me to Zivah."

I hold my breath as Scrawny takes to the air. He flies awkwardly, and it takes him just a hair longer than usual to get aloft. Is he hurt? Then he lands a short distance away and looks back at me expectantly. I go light-headed with relief.

"He knows where Zivah is," I say. "Let's go."

There's the problem of getting Arxa onto the stretcher. I don't want to jostle him in this state, but there's no way around it. Finally, Walgash takes his arms and I take his legs. The commander is deadweight as we lift him on.

"You take the front of the stretcher," Walgash says.

I'm not exactly eager to turn my back to Walgash. It makes me too vulnerable.

"You take the front," says Walgash. "Or we end the truce. For all I know, Zivah's not even in this forest."

"You'll never find her if you kill me," I remind him.

"You have nothing to worry about, then."

I grit my teeth. Fine. If he didn't kill me in open battle, I'll trust him not to stab me in the back.

Scrawny's definitely flying a bit funny, but he doesn't look distressed. In fact, he seems to be enjoying his newfound importance, leading the way with all of us following. Maybe that's why he took so readily to Zivah, since before he met her he was always the subordinate crow. One thing the crow's not good at, though, is picking a good trail for two men carrying a third. It's rough going over uneven ground. I'm jumpy at every shift of the stretcher, thinking that Walgash is about to pull something. Twice, we almost dump Arxa onto the dirt. But my spirits lift as Scrawny leads us to a granite rock face. Rock means caves, and there Zivah will likely be. It's getting dark, and soon every shadow looks like her. Finally, we catch up to Scrawny and he doesn't lift off again.

That's when I see her.

She's standing near a stalk of bamboo, looking intently at something within its leaves. A low whistle drifts from where she stands, and the long, supple shadow of a snake bobs an arm's length above her. Still whistling, Zivah raises her arm to the creature.

It strikes. I swallow a yell.

Zivah clutches her arm where it bit her. For a moment, she doesn't move. Then, quietly, she whistles again and lifts her arm once more. This time, the snake coils itself around her arm. She holds the creature by the base of its neck, examining its fangs, before carefully returning it to the tree.

Goddess. The word pops into my head, an echo of the rumors I'd heard. And indeed, she does look like a goddess. Not the immaculate deities found in temples—even in the growing twilight I can tell that her clothes are old and torn. Hair has come out of her long braid, and if I go closer, I'll likely find dirt on her face and arms. But there's something about her, something that calls of blood and earth, and the sight of her sends shivers across my skin.

A twig breaks under my feet, and Zivah's head snaps toward the sound. "Who's there?"

THIRTY-NINE: ZIVAH

When he says his name, I'm afraid to believe it's really him. I'm terrified that this is a new manifestation of my fever, a hallucination to tease me. But if it's a hallucination, it's painfully real. I recognize his voice: familiar, hopeful, and scared. And though his face is in shadow, I recognize the width of his shoulders, the lines of his arms, the way he shifts his weight as he walks.

Dineas steps into the light, and my heart goes still. His eyes meet mine, the same eyes that had searched desperately for an anchor as he came out of fever delirium in Sehmar City. The same eyes that had clung to my every move as I left Monyar for the second time.

It's him. He's alive.

As he steps closer, I see that he's carrying a stretcher. Fear shoots through me when I see the Amparan soldier holding the other end, but then I recognize Walgash from Neju's Guard, and I don't know whether I should be more or less afraid.

"We bring you a patient," says Dineas.

A patient, at least, is something I know how to deal with. The man on the litter is motionless and covered with blood.

"Bring him into the cave, quickly." I part the vines covering my cave entrance and make sure the snakes are a safe distance away. Walgash and Dineas have to tilt the stretcher to get it through the crevice. He and Dineas lay the patient down, and that's when I catch a glimpse of the injured man's face.

I draw a sharp breath. Arxa's eyes are closed, he struggles to draw breath, and his face has a grayish cast. When I place my finger on his wrist, I can hardly feel his pulse. "How was he wounded?"

"Sword through the ribs." From the way Dineas says it, I know it was his sword.

I have other questions. If Dineas wounded Arxa, why didn't he kill him? Is Walgash a friend or an enemy? But the man on the floor of my cave is dying, and he won't wait for questions to be answered.

"His lung's collapsed. He needs treatment, quick," I say. "Walgash, take him off the stretcher and lay him down. Dineas, there's a fire pit near the mouth of the cave. Build a fire and throw some rocks in the flames. You'll find some bamboo segments near the wall that you can use for water."

I scan my stacks of dried herbs, deciding on the last of my puzta flowers and syeb petals to stabilize the wound, and spine-leaf root to seal it. Dineas walks past me with canisters of water as I fill an improvised bamboo bowl with my selections.

I touch his elbow as he goes by. He shudders, even as the feel of him sends a tingle up my arm. "How did you find me?"

"Goddesses don't stay hidden for long," he says.

He looks at me like a man who's found a flower in the dead of winter. If only he knew the extent of my failures.

Walgash clears his throat. Dineas and I jump apart, and I turn back to my herbs. There's no time to grind them thoroughly, and it doesn't help that my hands shake when I grasp the grinding stone. I notice Dineas watching me from the fire, and I angle my body so he can't see my tremors. For a short while, all three of us work silently in our scattered places, guided by the light of the flickering flames. Once I have a rough poultice, I join Walgash where he sits near the general. He's hunched over, shoulders rounded and tense.

"Do you come as a friend or an enemy?" I ask.

"I come as someone who doesn't want to see my commander die."

For the second time in two years, I hold Arxa's life in my hands. This time he's more than an unknown patient. He's the father of my friend, the potential destroyer of my people. "You have my word I'll do my best to cure him," I say. "I swore to Mehtap that I wouldn't harm her father."

Walgash rolls his shoulders uncomfortably. "What can I do?"

"Remove the bandages around Arxa's chest," I say. "There's warm water if anything sticks."

"Can I help?" Dineas says at my ear, his voice low and uncertain. I can almost feel his breath on my hair.

"Yes, help me slather the poultice onto bandages."

The bandages are leaves, actually, that I've woven into mats. Dineas stretches them flat for me as I apply the paste. The skin of his hands is rough and windblown from his travels, and his fingers come close to mine as we work. If I stretch out my arm just a little bit, we would touch.

After I finish, Walgash and Dineas steady Arxa as I rewrap his wounds.

"Will he live?" Walgash asks. His expression is stoic, but I hear the fear in his voice.

"The cut leading to his lung collapse was not a large one," I say, "or he would have been dead before you found me. Now that the cut is sealed, it's up to the Goddess. Arxa needs rest most of all. It will be many days in the best of circumstances, and I work better without distraction. It's best if you leave him here with me."

Walgash doesn't look surprised at my words, though he

fidgets with a patch on his armor as he considers them. He's a fearsome warrior on the battlefield, but right now he looks like an uncertain youth with his tutor.

"You swear you will do him no harm?" he asks.

"I've made vows to my Goddess," I remind him. "I'm bound to heal."

He takes a long look at Arxa, then moves reluctantly toward the cave opening. After several steps, though, he turns back. "Tell your people to surrender. You don't know what our soldiers and our weapons can do."

When neither of us answers, he heads for the cave entrance again, only to turn and address Dineas. "Did your kinsmen really exile you?"

I look to Dineas in alarm. He nods.

Walgash adjusts the sword at his belt. "If you had a choice between joining their side and ours, what would you choose?"

Dineas's expression doesn't change. "I am Shidadi," he says.

Rather than angry, Walgash looks satisfied. "I wouldn't have believed you if you'd said anything else."

He leaves. And just like that, Dineas and I are alone with Arxa.

HE'S ALIVE.

I can't stop looking at him. I take in his face, the flecks of gold in his eyes, the curve of his cheekbones. He looks at me with the same hunger as when we last parted, and it causes my stomach to tighten. My fingers are restless with the memory of his skin.

"I thought you were dead," I say. "I found your mother's bow."

He swallows, and it takes him a few attempts to speak. I still get the sense that he's worried I'll vanish. "I lost it...the bow. I went down by the beach to scout, and Walgash caught me—"

"You were looking for me."

"Yes." Like me, he seems frozen in place.

He's alive. It's more than I had dared hope for, but now that he's here, I'm at a loss. Shouldn't I be throwing my arms around him? Shedding tears of joy on his shoulder? Telling him how the thought of him dead might have destroyed me, had Scrawny not been there?

"Sarsine's dead," I blurt out.

Sorrow crosses his face. "I suspected as much, when I didn't see her here."

His words bring a fresh pang of grief. "She died bravely. I'd be dead if not for her."

"Zenagua guide her soul," Dineas whispers.

Perhaps it's just my imagination, but the fire seems to burn more brightly. For a moment, we stand silent, and I send up one last prayer for her. Dineas's lips move soundlessly as well. The past weeks have been hard on him. His clothes are worn and dirtied, fitting loosely on his frame. He's thinner now than he was even after we returned from Sehmar.

"Dineas, what did Walgash mean, when he said your kinsmen exiled you?"

A shadow enters his eyes. "There was an ambush, and the leaders thought I was behind it. I've been wandering the mountains since."

"Alone?"

He stares at the cave wall without seeing it.

"Dineas?"

"My ghosts came back," he says, his voice barely louder than a whisper.

Ghosts? And then I understand. "Your past."

"My fears. My friends. My enemies."

"You had visions again. Out in the forest?"

Finally he looks at me, his eyes haunted. "It's never been that bad before."

His words usher in a wave of guilt. I take his hands, and he grips me tightly back. "You've been through something the gods never intended. I shouldn't have done this to you."

He shakes his head. "Don't blame yourself. I was already haunted by my past before our mission, just in different ways. I lost something in Sehmar, but I also gained something."

Dineas draws a slow breath and continues. "I was so confused when I first came back from Sehmar City with *his* memories tearing me apart. I didn't know if I was Amparan or Shidadi. I didn't know if I could even decide who to fight for. But then I realized it was still me doing the deciding. I simply know more."

"Is it painful, knowing too much?"

"Sometimes. But it's better to know. Before our mission, I had ideas of what was good, what was brave, what was cowardly. And all this time, I was wrong. If I hadn't been forced to forget all that, I would have passed over a beautiful thing. The man I was in Sehmar and the lessons he learned are a part of me now. I wouldn't give that up."

A shiver goes up my spine at the mention of his other self. *I know I'm not him,* he'd said. I remember the resignation in his voice, the silent apology. And I remember the kiss that followed, the vulnerability of it, and I realize how much courage it had taken him.

He's looking at me now in that same wistful way. "I've missed you," he says.

I would have passed over a beautiful thing.

My heart beats an unsteady rhythm. Though his eyes beg for a reply from me, my lips are frozen.

After an eternity of silence, Dineas lets out a frustrated groan and runs his fingers through his hair. "Zivah...do you think about the morning I sent you off with Sarsine?"

"Yes." Even now, I feel the phantom brush of his lips against mine.

A flash of hope enters his eyes. "Do you..." He pauses, takes a breath. His voice is raw when he continues. "Do you think back on it fondly?"

I still can't speak, but the memories flood through me now—those nights traveling with Sarsine when I stared up at the stars and prayed Dineas was safe. The times I'd curled my fingers, wishing I could hold his hand. The pain that ripped through me, when I feared he'd died.

"Yes," I whisper.

Relief floods his face. The air between us thrums with energy. *He's so close.*

My entire body aches to touch him, but I gather my resolve and put my fingertips against his chest, pushing him gently away. "Nothing's changed." It's a last desperate reminder that I'm still sick. That anything we start is doomed.

He brushes my hair away from my forehead. Strange that hands so calloused could still feel so feathery soft on my skin. "You know he didn't care," he says. "And neither do I."

I don't want to resist anymore.

Closing my eyes, I cup the back of his head and bring him to me. The first touch of his lips is a lightning bolt. My legs go soft, but I cling to him, and he tightens his arms around me. As the first jolt fades away, our kiss becomes slow and lingering, a wave of overwhelming relief after a lifetime of waiting. He smells of the forest, of earth, and of battle, and he feels solid, wonderfully real. As I link my hands behind his neck, all I'm aware of, all I want to be aware of, is the gentle weight of his chest against mine, the press of his hand to the small of my back, the cords of his muscles beneath my hands.

A jolt of pain through my temple. A flash of light across my eyes. I cry out.

Dineas catches me as my knees buckle. *Why now?* I want to scream, but I don't have it in me.

"Zivah? Zivah!"

The worst of the pain recedes, but its echoes persist in my skull as Dineas lowers me to the ground. I pull away, keeping my face turned toward the ground as I untangle myself from him. It's as if my body were reminding me what I'd forgotten. No words of love, no gentle touch, can change my fate.

"Zivah." He's frantic. "What's wrong?"

His fear breaks my heart, but I can't protect him. "My headaches are getting worse."

It takes a moment for my meaning to dawn on him. And when it does, he closes his eyes. For the second time tonight, grief plays across his face.

"I should have told you," I say.

He shakes his head. "It wouldn't have mattered," he says. "I just wish..." He stops. Turns away and clenches his fists before turning back. "How much time do you have?"

"I don't know. Weeks or months."

He looks at me, and I wonder if he might shatter on the spot. "Zivah..." he whispers again. And once more, he wraps his arms around me and pulls me in, holding me as if I might dissolve into mist. I lay my head on his chest and close my eyes, waiting for the pain to subside.

I WAKE up alone on the cave floor. My head rests on a folded leaf bandage, and my cloak serves as a blanket. I sit up in a panic, and then I see Dineas tending the fire.

"Does it still hurt?" he asks.

I shake my head.

"Good," he says, though he doesn't take his eyes off me.

The pain's gone, though I still feel as if I'm moving through a fog. "How long did I sleep?"

"A few hours."

Hours? I throw off the cloak. "Arxa."

Dineas moves aside to give me a better view of the general. "He hasn't stirred."

I climb unsteadily to my feet and make my way over to my patient. He's still pale, though he seems to be breathing more easily now. I check his bandages and find blood, but less than I'd feared.

Dineas watches me work without comment. Finally, when I'm satisfied, I join him by the fire. He holds out a hand to help me down. After a moment, I lean my head into his shoulder, and he puts his arm around mine. I'm surprised at how natural it feels. It's the first time since we left Sehmar City that there's no wall between us.

"What will you do now?" I ask.

"I haven't thought that far ahead, to be honest," he says.

"It will take time to nurse Arxa back to health," I say. "And then..." I trail off. We're still stuck where we were. The Amparans still hunt our people.

"The rumors say you've been treating Amparans," says Dineas.

He says it with a mild enough tone that I answer without justifying myself. "I have."

He nods, his expression again carefully neutral. "The soldiers you've healed. Do you let them go back to their battalions?"

"I do. Though it haunts me, the thought that one of them might go on to kill someone I love." I glance at him, trying to gauge his expression. "You don't approve."

He struggles for a moment. "No. I don't approve. But I don't know what else you could have done."

A year ago, Dineas would have condemned me on the spot. I marvel at this change. "You told Walgash you were still Shidadi, even though they exiled you. Why?"

He's silent for a long time. "I still fight like a Shidadi," he says. "I still speak and think like one. It'd be better if I could hate them all, but it'd be like hating the bones in my hand."

"Our hearts are not so easily changed," I say. "Nor what runs through our veins."

"No." He plants a kiss on my eyebrow. For a long moment we sit side by side, watching the flames. Though the truth of my illness remains, there's relief in finally being together.

"Did you find Kione?" he asks.

"We did. She worked in the kitchens when Arxa's battalion was infected. They were given special flour rations with which to cook for the troops, and she thinks the rations were infected with rose plague."

"Do you have evidence?"

"No." It still hurts to say it.

Dineas can't quite hide his disappointment. "It's all right," he says. "We'll find another way." But I know we're both thinking the same thing. We're running out of time.

I can feel him gathering himself to ask another question.

"How did Sarsine die?"

Sarsine. Once more, a twinge in my chest. "She was killed after we returned to Monyar."

"On the beach?"

"No, we didn't land at that beach. We turned around when we saw that something wasn't right. There were soldiers on the beach, and a strange Amparan ship. It was too small to be a warship but larger than a rowboat, and it was simply floating out on the ocean."

Dineas sits straighter. "A ship, waiting in the ocean? Did it have a purple flag, or any kind of seal?"

"I looked for markings on the ship. I didn't see any." But the mention of purple and a seal tugs at my memory. I remember then, the men who'd killed Sarsine and the ring they'd carried. "I did see a strange seal." I slide out from under his arm and fetch my bag. It takes me a bit of rummaging but I find the ring and hand it to Dineas.

Dineas rolls the seal between his fingers. "This is Kiran's

seal. The boat you described is his personal vessel. Where did you—"

"It was on the body of one of the men who killed Sarsine." And slowly it sinks in. "Kiran wants us dead. Baruva must have told him we're trying to find evidence against him."

Dineas calls down a dozen curses on Kiran. "This tells us, at least," he says when he runs out of breath, "that we're on the right track."

There's a shuffling sound behind us. Arxa moans, and I rush to his side. The commander is hot to the touch, and sweat runs down his face.

"It's too hot in here," I tell Dineas. "Help me get his clothes off."

Arxa's tunic is already slashed open from when we bandaged his wounds. Now we pull off what's left of it, and his trousers as well, leaving him in his loincloth. It's a strange feeling, seeing the almost naked commander lying comatose on the ground.

"Here," I say, holding my hand out for Arxa's tunic. It's caked with so much blood that I doubt it'll be usable again, but I fold it just in case. One corner of the tunic is particularly stiff. At first, I think it's just dried blood, but then my hand runs across a seam—there's a hidden pocket. I pull out what looks like half of a blue handkerchief sewn together with a white handkerchief.

"Do you know what this is?" I ask Dineas.

"It's a cloth used to command messenger pigeons. Arxa had this?"

He examines the cloth, frowning, as I pull out something else. It's a parchment which turns out to be a map of Monyar - Peninsula. Trails are marked, as well as a circle around a spot far north near the mountains. Several areas midforest are shaded in as well.

"What about this?" I ask Dineas.

He takes the map and scans it briefly. Then he stares, disbelieving. "This was on Arxa's person?" he asks.

"Yes. In the same pocket."

Dineas grips the map as if it were an enemy that might flee. "This is a diagram of our fighters' positions," he says. "And that's the location of the Dara camp."

My stomach plummets. "Where my family is."

He rolls the parchment back up, and I can tell the effort it takes him not to crush it. "I have to go," he says. "There's a traitor in the Shidadi camp, and I know who it is."

FORTY: DINEAS

I can feel Zivah's eyes following me as I leave her cave. It's hard to go. To have had those few moments with her, to actually hold her in my arms, only to have to abandon her again...But I need to warn my tribe. The Amparans know where they are and could be marching already. Curse them. Curse this war.

Zivah's voice echoes in my mind, and the memory of holding her teases my skin. The silky softness of her hair, the touch of her lips. But mixed with those are other images: her eyes squeezing shut as the headache took hold, the press of her forehead against my cheek, warmer than it should be. I want to yell at the heavens, shake my fist at Hefana. Haven't we been through enough?

But Hefana doesn't answer. She never does.

I follow Arxa's map north. What bothers me is how specific it is. Whoever drew the map marked out the locations of all our fighters, from the main camp, to the small group that shuttles supplies between the Dara and the Shidadi, to our raiding parties roaming the southern stretches. The location of the main Shidadi camp is close to what it was when I was exiled, but it's not quite the same. Which means, either the map is out of date, or it's very, very current. And somehow, I don't think it's the former.

For all that time I've spent wandering, the Shidadi camp is only a day's hard march away, according to the map. That's plenty of time, though, for a whole host of feelings to vie for attention in my head. Why am I risking my life to save a tribe that's turned me out? And that's assuming they even listen to me. Perhaps they'll simply kill me on sight.

I slow down as I get within scouting range of the camp. As much as I'd like to charge in with an accusation, that plan would almost certainly get me killed. I need to talk to Gatha. The question is, will she talk to me? After some thought, I tear an edge off Arxa's map and scrawl a message on the back with a sharpened charcoal from Zivah's fire.

I have evidence of the real traitor. Please talk to me tonight. Bring fighters from our tribe if you don't trust me, but don't tell the other tribes. Please come.—Dineas

"Find Gatha," I tell Slicewing. She flies off, and I settle down to wait.

As evening falls, Slicewing still hasn't returned, which is actually a good sign. Slicewing doesn't like wandering around in the dark, so if she hadn't found Gatha, she would have come back to me soon after sunset. As insects start to sing, I rehearse what I'll say in my head. Gatha must believe me, after I show her the evidence. She must.

There's a flutter of wings, and Slicewing lands on my shoulder.

Gatha's voice comes out of the darkness. "Don't move, Dineas. You have arrows on you."

I freeze, imagining the archers I can't see in the bamboo around me. "I'm alone."

"I have scouts making sure of that." She steps out where I can see her. There's no longer a visible bandage around her chest, though she still moves a bit stiffly. She fixes me with a humorless gaze. "I'll admit I'm glad to see you alive, Dineas, and your note intrigues me. But I have to be careful. Lay down your weapons."

Asking a Shidadi to lay down his weapons is like asking him to strip naked, but I do what she says. My arrow and quiver comes off my back, followed by my swords off my belt. Then come the daggers in my boots and at the small of my back. I toss my belt pouch to the ground as well.

"Hands in the air," says Gatha.

All I can think, as she pats me down, is that I used to be one of her elite fighters.

Finally, Gatha steps back. "What do you have to say? Don't disappoint me, Dineas."

Here goes. "You're in danger. The Amparans know where we are, and they know where the Dara are."

"Explain."

Where do I even start? "When I left the camp, I wandered the mountain." I find myself unwilling to tell her all of what actually happened on the mountain. "I'd planned to leave the Shidadi behind, but then I crossed paths with a raiding party led by Taja."

That gets Gatha's attention. The party must have returned by now, and she must know of their failure.

"Did you see their attack?" she asks.

"I didn't warn Arxa," I say, answering her unspoken question. "I followed the raiding party, and I watched the fight. When Arxa ran, I chased after him. And when he jumped off a cliff, I intercepted him farther down the river and stabbed him through his ribs."

Gatha leans forward. "You killed Arxa?"

"No. I took him to Zivah, who bandaged him up."

"You told us you didn't know Zivah's whereabouts," she says.

"Slicewing found her."

I know just how convenient that sounds, but Gatha motions for me to keep talking.

"Arxa was badly wounded, but Zivah is a skilled healer. He may yet survive. When we removed Arxa's clothes, we found something." Slowly, I motion that I need to get something from my belt pouch. Gatha nods, and I pull out the map. "The camp is marked here, along with our current positions."

I hand it to Gatha, who holds it to the moonlight. "This is everything," she murmurs. "They know everything."

"There's more. I also found this." I take out the handkerchief. Any Shidadi would recognize it as a signal for messenger pigeons.

Gatha is silent a long time. "What are you saying, Dineas?"

"You know what I'm saying. The Amparans don't train their messenger pigeons with colored cloth, but Shidadi do. Vidarna does."

"There are others in his tribe who use pigeons."

"But they wouldn't know our locations in this much detail. It explains why he's so particular about other people working with his pigeons. And do you remember Vidarna saying something once about Kiran watching the war from his ship?"

Gatha frowns. "I may."

"I thought it was just a turn of phrase at the time, but Kiran is actually at sea right now, commanding from a ship. Nush of the Rovenni told me, and Zivah's seen it in her travels. Vidarna knew where Kiran was, and he slipped up."

Gatha rubs at her temples. "The evidence is slim."

"You kicked me out of the tribe on less," I say, and I can't help the bitterness.

"You're right," says Gatha. "If what you say is true, then we have wronged you greatly. But you're not a warlord. We need more evidence, if we're to discredit someone of his stature."

"I'll get you more evidence," I say. "But I need your help."

FORTY-ONE: ZIVAH

Soon after Dineas leaves, the headache returns. I'm standing by the fire when it happens, and I crumple, clutching my forehead and backing away from the flames until I'm leaning against the cave wall. Flashes dance in front of my eyes. The pain makes me clench my jaw, which in turn makes the headache worse. I take deep breaths, willing myself to relax, but it just goes on and on. Finally, after what seems like hours, the throbbing dies away, and I slump against the stone. Everything —my arms, my head, my eyelids—feels heavy.

Sluggishly, I take stock of my surroundings. Arxa is still unconscious. I don't think he's moved, though it's possible that I simply hadn't noticed. Over the next hours, the skin around his chest wound becomes redder, which worries me. Soon, a putrid fluid starts draining from the lesions, and he starts to run a fever. I do my best to clean his wounds. When I feel well enough to leave the cave, I hike the mountainside for nadat root, which I pulverize for juice to squeeze onto his wound. The redness subsides somewhat, but not enough. He continues to drift in and out of consciousness.

The sleep herbs I give Arxa keep him from full clarity, and

he's confused when he wakes. When he sees me, sometimes he thinks he's ill again with the rose plague. Other times, he seems to realize that he shouldn't be here with me, and he yells for his troops.

Even as I care for him, I worry about Dineas. I don't know what his people will do when he returns. Will they listen to him? Attack him as a traitor? Will the Shidadi muster up a defense in time? Whenever a shadow darkens the mouth of my cave, I look, hoping it's Slicewing.

On the third day, I hear footsteps outside the cave. Though I wish for Dineas, it's unlikely to be him. Even if he delivered his message unscathed, he'll need to stay and help prepare for battle. More likely, it's Amparan soldiers. I stay quiet, hoping that they'll pass on by, but the footsteps come steadily closer.

"Is this it?" The voice is female, and very familiar.

I rush to the front of the cave, disbelieving, and peek out the entrance. Sure enough, Mehtap stands outside, surveying the surroundings. With her is Sisson from her caravan and Walgash.

What is she doing here? As Walgash leads her to the cave entrance, I step outside. "Mehtap?"

Her eyes land on me. "Zivah," she says. "I spoke to Kione."

MEHTAP TURNS bone pale at the sight of her father. She covers her mouth with her hands, and it takes her a moment before she can gain enough composure to speak. "Can he hear me?"

The ashen-faced Arxa lies in deep slumber, his wound tightly bandaged. His chest moves steadily, but weakly.

"I gave him potion to sleep," I say, "but he may be able to hear you in his dreams."

Mehtap draws close. She touches his hand quickly, as one might test a hot stove, before wrapping it in her own.

"If only I had the courage to tell you the truth," she whispers. And I know that she's thinking about how she assassinated

Emperor Kurosh. The tableau of father and daughter is heart-breakingly raw, and I get the acute sense that I shouldn't be here. She doesn't seem to notice when I quietly slip out of the cave and sit outside the entrance. Walgash and Sisson stand a stone's throw away, talking between themselves. What a bizarre mix of people we are: an elite Amparan soldier, a Dara healer, a lady assassin, her escort, and a comatose general. The tangle of loyalties is dizzying to consider. I don't know if I should be glad for their presence or fear for my life.

When Mehtap joins me a while later, her eyes are rimmed in red. She sits down next to me and leans against the granite mountainside.

"I keep on trying to work up the courage to tell him," she says. "He thinks I'm his perfect daughter, yet he would despise me if he knew."

"Why do you want to tell him?" I ask.

"If I don't deserve his love," she says, "I shouldn't have it."

For a while, neither of us says anything.

"I didn't want to believe what you told me about Kiran," she says. "But you gave me a name, and I had the means to go find her. It would have been foolish of me not to look further. I found Kione, though she was afraid to speak to me at first. I think she worried I would disbelieve her and turn her over to the emperor. But eventually she told me everything."

She fixates on a distant spot, and her lips flatten. "I came in search of my father after that. When I arrived at the army camp, they told me he'd gone missing. I feared he was dead, and then Walgash pulled me aside and told me he knew where he was."

Mehtap wipes at the corner of her eye. "I knew Kiran at court growing up. He was only a few years older than I, and very ambitious. Did you know his mother was a lower-ranked wife? She had to fight to get him named crown prince, and I think Kiran just never stopped fighting. He often talked about the glory of Ampara, of how we needed to safeguard it, to always be on the attack lest we be overtaken ourselves. I remember Father warning him against his ambition, but I never thought he would go this far." She chuckles. "But then, who am I to condemn him for going too far? I'm just as bad as he is. But Father isn't. He believes in Ampara. He would never have done what I did to Kurosh, and he would never knowingly serve an emperor who's committed Kiran's crimes."

Mehtap continues. "I think Kiran has more plans we don't know of. Walgash tells me he got pulled out of Neju's Guard to serve in that unit on the beach. Everyone in that unit is umbertouched—Kiran says it's so they can take on more dangerous missions and fight without worry of rose plague. But we all know there's no real need for such a battalion, because the only one who has used rose plague in battle is Kiran himself."

An umbertouched battalion..."So you think Kiran means to cause more harm."

She nods. "Walgash is suspicious too. He didn't say as much, but I can tell. I don't think he would have taken me here otherwise."

Those are foreboding words. I think of my family some-where in the mountains, of the traitor in the Shidadi camp, and I pray that Dineas was able to warn them. "We need to tell your father about Kiran."

"Not just my father. There are other generals and comman-ders who feel the same way. They should know what kind of man they really serve. We need to find evidence."

There it is again, evidence. I'm so tired of telling people of my failure. "I've been trying. I've searched Baruva's quarters twice, and I found nothing."

"We just need to get him to confess," says Mehtap matter-of-factly. "He's here, you know. On the beach near Kiran's ship."

"Baruva's here? What is he doing?"

She shrugs. "Nothing good. But I'm sure he knows something. It's just a matter of finding some way to persuade him to be honest."

"Are you talking about torture?"

She grimaces. "That has crossed my mind, though I don't think I have the stomach for it, even if Baruva would do it to his own enemies. But if it's the only way..."

An idea comes into my mind. "It might not be," I say.

FORTY-TWO: DINEAS

Gatha leads me into camp with my hands bound, surrounded by the ten fighters she'd brought with her when she met me in the forest. Word spreads quickly that I'm here. A handful of Shidadi appear out of the foliage to follow us, shooting me curious glances, and then more after that. It's as if I'm at my own funeral procession.

Finally, I see Vidarna coming toward us, followed by Karu. Vidarna's composed as always, and dignified. A Shidadi among Shidadi. Karu regards me with suspicion. *No, I'm not the one you need to fear.*

"What is this, Gatha?" says Karu. "I thought you'd exiled him."

"I found him lurking just out of scouting range," says Gatha. "His presence here raises some questions."

"It certainly does," says Vidarna.

Gatha lifts two fingers. Two of her fighters grab Vidarna by the arms, as others go for his weapons.

"What—" Vidarna struggles against them, kicking one of Gatha's fighters and sending him sprawling as shouts of confusion come from the crowd.

"Order," calls Gatha over the shouts. "Order! All will be explained."

Miraculously, voices die down, though the scene still crackles like dry brush on a hot day. Vidarna stands disarmed and restrained by Gatha's fighters. Every member of Vidarna's tribe has a hand on his weapon, as do many of Karu's and Gatha's, for that matter. Karu stares openmouthed and silent. Gatha looks at all this, and then steps in front of Vidarna to address the crowd.

"Forgive me for the break from tradition," she says. "There have been accusations brought against Vidarna. Accusations which he is free to dispute, but they need to be investigated immediately and without warning, if he's to clear his name with no room for doubt. While Dineas was in exile, he fought and wounded an Amparan officer. He found a map on the officer's person marking our current locations, and he found this." She holds up the colored cloth.

Murmurs start up again at the sight, but Vidarna's voice cuts through them. "I won't stand to have my name impugned. Even if that cloth really was found on the Amparan's body, I'm not the only one who uses pigeons. It seems it's not enough for Dineas to betray his people. He must make it look like others share in his guilt."

"It's true that there are others with pigeons trained in this manner," says Gatha. "But you are the only one who knows our positions to the detail drawn on the map. If you claim your innocence, then let us do one simple test. Send your pigeon Whiteclaw out with the cloth. We'll have one of our crows follow."

"This is insulting," says Vidarna.

"Insulting perhaps," says Karu. She takes several steps closer, and her one eye is sharp. "But it's an easy way to clear your name."

"Crows are fickle," says Vidarna. "They'd be just as likely to fly off by themselves."

Mansha, the woman whose ear I severed when I served in Neju's Guard, steps forward. "My crow Digger is more responsible than most. He can trail the pigeon without getting distracted."

Gatha addresses Vidarna again. "There's no good reason to refuse," she says.

A vein pulses in Vidarna's forehead. For a moment, I think he might try to fight. But then he simply snaps, "Let's get this done, then." He whistles for his pigeon. Gatha flashes the handkerchief in front of the bird's face, and it takes off. Mansha commands her crow to follow.

The next hour passes painfully slowly. Gatha's soldiers allow Vidarna to sit, and I follow suit, resting my aching legs. I itch to get rid of the ropes at my wrist, but I know Gatha would refuse if I asked her. The area around us is crowded with Shidadi, but no one speaks, and everyone's eyeing everybody else with suspicion. It seems like the slightest provocation would set us all aflame. For the first time, the ramifications of what I've done sink in. Maybe the crow will bring back something incriminating. Maybe this entire plan will fail. Either way, I don't know if our Shidadi alliance can survive this.

Finally a ripple goes through the crowd. "The birds are returning!" someone shouts. Indeed, the pigeon's flying back, followed by the crow bearing something in his beak, which he drops into Mansha's hand. She holds up a silver cord for all to see.

"That's the silver ribbon of Neju's Guard, Arxa's elite," I say. "I wore one myself."

"Rubbish," says Vidarna. "It's simply a silver cord."

Karu takes the ribbon from Mansha. She rubs it between her fingers and examines the weave. Then her expression abruptly changes. "Seize Vidarna's belongings," she says to three men next to her. "Sift through it all."

Vidarna jumps to his feet, but Gatha's guards are ready for him. They restrain him again, and this time they tie his hands. Several of Vidarna's fighters rush forward, drawing their weapons, but others from our tribe form a wall between them and Gatha.

I can't look.

"Sheathe your weapons!" shouts Gatha. "Your loyalty is to your people, not to Vidarna. If he is innocent, no harm will come to him, but if he is guilty, he no longer commands you."

Two of Karu's fighters approach. "Here are Vidarna's bag and cloak," they say, laying the prizes at Karu's feet.

"Sift through it," says the young warlord. "Search every pocket."

"Get your hands off my belongings," says Vidarna. His face is flushed, and he pulls against the men holding him.

A woman looks up from examining Vidarna's cloak. "There's something sewn into the lining." Karu holds out her hand, and the woman gives her a ring of purple stone.

Gatha's face darkens. "Is that what I think it is, Dineas?"

"The emperor's seal," I say. "Someone holding it would be granted access through the empire front lines."

Shocked exclamations come from the crowd. Gatha shakes her head incredulously. "What do you have to say for yourself, Vidarna?"

Vidarna bares his teeth. "It's folly to think we can beat the Amparans," he says. "In exchange for the location of the Dara camp, they promised safety to the Shidadi."

"We promised the Dara our protection," says Gatha.

"They're a deadweight on our war effort," says Vidarna. "This alliance will get us all killed."

Gatha's eyes narrow dangerously. "They've provided us with food and medicines throughout this war. And we gave them our word." She raises her voice. "Order your people down. Your fate is sealed, but not that of your tribe's. If you're a true warlord, you won't let them destroy themselves fighting their own kin."

The forest itself seems to go quiet waiting for Vidarna's next move. As the old warlord looks from Gatha to the fighters thronged around him, I scan the faces of the Shidadi. I see surprise, betrayal, and incredulity. Gatha and I had talked about whether anyone in his tribe could be complicit. Neither of us had thought it possible to keep something this large a secret, but it's hard to know for sure. Now, looking at the faces, I'm convinced that most, if not all, of them did not know.

Vidarna drops his head. "My tribe had no hand in this," he says. "I take full blame and responsibility."

Gatha regards him with a stony gaze. "So this is how low we've fallen," she says. "Dineas, forgive us. We have wronged you." She looks into the crowd now and raises her voice. "Brothers and sisters from Vidarna's tribe, I do not hold you responsible for your warlord's wrongs. But if you stay, I must know you to be true. I do not ask to be your warlord, but I do demand your loyalty if you stay under my command. If you cannot give me that, then leave now. You have my word that we will not harm you. If you choose to stay, you will swear your sword to me in Neju's name. The choice is yours, but it must be made now."

Nobody moves. Somewhere, someone coughs. I look from Gatha, staring down the crowd, to Vidarna's grim countenance, and then to the Shidadi fighters all around me. And I'm painfully aware that we could still end up destroying each other right here.

A woman clears her throat. Taja, the fighter from Vidarna's tribe who'd led the raid against Arxa, steps forward. "You have my sword, Gatha. Neju strike me down if I go back on my word." I try to imagine what it would feel like to risk your life on such a dangerous mission, only to find out your warlord has been undermining you. I wonder if Vidarna had tried to warn Arxa about the raid.

A sigh passes through the crowd. Another fighter steps forward and pledges his sword to Gatha, and then another. A woman I don't recognize says she will leave for the mainland, and Gatha tells her she must leave by the end of today. Most of Vidarna's fighters, though, make the decision to stay. One by one, the fighters take out their swords and bring Neju's wrath upon themselves if they lie. As I watch, I should feel vindicated, but instead there's something tugging at the corner of my mind. I feel like there's something I'm overlooking, almost as if I had a memory that's been buried. Images flash through my mind—the catapults and the tiny bundles of flour at the beach, Kiran's seal everywhere, and his ship on the waters. Why would the emperor be on the beach instead of on land with his men? I remember now the umbertouched soldiers at that outpost, and I wonder if they were all umbertouched. I think about Walgash's warning, *You don't know what our soldiers and our weapons can do.*

And suddenly, I know what the Amparans are going to do.

FORTY-THREE: ZIVAH

We leave Walgash with Arxa. The rest of us—me, Mehtap, and Sisson—travel south to Kiran's beach in search of Baruva.

The forest is quiet as we travel. It's the quiet of hidden threats, though, and the silence winds up my nerves instead of soothing them. I wonder how Arxa fares back where I left him. Is he still alive? And if we manage to find any evidence, would he believe it?

We travel as fast as we can. I ride the donkey, Mehtap has a mountain pony, and Sisson walks. Both Mehtap and I are limited by our illness. Several times a day, one of us has to stop and wait for a particularly bad headache to pass. When we're well enough to move, though, we go without stopping, eating meals as we ride and pushing ourselves not to lag. Occasionally, I see an herb that I want, and I direct Sisson to pick it.

Sisson walks close to Mehtap as we travel. Several times I see their heads bent together in quiet conversation. And once, when they think no one is looking, he touches her hand, and she looks at him with open, unguarded eyes.

LIVIA BLACKBURNE

During a rare stop to refill our waterskins, Mehtap speaks to me. "This is what Ampara is, isn't it? It took the plague for me to see the truth of it. The emperor cares only for his own glory, and those that get in the way are tossed to the side." She tilts her head thoughtfully. "Why did the gods decide to make him emperor? Why did they make you Dara and make me Amparan? Is it the same way they decide who gets struck with the plague? Sometimes I think our lives are just one big dice game to the gods."

Her plainness of speaking makes me scared on her behalf. Say what she might, Mehtap is still a general's daughter. "Have you thought fully about the consequences of what you're doing?" I tell her. "If your father believes you, you'll be driving a rift between your family and the emperor. You know what Ampara does to her enemies. Are you willing to pay that price? Are you willing to have your father pay that price?"

"My father would not want to serve a lie, whatever the price. As for me, my days are numbered no matter what I do."

My days are numbered. She says it so matter-of-factly, and my eyes drift to Sisson a short distance away. Mehtap follows my gaze, and her serene smile gives me permission to ask.

"He's more than a friend, isn't he?"

There's a glow about her as she speaks. "You come to know your companions well, when you're traveling across the empire."

Sisson looks over at us, and I have a feeling he knows we're talking about him. I can't help but wish I knew more about him, and whether he could be trusted.

Mehtap laughs. "There you are, being the protective older sister. I can see it in your face. But what can he gain from being with me? I won't live long enough for him to curry any favor from my father. And if he simply wants someone to entertain himself with, well, there are plenty of girls who don't get splitting headaches in his embrace, and who don't have powerful fathers who will defend their honor."

She does have a point.

Her eyes turn solemn. "He knows what I've done, and he hasn't given me away."

"You told him?" What reassurance I felt before evaporates. The girl is too trusting.

"He guessed," she says. "He said I wore my guilt like an over-burdened camel whenever the emperor was mentioned." She rolls her eyes. "Romantic, isn't it? He told me he would leave it up to the gods to judge my past, and that he's only concerned about the present and future." She continues, more subdued. "To be honest, what I worry most about is whether it will be too hard for him when I'm gone."

Dineas's face appears in my mind's eye, and I blink it away.

Mehtap gives me a knowing look. "But I came to realize that if I love Sisson, then I need to trust him to make his choices wisely. I can't protect him from grief, and it wouldn't be right for me to do so."

It's clear that she's speaking more for my benefit than for hers. "You disapprove of how I've treated Dineas," I say.

"I've wished happiness for the two of you since the early days of our friendship," says Mehtap. "Long before I saw you turn him away in the emperor's garden." She smiles when I raise an eyebrow. "Yes, I overheard the two of you speaking that night. You have a good heart, Zivah. You want to control every-thing. You want to protect everyone, but you can't, even in the best of circumstances. Let Dineas decide what he's willing to risk."

"And me, what should I decide?"

She smiles. "You should decide on the world," she says. "Feel everything. Experience everything while you can. Trust me, I know. I was locked up like a proper lady even before the plague hit me. If I hadn't stepped out of those walls. I wouldn't be here. I wouldn't have met Sisson." She looks at her palms and spreads her fingers wide. "Rose plague might keep us from living a long life, but it can't keep us from living a full one."

FORTY-FOUR: DINEAS

"The Amparans are going to infect the Dara with rose plague," I say.

Gatha stares at me. "What are you saying?"

I don't blame her for thinking I've lost my mind. It all seems crazy to me as well. "When I scouted the Amparan outpost on the western beach, I found catapults on the beach and a tent filled with bags of flour. Why would they have catapults when we have no city walls to breach? And the bags of flour were small, more suited for a household's use than to feed an army. It was strange, but I didn't think much about it at the time. Then Zivah told me tainted flour was what Baruva used to infect Arxa's troops. Thing is, though, the flour doesn't have to be mixed into food to infect someone. Bags that small can be catapulted into the air and shot so the flour gets dispersed over the people below. I promise you, the battalion's dragging those things through the mountains now toward the Dara camp."

"Are you sure of this?" says Gatha.

"As sure as I can be. You must decide whether to trust me."

Gatha's quiet a good long while, her chin in her hand as she studies a spot on the ground before her. Finally she looks up at me. "What would we need to stop this attack?"

"There are roughly a hundred soldiers, probably all umber-touched. If I had to make a wager, I would say they're all headed there. We need to get to the Dara camp before they do and empty it of everyone inside. And then we need to destroy the catapults and burn all their flour bundles. For that, I'll need the help of every umbertouched fighter we have."

Karu steps forward, a fiery expression on her umbermarked face. "I misjudged you, Dineas, and I won't do so again," she says. "I will fight under your command." I don't miss the significance of this—a warlord volunteering to follow my orders—and the sharp intakes of breath around me show that others don't either.

Gaumit is the next to step out. "I, as well."

"Thank you," I say.

I look around, but the rest of the faces around me are unmarked. Three of us against an entire battalion...Neju help us.

"You have your umbertouched fighters," says Gatha, "but I won't divide our troops after all that's happened. We all march to the Dara camp, and we'll all defend the evacuation."

Within an hour, every fighter is ready to go. We have less distance than the Amparans to travel, but that means very little since we have no idea when they started. Gatha sets a grueling pace, following the length of a wide valley that gets narrower as we march. Once night falls, the going gets trickier, but we push grimly on, one step in front of the next until the moon sets, and Gatha finally allows us a few hours of rest.

Dawn brings more marching. Finally the two walls of the valley meet in a half-moon cliff that towers in front of us. It's hard to spot the camp at first, but eventually I see movement in the bamboo ahead—a flash of tunic, a shifting in the leaves. There are no sounds of fighting, and I breathe a sign of relief.

A runner comes to greet us as we come down the trail.

"I need to speak to Tal," says Gatha. "Right away."

"And Kaylah," I add. Gatha nods.

As the runner goes off in search of them, villagers gather around us. I see young and old Dara faces, equal parts curious and scared. Though the Dara have never been an extravagant people, it's clear that they're living even more simply than before. Everyone wears old, beat-up clothes, and some of the women have given up their aproned dresses for tunics and trousers. Children have unkempt hair and dirt on their faces. I look around for Zivah's family, but I don't see them.

Then the crowd parts, and Tal strides toward us with Kaylah on his heels. "Gatha. What has happened?"

"We need to speak, alone," says Gatha.

Tal raises his eyebrows, but he and Kaylah follow Gatha and me a distance away.

"I hope that was truly necessary," says Tal when we stop. "It's not our custom for the leader to keep secrets from his people."

"You'll tell them soon enough," says Gatha. "We need to empty this camp. There are Amparans coming, armed with plague-infested weapons."

Tal's mouth drops open.

Kaylah takes a half step forward. "What kind of weapons?"

"Tainted flour," I say. "They plan to lob bags of it into the air and scatter it over the camp."

"You're sure of this?" asks Tal.

"Sure enough to march our fighters here through the night," says Gatha.

Both Tal and Kaylah fall quiet as they digest the news.

Tal breaks the silence first. "How much time do we have?"

"We don't know," Gatha says. "Act as quickly as possible, and, Kaylah, if there's anything you and your fellow healers can do to protect us..."

Kaylah nods, assuming an air of authority. "We need to store food and water in earthen jars, and every jar must be filled and sealed well enough to survive a fire. Everyone should be instructed to ready their heaviest cloaks, gloves, and scarves, to wear if we're attacked. I'll consult with my fellow healers as well, but this is where we should start."

Tal steps back and starts delivering orders. As Kaylah rushes off, Gatha signals for the Shidadi to gather around. "I need scouts," she says. "Scouts and crows to go in all directions. We're looking for a battalion of a hundred or so men with catapults and bundles of flour." She sends out twenty scouts in groups of two, each with a crow.

After the Shidadi scatter, I walk through the camp looking for Zivah's family and trying to get a better sense of the terrain. The residents have taken pains not to leave much of a mark on the forest. Most of the bamboo still stands, though small patches here and there have been cleared for gardens. I wonder what crops they're planting, given that they never know how long they'll be able to stay in one place. A few families have strung up mats of leaves between stalks for shelter, though they wouldn't last long in a hard rain, and wouldn't provide much cover if plague were to rain down from the sky. As word spreads, I see more and more people frantically packing and setting out clothes.

Finally, I glimpse a familiar face—Zivah's sister Leora crouches underneath a mat, folding clothes. Her belly is so large now that I'm convinced the baby could come out this second, and I wonder if she should really be squatting in her state. She sees me coming and stands nervously, putting a hand to her back as she straightens.

"Zivah is alive," I say. "And she's back in Monyar."

Relief floods Leora's face. "Is she well?"

She's alone in a cave with a dying Amparan commander, in a forest infested with Amparan soldiers. Even if those soldiers don't find her, even if she survives this war, she will still die.

"As well as can be expected," I say.

Nearby, Zivah's father and a man who I guess is Leora's husband have untied a large piece of cloth from some stalks of bamboo and spread it out for folding. "Keep that out," I tell them. "Use it to cover yourselves if there's an attack."

"Dineas!" Alia runs up now. Her braid bounces wildly, and her clothes are covered in patches. "Will we have to fight the Amparans?"

"Let's hope not," I say, remembering my promise to Zivah. "A fight is nothing to wish for." A flash of annoyance crosses Alia's face, but a runner comes by before I can give it much thought.

"Gather in the meeting place for news!" he shouts.

Leora gives me a questioning look. "So soon? Wouldn't our time be better spent gathering our belongings?"

All I can do is shake my head. News that comes so quickly doesn't bode well. "Where's the meeting place?" I ask.

"This way, I'll take you," Alia says, and pulls us in the direction the runner had come from. Other bewildered people walk the same way, though most of them pass us because we go at Leora's pace. We reach a patch of forest that's less thickly wooded. Dara sit in clusters between the bamboo, whispering among themselves. A handful of Shidadi stand along the perimeter, fingering their weapons and scanning the forest. At the front of the crowd, Tal stands next to Gatha.

Tal raises his hands for people to quiet down. "I'm sorry to call everyone out here so soon after the order was given to move camp. Our situation changes with every new report from our scouts."

Murmurs greet his words. It's strange to me how open Tal is in sharing information with the village.

Tal raises his hands for silence. "We learned this morning that a traitor has revealed the location of our camp to the Amparan army. We suspected that an umbertouched battalion of a hundred soldiers was headed toward us, armed with the rose plague. As we've prepared to move our camp, Gatha sent out scouts to locate them."

The crowd falls into nervous silence.

"The scouts didn't find the umbertouched battalion," says Tal, "but it appears that the main Amparan army, equipped with the traitor's knowledge, has moved much more quickly than we anticipated. There are ten thousand troops less than a day's march away, and they have blocked off our path for evacuation."

FORTY-FIVE: ZIVAH

We don't encounter any Amparan scouts as we near Kiran's beach. At first I think it's a stroke of luck to get so close without a warning call from Scrawny, but no one's fortune is this good.

"Something's not right," I tell Mehtap and Sisson.

Still, there's nothing to do but to keep going. When we finally get to the cliff overlooking the water, we realize why we've met no scouts.

"They're all gone," says Mehtap.

Signs of the soldiers are everywhere—rocks have been trampled into the mud, scraps of fabric blow in the wind, and ashes from old campfires are scattered over the sand—but there is not a single person here.

"You're sure Baruva was here?" I ask Mehtap.

"Walgash said he was," she says. "But the entire battalion must have moved on."

An entire umbertouched battalion has begun to march, and the Amparans know where my people are. I feel as if I've swallowed a stone.

"Maybe they left some clues," I say, and step out onto the

trail. It's rocky and steep. Seagulls hop on the rocks below, picking at the detritus left by the army. We hike down carefully and then spread out to look for clues.

"There was a large tent set up here," says Sisson, pointing to a spot where the rocks had been cleared away.

"It looks the same size as Baruva's tent at Taof," I say. I bend down to pick up a length of yarn as long as my finger—the tassel on a fine silk rug. Apparently Baruva's still fond of his comforts. "Are we sure Baruva left with the battalion? I can't see him as a battlefield healer."

"I'm not sure," says Mehtap, "but I don't know where else he might have gone."

I suppose she's right. "Perhaps we can still catch up to them."

It's easy enough to follow the battalion's path. One hundred men dragging equipment don't hide their tracks very well. The tracks are fresh and get fresher as we go. As we add our footprints to the ones already there, mud from the churned ground sticks to our shoes and stains the bottom of our trousers. Finally Scrawny calls a warning, and we slow down.

Sisson volunteers to scout, loping away with the efficient grace of a professional soldier. He returns with a satisfied smile. "He's set up his tent at the edge of camp. I saw him walking around—not so fond of the soldiers from the expression on his face."

"At the edge of camp?" I ask. "Not separate from them?"

"No," says Sisson.

"How many soldiers nearby?"

"A good twenty right outside his tent," he says.

Truth is, getting Baruva away from the soldiers was the one part of the plan I hadn't figured out.

"We can go in after it's dark," says Sisson. "Sneak into his tent."

"We'd have to find a way to subdue him and carry him out without waking anyone," I say.

"You could give him a sleeping potion," says Mehtap.

"I could, but I don't have enough darts for all the soldiers around him."

We fall silent. Mehtap rubs at her temple. Sisson lays a concerned hand on her shoulder, and she acknowledges it with a pat.

An idea comes to me. "Sisson, do the soldiers share a group privy?"

He raises his eyebrows at my question. "I wasn't looking for one, but general protocol is to dig an open trench a short distance from camp."

"And all are required to use it, right?"

"Yes. Makes the rest of the place a lot more pleasant for everyone."

"It's just a hunch," I say, "but Baruva doesn't strike me as the type who will stoop to sharing a privy with a crowd of soldiers. It just might be worth it for him to sneak away without his bodyguards. Let's watch this area for a few hours. I'll go west with Scrawny, and you two go east."

Mehtap frowns. "Are you sure?"

"It's the best way to cover the area. I feel fine, and I'll have my blowgun." I try my best to look confident. It's true, though, that my fever seems to have given me a few hours of respite.

Sisson wavers for a moment, but simply says, "Send the crow if you run into trouble."

The forest is quiet as I head west. There are none of the usual birdcalls in the branches around me. That, along with the abundance of trampled vegetation, makes me believe that there's a battalion of soldiers nearby. I walk a little ways before ducking behind a thicket. I'm too far to see the camp from my hiding place, but hopefully I'm close enough to intercept anyone that Scrawny sees.

Scrawny calls twice over the next hour, but it's for scouts both times, and I duck low as soon as I see their armor through the leaves. Finally, Scrawny calls again. This time, instead of armor, I glimpse a finely woven golden-brown tunic. I feel a twinge of recognition. That outfit still isn't well suited for hiking the forest, but better than his embroidered robes, I suppose.

Baruva makes his way gingerly through the bamboo, his nose wrinkled in a permanent expression of distaste as he looks this way and that. I trail him, staying as far back as I can without losing sight of him. Finally, he stops, looks around one more time, and ducks out of view. I speed up now, putting on gloves and getting a dart ready for my blowgun.

Baruva's head appears again through the leaves. Stepping slowly, I take aim, though my traitorous arm won't stay still. I take a breath, hold it, and shoot. The dart goes wide, and I suppress a cry of frustration.

As I grab for another dart, Baruva looks in my direction, and his eyes open wide. He stands to run.

No. The thought of him getting away again lends speed to my hands. In one quick movement, I aim and shoot again.

He slaps the back of his neck with his palm, and then he falls.

FORTY-SIX: DINEAS

It's a while before the crowd quiets enough for Tal to give us more details. The camp is built at the base of a half-moon granite cliff facing southeast. The trails that lead up the cliff are steep and narrow, which makes the campsite easier to defend because you can only move in from the south, along the valley. At the same time, we didn't think the valley was so small as to become a trap. What we'd failed to take into account was the sheer size of the Amparan army, and how close they were able to get without us seeing. With a big enough cover, even the widest of bowls can be turned into a flytrap.

With escape to the southeast blocked off, our only way out is to climb the trails up the cliff and hike down along the ridge. It's hard travel, especially for the young and infirm, and people will only be able to go two or three abreast. It will take many days to get everyone out this way, and we'll have to hold off the army in the meantime.

I keep wondering about the scouts' reports. Why couldn't they find the umbertouched battalion? Where could the battalion be, if not here? I suppose at this point it doesn't matter. I'd been so worried about plague weapons, I'd forgotten to worry about anything else, but this is a grim reminder that rank-and-file Amparan troops can leave us just as dead.

After Tal dismisses the gathering, some of the Dara race back to their campsites, while others huddle and console each other. Leora stands wordless, one hand on her belly.

Alia looks up at me. "I may have to fight after all."

Though I'd been fighting for years at her age, her words make me sad. "We might not need you. We're not as big as the Amparan army, but we still have several hundred fighters. With a well-planned defense—"

This time, the anger across her brow is much harder to miss. "That's not what you said before."

Her rage catches me off guard. "What?"

"You had no problems with me fighting when you were teaching me. Zivah made you promise to keep me safe, didn't she?"

I rub at the back of my neck. She knows her sister well. "She's worried about you."

Alia tosses her braid over her shoulder. "So you want to hide me away like some useless bauble? I've seen the way you Shidadi look at us. Like we're a burden, a village full of children to be taken care of." She stomps her foot. "This is my home too. These are my people." Before I can reply, she takes Leora's hand. "Come, Mother and Father will be looking for us."

Leora shoots me an apologetic look over her shoulder as they leave. I wonder if I should follow, but Gatha's here in the middle of a crowd of Shidadi. She acknowledges my approach with a nod as she gives instructions to one of the chief Dara builders.

"Put up the fence," Gatha says to the woman. "At least we had the foresight to construct the walls, but let's not use them until we must."

The "wall" is an earthen berm around the camp, and the "fences" are rows of sharpened bamboo stakes to be erected in front of it. Everybody knows, though, that defending those fortifications would be a last stand.

After the builders leave, Gatha waves me over. "We must slow them down," says Gatha. "Buy time for everyone to escape and disappear. Karu's tribe will defend these fortifications. The rest of us go out to meet that army. We'll wreak havoc on their camp and do all we can to cause disarray. We're an army of hundreds against an army of thousands. But we will make it look to them as if they're fighting a force of ten thousand."

SUNDOWN FINDS me with fifty other fighters, face smeared with mud, creeping along the hills overlooking the edge of the Amparan camp. Occasionally, the wind blows hard enough that we can see campfires through the leaves. I know, from an earlier glimpse, that they're camped in clusters of ten, and about half have their weapons on them right now. This part of the camp carries the standard of the third battalion from Sehmar. Word around the palace was that their commander gained his position through ingratiating himself with the old emperor instead of rising through the ranks. He's rigid in his thinking and cuts corners when training his troops, drilling them in old-fashioned formations that don't make sense in this wooded and uneven terrain. If we drive at their weaker fighters, the others will fall as well.

Our crows fly overhead, warning us of any approaching enemy. Already, one Amparan sentry has been silently disposed of. That means, though, that the clock has started to run, and we'll need to attack soon. Waiting is the worst part of an ambush. My muscles refuse to uncoil. I'd much rather be fighting.

Gatha crouches a few paces ahead of me, motionless. She's in one of the few positions with a view of the valley below. I don't know where she gets her patience, but she's steady as the rocks on the mountain. Somehow that discipline overflows to the rest of us.

"Archers," she says. "Three volleys."

I draw my bow—a new one from one of Karu's fallen fighters—and fire three arrows one after the other into the sky over the camp. The soldiers around me do the same. Shouts drift toward us as the deadly rain makes contact.

"Go," says Gatha.

Amazing how a single word can get my blood racing. I charge, caught up in the momentum of my fellow fighters, and I pray that Neju is on my side this evening. Or if not him, then Zenagua.

As I reach the floor of the valley, I get my first clear view of the Amparans. The camp is in confusion after our arrows. Soldiers struggle to strap on their armor and weapons and step into some semblance of a formation. I draw my swords and charge full pitch into two Amparans, bringing my left arm up to block one man's blow. My right sword blocks the other's and then arcs back down to cut him across the throat. He falls, and another man takes his place.

It becomes a rhythm of block, strike, turn to meet the next soldier. Some are better fighters than others. One man's face morphs into Arxa's. He almost slices off my hand, but a Shidadi next to me stops the blow and runs him through. There's no time to think before the next man comes. That's the problem. They keep coming, and the new troops are far less confused than the ones we charged. Our forward progress stalls.

Finally, I hear the blessed call for retreat. We fall back in ragged bursts. I knock the sword out of an Amparan's hand, then run back a few steps before turning to meet another soldier coming at me. Gatha's a few steps ahead of me, fighting her own retreat. Out of the corner of my eye, I see someone stab her in the thigh. She goes down.

"Gatha!"

It feels like an eternity, edging my way closer to her. A sword flashes to my right. I'm too late to block it, and searing pain burns across my rib cage. I scream, doubling over, though I'm vaguely aware that I can still move. Step by step, I move closer to Gatha and thread my arm under her shoulders. Other Shidadi close ranks around us. Little by little, we edge our way toward the forest, until a volley of arrows over our heads thins out the Amparans still coming after us. We turn and break for the hills.

FORTY-SEVEN: ZIVAH

Sisson carries Baruva over his shoulder to a cave we'd scouted on our journey here. Mehtap stands guard while he unceremoniously dumps the healer onto the floor.

"What do you need?" Sisson asks me.

I look down at Baruva crumpled in the dirt. "Water, mortar, and pestle. A small fire, once it's dark enough to hide the smoke. Bring out the herbs we gathered on the way as well. We don't have long before they realize he's missing."

I instruct Sisson to spread out the plants he gathered for me on our trip. "I need you to be my hands." I realize as I speak that Baruva used the same term for the slaves that did his work. Today, though, Sisson protects my patient instead of me.

Among the herbs we've gathered is a small, thin brown root, and I point to it. "Crush that one with the pestle."

Sisson is obviously new to healers' tools. He holds the pestle gingerly, but gamely gets to work. Milky white fluid oozes out of the pulverized root. "What does it do?" he asks.

"We use it to induce fever." It's the same herb I gave Dineas to fake his rose plague in Sehmar City. "Squeeze the juices into Baruva's mouth."

He takes ahold of Baruva's cheeks so that the man's mouth opens like a fish.

"Make sure it doesn't just dribble back out," I tell him.

After the root, I nod toward the berries. "You'll have to work quickly to get the stain set and the juice washed off before he wakes. We don't need to cover everything. Only the parts of his skin that he can see."

The berries bleed a sweet-smelling red juice. As Sisson smashes them into Baruva's skin, I turn to the last ingredient, syeb flowers, and start the painstaking work of detaching the pollen pods from each flower and shaking the yellow powder into a bowl. I'm glad that rose plague affects the edges of my vision more than the center, or there would be no way I could do this. By the time I have enough pollen to cover a fingertip, Sisson is sponging the berry juice off Baruva. The resulting marks have a bluer shade than real rosemarks, but I hope the firelight will camouflage the difference.

Sisson raises his eyebrows at the finished outcome. "Not bad."

Indeed, the result is better than I'd hoped, and I push aside the misgivings that bubble up at the sight of Baruva drugged and painted before me. I'm bending the rules once more, and only the Goddess can judge me. "Now we wait."

We sit in the cave in hushed silence, watching our comatose patient.

"How is his temperature?"

Sisson checks. "Seems to be warmer."

After a while, Baruva starts to stir. He curls his fingers, and then bends and straightens his leg. I look to the cave entrance and catch Mehtap's eye before getting on my knees and creeping closer to the healer. "Wake up, Baruva."

He groans.

"Wake up. You've been asleep a long time."

Baruva opens his eyes a tiny bit, then closes them again. A

moment later, he forces them back open. His eyes focus on me, and slowly, recognition dawns on his face.

Mehtap's expression, as she comes to watch, can only be described as that of a snake who's cornered a mouse.

"Where am I?" says Baruva. I hear the panic in his voice. He puts his hand to his temple and winces. The fever root causes sharp headaches. "What have you done to me?"

"I'm surprised you need to ask," I tell him.

He looks down at his hand, and then he looks again. He starts to shake. "It's not possible. I was just—"

"You've been asleep a long time."

He shakes his head. "You wouldn't do this," he says. "You wouldn't use your disease as a weapon."

And now Mehtap comes to kneel next to me. "Hello, Baruva," she says.

"Mehtap..." he says warily.

Mehtap gives a sweet smile. "You're right. Zivah wouldn't, but I would. Can you blame me, after all the trouble you've caused?"

Baruva wipes the sweat off his forehead. "When the emperor finds you, nothing will save you from his wrath."

"Perhaps," says Mehtap. "But you must admit I have very little to lose, and you'll be dead."

Slowly, horror spreads across Baruva's face. It's the look of a man who's just realized that all his efforts have come to naught. I know what a helpless feeling that is, and part of me almost feels sorry for him.

"You might not yet die," I say to Baruva. "Some people expel the disease from their bodies."

And now I take out the bowl of syeb pollen. I let Baruva see the yellow color in the firelight and hope that it's close enough to the real thing. If he's observant, he'll see that it doesn't quite have the same iridescent shine of suona. The smell of the syeb, though, is very convincing.

The imperial healer takes a long look at the bowl, and then he looks up at me, furious. "You demon," he says. "You did take it. How did you hide this from my guards?"

"You have a theory of how rose plague works, don't you? That it starts in the liver and spreads through the blood to the skin?"

He stares at me, sputtering.

"You're right," I say. "And you know what I've learned through my own studies? The suona pollen doesn't just help the rosemarked live longer. If you use it early enough, it will fight off the disease completely."

"Liar," he says, but he can't quite hide the hope in his voice.

I can't blame him, since I myself yearn for these lies to be true. I hope I've mixed in enough truth to reel him in. "It's up to you to decide whether you believe me."

His eyes track the bowl as I move it away.

"And I suppose you want something from me in return?" Baruva says.

"We want a confession," says Mehtap. "Signed in your own hand and sworn before all of us as witnesses. Include enough details to make us believe it's you. I want everything. Tell us all you've done, and all that Kiran's done. The history of your crimes, the documents that you received."

Sisson comes closer and hands Baruva a pen and a piece of parchment. Baruva stares at the pen. He curses, but he doesn't put it down.

"The choice is yours," says Mehtap. "But don't wait too long, or it will be too late."

FORTY-EIGHT: DINEAS

We limp back to the camp, carrying those who can't carry themselves. The Dara meet us with water, bandages, and food, and the Shidadi gather in clusters, nursing wounds, eating, and repairing armor and weapons. A Dara healer named Zad bandages the cut on my chest. The bandages feel restrictive, but he tells me to be grateful the sword didn't cut anything important. Next to me a healer from Vidarna's tribe bandages two of her fellow tribesmen. Among my own tribe, I see many cuts, one broken bone, and a dislocated shoulder. In addition, three were killed, Zenagua guide their souls.

Against an army that stretched as far as the eye could see, it could have been far worse. We killed far more than we lost, and caused mayhem on top of that. But it hadn't been enough. As things settle down, I climb the narrow cliff trail behind the camp until I get a good view of the valley. Amparan campfires wink between the leaves. Even after today's attack, they're confident enough to rest. And why shouldn't they be? Their campfires number more than our troops. We're gnats to them, a swarm to be swatted out. As for us? We're huddled in the darkness with arrows pointed over the wall. One thing I will say, though. The hours after that first attack evoke in me a deep pride for my fellow fighters. Others might be demoralized after such a battle, but the men and women that gather here tonight are focused on what lies ahead.

Footsteps crunch in the dirt. My hand jumps to my sword, but it's Gatha. She walks with a heavy limp and a cane, and joins me in looking down the valley.

"It was a valiant effort," she says. "I can't find fault with anyone."

"But it's not enough," I finish.

She shakes her head.

"Neju help us, then," I say.

Below us, the Amparan fires flicker like stars. I wonder what Gatha's next orders will be.

"Tell me something, Dineas," says Gatha. "Was I wrong to send you to Ampara with Zivah? I didn't foresee how high a price it would demand from you. Did I fail you as a warlord?"

I've seen Gatha make all kinds of decisions on the battlefield and off. She's given orders that have ended in devastating defeats, costing us dozens of lives and driving us farther away from our homeland. Not often, of course—she's good at war— but all the same, she's failed many times. Not once, though, in all these years, have I ever heard her voice any doubt. Not once have I ever seen her waver in that confidence the rest of us lean on. And I realize how much of a toll this past year has taken on her.

"You weren't wrong to send me," I say. Now that I look back on my mission, I realize how much good there was. The chance to see the world without the shadow of my past. Friendship, though it was with unlikely comrades. A fleeting chance for love.

"I'm glad to hear you say that," says Gatha. "It weighs on my conscience."

"My blade will always be yours."

"That I am also glad to hear."

I believe her. But even so, I know she'll never ask for my loyalty again. Her guilt won't let her.

She leaves me there, looking out over the Amparans. I don't know how long I stay there, but the sky starts to turn gray.

"Is someone there? Please help!" The panicked voice comes from higher up on the trail.

I draw my sword. "Who's there?"

"The scouts sent us down." It's an old woman talking. "They said we could find healers here. Please help. My husband's wounded, and we've been walking for hours."

I can see them coming down the path now, an old Dara couple. The man has a cut on his leg. I hurry to their side and swing the man's arm over my shoulder. "Why were you on the ridge? Everybody is supposed to stay in the camp tonight. More people can leave in the morning."

"The soldiers," she says. "The scouts warned us to turn back, but we were too slow. The others were cut down."

Soldiers? Cut down? And I finally realize with horror that this couple was part of the group that fled by the cliff paths earlier today, the first wave to leave.

"There were soldiers on the trail?"

"Amparan soldiers," she says. "With mules carrying giant loads, climbing the ridge trail."

The umbertouched battalion. So they'd taken the strenuous march up the cliff, hauling their weapons with them. And they stand in the way of our escape.

"Gatha will need to hear about this," I say. "Did anyone else escape?"

"I don't know," says the old man. "We scattered into the trees."

The man stumbles twice on our way down. At the base of the trail, we find the camp in disarray. Torches have been lit and wedged onto hacked-off stalks of live bamboo. Shouts and commands overlap each other in every direction. Both Shidadi and Dara race around frantically as crows weave about their heads. A Dara boy rushes past me, and I grab him by the arm. "What's going on?" I say.

He looks at me, his eyes wide. "The Amparan army is advancing."

FORTY-NINE: ZIVAH

We leave Baruva in the cave to sleep off the fever. He'll wake in a few hours with a lingering headache and sticky skin, but should otherwise emerge unharmed. In the meantime, we need to get out of the area before the Amparans send out search parties.

Mehtap rolls up his confession and carefully tucks it into her belt pouch.

"Will it be enough?" I ask her. "What if Baruva denies writing it?"

"Father will believe me if I tell him I witnessed it."

"And then what happens after that?" I ask.

She closes her pouch and meets my eyes. "I don't know."

Once again, we go as quickly as we can. Our steeds are cooperative, and so are our bodies, for the most part. It's nearing dusk by the time we get back to my cave, but there's enough light for me to see that the entrance is still well camouflaged. The vines fall differently than when I left, and the undergrowth around the mouth of the cave has been slightly disturbed, but not more than I would expect from a few days of wind and wandering animals.

Carefully, I brush aside the vegetation. There's one snake clinging to a vine above the doorway, which I wrap around my arm. Inside, it's completely silent. The air is musty, with hints of smoke. It takes a while for my eyes to adjust to the darkness. Slowly, the features of the cave start to materialize. The fire has been kicked out, and the dirt is scuffed. My supplies piled alongside the far wall have been knocked over.

Arxa and Walgash are missing.

The hair on the back of my neck stands on end. "Start a fire," I call to those outside. "I need a torch."

I scan the cave again, but it's a small space. There's no place for anyone to hide.

"Is everything all right?" Mehtap's voice drifts in. "Is he all right?"

I wipe my sweaty palms on my apron. What happened here? Arxa had been feverish, barely able to stand. Had Walgash carried him away? Or someone else?

Torchlight flickers at the mouth of the cave. "Zivah?"

"Wait—" I say, raising my hand.

But Mehtap is already stepping in. "Can I see him? How is—"

She cuts off. Scans the cave just as I'd done a moment before. And then she blanches. "What happened?" she whispers.

By the light of Mehtap's torch, I can see bloodstains along the floor leading toward the entrance.

"I don't know," I say heavily.

"You don't know?" She looks around again, and her voice grows more shrill. "They can't have gone far." She runs out of the cave.

"Mehtap, wait!"

She ignores me. "Father!" she calls. I hear rapid footsteps, and then another piercing call. "Father!"

It's her panic that finally forces me to gather my wits. "Mehtap, stop!" I run out after her. Sisson stands at the cave mouth, staring after her.

"Where'd she go?" I shout at him. "She'll bring everyone within a league of this place down on us."

"Father!" Mehtap calls again, and I run toward her voice, dimly aware of Sisson behind me.

Finally, I catch up to her. She stands, panting, looking out into the dense woods. I grab her by the arm. "Quiet!"

She wrenches her arm out of my grasp. "If any harm has come to him..."

"We don't know if it has," I say. "Maybe Walgash took him somewhere safer." But the blood, and the mess.

Four Amparan soldiers step out of the trees. One aims a bow at us. A cold sweat breaks out over my skin.

"We are rosemarked," I say. "Keep your distance."

The soldier closest to us curses. "Both the women are rose-marked. Not just the healer."

The healer? But I'm not wearing a sash.

Mehtap raises her hands. "I'm Mehtap, General Arxa's daughter. Is my father with you?"

The first soldier gives a bark of a laugh. "Your pedigree won't help you with us."

And then I realize that these soldiers aren't wearing standard Amparan livery. They're dressed in nondescript but fine armor, just like the men who'd killed Sarsine. Kiran's men. Had they seen us at the beach? Did they track us from the camp?

"Imbeciles," says Mehtap. She speaks imperiously, though I can sense the fear behind it. "If you lay one finger on me and my father finds out, you and your family will hang."

The soldier's face hardens. "Shoot her," he commands the archer next to him. The archer hesitates.

"That's a command," the leader says.

The archer draws his bow. Mehtap flinches.

"No!" I yell.

A twang of a bowstring. A blur of motion, and Mehtap

screams. I look at her, steeling myself for what I might see, but she remains standing, and she keeps screaming.

In front of her lies Sisson, eyes dull. Blood streams out of the arrow wound in his chest.

Mehtap crouches next to him, collapsing into ragged sobs. "Not you. It's not supposed to be you."

She looks up at the lead soldier, bares her teeth, and runs at him. It's a strange sight. Small, unarmed Mehtap charging at a fully armored soldier. Perhaps that's why the archer is late to draw another arrow. Perhaps that is why Mehtap is already halfway to him before he shoots her in the stomach.

And now I'm the one to scream.

Mehtap stumbles, but she keeps running. The soldiers back away but not quickly enough. She flings her hand out toward them as she collapses. Several soldiers, including the leader, stare aghast at her blood splattered on their tunics. They draw their weapons, and I reach for my blowgun, though I know I'd only be delaying my death.

A familiar voice booms out from the trees. "Disengage!" It's a voice that's used to giving orders and used to being obeyed.

Miraculously, everybody stops. The man who'd shot Mehtap backs away. I loosen my grip on my blowgun as the soldiers around me lower their swords.

Arxa stands at the very edge of the battle, leaning heavily on a stalk of bamboo. He clutches his side with his hand, and his face is drawn in pain.

Nobody makes a sound.

Wounded and weak as he is, Arxa still carries an air of authority. His eyes travel from one man to the next, and then fall on Mehtap, lying on the ground in a pool of blood. He stares, his face twisting in disbelief as he staggers, then falls to her side.

"Mehtap. Why are you here?"

"Step away, General," says the lead soldier. "We have orders to execute her."

"Orders from who?" I've never heard Arxa sound so dangerous.

"The emperor," he says. "For treason."

"Leave her be," says Arxa, standing up. "I'll take this up with the emperor."

"We have our orders," the soldier says again.

"Leave her be," Arxa says again, his voice rising.

I can't breathe, and I can't look away.

The soldier sets his jaw and draws himself taller. "Step aside, General, or we will go through you."

"Go through me, then!" Arxa's challenge rings in the air.

The soldier hesitates, gathering his resolve. He raises his sword.

Arxa doesn't move, just stares him down. I feel another scream building up.

Then suddenly an arrow protrudes out of that soldier's chest. Two more fly through the air and skewer his companions. There's a flash of metal, and then the last man falls, felled by Arxa's sword.

Walgash comes out of the trees. My knees give way.

Arxa kneels again by Mehtap's side. "It's all right, my gem," he says, and his voice shakes. "Just stay still."

I look on in horror, wishing I had bandages even as my healer's instincts take stock. The arrow is embedded deep in Mehtap's abdomen. The blood spurts out too quickly. There is no way to stem this flow.

I see now that Arxa is doing the same thing, assessing his daughter's injuries with the expertise of one who's lived his life on the battlefield. "No," he whispers. It's the first time I've seen him even come close to losing control. He cradles her head in his hands, his gaze jumping from her face to her bleeding midsection and back again.

"Why are you here?" he repeats over and over.

Mehtap stirs in Arxa's arms. She directs a glassy gaze at him, and for a moment, she smiles. "Father."

Slowly, in fits and spurts, she inches her hand toward her purse. Her fingers are clumsy, and she drops it.

Arxa picks it up for her.

"Open," she whispers.

Arxa reaches in and takes out a rolled parchment. He grips it so hard that I fear he might crush it to dust.

"Don't fight a traitor's war," Mehtap says. "You deserve better."

Arxa unrolls the parchment and looks at it, uncomprehending. "What is it?"

"It will explain..." Mehtap says. Then her face takes on an expression of intense determination. "Father, I need to tell you. I've done something horrible...." She gasps in pain.

"Don't speak, Mehtap," he says. "Don't speak. I love you."

She screws up her face. I can tell she's going to try again, but then pain lances across her features once more.

She lays her head on her father's arm and falls silent.

FIFTY: DINEAS

The forest groans around our camp, a bedlam of cracking twigs, shuddering leaves, and thousands upon thousands of footsteps. Soldiers come out of the foliage along the entire width of the valley, advancing toward our walls until they stop just outside of arrow range. And there, they stay.

Over the next hours, more Dara flee back down the cliff trail. Some have been wounded by soldiers. Others bear injuries from falls as they fled. The lucky ones made it back unharmed but frightened. Gatha asks endless questions of those who return, trying to figure out if the tainted flour had been used against them. It's hard to know. No one had seen much in the confusion, but on Kaylah's advice, Tal confines all the returnees in quarantine.

I speak to the returners as well, gleaning every detail I can on the battalion coming up the trail. It's hard to untangle the conflicting stories, but it seems like a standard battalion of a hundred is headed our way, and they climb the trails with pack mules carrying wooden beams and bundles of what look like food. Their progress up the mountainside is slow, but they're probably less than a day away.

If they reach the top of the ridge, they could catapult the rose plague bundles over the edge. The tainted flour would rain down over the entire camp.

"You must stop them," says Gatha. "If they fire the catapults, then it doesn't matter whether we can hold off the army at our gates." We're standing together on the camp's fortifications. Below us, the main Amparan army waits in the valley, as numerous as the trees. They're all armed, with weapons at the ready, but they don't move. They're trying to frighten us, make us wonder when it will finally happen. I hate to admit it, but it's not altogether ineffective.

"Why would Kiran send his entire army after us if he had the rose plague planned all along?" I ask. "Why put his troops in harm's way if the plague will do his conquering for him?"

"Maybe he's not sure the rose plague would work," says Gatha. "Maybe he wants to keep us from fleeing. Maybe he doesn't want to use the plague weapons if he doesn't have to. Maybe he's fickle."

If the army breaches our walls, we die. If the battalion on the cliffs gets too close, we die. Zenagua must yearn for our company.

"When do you think they'll storm the walls?" I ask.

"I think they'll wait for dawn, but we must be ready for anything." She hands me a tablet. "Gaumit and Karu will go with you to the ridge. Seventeen other fighters without umbermarks have also volunteered to fight under you. I told them to meet you at the bottom of the ridge path in a half hour."

I look at the names on the tablet. Twenty against a hundred is far better odds than the rest of our fighters will have.

"You may have to order our unmarked fighters close to the plague weapons," says Gatha. "Be prepared for that."

That's a sobering thought. I wonder why it's so much easier to order someone into a fight than it is to order someone into a fight with rose plague.

A blast of horns sounds just then from below. There's a mighty shout, and the Amparan army surges forward. For a moment, I stare uncomprehending.

"They're attacking. Take your stations!" Gatha shouts. "Go, Dineas. This is not your place."

As I run down the back of the berm, Gatha shouts, "Arrows!" The twang of a hundred bowstrings sounds behind me.

If I thought the camp was in chaos before, this is a hundred times worse. Shidadi zigzag through the bamboo to their stations. Dara run to help as well—some toward the wall with spears, others gathering with shovels, buckets, and tools of every kind to fortify the walls.

"Arrows incoming!" someone shouts just as I catch a glimpse of flame through the leaves above me. I crouch at the base of a thick stalk of bamboo, throwing Gatha's tablet over my head and wishing for a shield as a rain of arrows comes down, some with fireballs at their tips. Screams echo as some find their mark. A few steps from me, a fighter from Karu's tribe falls with an arrow through his collarbone. Next to him, another arrow smolders in the underbrush. A small, familiar shape runs past me with a bucket of dirt.

"Alia!"

She stops in her tracks, her bucket swinging in a wild arc. She looks as if the slightest touch will knock her over, but she sees me, and her chin lifts.

"You shouldn't be at the front lines," I shout.

"These are my people. This is my life." She runs to the smoldering arrow, dumps dirt on it, and stomps it out.

Do I stop her? Carry her bodily back to her parents? Zivah would want me to, but I've seen the fire in Alia's eyes.

"Alia, wait!"

I take a step toward her. She shifts her weight from foot to foot, ready to flee, but I go past her to the fallen Shidadi from

Karu's tribe. His lifeless eyes stare toward the fortifications. I take his shield and hand it to Alia.

"Take this."

I can see her struggling to quell her disgust at taking a dead man's shield.

"Take it," I say, louder now. "Keep it over your head."

She sets her jaw and accepts the shield. I grip her shoulders. "If they breach the wall, take a sword from one of the fallen and fight your way out of here, you understand? Just as I taught you."

She nods.

"Neju guide your steps."

As she runs off, I hope to the gods I haven't sent her to her death. But there's no time to wallow in doubt. I'm still out here unprotected, and I have a job to do. Problem is, I don't know where any of my soldiers are.

Someone shouts my name as I run toward the ridge trail. It's Gaumit, his umbermarks stark in the light of the flames.

"We need to go," I shout. "Where's Karu?"

We find her waiting at the bottom of the trail, her weight on the balls of her feet, her one eye fierce. With her are Hashama and ten of the fighters that Gatha had assigned to me. I don't know where the others are, or whether they will come. "We don't have time. We have to go." I leave the tablet of names at the bottom of the ridge and scratch a message in the dirt for anyone else who comes later to catch up.

"Hashama," I say. "You're the fastest runner. Can you go on ahead and scout? Take Slicewing with you."

"For Sarsine," he says, as serious as always. For once, my expression is just as grim as his.

He charges up the side of the mountain while we follow at a slower pace. As we climb, we get a better view of the Amparans storming the walls. Arrows fly in both directions as Amparan soldiers run up the berm. When they're slowed by the bamboo stakes up top, Shidadi drive them back with long spears.

"Keep climbing," says Karu. "You can't help them by watching."

Easier said than done. We hike in the darkness with the death cries of our kin growing ever fainter below us. By sunrise, we're on top of the ridge. War still rages in the camp below, though we can no longer tell which soldiers belong to which army. The other side of the ridge overlooks the open ocean. A familiar ship floats in the distance. Apparently the emperor has decided to come closer to the fighting.

"Do you have a plan?" asks Karu. The salt-laden wind whips at her tunic.

"I'm working on it," I mutter.

Slicewing flies toward me, circling once over my head before landing on my shoulder. *Two hours away,* says the note she carries. I thank her and send her back.

I look at the narrow twisty trail on this ridge, and the boulders on either side. "We need dried bamboo. Lots of it, and twenty torches." There aren't many plants this high up, so I send soldiers back down the trail to gather some. "You have an hour," I tell them.

Meanwhile I start the others gathering the dry grass growing between rocks to use as kindling. I breathe a sigh of relief when an hour passes and the men I sent down the mountain return with armfuls of dried bamboo.

"Good," I say. "Separate them into batches and plant them along the path. Better if they're out of view."

Slicewing returns. A quarter hour away.

Everything depends on timing this right. "Give me fire," I say.

Behind me, someone strikes a flint and nurtures a small flame to life. We pass him torches to light, one by one. I take a lit torch, as do seven others.

"This better work," mutters Gaumit.

"It has to," I say. "The Amparans can't be this disciplined."

We take cover to wait. A crow caws in the distance. They're here.

"Light the bamboo!" I command. The eight of us with torches bend low and run each to a bamboo bundle. The dried stalks smoke as I hold my torch to them, making my eyes water, and then a small orange flame catches. I wait until I'm sure it'll burn, and then I run back a safe distance.

I'm hearing footsteps now, both human footsteps and the *clip clop* of horseshoes on rock. The first Amparans come around the bend and slow at the smoke. The procession stops and a few soldiers come forward to investigate.

The bamboo starts to pop. A few mules shuffle nervously.

"Arrows!"

We let loose a barrage of arrows as the fires we started gain strength. Pops and explosions fill the air. One mule turns and races back down the trail. Soldiers dive out of the way, while several of their slower comrades get trampled or tossed off the cliff. As chaos spreads, more mules bolt, losing their cargo and scattering the soldiers around them.

"Forward!" I yell. With a mighty shout, we charge, the three umbertouched fighters leading the way. As we get closer, the untouched fighters slow, though they still back us up with shouts and arrows.

Five Amparan soldiers take formation against me, Karu, and Gaumit. We don't slow, just raise our blades to meet them. I run a soldier through, and he falls to the ground. As I face the next soldier, I'm aware of Karu and Gaumit desperately battling next to me. More soldiers come. More fall. The wind shifts constantly, blowing smoke into my face, and then away. My throat burns. My eyes water with the effort of staying open. And then the wind switches again, and I realize there are no more enemy soldiers within striking distance.

I glimpse a large sack that's fallen off a mule. With a quick glance around, I grab it and untie the rope tying it shut. Small flour bundles spill out. I grab an armload and throw them into a fire. Small fireballs ignite with each one, and I back away with each toss. Then I open a second bag and throw them in too. Karu and Gaumit join me.

The volley of arrows behind me continues to fly. Several Amparan archers return fire, but we have the advantage of high ground and range. Twice, we're charged by swordsmen, but our archers thin out their ranks, and Karu makes quick work of the three who make it through. Farther down the trail, someone calls a retreat. The remaining Amparans flee down the ridge, and then suddenly it's quiet.

"Quick," I say. "Everything must be destroyed."

There are more bags strewn along the path, along with disassembled catapult parts. Most of the bags contain pouches of flour. Others have earthen jars, also filled with tainted flour. I wonder if these are supposed to fly farther than their softer counterparts. They go in the fire too. Handful by handful, we destroy it all. My face and my fingers grow hot from the flames. Finally, Gaumit brings the last batch. He starts to heave them into the fire, but I stop him.

"Wait. Don't throw them away." And I gaze out to sea.

THE CLIFF FACE is almost completely vertical. There's a reason the battalion took a three-day march up the mountain range instead of sailing here by sea. It'd be impossible to get that many men and all those machines to the top of the ridge from the beach below. But what about getting three Shidadi with jars of rose plague flour down the cliff face from the top of the ridge? Impossible, or just very ill-advised?

I peer over the edge, trying to ignore the shaky feeling in my legs. The wind buffeting me from three directions doesn't help.

I see a few ledges on the way down—four of them, I count. They should offer a chance to rest.

At least we have a lot of rope.

"Get the rope off these catapults." I gather three coils, knot them together, and tie the end to a sturdy boulder. I double-check each knot and then check them a third time. After that I tie a second shorter rope around my waist and affix that to the boulder as well—this one will catch me if I slip. The flour jars, I cram into a sack at my waist along with several more lengths of rope to use on the way down.

I grin at Karu. "Ready to climb?"

"No one has ever accused you of being too cautious," she says, dusting off her hands.

I lead the way, grabbing ahold of the rope and backing up toward the edge. "Neju help me," I mutter, and step off.

I don't know if it's my imagination, but the wind picks up as soon as I'm hanging in midair. The rock face is slippery below my feet, and the rope feels far too thin for such an enormous task. I keep my eyes straight ahead and lower myself hand over hand. The rope swings wildly from side to side, and the sky tilts. *Don't look down. Don't look around.* When my feet touch the first shelf, I pull myself in and take a long, shaky breath. Then I put my back against the rock face. The view of the ocean is impressive, but somehow I'm not in the mood to enjoy it. I tie a second safety rope to an outcropping here, and untie the first one to be pulled up by Karu.

It gets easier as I get farther down, though my arms start to ache. Granted, I'd be just as dead falling from the top of the cliff as from the middle, but it's still a much less nausea-inducing view. Finally, I touch down on solid ground and wait for my stomach to settle. Karu follows, and a very pale Gaumit arrives just moments before sunset. We're in a bamboo thicket, only a few dozen steps from the beach.

"What now?" Gaumit asks.

And here's the hard part. There's no good way to get onto the emperor's private ship. He has far too many soldiers guarding him. Swimming is out of the question in these waters, and taking a boat, even if we had one, would get us shot out of the water.

I turn to Karu. "You still have the emperor's seal that you took from Vidarna, right?"

She produces it from her bag.

"Let's see how far that seal can get us." I glance around. "I saw a rowboat on the beach."

"We're not going to row right up to the ship, are we?" says Gaumit.

"Have a little faith in me."

I whistle for Slicewing to scout, and then we make our way onto the narrow expanse of sand. The rowboat I saw earlier sits at the high tide line. I glance around, making sure it's dark enough to hide us from Kiran's ship, then run over to the boat. It's a fairly standard vessel with two benches stretched across the middle. I take out my earthen jars and wedge them underneath the seats.

"They'll search us before letting us on board, so we'll have to stash these where we can grab them after we're searched. Put yours along the path the boat will take when it's dragged back into the ocean," I say. "Your best guess for where you'd be able to get to it."

Karu buries hers in the sand so that all but the tops are hidden. Gaumit wades into the ocean and ties his jars to some submerged rocks. Slicewing gives a warning call then, and we hurry back into the bamboo thicket.

"Leave anything you're attached to over here," I say, and start piling my weapons on the ground, though I hang on to my knives.

Slicewing gives another warning call, and I see two soldiers coming down the beach. One bears a torch. *Neju help us.* I raise my hands in the air and step into view as Karu and Gaumit follow my lead. The soldiers immediately draw their weapons.

"We have a message for Emperor Kiran," I say. "Vidarna sent us, and we bear the emperor's seal as proof."

The Amparans approach us warily. "Let me see the seal," says the torchbearer. I do my best to project confidence as I hand it over. He takes it and inspects it on all sides.

I hold my breath.

The torchbearer gives a curt nod. "I'll signal the ship."

The other Amparan keeps a close eye on us as the torchbearer steps out toward the water and waves his torch in a signaling code I recognize from Neju's Guard. Lights from the ship wink back.

After a while, a longer rowboat lowers onto the water from the ship and glides toward us. I count five soldiers on board. Their leader wears the sash of a commander, though I don't recognize him.

"Are you sure the seal is authentic?" he asks the torchbearer as he steps out onto the sand.

The torchbearer hands him the seal, and the commander inspects it much as before.

"Vidarna was injured in the fighting," I say, "so he sends us in his stead."

Once again, we're subject to scrutiny. "Everyone who sees the emperor must remove his weapons," says the commander. He signals one of his soldiers to pat us down. The bastard finds both the knives in my boots and confiscates them. I see him take a dagger from Gaumit as well. When we've been inspected to the commander's satisfaction, he nods. "Come with us."

I'm kicking myself now for hiding my earthen jars in the other boat. Still, there are four more we might be able to get. Karu walks ahead of me, and I see her angling herself toward the jars she buried. I catch up with her, and as we near the jars, I trip.

"Agh!" I spit out a mouthful of sand and let out a string of curse words that raises a few eyebrows. Karu crouches down to help me, and I climb back to my feet, still cursing loudly.

"Watch yourself," says the Amparan commander.

"Sorry," I mutter. In the corner of my eye, Karu sneaks something underneath her tunic.

In the boat, it's us plus the five Amparan soldiers who came over on the vessel. I sit at the stern and watch as Gaumit casually leans over the edge and tries to grab a jar he'd tied to the rocks. It slips through his fingers and bobs on the water toward me. I'm about to make a grab for it when I notice the commander watching. There's nothing to do but watch the jar float away.

I'm trying my best not to gouge holes in the boat with my nails as we move into deeper water. We have no weapons and only one rose plague jar. How are we going to keep the jar hidden until we're in the same room as Kiran?

"Is Vidarna alive?" asks the commander from the prow.

"Alive, but too wounded to travel," I say. "Took an arrow in his thigh."

"And why send three of you in his place?"

"To make sure we convey the message correctly."

"I see," says the commander.

And then he draws his sword and slices Karu across the throat.

It happens so quickly that I don't have time to scream. Karu pitches over, her blood spilling onto the deck. I dive forward just in time to avoid getting decapitated by the soldier next to me and land next to Karu. She's facedown and twitching, and there's no time to think. I feel around her midsection until my fingers close around a jar. As the commander swings his sword again, I dive over the side of the boat.

Ice-cold water squeezes the air out of my lungs. The salt hurts my eyes. I can't see a thing, but I dive deeper down until I can't hold my breath any longer, and then I kick my way back up. I get a mouthful of seawater the moment my head breaks through. The ocean's surface dips and rolls. I can't feel my limbs.

I've gone farther than I expected. The rowboat is in chaos, and I can't tell if Gaumit is still alive. I turn my head to look for Kiran's ship and get another wall of salt water in my face. I go under again, my nose and windpipe burning, and it's all I can do to kick my way up to the surface. As I cough and sputter, I remember the earthen jar. By some miracle, I'm still holding it.

The shadow of Kiran's ship looms in the distance. It's far, but closer than the shore. Tucking the jar under my arm, I swim toward it. At least the waves help. Each swell pushes me closer. After a while, I stop trying to swim and just let the current take me. As the boat looms higher, I keep my head low and kick to adjust my direction. If I miss it on the first pass, swimming back against the current would be a lot harder.

As the next swell pushes me forward, I reach with my free hand for a span of netting along the side of the boat. My fingers close around a rough, slippery strand, and my arm nearly gets wrenched out of its socket as the current tries to carry me past. Gritting my teeth, I haul myself up the netting. The wind hits me like a thousand darts, and I will myself to move faster.

The boat pitches back and forth as I climb one-handed up the side. My fingers are so numb I can hardly feel the net, but somehow, I keep grabbing, and finally throw myself over the rail to find myself near the stern of the ship. Crates of messenger pigeons line the walkway, labeled with the destinations they were trained for. As two soldiers run at me, I grab one of the pigeon crates and throw it at them, then duck and slam into the first soldier's legs so he stumbles back into his comrade. In the confusion, I wrestle his knife from his belt and run him through. As he falls, I yank out the dagger and throw it at the other soldier. The blade embeds itself in his neck.

There's a door at the end of the walkway. I yank it open and step in, slamming it shut behind me and pulling the bolt. Of the six men in this room, five have weapons drawn. I hold the jar over my head. "Come any closer and I smash this against the wall."

Everyone freezes. I catch a better glimpse of the soldiers and the man they're guarding. Emperor Kiran looks as I remembered, young and strong, with his father's wide mouth and heavy brows. He wears military garb, even though he's currently sitting behind a large desk. I see a flash of recognition in his eyes.

"I took this from your catapults," I say to Kiran, still holding the jar high. "You recognize this, don't you, Your Imperial Majesty? If your men come near me, I will dust this room with the plague."

Kiran scrutinizes me. "Dineas, the Shidadi traitor. I lent you a handkerchief once to bandage your dying friend. Do you remember?"

"I do, Your Majesty. And then you invaded my homeland."

"And now you're here to save your homeland," he says. His voice is strong and his accent refined, as an emperor's should be. "That's brave of you, but misguided. You'll never make it out of this room alive."

"It'd be worth it," I say.

Kiran doesn't blink. "Your jar of flour won't go very far here," he says. "It's meant to be thrown and broken high up in the air. It won't do much if my men simply shoot you and it drops. It might not even shatter."

"That might be true," I say. "Or perhaps your men will miss, or I will not die right away. And I'll lob it to the ceiling with my dying breath."

"What do you want?" he asks.

"I want your men to signal to shore a command for all your troops to retreat. And I want an edict, signed with your seal, sent to Sehmar City announcing that you grant independence to Monyar Peninsula."

The signal is fleeting, almost impossible to see. It's a mere lift and twist of Kiran's fingers, and he doesn't even look away from me. But I see his guard shift his weight and it's just enough time to react. When the man rushes me, I dodge to one side and kick his legs out from under him. He crashes to the floor. I dart forward and grab a stone paperweight off Kiran's desk. Now I lift it up along with the jar, one in each hand.

"I wouldn't try that again, Your Majesty. I'm closer now."

Indeed, it's a big desk, but if I leaned over, I'd be able to touch him. He sits back in his chair, his eyes trained on me. I wish I could see more fear in them, but all I see is calculation.

"Are you really ready to die, Dineas?" he asks. "This could go differently. I could give you my seal and a letter to one of the outpost treasuries. You could live out the rest of your life a rich man in Mishikan."

I move the jar and the weight away from each other, giving myself distance to smash them together. "You know nothing of our people if you think you can bribe me."

Kiran doesn't reply.

"My patience grows thin, Your Majesty," I say.

Maybe Kiran sees something in my eyes, because he turns to one of his guards. "Send a torch signal to shore to stop the attack, and fetch a pigeon to Sehmar."

"Have the torchbearer stand where I can see him through the window, and have him relay the message right away. If there's any hint of another message being relayed out of my sight, I break the jar." I add, "Also, be sure you bring back a pigeon trained for Sehmar. If it's the wrong one, I break the jar."

A flicker of surprise crosses Kiran's face, and the first hint of doubt.

"I was an Amparan soldier, Your Imperial Majesty. I know your protocols."

Every muscle in my body is taut as Kiran's soldier leaves the cabin to relay the emperor's message. It's nerve-wracking, watching the message relayed outside as I try to keep an eye on the soldiers inside, but nobody tries anything stupid. I jump when the door to the cabin opens again, but it's just Kiran's guard, and he brings a pigeon I recognize from the Sehmar City cage.

"Your man did well," I tell Kiran. Once the torch message is sent, soldiers onshore will relay it to the army through pigeons or drums. "Now I need your edict for Sehmar City."

Kiran glares at me, but he reaches for a piece of parchment and writes the edict in a deliberate, fine script. He pushes it across his desk for me to inspect. One of his men tries to move toward me as I read, and I raise the jar in warning.

"Now stamp it with your seal," I say.

Kiran hesitates.

"Do it now."

He drips candle wax on the parchment and stamps it with his ring. Then, after another warning glare from me, he ties it to the pigeon's foot.

The door slams open, and someone comes barreling toward me, knocking me off my feet. My attacker—my very large attacker—falls on top of me, knocking the air out of my lungs. As I struggle to breathe, the man wrestles the jar out of my hand, then punches me in the stomach. Gods, the man can punch. Gagging, I blink the tears from my eyes and look straight up into Walgash's face.

Walgash? I stare at him, too shocked to move. Why is he here? I steel myself for a second blow, but he climbs off me. Umbertouched soldiers swarm around him and haul me to my feet. As I strain against their grips, General Arxa walks in.

Though the general stands with the support of the door-frame, his eyes burn with rage that's anything but weak. I back up despite myself, only to bump into the men holding me. Emperor Kiran watches and smirks.

"Why are you here, Dineas?" Arxa asks.

"Same reason as before, General. I want to free my people."

Arxa looks at the pigeon in Kiran's hand. He takes it from the emperor and reads the edict attached to the bird's foot. I try to swallow the stone in my chest, the urge to scream my rage. So close. I'd been so close.

Then Arxa rolls up the message, ties it to the pigeon, and releases the bird out the window.

"Arxa," says Kiran, and now I see true doubt in his eyes.

But Arxa ignores him. When the emperor's soldiers move toward the general, Arxa's troops push themselves in front of their commander.

Arxa turns to me. "There is a rowboat next to this ship with my men on it. They will row you to shore."

I gape at him.

"Do you hear me, Dineas?"

"I heard what you said, Commander." What kind of game is he playing?

"Do you know me for a liar, Dineas?"

"No, sir." That "sir" still comes out so easily.

"Then go before I change my mind."

I don't need to be told again. I catch a glimpse of Walgash as I edge toward the door—wildhaired, dangerous, his fist clenched. I can still feel the imprint of his knuckles in my stomach. At any moment, I expect Arxa to spring his trap, to signal his soldiers to execute me, but no one moves.

At the door, I turn to Walgash once more. "I told you my blood was Shidadi," I say. "But I wish you well, Walgash. I always have."

He stares me down. And then he jerks his chin toward the door. "Watch the threshold," he says.

I don't tempt fate by staying any longer.

FIFTY-ONE: DINEAS

A rxa's soldiers don't speak to me as they row me to shore. I'm pretty sure Arxa's command is the only thing keeping them from throwing me into the ocean. Still, they deliver me safely, and I wade onto land. I can't wrap my mind around what happened. Why did Arxa let me go? Why did he let Kiran's message leave the ship when he could have simply put the pigeon back in its cage? Saving his life doesn't seem like enough of a favor for him to betray his emperor so completely.

Once on the beach, I find and destroy the jars of plague we'd left there. Then I retrieve my weapons. Guilt overtakes me when I see that Gaumit's things are still there. He's likely dead, then, like Karu. I take Karu's gear, leaving Gaumit's in the slim chance that he's alive, and set out to find a way back to camp.

The return journey is much longer than the journey down, since I can't very well climb up the cliff. I walk south from the beach to find a passable trail up the ridge, but I only make it an hour before the last few days catch up to me, and I'm barely able to find an alcove in the mountainside before I collapse. It's evening by the time I wake.

Eventually I come across the path taken by the umbertouched battalion. It's pretty hard to miss the hoofprints and trampled ground that mark their passage. As I climb, I find several more bundles of rose plague flour, which I promptly burn.

It takes me two days to get to the place where we staged our ambush of the umbertouched battalion. Burned bamboo fragments lie strewn around the path, and again, there's no one here. I sprint to the top of the ridge and take my first glimpse of the camp below.

The first thing I notice is how quiet it is in the valley. There's no enormous army and no sign of battle. From this height, the earthen berms surrounding the camp are thin lines, and the walls of bamboo spikes mere twigs. Dread hits me when I see breaks in the line and places where the twigs have fallen. But I do see people walking around, small as ants. I hurry down.

I come off the ridge trail into a camp full of activity. Several Shidadi and Dara are cooking at a campfire, while a Shidadi man dumps clothes into a pot of boiling water. A Dara woman carrying bandages hurries past me. I'm wondering where to find Gatha when I see her limping toward me. Her arm is in a sling.

"Dineas, son of Youtab and Artabanos," she says, strong and sure as ever. "Welcome back."

GATHA TELLS me that the battle came very close to ending differently. Twice the Amparans knocked holes in the camp's defenses, only to be repelled by a concerted effort from the defenders.

"We wouldn't have lasted much longer," she says. "But suddenly a retreat signal was blown and the soldiers withdrew. We thought it was a ruse at first, but the army marched away and our scouts say they're still marching south. We could only guess at why. I'd heard from your fighters that you went after the emperor, and thought perhaps that meant you had some success."

I tell her all that had transpired on the emperor's ship. "It was a foolhardy plan. Got Karu and Gaumit killed."

"They died saving our lives," says Gatha. "Zenagua will honor that."

I breathe yet another prayer to the goddess of death. "What happens now?"

"We treat the injured. There are many, so it'll be a while before we can leave this place. I've given the order to treat the Amparan prisoners as well. When the time is right, we'll contact the emperor about their return."

"That's far better than they treated us." Though I know Gatha's mercy has strategic motivation as well. Live prisoners make much better bargaining chips.

"Dineas!" I turn at the familiar voice.

Alia doesn't stop running when she gets close, just throws her arms around me, knocking me back with the force of the impact. "You're safe."

She clings to me, and I thank the gods she's alive. Her braid looks lopsided, and I realize it's because the hair on the right side of her head has been singed short. Her right ear, temple, and the side of her neck bear deep red burn scars.

Alia raises her hand self-consciously to her burns. "I got a little too close to one of the fires," she says. "Kaylah tells me I'll have a scar."

"A scar is a mark of honor," Gatha says.

"Zivah wasn't happy to see it," Alia says, though she stands a little straighter.

It takes me a while to comprehend Alia's words. "Zivah's here?"

"She arrived yesterday," Gatha says. "She's living outside of camp."

"I'll take you," says Alia.

Gatha smiles as she waves me away.

Alia leads me south, over the berm and into the trampled forest, until the sounds of the main camp fade behind me. Though I'm curious to know her role in the battle, I don't ask. It's always better to let a soldier decide whether to relive a fight. Alia, for her part, is quieter than I've ever seen her. And while her eyes stay focused on the trail, she's not quite looking at it either.

I'm starting to worry when she finally breaks the silence. "I kept the shield over my head," she says softly. "Just as you said."

"Good. I'm glad."

She nods imperceptibly. "It was hit twice by arrows. Once in the middle, and once on the edge. The first time, the impact knocked me over. I didn't realize how fast and heavy the arrows would be."

"You kept your shield up. You did well."

She looks at me out of the corner of her eye. "A shield can only do so much, though, right?" she says shakily. "There were people all around me hiding under shields, planks, hides, anything they could get their hands on, and they still died." Her words come faster now. "One man got an arrow in the thigh, and then another one in his gut. He was so close I could have touched him."

"Alia—"

She charges on, one syllable running over the next. "And another woman got caught with a jar of burning pitch. And then there was another—" She stops. Clamps a hand over her mouth as she struggles to compose herself.

"Alia," I say again.

She hunches her shoulders. Her chin trembles. And I remember it's her first battle, her first real taste of war.

I put my hand on her shoulder, as Gatha would. "Alia, look at me."

Reluctantly she raises her head.

"You did well."

She dissolves into wracking sobs, and there's nothing to do but to help her to a boulder and rub her back as she cries into her hands. How old had I been when I saw my first death on the battlefield? The memory is hazy for me, a jumble of screams. I don't remember the details, but I remember the fear and the smell of blood. War's been part of my life for so long that I've lost sight of just how senseless it all is. And I wonder if it's too much to hope that we could be free of it. That this would be both Alia's first battle and her last.

A GOOD DISTANCE down the valley, a tent's been set up. Alia leads me within view of it.

"Give Zivah my love," she says. As she walks away, she turns around once more. "Thank you," she says, and then she disappears.

There's a fire burning brightly outside the tent. Wounded fighters lie around it, though I see no healer. As I come closer, the fire sends sparks toward me, and the flames dance a welcome.

Zivah ducks out from inside the tent, and my throat tightens. Her braid hangs over her shoulder, and her forehead is covered in a sheen of sweat. She squints in my direction. "Keep your distance," she calls. "I'm rosemarked." Then I step out from the trees. Zivah's eyes land on my face, and her mouth falls open. Something softens in her brow.

I step closer. "I'm umbertouched."

A hint of a smile pulls at her lips, though there's deep sadness in her eyes. A lifetime ago, when she'd found me in her shed, we'd traded the same words.

"You're alive," I say.

"As are you." There's the same exhaustion in her voice as I'm sure coats mine. We gaze at each other, as if both unsure that what we see is real. She gestures toward the wounded around her. "I convinced them to give me the ones nearest death. There aren't enough healers to go around."

"Never a moment's rest for you," I say.

"Not when there's work to be done."

"Did you find Baruva?"

She nods. Her lips quiver just the slightest bit, and she looks away. "Mehtap's dead," she says. "She died in her father's arms."

"I'm sorry."

She draws in a deep breath, composing herself. "She gave Arxa the evidence before she died. He didn't say anything to me after that, just left with Walgash. I don't know where he went."

"Arxa found his soldiers and boarded Kiran's ship while I was there," I tell her. "He could have killed me, but he let me go. I don't know what happened after that. I suppose time will tell."

She nods, and her eyes lose their focus. "Mehtap tried to confess her crime to Arxa as she lay dying, but she didn't have a chance. He may never know how the old emperor really died."

"Do you wish he did?"

She shakes her head. "No. There was much good in her, even if she lost her way at times. Better for him to remember her that way. I'm glad she was with her father when she died." Zivah wipes a hand across her eyes. "It's funny. We think, when we get the rosemarks, that we know our future. That we know how we'll die, but even that certainty is an illusion. Nothing's ever promised us by the gods, is it?"

There's nothing much I can say to that. So I simply wrap my arms around her. She leans her head on my chest, and for a moment, just for a moment, we rest.

FIFTY-TWO: ZIVAH

We hold our breath for days following the battle, fearing news of the Amparan army turning around and coming back north. Day after day, though, our scouts send back the same message: *Imperial army on retreat.* Within days, they return to Central Ampara. When the bridge of warships is dismantled, we finally dare to rebuild. The Dara return to our homes and begin the long work of putting the village back in order, building new cottages and redigging wells, remaking the fields that had been trampled, and flooding the ones that are now stained with blood.

My own cottage somehow escaped the worst of the battles. The door was ripped off the shed, and dirt had been tracked inside from some unknown squatter. But after a few days' work, everything is put back together, and I move back in.

Dineas comes to visit often. I'm always glad to see him, but as my health worsens, I'm not always good company. When my headaches confine me to bed, he sits with me and holds my hand. On good days, he helps me capture venomous creatures for my collection. Like many of the Shidadi, he's a bit at a loss for what to do now that there's no more fighting. A few times, he's mentioned wanting to see Mishikan, but he always has some excuse to stay.

Kaylah does what she can to help me. She mixes me potions to help with the headaches and tremors, many of them from Baruva's notes. We spend many hours talking about suona pollen, syeb pollen, and the possibilities for better treatments. The long discussions are hard on me, but I insist on having them. There are more experiments to be tried, more questions to answer. I fear that my time may run out before I can do everything, and I want to make sure someone carries on the work.

It should bother me, the progression of my illness, but as my death approaches, I find myself at peace. I think of the soldiers I treated in the wood, the people I've watched cross from this world to the next, those who fought, and those who went peacefully. I think of the soldier who said, *It's simply another journey.* I'd held his hand as he said it, made comforting sounds of agreement. But now I find that I actually believe him. When the time comes for my fever to take its course, I will be ready.

Kaylah and I have just finished a long discussion one afternoon, when my old master puts away her pen and looks at me thoughtfully. "When you were alone in the forest, separated from the rest of us, you treated the wounded Amparan soldiers you came across."

"That's right," I say. I'm not sure what she's getting at. My actions during the war are no secret, and fairly old news by now. I'm sure some people think me a traitor, but few people would openly condemn a woman already at death's door. "I didn't want to do it, but I couldn't not."

"That level of obedience to your vows is no small thing," she says. "Of all the Dara healers, you were the one who chafed the most against the Goddess's commands. Yet I never treated Amparan soldiers in the war, nor did any of the others."

I grip the arms of my chair and push myself shakily to my

feet. "Don't make me out to be more perfect than I am. I still used my herbs to coerce Baruva into confessing his crimes."

Kaylah tucks her notes under her arm and stands to leave. "Perhaps perfection is not what the Goddess asks for."

FIFTY-THREE: DINEAS

Watching Zivah fade is the hardest thing I've ever done. She tries to hide how bad it is, but I can see the strain in her face, the circles under her eyes. She was thin already from the war, and she gets even thinner now. On bad days, her hands shake so much that she can hardly get water to her lips.

The worst part is that there's nothing I can do. Kaylah, at least, mixes remedies to help, but I can only watch her suffer. If only the plague were a soldier that could be felled.

Despite my uselessness, Zivah still smiles when she sees me. She's asked me several times what I plan to do now that the war is over, and I think she feels guilty for keeping me here with her. If she expects me to leave her here alone, though, she's gravely mistaken.

One morning, we're out in Zivah's garden when Scrawny (who has basically become her bird by now) gives a big squawk and launches himself into the air. A few moments later, Preener lands in a cloud of dust—a grand entrance worthy of his long absence.

"Preener, you ridiculous bird," I say. "What news does Nush send now?"

The crow simply shakes the dust off his feathers. Zivah and I hold the note between us and read.

There is great unrest in Sehmar City. Commander Arxa has taken Kiran under guard and accused him of high treason against the empire. Generals and officials alike are taking sides, and it may be years before it is all settled. The imperial physician Baruva has gone missing. No one has seen him since he disappeared in the last days of fighting. Perhaps this beast of an empire can be felled after all. —Nush

Kiran taken under guard. Generals taking sides. It's hard to believe what's happened with the mighty Amparan empire.

Zivah folds up the note and hands it to me. "When the dust settles, Arxa could end up as emperor. What would you think of that?"

I think back to my last encounter with him on the boat, how surprised I'd been when he let me go, how confused. "I just hope I never have to face him in battle again."

Zivah's frowning now, and I put out an arm to steady her. "Headache?" I stand to fetch her some tea. I've become quite good at mixing Kaylah's brews.

She shakes her head. "No, I was just thinking. There's one thing that has been weighing on my mind since the war ended. I'd believed it out of my reach, but I wonder now if Nush can help me. Can you do something for me?"

"Only if it doesn't involve scorpions."

That gets a wan smile. "I'd like to dictate a note to Nush. But please, don't argue or question me over it."

"What could you possibly want to write that I'd argue with?"

I'd spoken lightly, but she's surprisingly solemn. "Will you do it? I could write it myself and pass it over the fire, but it's still safer if you write it. Your handwriting is better these days anyways."

I fetch a pen, ink, and parchment from her cottage, and we settle down under her awning.

Zivah takes a deep breath through her nose and rests her

hands on her too-thin legs. "I want to write two notes. The first one is to Nush. Tell him, 'Your news is encouraging. I hope the unrest hasn't put your people in danger. Do let us know if we can lend any assistance. I would like to request a favor. If you can deliver the following letter to Kione at the Khaygal rose-marked compound, I would be very grateful.'"

Kione's name catches my attention. I set the first note out to dry.

Zivah starts dictating again. "'To Kione. In Baruva's manor near Khaygal there is a garden with bushes trimmed like animals. Hidden within the branches of the trumpeting elephant is a jar of suona pollen. A pinch a day extends the life of the rosemarked.'"

I stop and stare. "Is this true?"

"You promised you would simply transcribe."

Yes, but I didn't expect her to reveal something that could keep her from dying. Zivah looks at me, pleading, and with great effort I stay quiet.

She continues. "'If your resourceful friends can obtain this for you, please share it among Baruva's former slaves. It should rightly be yours.'"

My pen slips, leaving a thin trail of ink. "You never told me about this."

She meets my gaze calmly, apologetically. "It was half a continent away."

"Where did you find it?"

"I found a note in Baruva's journals that made me think he had something hidden in his garden. I dug up the pollen, but I had to hide it before they captured me."

I stare at the parchment, wondering if I put my pen to it again, if I would crush the nib. "And you'll give it all to Kione?"

"It was never mine to give." She looks at me sadly, though I don't know why I'm the one being pitied.

There's a pounding in my ears. "You traveled across the

empire to find that pollen. It wasn't exactly an easy journey." I hear my voice rising. "Doesn't that mean anything?"

She shakes her head. "It was less than a year of my life," she says. "These slaves were with him for many more. Baruva built his wealth and his fame on their labors. The suona belongs to them."

"Maybe, but nobody would have known it was there if not for you." I can't believe she would let something like this pass through her fingers. I open my mouth to speak again, but then I notice she's crying. Well, perhaps not crying, but her eyes shine more than usual.

"Dineas," she says. "You said you were willing to let me go. Please don't make this harder than it already is."

I stare at her, take in the resolute tilt of her chin, the pleading in her gaze, and something inside me threatens to break. But I clench my jaw and finish the note. When she asks me to attach the parchments to Preener's leg, I don't put up a fight.

"Thank you," she says as the traitorous crow flies off.

I LEAVE Zivah's cottage soon after Preener flies away. She doesn't stop me, even though we both know I usually stay much later. But I need to be away for a while, somewhere she can't see me. Tomorrow I'll go back and be strong for her, but I need this afternoon to grieve.

I'd almost fooled myself into thinking I had come to peace with her illness. All those things I'd told Zivah about loving while we can and being unafraid of the consequences, I'd said it so many times I'd convinced myself as well. But after hearing about the suona pollen, that small ray of hope that Zivah won't even try to chase...all my grief and doubt come back.

I walk up the mountainside toward the Shidadi camp, but when I get close enough to see my kinsmen through the leaves, I turn and head farther up. I've no desire to see them right now. I get along fine with them since the war—I'm a hero now. The younger fighters look at me with awe when I pass them, and older ones quiet when I speak. But too many people have died in the past months for me to feel at home with my people. Tus, Frada, Gaumit, Sarsine, Stateira, Pouriya...The list goes on. Gatha's the only one remaining who still feels like family, and even with her it's not the same. We've disappointed each other too many times.

As I climb higher, the bamboo thins out and the wind picks up. I find myself atop a cliff again, the one with the altar to Yaras where I'd talked to Sarsine ages ago. The strait below looks empty without warships spanning its width.

I'd never leave Zivah to die alone. I'd spend a thousand years in the Amparan dungeons before I abandon her. But now the fears I'd kept at bay come back to prod me. We have a few weeks together, maybe months if Hefana smiles on us. And after she passes, what then? Where will I go?

Footsteps sound behind me. My hand is halfway to the knife in my belt when Hashama's voice calls out, "Dineas, it's me."

I relax my knife hand, though I can't say I'm thrilled to be found. I haven't forgotten the risk Hashama took to support me when everyone else thought I was a traitor. He is a good man, but I'd rather be alone right now.

"Hashama."

He comes to stand beside me and looks out onto the water. "Out here to think?"

"To think," I say. "And for some time alone to clear my mind."

I might imagine it, but I almost think I see a hint of a smile cross his face. Can't be, though. This is Hashama.

"I won't keep you long, then," he says. "I wanted to let you know that our tribes voted on Karu's and Vidarna's successors today. Taja from Vidarna's tribe will take his place. And Karu's tribe has decided to join Gatha's rather than return to Iyal."

I'm not that surprised that Karu's tribe has decided to join us. They were the smallest to begin with, and the war thinned their numbers even more. "And what about you? Will you go back to Central Ampara with Taja?"

He shakes his head. "I'll stay here."

I turn to him. "Really?"

"My closest friends in my tribe have gone to rest with Zenagua," he says. "It wouldn't be the same."

I know how he feels. "We'll be happy to have you."

"And what about you?" he asks. "What will you do?"

And there it is again, the question I don't want to face. "I'll stay here for now, until Zivah...no longer needs me. And I'll decide my place after that."

"There are plenty of places for you," he says.

"Thank you." But I wonder why I can't think of any.

Hashama rummages through a bag slung over his shoulder and pulls out a curved piece of scrap wood. "This is yours," he says.

I take it, though it doesn't look like anything I've ever owned. But the moment it touches my hand, my heart does a somersault, because I would know the feel of that wood anywhere, the finish lovingly maintained with oil and wax, the curves worn smooth from use. I turn it over, hardly daring to breathe, and run my finger over my mother's carved initials.

"I'm sorry it was broken," says Hashama. "But I guessed you'd want it anyway."

I cradle the bow in my hands, not quite believing it's real. "Where'd you find this? How?"

"Mansha from your tribe overheard Zivah talking about it. She roped me and a few others into combing that beach where you lost it. For some reason, they decided that I should present it to you, even though it was Mansha's idea, and a girl from Karu's tribe was the one to actually find it."

Mansha of all people. I don't think I've spoken ten words to her since I came back. "I cut off Mansha's ear last year in battle."

"So she told me," says Hashama.

I squeeze the remnants of the bow, at a loss for words.

"There are plenty of places for you," Hashama says again. "When you're ready." He stands up. "I'll leave you to your thoughts."

I reach to take his hand, but I jump back because his face shifts and blurs until Walgash stands before me.

We're standing just inside the door to our barracks, half-hidden behind the first bunk and several hanging cloaks as we spy on Naudar in the middle of his morning routine. Actually we're not very well hidden at all. No man Walgash's size can take cover behind a single bunk and a cloak, but Naudar's too engrossed in his grooming to notice us. It doesn't matter how early our training is, he always gets up early to wash his face, press any clothes that need it, and comb cedar-scented oil through his hair.

"I can't believe I let you talk me into this," I mutter to Walgash.

The big man simply grins. "Just look at that peacock. He has it coming."

Naudar frowns into his copper hand mirror and smooths his right eyebrow.

Walgash has a point.

Other soldiers pay us no attention as they get ready, too bleary-eyed to notice anything but what's right in front of their faces. Walgash elbows me as Naudar reaches for his jar of cedar oil and pours a small amount into his palm. He's rubbed one hand over his hair, when he stops and sniffs at his palm.

Walgash chortles silently.

Naudar sniffs his other palm. Fish oil from the bayside cities has a very distinctive scent. Then his head whips toward us as Walgash guffaws.

"Is this fish oil?" Naudar says, aghast. His eyes lock on us. "You two..."

As Naudar charges toward us, Walgash gives me a pat on the shoulder and beats me out the door. I follow, but my foot catches on the raised threshold and I go flying. As I spit dirt out of my mouth, the scent of fish wafts in my direction, and then Naudar is on my back raining blows on my shoulders, arms, and back. He's pulling his punches—otherwise I'd be dead—but he's sure aiming to leave bruises.

In the background Walgash laughs even harder. "Dineas, you clumsy dog. Watch the threshold!"

My vision clears, and Hashama is staring at me. "Are you all right?"

I take a few moments to blink the scene away. I wonder where Walgash is now. Is he fighting by Arxa's side? I wonder if our paths will cross again.

"I'm all right," I say. And I'm not lying.

Hashama gives me a long look and then apparently decides to believe me.

"Hashama," I call out as he's walking away.

He turns.

"Thank you."

There it is again, maybe the hint of a smile, before he continues down the trail. It makes me wonder if perhaps he'd smiled all along, and I just hadn't noticed.

FIFTY-FOUR: ZIVAH

I know I broke Dineas's heart with that letter to Nush. That moment when he realized what I intended to write, his look of sheer desperation nearly undid me. The raw pain in his eyes was exactly what I tried to avoid by resisting his courtship. But we've chosen our path now.

The wedge driven between us by that note doesn't stay there for long. After leaving early that afternoon, he comes back the next day and tells me I did the right thing. I suspect he's lying to make things easier for me, but there also seems to be genuine peace in his eyes. We don't speak of Nush or the suona pollen again.

A month after the final battle, Leora goes into labor. I'm a wreck, pacing the length of my cottage and demanding constant updates by crow. It's all I can do not to send Kaylah instructions for delivering the baby. Finally, after a grueling two-day labor, I get the long-awaited message.

A healthy girl! We will name her Elannah.

A week later, Leora brings her to see me. I make her stay ten paces away, and even then, I'm terrified. But the sight of the wrinkled little face with Leora's eyes and nose, suckling at her breast, heals parts of me I didn't even know had been wounded.

Over the next weeks, I have good days and bad. The headaches come strong some evenings, but other days I can forget my illness. I still experiment with herbs, and I still look for a cure, though I'm less reckless now than I used to be. Part of it is because I'm too weak to recover from any catastrophic failures. It's more than that, though. I simply don't feel the same urgency or desperation.

One morning, as I'm resting outside my cottage, I glimpse an unexpected visitor in riding leathers. The Rovenni trader Nush comes down my trail, with Preener on his shoulder. I stand to greet him. "I'm glad to see you, Nush," I say. "How are your people?"

"We are well, though moving around a lot," he says. "With all the unrest, we suspect that many people will soon be after our horses. We have no intention of sending them into a conflict such as this, so we are making ourselves scarce." He takes a seat in one of the visitor chairs and lays a small pouch on the ground. "I bring a message from Kione. It must be an important one, as she made me swear on my steed that I would bring it safely."

There's only one thing I can think of that Kione might send. I pick up the bag and try not to hope for too much. There's a note attached.

We felt it right to share the suona with you. Take this portion with our regards.

Just two short sentences, scrawled in uneven script, yet it's enough to stop my breath. My hand is unacceptably clumsy as I untie the thong holding it closed. Inside the pouch is a jar sealed with wax. I cradle it between my fingers as I sit back down—I don't dare open the seal while I'm standing. Sweat breaks out over my skin.

The lid pries up to reveal a handful of the pearly powder. It's not much—a year's supply at most. But it's a year more than I had expected.

"Is it useful to you?" Nush asks.

I can't bring myself to breathe, much less speak. I nod my reply.

"I'm glad."

I sit, clutching the jar, for a long time after Nush leaves. What if I drop it? What if the lid falls off, trailing a month's worth of golden dust? But finally I gather the courage to take the precious pollen inside. I already have a pot of tea warm over the fire. For a moment, I wonder how large a pinch I should put in my cup.

The tea still tastes the same. Perhaps I detect a slight astringent aroma. Unbidden, the memory of Mehtap pouring tea in her villa comes to me, along with a twinge of sadness that I cannot share this with her.

I don't know what I expected after I drink, but I feel exactly the same. The light headache that had clung to me all day remains, and the only difference I detect is a warmth in my throat from the tea. It's silly, of course, to expect a change right away. That evening, my headache doesn't get better, but neither does it worsen. My fingers still shake as I prepare dinner, and I try to stave off disappointment as I fall asleep.

I wake the next morning to a tugging at my scalp. Scrawny stands on my pillow, picking through my hair.

"Scrawny!" The bird jumps away as I wave my hand groggily in his direction. He leaves ash streaks on my pillow—the bird must have come down the chimney. "Do you have anything for me?"

There's nothing on his foot, and he seems more interested in poking through my bedclothes than giving me a message.

"Just here for company?" There's no point in going back to sleep, so I put a dress on over my shift and pad over to the fire.

That's when I realize my head is clear. No pain except the

slightest lingering echo. Everything in my vision is crisp and sharp, sharper than it's been in a long, long time.

I collapse into a chair. The clatter raises a squawk from Scrawny.

"I'm fine," I tell him. Quite possibly, I'm more than fine. For once, my body's holding firm. It's my mind that made my legs give way.

My mind whirls, and my veins pulse with an expectant energy. *It's only a year,* I remind myself. But it's a year more than I expected to have, and even that possibility is equal parts exhilarating and frightening. When I find the strength in my legs, I coax the embers of my hearth into a new fire and boil some more water. Carefully, I take a second pinch of pollen from the jar.

I've about finished my tea when Scrawny caws and takes wing out the window. A few moments later, Dineas appears at the top of the path, carrying a bag over his shoulder. He smiles a greeting. I wonder if I look different, if the absence of pain shows in the lines of my face.

Dineas dumps his bag on the ground in front of me. It's filled with foraged bamboo shoots, and I raise a questioning eye.

Dineas shrugs. "They looked good, if you trust my plant lore."

"I trust it more than I used to." Should I tell him? Should I wait? I pull at the hem of my apron.

"Why did Nush come to see you yesterday?" he asks.

"Been watching who comes and goes, have you?"

"Old habit, I suppose," he says, unrepentant. "I wouldn't have lived this long if I hadn't learned to keep a good lookout."

I hesitate, worried for a moment that saying something too soon would render it false. "He brought me a gift."

"Oh?"

"A gift of time. Not much. A year, perhaps."

Dineas is uncomprehending at first, until I lead him inside

and carefully show him the sealed contents of the suona jar. Despite my warning, hope lights up his face.

"Suona pollen," he whispers.

"It was a generous gift," I say. "From some people who have suffered more than their share."

For a moment, we're both silent.

"A year at most?" he says again.

"Yes." There's a buzzing along my skin.

Dineas stares at the jar, blinking, and a myriad of emotions cross his face—joy, hope, fear. His eyes search mine. "And how will you live this year?"

It's a good question. Having a year suddenly added to my life is disorienting, like coming out of a cave into the open air. But seeing Dineas in front of me clarifies my thoughts. "I'd like to live it similarly to how I'm living now. Rest, work on new potions. Learn more about suona pollen and see if it's similar to the syeb flowers in these hills. Also, I discovered some rather beautiful corners of Monyar during the war. I'd like to see them again. I'd like to watch Elannah grow." My voice catches. "From a distance of course. See her learn to walk."

Dineas takes in my words, only half looking at me as he bobs his head. Then he gives me a crooked smile, one worthy of his most outrageous schemes. "Want company?"

The corners of my lips lift in response. "It might be monotonous, as I'm planning to do a lot of sitting around. I've had my fill of adventure."

"Monotonous might not be so bad a thing. But I wouldn't be so sure we can count on the next year being that way. Did you think, when you first became ill, that you'd end up freeing your people from Ampara? Who knows what another year might bring?"

He steps closer to me, more optimistic than I've seen him in a while. In fact, he looks almost like the other Dineas of Sehmar City. I think back to that night we spent in the emperor's garden a lifetime ago. The heady scent of flowers, the yearning to say yes to love. "Mehtap told me I should do everything and experience everything while I can. She told me that trying too hard to control things would shut me away from the world as surely as any rose plague."

"Mehtap was a smart girl."

I look into his eyes, and they are earnest. Not naive, like the Dineas of Sehmar City, but wise. And hope, true hope, bubbles up within me. The journey ahead may be short, or perhaps the Goddess has more in store. Either way, Dineas is a traveling companion I've grown fond of.

And so I reach out, and take his hand.

NOTE FROM LIVIA

Thank you for reading *Umbertouched*! If you enjoyed it, I hope you will consider writing an online review. They really help get the word out about the book.

If you'd like to hear about my other work, consider joining my mailing list. Subscribers are the first to know about new books and special deals, and also receive two free short stories. You can sign up for the newsletter at:

www.liviablackburne.com

MIDNIGHT THIEF

BY LIVIA BLACKBURNE

An exceptional thief...

Kyra specializes in nighttime raids, using her sharp senses and uncanny agility to plunder Forge's wealthiest homes. Then she meets James, the deadly but intriguing Head of the Assassin's Guild. He has a job for Kyra: infiltrate the impenetrable Palace compound. The pay is good, and the challenge appealing.

But as Kyra establishes herself in the Guild, things start to unravel. Her assignments become increasingly violent, demanding more than Kyra is willing to give. And as she grows closer to the darkly attractive James, she can't shake the feeling that his plans run deeper than he claims.

A knight sworn to vengeance...

When Tristam's best friend is killed by Demon Riders—barbarians riding vicious wildcats—he vows to defeat them. The young knight throws himself into his quest, only to find his efforts thwarted by a mysterious and very talented thief.

When a twist of fate throws Kyra and Tristam together, they realize that Forge faces greater dangers than either of them had imagined. They must make a choice: continue to fight each other, or work together to unravel the truth. As sinister forces close in, Kyra and Tristam discover a shocking secret that will change their lives forever.

ONE

This job could kill her.

Kyra peered off the ledge, squinting at the cobblestone four stories below. A false step in the darkness would be deadly, and even if she survived the fall, Red Shields would finish her off. She stared a few moments more before forcing her gaze back up. The time for second thoughts had passed. Now she just needed to keep moving.

The jump ahead was two body lengths long, so Kyra backed away from the ledge. Ten steps, then she drew a breath and sprinted forward. She pushed off just before the drop, clearing a gap of three strides before softening her body for the landing. There was a slap of soft leather on stone as she hit the next ledge. The impact sent a wave of vibrations through the balls of her feet, and Kyra touched a hand to the wall for balance.

Too hard, and too loud.

Silently cursing her clumsiness, Kyra scanned the grounds, looking for anyone who might have heard her. If she squinted, she could make out faint outlines of buildings around her—some as high as her ledge, some even taller. The pathways below were lined with torches that flickered, casting shadows that played tricks with her vision. Since she couldn't trust her eyes, she listened. Other than the wind blowing across her ears, the night was silent, and Kyra relaxed. Tucking away a stray lock of hair, she set off, dashing deeper into the compound.

Two days ago, a man had come to The Drunken Dog, introducing himself as James and asking for Kyra by name. He'd moved with a deliberate confidence, and his gaze had swept over the room, evaluating and dismissing each of its occupants. When Kyra had finally approached him, James laid out an unusual offer. There was a ruby in the Palace compound. He wanted her to fetch it for him, and he was willing to pay.

"The Palace is guarded tight," Kyra had told him. "If you want jewels, you'll better get them elsewhere."

"This ruby's got sentimental value," he'd replied. Kyra didn't consider herself the most astute judge of character. But she also wasn't an idiot, and she'd swallow her grappling hook before she'd believe that this man would do *anything* for sentimental reasons. The pay he offered was good though, and the job an intriguing challenge. The Palace was a far cry from the rich man's houses Kyra usually raided, with their handful of sentries guarding two or three floors. The Palace's massive buildings were patrolled by so many guards it was impossible to walk the grounds undetected. Rumor had it that even the rooftops were closely watched.

Which was why Kyra was neither on the ground nor on the rooftops. Instead, she balanced on a ledge outside a fourth-floor window, darting from shadow to shadow. The moon had not yet risen, and darkness concealed her from the Red Shields below. Unfortunately, it also hid the ledges from her own sight; the boundary between stone and air was easy to miss. From time to time, she slid a foot out to check her position, tracing her toe along the edge to fix the border in her mind.

Yes, she could die tonight. But as Kyra crept through the darkness, her doubts faded against the excitement of a challenging job. Those who knew her understood her skills. They knew she had no fear of heights and never lost her balance. But not even Flick, the closest thing to an older brother she had, understood the sheer joy that came over her every time she raced through the night. There was something about the way the darkness forced her to rely on her other senses, the way her body rose to the challenge. Her limbs silently promised her she would not fall, and by now she knew she could trust them.

The buildings across the path gave way to a courtyard with three trees, and Kyra slowed her pace, counting windows as she passed. The seventh from the southwest corner, James had said. These outer palaces were guest rooms for country noblemen visiting the Council. They were built securely but emphasized comfort more heavily than the fortresslike inner compound. And thus, they had glass windows instead of shutters, making it easy to see that the bedroom inside was dark. A minute fiddling with the latch, and the pane swung open on greased hinges. There was a shape on the bed, snoring in the loud and punctuated way of men who had indulged too much in rich food and drink. Kyra wondered for a moment what it would be like to get fat, to eat so much and work so little. No matter. Tonight, the nobleman would share some of his bounty.

She started with a dresser next to the bed, coaxing open the top drawer. Silk caught the dry skin of her fingertips. Apparently, the nobleman had a penchant for embroidered silk handkerchiefs. Not the jewelry box she sought, but Kyra took one and slipped it into her belt pouch. After checking the rest of the dresser, she moved to the desk. The latch gave easily to her pick, but there was nothing inside but documents and seals.

The sleeping nobleman shifted, and Kyra dropped to the floor. He rolled over, snorting loudly before his breathing once again settled. Kyra counted ten breaths, then went to the chest, taking care with the hefty cover. The top layer was fabric. Soon, she was up to her elbows in velvet night-robes, but still no ruby.

If there was a jewelry box, it almost certainly would have been in the dresser or the chest. James had assured her that the nobleman wasn't the type to hide his jewelry. Could he have been mistaken?

She combed the room again, feeling along the floors and walls for trapdoors, even running her hands over the bed's thin mattress. Still nothing. Kyra bit her lip. The moon was rising, a thin crescent above the horizon that announced the coming dawn. She'd already stayed too long. Taking one last glance around the room, she crept back out the window.

Getting out was harder than coming in. Her limbs were slow from a night without sleep, and her nerves were frayed from being so long on her guard. By the time Kyra reached the meeting spot two blocks outside the Palace, the sky was visibly lighter, and she was in a considerably worse mood.

Two men awaited her at the street corner. They hadn't seen her yet, and she took a moment to study them. The first was solidly built, with a stubborn jaw and brown hair curled close to his head—Flick. When Kyra had first told him about the job, he'd listed all the reasons she should refuse, from the dangers within the Palace to his suspicions about James. Her friend's arguments had been more reasonable than Kyra cared to admit, but by then she'd already decided. Since Flick couldn't dissuade her from going, he'd insisted on escorting James. The two men had watched her cross the wall a few hours earlier, and now they awaited her return. Kyra felt a twinge of guilt when she saw the tense set of Flick's shoulders. He'd been worried.

Behind Flick, Kyra recognized James. He was slimmer but taller, with pale coloring and a wiry, athletic build. He exuded confidence, studying everything around him with languid readiness. His expression was impossible to read.

Both men's eyes flickered to her hands as she came closer, then to her belt.

"It in't there," she said, answering their unspoken question.

Perhaps her voice was sharper than it should have been, but she was tired.

There was a brief silence as the two men digested her news. Finally, James spoke. "What do you mean?"

"I flipped the whole room—the dresser, desk, the chest at the foot of the bed. No jewelry box."

"You searched the entire room?" James raised an eyebrow.

Kyra spat on the ground. "Look, unless he sleeps with the rock in his small clothes, it wasn't there."

"Maybe you went to the wrong place."

There was a hint of derision in his voice, and it galled Kyra. Trying hard to control a flush of anger, she reached into her belt pouch for the handkerchief she'd taken from the noble's dresser. She flicked it at James, who snatched it out of the air with surprising quickness.

"This handkerchief's got the fatpurse's initials embroidered on it. See if it matches your mark."

Kyra made no effort to hide her frustration as James inspected the embroidery. Payment for the job depended on handing over the jewel, so she'd taken a long and dangerous night's work for nothing. She felt a hand on her shoulder. Flick, knowing her temper, was silently warning her not to push anything too far. Kyra gritted her teeth. James studied the handkerchief, after a while not even looking at it, but through it. Finally, he looked up, and his demeanor abruptly changed.

"Very well," he said, voice now smooth and agreeable. "Mayhap he didn't bring the stone to the Palace." James untied a pouch from his belt and tossed it at Kyra, who almost didn't react quickly enough to catch it. "That's the agreed-upon price, plus some extra. I believe this will cover your effort."

Without another word, he turned and walked away.

ALSO BY LIVIA BLACKBURNE

Midnight Thief Series:

Poison Dance (novella)

Midnight Thief

Daughter of Dusk

Rosemarked Series:

Rosemarked

Umbertouched

Short Stories:

Lord of Time

Other YA Fantasy:

Feather and Flame

Picture Books:

I Dream of Popo

ACKNOWLEDGMENTS

I wrote *Rosemarked* while pregnant with my daughter. It therefore follows that writing *Umbertouched* occurred at an even more exciting (and discombobulating) stage of my life. Large portions of the first draft were dictated during 3 a.m. nursing sessions, and I turned in the last round of substantial revisions shortly before my daughter's first birthday. It takes a village to raise a child, and it takes a village to publish a book. As for writing a book while raising a child...well, let's just say that these acknowledgments are more heartfelt than ever.

First off, my editors! Abby Ranger, who bravely waded into that sleep-deprived first version and figured out exactly what worked, what needed to go, and provided a much-needed road map for me to find the heart of this story. And Rotem - Moscovich (four books in now!), who huddled with me to brainstorm everything from the progression of Dineas's hallucinations to the progression of Zivah and Dineas's romance, who always managed to come up with great ideas for the questions that stumped me, and who never failed to make delighted noises at my baby pictures.

And then the rest of the Hyperion team. Cassie McGinty, publicist extraordinaire, supernaturally organized and always there with an encouraging word. Heather Crowley, always a reliable presence and a cover copy wizard, as well as the art and marketing departments, and everyone else who works behind the scenes.

Jim McCarthy was a constant cheerleader and sounding board throughout (and also exclaimed at baby pictures). Thanks for chasing that *Rosemarked* RT review all over town!

Many thanks to Courtyard Critiques: Amitha Knight, Rachal Aronson, Jen Barnes, and Emily Terry, for your reactions to my early drafts and your patience with my spotty and somewhat distracted attendance during those early months.

Beta readers provided much needed encouragement and ideas for enriching the story: Lauren James, Jenna DeTrapani, Emily Lo, Nicole Harlan, Bridget Howard, and Annie Earnshaw.

Other readers offered advice on their areas of expertise: Lisa Choi, MD, provided feedback on the various wounds and treatments in the story. Chris Lenyk once again gave pointers on the military aspects. Al Rosenberg read the story with an eye to terminal illness, and Lily Maase graciously discussed the psychological impact and experience of PTSD.

And last but most definitely not least, a heartfelt thanks to my family, without whose support this book would never have been turned in on time. My mom for spending countless hours watching my daughter while I holed up and wrote. My dad, for all those grocery and library runs, and for sharing my mom with us. My husband picked up the slack in so many ways, from dishes to childcare to absorbing my deadline grumpiness. Thank you to my family-in-law, for your support and encouragement from a distance, especially my mother-in-law, who must have handed out several thousand bookmarks by now. And of course, thank you to my dear daughter, the inspiration behind Leora's baby. I hope you aren't too badly traumatized from all those plague and war scenes Mommy dictated during your early infancy.

ABOUT THE AUTHOR

New York Times bestselling author Livia Blackburne wrote her first novel while researching the neuroscience of reading at the Massachusetts Institute of Technology. Since then, she's switched to full time writing, which also involves getting into people's heads but without the help of a three tesla MRI scanner. She is the author of *Midnight Thief* (An Indies Introduce New Voices selection) and *Rosemarked* (A YALSA Teens Top Ten nominee), and the Disney Mulan reimagining *Feather and Flame* as well as the picture book I DREAM OF POPO , which received three starred reviews and was included in numerous Best of Year lists.

twitter.com/lkblackburne
instagram.com/lkblackburne
facebook.com/livia.blackburne
amazon.com/Livia-Blackburne/e/B004GNAGEW

Printed in Great Britain
by Amazon

18813729R10212